Inescapable

NATASHA ANDERS

Chapter One

I ris Hughes glared at the dead end in front of her.

"What in the actual *fuck*?" she whispered in disbelief, diverting her glare down to the satnav—or *GPS* as they called it here—on her dashboard.

"Please continue straight ahead for another 1.2 kilometers," the robotic voice unhelpfully informed her. Ugh, why hadn't she taken the time to switch to miles before starting her journey? She'd completely forgotten that South Africa used the metric system. But aside from that, she had more immediate problems.

"Straight ahead? There *is* no straight ahead." Iris cast a strained look at the overgrown forest around her—the sun had set ten minutes ago—it was rapidly getting dark and the trees were starting to loom threateningly. She couldn't afford to get lost, not at this time of day, on an unfamiliar road, in a foreign country.

"*Shitshitshit*," she muttered, reaching for her mobile, hoping the phone's GPS would be more forthcoming than the one in the car.

She peered at the screen, alarmed to note that the battery was in the red. Not great. Since the charging cable was somewhere in her luggage in the car's boot.

"Genius move, Iris," she groaned. When she'd picked the car up at the airport what felt like hours and hours and *hours* ago, she'd considered going through her bags to try and find the damned cable, but in the end had decided that getting on the road faster would be best. It now looked like that decision had come back to bite her in the bum. Her phone hadn't been charged since before she'd boarded her flight some twenty-something hours ago. She'd used it only sparingly on the nightmarish, eons-long flight over, but despite her valiant attempts to save it, the battery—at only five percent—was on its last gasp.

Praying that it wouldn't die on her, she hastily put the address into the search bar, and it immediately calibrated a different route to the car's satnav.

"Bastard," she growled at the car. It looked like she'd have to backtrack and take a turn she'd passed about half a mile back.

Still swearing underneath her breath, she put the car in reverse. There wasn't enough room to turn around on this narrow, overgrown road, which meant she'd have to drive in reverse until she came to the turnoff. Thankfully, the car had a rearview camera and she periodically checked the image and the mirrors as she drove. The camera lens was foggy and didn't provide her with a clear view of the road, and so it came as no surprise when one of the back tires hit something unseen and the car rocked alarmingly.

"Damn it," she muttered, swerving slightly to avoid the front wheel hitting the same obstacle. The car was "limping"—for lack of a better word—along now, telling Iris that the affected tire must have sustained serious damage.

She braked and peered onto the gravel track in front of the car, looking for whatever had caused the problem. She winced when she spotted what looked like a tree branch just off to the side of the road. *Ugh,* it must have fallen shortly after she'd already passed this spot on her way to that blasted dead end because it definitely hadn't been there before.

It was frighteningly windy outside—the strong gusts buffeted her tiny rental car even while she sat there pondering the wisdom of getting out and checking the tire. She couldn't very well continue driving without assessing the damage, but the thought of getting out into the darkness that had enveloped her surroundings in such a short time was more than a little daunting. If one branch had fallen, surely there was a danger of more dropping. It couldn't possibly be safe out there. Iris had researched the Knysna area in the Western Cape of South Africa on her flight over from London and knew that the area was populated by wild cats; caracals, leopards—and also most fearsome of all—honey badgers.

What if there was a honey badger out there looking to fuck some shit up? She couldn't risk it.

She put her foot back on the accelerator and inched along slowly, trying to ignore the flapping, grinding sound coming from the left rear wheel.

Crap, the car was starting to wobble badly. Iris braked again and this time switched the car off, before dropping her forehead and thumping it softly on the padded steering wheel.

She was going to have to get out and check.

"Dear God, please don't let me be eaten by a wild animal, thank you, amen." She unbuckled her seatbelt and opened the door, only to have it rudely snatched out of her grasp by the violent wind.

This was going to suck.

The wind tore at her clothes, snatched the breath from her lungs, and extended icy, intrusive fingers into any gaps between her clothing and skin.

It was ice cold. This was South Africa; shouldn't it be warm or something? Why was it so damned cold? She felt cheated and indignant about this shitty weather. Were all those pretty pictures she'd seen of Cape Town during her quick online research of the area a total lie? So far, she wasn't at all impressed with anything about the place. Nothing but gray skies, over-crowded roads, and stormy oceans.

Oh, and really rude, impatient drivers.

She could get all of that back home.

She glared down at the completely flat rear tire balefully and screamed in frustration. Annoyingly, the sound was torn away by the wind.

Jesus, had her biological father ever had to work this hard on any of his assignments? Because this felt like piling on.

She knew the car had a spare. It had been drilled into her by her dad—the one who'd raised her—to always check for that when renting a car, but she doubted she'd be able to get the tire changed in this crazy wind. Her best option was to walk while she still had enough battery power on her phone to follow the GPS.

She checked the map again... it looked like a ten-to-fifteen-minute walk. Probably closer to half an hour in this weather, lugging her small carry-on bag that at least contained a pair of clean undies. She could call a tow truck or mechanic in the morning and get the rest of her stuff then too. For now, it would be best to get to the house and shelter.

Provided the GPS was right this time. And her phone didn't die. And she didn't tumble off a cliff in this blackness—because putting on her phone's flashlight when the battery was this low was not an option.

God, maybe she should just stay in the car, dig out her cable, charge her phone, and call for help in the morning. Surely that would be the best option?

But it had only just gone six p.m. and the sun wouldn't rise until just before eight in the morning, and she was not keen on staying out here for fourteen hours. Also—she checked her phone—yeah, there was no mobile service out here. Which meant she'd have to trek to Trystan Abbott's place before calling for a tow truck anyway. Might as well bite the bullet and do it now. Better than spending an uncomfortable night in the car.

"This is so dumb," she told herself as she got her carry-on wheelie suitcase out of the boot. "This is how people get murdered. Or eaten by animals. Or abducted by aliens. Or attacked by sharks, or zombies, or frikking vampires."

Still, she was going to do this. She had to do this—it was the shittier of the two options available to her, but the most logical one.

She zipped up the puffer jacket she'd bought at the airport after discovering how cold it was, and put one resolute foot in front of the other as she continued to backtrack until she came to the turn she hadn't even noticed earlier.

A reckless five-second switch to her phone's flashlight told Iris that the road was lined with tall skeletal trees whose bare branches entangled many meters above her to form a brittle canopy above the road. The branches squeaked and scraped against each other in the strong wind, which was now blowing straight at her. The occasional gunshot-loud *crack* warned her that more branches were likely breaking and falling, making this foolhardy course of action even more treacherous.

One bright spot, the GPS didn't seem to indicate any cliffs in the surrounding area, but that didn't preclude deep ditches and holes, of course.

And now that the thought had crossed her mind, she kept imagining herself plunging into one with every step she took.

Thankfully, the howling of the wind was loud enough to drown out any potential howling from animals, which meant it was easier to put the threat of death by animal mauling and predation from her mind.

Sometimes she cursed her over-active imagination.

In fact, it was the absolute worst thing for her to have. She was trying to be a journalist over here, not an author of gruesome horrors.

She could use this in her feature. Set the scene...

It was there—among the dead trees, stormy seas, and wild

animals—that I finally tracked down the elusive Trystan Abbott. The legendary actor hiding in a remote cottage in the wilds of—

What was that?

She stopped dead in her tracks and canted her head to the side as she tried to ignore the wind and listen for the sound she thought she'd heard beneath the cacophonous wind.

A growl. She was sure of it—a low, menacing growl that—

There it was again.

Oh God, she glanced down at her phone. According to the map, the house was straight ahead, just fifty meters away. She couldn't see it. But it had to be there. It just had to.

She picked up the pace, but felt almost certain she was being stalked. She was practically running by now and when the trees abruptly ended and the gravel road changed to paving beneath her feet, she let out a grateful cry at first sight of the huge, creepy house, with its unlit windows, and dropped her case as she darted through a small garden toward what looked like a back door.

She pounded frantically at the door, but the lights remained dark.

She hammered on the door again.

"Open up. Please. Open the door!"

She heard the growl again, louder, closer. She gulped in terror and switched her phone to flashlight mode and swung around. *There!* By the fence. Eyes, illuminated by the light. She kept the flashlight focused in that direction, striving for a better look, when the phone finally died on her, plunging her into absolute darkness with a creature that looked about waist high to her five-foot-five-inch height.

She mewled in terror and plastered her back to the door, her left hand reaching for the doorknob, hoping that someone who lived this far from the rest of humanity would keep his doors unlocked. But the doorknob didn't turn and the door wouldn't budge.

Iris closed her eyes and asked for forgiveness for all her sins. She hoped her parents would understand what had driven her to come all this way. Hoped they wouldn't be too disappointed in her... chasing a man, a story, a dream she wasn't even sure was her own.

She was only twenty-six. She still had so much she wanted to do, so much to see, so much to—

The door swung inward behind her back and Iris, weak-kneed and terrified plummeted backward into the void.

She hit the floor—arse first—*hard* and sat there for a moment trying to get her bearings. It was still dark and something huge stood above her, and for a second's blind panic she was sure it was the creature, until she recognized the two tall, solid structures straddled on either side of her waist as legs.

Long denim-clad legs.

"*Oh, thank you, Jesus,*" she breathed the reverent prayer as she smiled up at the man standing above her. She couldn't *quite* see his face or expression in the dim light, but knew it had to be Trystan Abbott.

"Not quite." The curt voice was at odds with what she'd been expecting, and she blinked up at him.

"What?"

"Not quite Jesus," he elaborated. "Probably the exact opposite."

Huh?

"Mr. Abbott?" She pushed clumsily to her feet, a little put out when he didn't offer to help her up. For that matter, had he *stepped aside* when she'd lost her balance at the door? It had all been quite confusing in the moment, but now that the panic was receding she was almost certain he had. When he could easily have caught her.

He answered her question with two of his own. "Who the fuck are you? And what are you doing here?"

She lifted her head to meet his gaze—able to see much better now that her eyes had adjusted to the gloom—and couldn't stop her mouth from dropping open in shock. She stared, aware that the astonishment on her face had to be insultingly apparent to this hulking man in front of her.

"M-Mr. Abbott?" Her voice trailed off uncertainly and she continued to stare, looking for anything familiar in this man's face. This couldn't possibly be the same man who'd been voted Sexiest Man in the Universe three years in a row.

That Trystan Abbott had the kind of classic leading-man good looks that harkened back to an era when Cary Grant and Audrey Hepburn had lit up the silver screen with their charisma and incomparable allure.

This guy—looking much older than his thirty-one years— had a long, unkempt beard and shaggy hair just brushing his big, broad shoulders and—while appearing clean enough—neither looked like they'd seen a comb in weeks. His lips were pressed into a thin, bloodless line, and his eyes—those familiar, famous molten silver eyes, the only things remotely resembling the man she was here to speak to—were narrowed into an intimidating glare. None of the magnetism and charm Trystan Abbott was famed for was evident in that frosty gaze, and a shudder of unease crept down Iris's spine. She'd had fond imaginings of witty discourse over cozy cups of coffee or tea. Free-flowing conversation, punctuated by the easy chatter and frequent laughter that had characterized all of the man's previous interviews.

"Who are you?" he asked again, impatience rippling along the edges of the question.

"M-my name is Iris Hughes." She fumbled around in her jacket pockets, hoping to magically produce a business card, but all she could find was used, crumpled up tissues, the receipt for the jacket, and a crisp pink South African banknote with a lion and cub printed on one side and a benevolently smiling Nelson Mandela on the other.

She stared blindly down at the useless bounty in her hands, wondering what her next move should be.

Don't be silly, Iris, she scolded herself. *Just tell him why you're here.*

That was easier said than done when one of the most famous men in the world was looming above her with that formidable glower marring his brow and narrowing his eyes. Her tongue and brain both seemed to have deserted her—not awesome when she'd hoped to dazzle him with her professionalism.

"Your, *uh*, that is, Mr. Quinn said he'd cleared this with you? The interview? I'm here for the interview?" God, why did everything she say have to sound like a nervous question.

The chill that shuddered down her spine had little to do

with the weather and everything to do with the added layer of frost that instantly transformed his silvery gaze into ice.

"Fuck off," he instructed with a snarl. "You're not welcome here."

He stepped back and moved to shut the door. Iris panicked and reacted without thinking, wedging her foot in the door before he could close it. She muffled her pained yelp when he slammed the damned heavy door on her trainered foot.

His glower got even darker when he grasped what she'd done and he—thankfully—eased the door back, removing the pressure. It had been an idiotic move and she had no one but herself to blame for her throbbing foot. But she refused to remove it, knowing that he would have no qualms about closing the door in her face.

"I have nowhere to go," she told him before he could say another word. Her words were rushed, desperate. "You have to let me in."

"I don't have to do a goddamned thing. *You*, on the other hand, need to remove your grubby self from my damned back porch."

"No, you don't understand. I can't leave. My car has a flat."

"That sounds like a you problem."

"Mr. Abbott... Look, your manager, Hunter Quinn, told me where to find you. It's my understanding that he'd arranged for me to stay here for the next three weeks. He said you were fine with that."

The sound torn from his chest *could* conceivably have been considered a laugh, if Iris hadn't—like the rest of the world— been very familiar with Trystan Abbott's infectious chuckle.

Instead, the noise he produced sounded menacing and feral and she flinched in reaction.

"I won't tell you again," he warned. "Fuck off, or I'll physically toss you out on your ass."

His words made her pause as she wondered if this hulking man was capable of physical violence. She took an involuntary step back and he slammed the door in her face, the wood coming within an inch of her nose.

She gasped in outrage and—as she cast a quick glance around at her dark, blustery surroundings—no small amount of fear.

She thumped at the door with the side of her fist.

"You can't leave me out here! Open up, please. Call Mr. Quinn... he'll clear this up."

The door remained firmly shut. She tried the handle.

Locked.

She redoubled her efforts, knocking and kicking at the wooden door in fear and frustration.

She heard a low, ominous growl from much too close behind her, and it reminded her that she was not alone out here and she screamed, the sound high-pitched and bloodcurdling.

The door was immediately snatched open again and she sagged in relief.

"Please, I think there's a wolf or wild animal out here. Let me in."

He peered into the darkness over her shoulder and refocused on her face with a sinister little sneer.

"Well, try not to let it eat you! You might give it indigestion."

"You can't leave me out here to face whatever that is," she said in horror. "It's illegal."

"So's trespassing, but that doesn't seem to bother you."

"You invited me to come."

"*I* did no such thing."

"Well, your manager did. He speaks on your behalf, right? I never..." Her voice trailed off on a helpless whimper. "Oh God, please just let me in. I'm sure it's a wolf. He's been watching me from the treeline."

"For fuck's sake, just piss off back to where you came from." His accent was mostly Americanized, but—despite her distraction and distress—Iris could still pick up an Aussie twang beneath that meticulously cultivated Hollywood drawl.

"We're in the middle of nowhere. My car is half a mile away. My phone is dead. I have nowhere to go and no way to get there. Just let me stay the night. If you really want me to leave I'll make a plan in the morning."

He laughed again, the same awful sound as before.

"Yeah right, and let you snoop around my house tonight? I don't think so."

"At least let me charge my phone, I can call an Uber or something."

"Again... these are not my problems. You got yourself here, you can get yourself the hell out of here too. I don't care how you do it."

"Without a GPS, I'll get lost. I could fall off a cliff. Die. That wild animal could maim or kill me."

"Don't worry, I'm sure the people who give a fuck about you

will eventually send out a search party to find your corpse in the woods."

"That's not remotely funny."

"I look like I'm kidding?" he asked without expression.

He looked as serious as a heart attack and that terrified her. He could quite conceivably leave her out here to fend for herself.

What a nightmare.

Strengthening her resolve, Iris allowed her shoulders to drop and in a quick move taught to her by her younger brother, feinted to the left and—when he reacted by instinctively moving in that direction—darted to the right and ducked under his arm into the kitchen. Once safely inside, she immediately darted behind the counter in an effort to put a barrier between them.

His back stiffened and he clenched his fists before turning to face her, murder in his eyes.

"Just one night. I'll sleep on the floor. I promise not to make a sound. Just call Mr. Quinn, he'll clear this up."

"You're trespassing and if you don't get out of my house right fucking now I *will* have you arrested."

"Oh, please do," she invited with an insouciance she didn't feel. Truthfully, the thought of being arrested and locked into a small space made her hair stand on end. But she wouldn't let *him* see that. "At least then I'd have a ride out of here and a place to sleep tonight."

He stared at her for an interminable moment and nodded decisively. He dragged his phone out of his front jeans pocket and swiped at the screen before he tapped a few times and then lifted the device to his ear.

"Although," she said, and his arm halted halfway up to his ear. "If you *do* call the police and someone recognizes you, how long before your private and cozy little hidey-hole is inundated by the public and press?"

"What the hell do you call this, if not an invasion of my privacy?"

"I'm one person, here to conduct an interview on your and Mr. Quinn's terms. You have all the control. You lose that the second you lose your anonymity."

His lips tightened and she felt a little thrill of victory when his thumb viciously jabbed at the *call end* button. He shoved the phone back in his pocket and nodded.

"Fine... follow me."

Go, me! Iris's inner voice cheered, as she meekly followed the big man out of the dark kitchen. He led her down a long, poorly lit hallway, into a darkened room, toward a closed door. Once there, he stood aside and held out a hand inviting her to open the door.

"You can stay there."

"Thank you so much, I promise I won't be a bother," she said, her giddy relief evident in her voice. "In the morning, perhaps you'd be willing to revisit the idea of an interview, especially after you have a look at my correspondence with Mr. Quinn, which will clear up this misunderstanding."

She pulled the door inward, still earnestly speaking to him over her shoulder as she walked through it. "And if you agree to..."

She stopped talking as she registered the cold air on her skin. A hand on her back shoved her roughly all the way through the door. It took her brain a second to absorb what was happening and, by the time she understood that she was outside again, the door had been shut and the lock engaged.

She appeared to have been led through a side door into a dark garden. She took a second to get her bearings—she had to be on the side of the house somewhere. She wasn't entirely sure how to get out of this space. There seemed to be a high hedge surrounding the patch of grass and trees, but there was no shelter from the elements. She'd been better off on the back porch, which had some cover and a swinging love seat.

But that... that *creature* was there. And Iris wasn't sure she wanted to venture back there again. There had to be another way into the house. Returning to the car without even the meager light of her phone was not an option, and she wasn't entirely confident of how to get back to the vehicle anyway. It was sleep outside in the cold and wind and, possibly, rain, with a wild animal on the loose, or do some actual breaking and entering.

Trystan Abbott had changed his mind about calling the police earlier, after she'd mentioned the possible loss of privacy if he did so. His reaction had revealed more to her than he'd likely intended to. He didn't want anyone to know he was here. And he wouldn't call the police because of that.

Which meant he wasn't likely to have her arrested for making her way back inside. And if she was wrong about that, then Iris only hoped that the police would be more reasonable than the elusive celebrity. They'd likely believe her story once she provided them with the correspondence between her and

Hunter Quinn. It was irrefutable evidence of her right to be here.

Iris thumped at the door in frustration.

"At least turn on the outdoor lights!" she yelled, more irritated than scared right now.

Seriously, what a dick. To think, she'd once been a fan of this arrogant arsehole. Not anymore. How excited she'd been when Hunter Quinn had agreed to allow her exclusive access to his most prized client. What an idiot she'd been.

She hadn't once stopped to wonder why *her*? An unseasoned journalist with zero bylines to her name. He'd taken one look at her, listened to her eagerly espouse her admiration of Trystan Abbott's phenomenal talent, and had leaned back with a sharklike smile and said that she was the exact type of writer he needed to do this in-depth piece.

Naturally, Iris had leaped at the opportunity. What a feather in her cap. Now she suspected that he'd chosen her because he thought she was easily manipulated. After all, an obvious fangirl like her would never have a bad word to say about his problematic client.

But that was before Iris had realized what a surly, uncommunicative hermit Trystan Abbott had become. Now she was intrigued to find out what had happened to cause this change in him. Unless . . . she tilted her head, brain working overtime as she thought about it, had he always been this way? Had that handsome, genial, joking man been the facade behind which this antisocial grouch had been hiding all along?

She thumped at the door in frustration.

"Come *on*. Turn the lights on. *Please!*" she demanded again, but it remained pitch black. She hovered uncertainly, not sure which way to turn or where to go.

This was terrible and Iris literally had no clue what to do next. Oh, how she wished she were back home, having dinner at her parents' house, fighting over the last roast potato with her brother. She would happily listen to her dad champion the benefits of running the business with him if it meant no longer being in this place.

The wind gusted around her, tearing at her clothes and hair, stealing the breath from her lips. She hugged herself in a futile attempt to trap the warmth and stamped her feet as she tried to think.

It was hard to concentrate when she was terrified. She kept looking back at the door, hoping he'd be standing there with a *hah, gotcha!* grin on his face, but as the minutes ticked by she resigned herself to the fact that this was not going to happen.

In fact, she wouldn't be surprised if he'd dismissed all thought of her from his brain and gone to bed.

"You can't stand out here all night, Iris," she berated herself. "Just move. In any direction. Anything is better than this."

She took a step forward and her foot immediately sank into something icy and wet.

"*Fuck, shit! Fuck!*" She lifted her foot and shook it. Her trainer had offered absolutely no protection from the water and her foot was completely soaked. Her toes had gone instantly numb from the cold. Probably a good thing, since it meant she no longer felt the pain after having it slammed in a door. God, this was just what she needed.

She took a couple of steps backward, away from whatever

the hell body of water lay in front of her, and once again stood there indecisively.

She heard a sound to her left and her head swung in that direction, but all she could see was the dark, high outline of the hedge against the slightly lighter sky. The sound came again, rustling in that hedge, and the hairs on the back of her neck stood up straight.

"Go away," she whispered. Then raised her voice and tried again. The thready, quavering sound that emerged from her throat was embarrassing, but at least it could be heard over the wind. "Go *away!*"

There was a soft, chuffing, animalistic sound in response and she backed up slowly as a dark shape separated itself from the hedge and prowled toward her.

"Get back," she implored, taking another step backward, but this time her wet trainer skidded against something slick on the paving and she lost her balance, and fell .

She impacted the hard ground with a pained *oof* and the massive dark silhouette saw its opportunity and surged toward her with a whining growl.

This is it, she lamented to herself, terrified as she lifted her arms to her face to protect her head from harm. She curled into a ball, hoping to make herself as small a target as possible. *This is how I die.*

Once again Iris's thoughts swirled to her family, her parents who had sacrificed so much for her and her brother. Her brother, who liked to act like a tough, independent guy but who called her every Sunday, *just to talk*. This would destroy them.

She mustered up enough resentment and anger to consider

Trystan Abbott's role in her downfall and she cursed him with every fiber of her being, but she refused to allow her last thought to be of that horrible man, and instead held the image of her family bright in her mind.

The massive *thing* stood above her, four paws straddling her body and Iris braced herself for unimaginable pain. She would have screamed if she'd had the breath for it, but she had none.

She would go out with not even a whimper.

Chapter Two

I ris felt hot, foul breath wash over her face, immediately followed by something warm and wet on her cheek.

Blood?

It turned out she had some breath left after all because she released it in a high-pitched scream. The creature above her stilled for a second before lowering its head again and this time the warm wetness stroked up from her open mouth to her forehead.

"Oh. Oh... *ew*, no... stop that!" Iris cried, her terror instantly turning to disgust as she realized that instead of being mauled, she was being licked to death. So gross. She pushed at the large shaggy head of what she now recognized as a massive dog and turned her face away from his tongue and wet nose. Ugh, she was almost certain he'd licked her gums while she'd been screaming.

How disgusting.

"Get away, Rover," she commanded, feeling foolish for having thought he was a wolf. *Were* there even wolves in South Africa? The dog's entire body was vibrating with the force of his tail wagging and he was still trying his best to lick every available surface of her skin. "*No. Sit. Down!*"

The last two commands yielded immediate results as the dog stepped away and, as far as she could tell in the darkness, sat obediently, before lowering himself into a down position.

"You're a good dog," she said automatically, and—now that her eyes were adjusting to the gloom—she could see the happy swipe of his tail at the obviously recognizable compliment. Iris sat up and reached for the gigantic floof, scratching the wiry fur around his perky ears, and moving her hand further down to discover a collar. "Do you belong to that horrible man in there? Does he just leave you out here at night? That doesn't seem right."

She felt around the front of the collar, looking for a tag of some sort, not that she'd be able to read it in the dark but...

Aah, there it was. A flat disk that Iris hoped was microchipped and tuned into an electronic pet door.

Fido over here was massive. Probably taller than Iris if he was to stand on his hind legs. If there was a pet entrance, it would be large enough for her to fit through.

"Where's your doggy door, boy? Can you show me? Can you take me inside?"

The full moon broke through the clouds to reveal an endearing fuzzy face, with a lolling tongue. The pooch tilted his head at the sound of her voice, his ears pricking attentively. He was a lanky, scruffy looking gray boy, with shaggy hair, and lively golden eyes.

"Come on, boy, let's go home," Iris invited again, and the dog continued to stare at her quizzically.

"Uh..." Iris wracked her brain, trying to figure out what would make him go inside. "Ball?"

He jumped up, turned in a circle—immediately getting her hopes up—but, after one rotation, sat down to stare at her again.

"Right. Okay. What about food? Are you hungry?" His head cocked comically at the last word, and he whined and shifted excitedly from paw to paw. "*Yes, you're hungry, aren't you? I am too. Let's go and get some food!*"

He nuzzled her hand with his big wet nose and then sat back with an expectant stare.

"Oh. No. I don't have the food out here. But we can get some inside, can't we?"

More staring.

"Come on, show me how you get into the house."

This pup just wasn't getting it. He gave Iris's hand a sympathetic lick and she groaned in frustration. She scratched his head and wondered what to do next.

The moon disappeared again, leaving everything pitch black. The wind died down abruptly and, after a brief lull, the skies opened up.

Iris yelped as the icy deluge instantly drenched her. The dog got up and shook himself vigorously, adding some dog-scented moisture to Iris's already soaked clothing. She sensed him moving away and Iris panicked, not wanting to lose her way into the house.

"Stay, boy," she implored. "Come here."

To her eternal gratitude she felt his big, furry body bump against her thigh reassuringly. He really was massive. She slid her hand up his narrow back toward his neck and lightly gripped his ruff. She didn't want to take hold of his collar in case he considered it a prompt to stay.

"Let's go."

His muscles tensed and he started walking.

"I'm putting all my faith in you right now, boy," she told him. "You could be leading me further into the woods only to abandon me there. Please don't do that. Don't be an arsehole like your owner. Be a better boy than him. Be the goodest boy ever."

The dog continued to amble along lazily, seemingly unperturbed by the heavy rain. Finally, after what felt like an endless amount of walking, they rounded the huge dark house and the ground started to slope downward...

Oh God, was she going to wind up over the side of a cliff after all?

But no, the stony ground beneath her feet gave way to gravel and then paving. And just ahead of them, she could see light creeping out from beneath a shroud of darkness, possibly a garage door?

The dog trotted toward the left and to Iris's relief a little door slid open as they approached, and the meter-by-half-meter square was more than big enough for her to crawl through. She stopped the dog, by tightening her hold on his ruff and when the mutt obediently came to a halt, Iris undid the collar and crouched to crawl through the opening. She remained close to the door so that the dog could walk through it as well. Once they were both safely inside, she refastened the collar around the dog's neck. After blinking a few times to adjust to the brightness in the garage, she gawked at the fleet of cars standing like silent metallic sentinels in neat rows within the brightly lit space.

Gleaming, sporty cars that had to be worth millions upon millions of pounds. She gaped, awed by the staggering display of wealth and found herself wondering why no one had known about Trystan Abbott's little bolt-hole in South Africa. Or even about his obsession with sports cars. It seemed like something that would have been revealed before in the many articles about the man. And yet, Iris hadn't found a single reference to either.

Curious.

She shrugged it off for the moment. She had much weightier matters to consider right now. Staying out of sight for one thing. She wasn't going to chance being kicked out into the cold again. Something told her that if he tossed her out a second time, she would not find her way back inside again. And God knew, she wouldn't survive the night out in the elements. Well, maybe she would, but it would be unpleasant and she'd likely develop bronchial pneumonia, or something equally nasty, as a consequence.

"What next, boy? I should probably find something dry to wear... Do you think your master is asleep yet?" The dog looked up at her with a quizzical tilt of his head and a thought occurred to Iris. "What's your name? It must be on your tag, right?"

She reached for the collar again and checked the round silver tag.

Luna.

"Oh, you're a girl. Sorry, sweetheart. You're so big, I naturally assumed you were a lad. Terribly gender normative of me, I know. Luna, such a pretty name for a very pretty, good girl."

The dog's tail lazily swept the polished concrete floor.

"How long should I stay down here before your master heads off to bed, do you think?"

The dog yawned expansively, displaying a daunting array of sharp white teeth. Iris gulped, grateful that Luna had proven to be such a darling, despite her terrifying first impression.

"And your dickhead of a master must have *known* I was referring to you, yet he chose to leave me out there completely petrified and expecting the absolute worse. That must have given him a nice little laugh."

Although, she couldn't quite imagine the bearded, hulking, formidably unsmiling man she'd encountered earlier finding anything amusing.

She wandered around the garage, inspecting the cars, and trying not to think about how very cold she was. She daren't touch any of the vehicles for fear of setting off alarms, and she held her hands tightly clasped behind her back as she leaned over the bonnet of a metallic green Aston Martin DB12. She wouldn't have known what it was if her brother hadn't been salivating over a magazine spread of this exact car a few months ago.

The personalized number plate on the front was puzzling. It read MILESH5-WP. A quick glance around at the other cars confirmed that they all had the same registration plates, with only the numbers differing. They ranged from MILESH1 to MILESH8, with one car—a bright red Mini Cooper—tagged as CHARIH1-WP.

How odd.

It niggled at something in her memory banks, but the more she worried at it the more elusive it became. She shoved it aside for now, hoping it would come to her later when she was a bit more relaxed. Although, right now, she wondered if she'd ever feel relaxed again. And warm. She doubted very much that she'd ever be warm again.

Luna got up and shook herself before ambling toward the single flight of stairs leading up to an open door. It was dark beyond that door, and Iris wondered if she should follow the dog. Surely Trystan Abbott wouldn't be lurking around in a dark room, so it should be relatively safe up there.

An involuntary shiver wracked her body and sent her teeth chattering. And warmer... it'll hopefully be warmer up there.

The dog was halfway up the stairs before Iris decided to follow her. It was ice cold down here, probably because it was underground. If she avoided any well-lit areas, she could well find a room to hole up in tonight and figure out what to do in the morning.

Right now, she was exhausted, frozen to the bone, as well as mentally and emotionally fried. She just needed a few hours to recharge her battery before facing the monster that was Trystan Abbott again.

She snuck up the stairs as stealthily as possible, wincing whenever one of the wooden steps creaked beneath her tread.

When she tentatively poked her head around the door at the top of the stairs, it was to find the darkened kitchen that he'd hastily shepherded her through earlier. At least it was somewhat familiar territory. Slurping sounds coming from the corner closest to the back door told her that Luna was enjoying a drink of water. As her eyes adjusted to the gloom, which was only broken by ambient light coming from a standing lamp in a long hallway, she saw Luna circle in a massive wicker dog bed, before sinking down with a contented sigh. The pooch then proceeded to lick her unmentionables with noisy gusto.

Iris left her to it and looked around the kitchen once again for a clue as to where to go next. She peeked down the dimly lit hallway and could see light coming from beneath the doorway at the far end of the corridor.

Danger! Keep AWAY!

Nope, she was definitely not going anywhere near that area. To her left was another—shorter—corridor that led to a closed door. She slowly made her way toward that door, careful to avoid bumping into any obstacles.

After what felt like an eternity, she gratefully closed her hand over the doorknob.

"*Fuck!*" The involuntary whispered exclamation burst from her lips when the hinges creaked, the noise resonating like a thunderclap in the night. And even while she froze, she told herself there was no way he would have heard that, not with the way the wind was howling and the rain lashing outside.

The weather seemed to have worsened since she'd found

her way into the house, which made her resentment mount. He had gone to *bed*, believing she was out there in this. What kind of conscienceless prick could sleep knowing that he'd tossed someone out into this weather without any warmth or shelter or even a fucking light?

She gritted her teeth and determinedly pushed the door even wider before stepping inside.

She had no idea where she was because she couldn't see in the blackness. She was going to have to risk a light. She felt along the wall to her left and found the light switch fairly quickly.

The room flooded with warm light.

Oh.

It seemed to be a self-contained suite of some sort, with a kitchenette, a tiny round dining table and a living room. She could see a bedroom and bathroom through a pair of open doors on the right.

It was tastefully decorated and comfortable. While it was extremely cold in here, there were—praise *Jesus!*—a couple of radiator heaters stashed in a corner next to the sofa.

This was perfect, it was far enough away from *him* for Iris to remain undetected for a while. Though she doubted the kitchen was stocked.

She carefully and quietly shut the door behind her. She switched on one of the table lamps next to the sofa before turning off the brighter overhead light. There, that was better. At least this wouldn't be as obvious to spot if he were to wander into the kitchen for a midnight snack or something. She would cover the threshold of the door with a towel or blanket later to block out even more light.

She shuddered again, the cold creeping into her bones. She moved the heaters to different areas in the open-plan room and put each on its highest setting, but she knew it would take a while for them to properly heat up the place. She did a quick tour of the bedroom and bathroom. The double bed had been stripped, but fresh linens were stored in the ottoman at its foot. There were sweats in the closet. Iris could tell at a glance that they were too big for her, but she wasn't fussy—she was just happy to have a change of clothes for now.

Iris fought back a pang of loss as she thought of her little neon pink carry-on case that had been left out in the rain. She hadn't spared it a thought when she'd ducked into the kitchen earlier, confident that she'd retrieve it once she and Trystan Abbott had resolved their misunderstanding. But it was still out there, probably ruined by the rain, with the change of clothes in there undoubtedly destroyed as well.

Luckily, she had her passport and phone safely stowed in her puffer jacket pocket.

She fished out her phone and stared at the dead device for a second, before heading to the little kitchen, where a quick root around the drawers yielded positive results. She latched onto the coiled charger cable with a muted, triumphant cry and left her phone charging on the bedside table.

She retreated to the bathroom and shimmied out of her clothes. God, wet denim was almost impossible to get out of, but in the end—after a lot of squirming and wriggling—she managed to divest herself of the garment. The rest of her clothing soon followed, all chucked into a sodden heap on the tiled floor next to the laundry basket.

It was as she stood there, naked, nipples and flesh pebbled, with a blue tinge to her damp skin, that the bathroom door—which she'd closed out of habit—slammed open with such violence it rebounded off the wall and shattered one of the lovely porcelain tiles. Iris's fight or flight instinct deserted her completely, while she defaulted to the lesser-known *freeze in utter panic* instinct.

Trystan Abbott stood framed in the doorway, his bearded face a study in rage and hostility.

Iris abruptly became hyperaware of the fact that she was naked and squealed—the sound pathetic and high-pitched—and crossed one arm over her boobs and cupped her other hand over her other bits. His eyes dropped, as if her movements had only now brought his attention to her nudity, and his lip curled in mocking contempt.

"Don't fucking flatter yourself. You have nothing there to tempt me, lady."

Iris could have curled up in a ball of utter humiliation.

Like she didn't know that. Trystan Abbott had been involved with some of the most beautiful women in the world and, while Iris mostly liked the way she looked, she knew she hardly compared to supermodels and A-list actresses.

Whatever. This horrible man's opinion of her looks didn't matter to her. What mattered was that she was nude and he was in her space.

"This is an egregious invasion of privacy," she said and then immediately wished the ridiculous statement back, when he bristled in outrage. Oh man, he looked on the verge of snorting flames... Iris could practically smell the brimstone.

"Are you fucking kidding me right now? You're intruding and *I'm* the one invading *your* privacy?"

Fair point.

He clenched his fists and his eyes gave her another sweeping once-over before he—mercifully—tugged an outrageously fluffy bath sheet off a railing to throw at her in disgust.

"Cover yourself up. I don't know if this is some desperate, pathetic attempt at seduction, but I'm not interested."

What? How in the hell had he arrived at that conclusion? She glowered at him as she gratefully—and hastily—half-turned away from him to wrap the towel around her shivering body.

"I'm only *desperate* to get w-w-warm and d-dry," she spluttered, annoyed when none of her outrage made it into her voice. Instead, she sounded timid and terrified. "So don't *you* f-flatter yourself."

Something that could have been considered amusement in anyone else sparked in his eyes. But that couldn't be the case since Iris was quite sure that Trystan Abbott was an unfeeling, soulless monster. Human emotion was beyond him.

"I should toss you out on your bare ass," he said, the sentiment all the more chilling because of the lack of emotion in that detached voice. She had no doubt that he was capable of doing exactly that and the notion terrified her.

"No. Please." The naked plea emerged on a whisper and she couldn't disguise her fear from him.

He glared at her for a long, silent moment, those famous eyes unreadable, his expression grim.

"I'm calling the cops. Until they get here, you're not allowed to leave this space."

Iris sagged in relief. It was better than being kicked out into the cold and stormy dark again.

"Thank you."

"Don't thank me, you're going to be prosecuted to the fullest extent of the law. I don't imagine being stuck in jail in a foreign land is very pleasant."

Being in jail probably wasn't very pleasant, regardless of the country within which one found oneself incarcerated, but Iris wasn't about to mouth off in this situation, and she nodded meekly.

"I understand."

She wasn't particularly concerned about the police. She was certain that the misunderstanding would be cleared up as soon as she was able to reach his manager.

He backed out of the bathroom, maintaining eye contact as he did so. Luna was sitting on the plush rug in the middle of the cozy living room, patiently waiting for her master. He dropped a cursory pat on the tall dog's head. She got up, shook herself, and followed him toward the door.

Iris stood framed in the bathroom doorway, watching the duo pensively, somewhat relieved that he hadn't made good on his threat to kick her out again. She doubted he would have given her time to dress had he decided on that course.

This was really much be—

Her thoughts ground to a halt as he removed the key from the inside of the suite door.

"What are you doing?" she asked, her voice raised in alarm.

"Ensuring that you stay put this time."

"You can't mean to lock me in here?"

"Can't I?" His lips curled and her blood ran cold at the sinister intent she could see in his eyes. "I did say you're not allowed to leave this space, didn't I?"

"I won't go anywhere, I'll stay right here. Locking me in is unnecessary."

"I'll be the judge of that," he sneered. "You think I'd give you free rein over my personal space, allow you to go snooping through my private things?"

"I wouldn't."

"You just broke into my home."

"Only because I didn't fancy catching my death out there."

"I'm happy I won't be finding out if that flare for the dramatic reflects in your journalism."

She ground her teeth again. God, she thought she might actually hate him.

It didn't help that his sentiment reflected her own self-doubt of... God, was it just an hour ago? It felt like this ordeal had been stretching out for hours, days, fucking *months*.

"I'm not exaggerating," she said, hating the juvenile sulky tone soaked through her words. "Have you been outside? It's grim."

His shoulders lifted in unconcern and he called Luna to heel, before they both stepped through the door.

"Don't lock me in here, Mr. Abbott. Please. I won't be—"

He shut the door in the middle of her plea and Iris stared at the closed door in consternation and alarm, moaning in horror when she heard the decisive turn of the key.

"Okay, it's okay," she consoled herself. "You're fine. You're safe, soon to be warm. At least you're not out in this crazy storm."

Even as she said the words the wind gusted, and rain and hail lashed against the windows. Iris shuddered. She told herself that was definitely an improvement on the situation she'd found herself in half an hour ago.

But she couldn't stop staring at the closed—*locked*—door.

"Plenty of space," she told herself out loud. "There's plenty of space in here. There's light. There's heat. Windows. Other ways out. This is fine. You're fine."

Verbalizing the positives helped calm her somewhat and she concentrated on her deep-breathing techniques, which helped.

After a few long fraught moments, she was finally able to unstick her feet from the floor and turn away from the door. It was just for one night. Everything would be worked out tomorrow, then all of this would be a distant memory.

One night in a locked room was a piece of cake. She'd be fine.

"Totally fine," she whispered.

She was shivering violently by now, and she slowly made her way back to the bathroom. There was nothing she could do except finally have that life-saving hot shower.

FORTY MINUTES LATER—AFTER the most satisfying shower of

her life—Iris made her way to the kitchenette, hoping against hope to find some food.

She kept her gaze firmly averted from the locked door. If she concentrated hard enough, she could almost trick herself into forgetting it was there.

She'd unearthed a blow-dryer from the bathroom vanity and rough-dried her wavy hair into a riot of staticky curls. The sweat suit she'd found was simultaneously too big and too small. It stretched obscenely over Iris's butt and thighs, while being too long in the arms and legs and too tight over her chest. She'd had to fold the sleeves and legs of the garments several times. The owner of the clothes was definitely taller and slimmer than Iris who was curvy with a tendency toward plumpness.

Iris checked the fridge first. No luck. The blindingly white and bright interior was devoid of even the smears of food from days gone by.

"So clean," Iris marveled and then sighed. She checked the freezer. Same result.

The cupboards yielded a box of unopened crackers, a couple of months past its expiry date, and—*joy*—a can of baked beans. There was also an open box of *rooibos* herbal tea and a half-full jar of instant coffee.

Her stomach growled impatiently at the sight of the meager bounty, and she was salivating by the time she managed to get the can opened. Preferring to have a warm meal, she blitzed the contents in the microwave, made a cup of tea, *sans* sugar and milk—since those items were nowhere to be found—and sat down to enjoy her humble feast.

Once she had assuaged her immediate hunger, she pushed

herself from the table to check on her phone. It wasn't fully charged, but it had enough juice so she could check her messages and attempt to reach out to Hunter Quinn. She took it back to the table and scrolled through her messages and emails, while finishing the rest of her meal.

She hoped that Mr. Quinn would sort out the confusion with his client tonight, so Iris would not be stuck in this room tomorrow as well, but just in case, she had set some beans and crackers aside for breakfast.

After messaging her parents and best friend, Evan Brooks, she sent a text to Hunter Quinn.

> Hi! This is Iris Hughes. There seems to have been an unfortunate miscommunication. Mr. Abbott wasn't expecting me and he hasn't responded well to my presence. Please could you call him to clear up this misunderstanding? He's kind of threatening to have me arrested. Thanks so much.

She stared at the text for a while, but it remained unread.

"Come on, Iris," she chastised herself. "A watched pot never boils."

Iris was a big believer in self-motivation. She often verbalized her problems and thoughts to herself—it was just easier for her to work out solutions that way. It did mean that she was often muttering to herself and giving herself little pep talks. She was aware that it made her seem a bit of an odd duck, but she was way past caring what people thought of her.

She checked the time. It was close to midnight. God, it had

been a long, *long* twenty-four hours and Iris desperately needed
to sleep. Mr. Quinn lived in London which was an hour behind
South Africa at the moment. She didn't think he was the type of
man to be in bed by eleven p.m. on a Friday night, but it *was*
pretty late to be expecting people to check their texts immediately.

> PS. I'm really sorry to be texting you
> this late.

She stared at the second message in satisfaction. Her
mother would be proud. Iris's parents had raised her to always
be considerate of others.

She set aside the phone for now. Her parents had already
sent a reply to her previous message, dramatically thanking the
gods that she was safe, and then immediately following that up
with a voice note asking if she had enough warm clothing. She
grimaced—of course her *parents* would know that the weather
here sucked. And, of *course,* they would have expected her to be
aware of that fact too. Yes, Iris had known that she was flying
into winter, but she'd expected it to be a mere nod to the season.
Light-cardigan weather at best. Not this ice-cold hellscape.

She reassured (lied to) her parents about being more than
prepared. And deflected their further questions about the
mysterious assignment she was on, telling them via voice note
that they would soon understand the need for secrecy.

They didn't push her further, wishing her a good night and
admonishing her to call them in the morning and to stay in
regular contact.

Hoping that her next call wouldn't be from jail, begging for bail money, Iris promised them that she would text and call regularly.

Evan hadn't yet replied, and Iris knew her bestie was probably out having a ball somewhere.

She cleaned the sparse dishes she'd used and went to the bedroom where she put her phone back on charge. After haphazardly making the bed—exhaustion making her movements sluggish—Iris crept under the covers and instantly fell into a deep and dreamless sleep.

Chapter Three

Iris had a moment's disorientation when she opened her eyes the following morning. A few seconds later memories of the previous night came flooding back and she went from pleasantly warm and sleepy to alert and tense in an instant.

She jerked upright and grabbed up her phone to check her texts. Nothing from Mr. Quinn. Worse, her messages to him remained unread.

Shit.

She would try emailing him and then calling him.

It had just gone eight a.m. here. It was probably a little too early to call him on a Saturday morning. But if she sent an email to his business account—the only address she had for him—he'd probably only check it on Monday morning. That meant—if Trystan Abbott was true to his word—Iris could quite conceivably spend the weekend in a jail cell.

God, she couldn't do that. She literally *couldn't*. She wouldn't survive it.

She was legitimately starting to freak out now. She only hoped that The Dickhead—as she'd start to think of her reluctant host—was in a more reasonable frame of mind this morning. Hopefully he'd be in the mood to give her a fair hearing.

She pushed the covers down over her legs with a groan. Seriously, she'd much rather bury her head under the warm comforter and not surface again until she knew for sure that the situation with The Dickhead—*TDH* for short—was resolved. But she knew nothing could be fixed by hiding her head in the sand, or under the comforter, as it were. She had to be proactive about this and figure this shit out.

She got out of bed and bit back a yelp when her bare feet hit the icy tiles.

She had nothing to wear on her feet, her trainers and socks had been left sodden after the misadventures of the night before and she hadn't found any type of footwear in the closet belonging to her mystery benefactor with the statuesque supermodel proportions.

All of which meant Iris had no option but to brave the cold floor in her bare feet. Not ideal.

She stumbled her way to the door and tried the handle again, just in case TDH'd had an attack of conscience and unlocked the door while she was asleep.

No such luck.

She hated this. Last night she'd been too exhausted to fully comprehend what being locked in here meant, but this morning she wanted to crawl out of her skin at the sheer terror of being trapped.

She needed to clear up this misunderstanding as soon as possible. She had to make that unreasonable man listen to her.

She put her ear to the wood, hoping to hear some signs of life. She heard faint music, and the low gravelly undertone of *his* voice. Which meant he was out there, awake, aware, and basically ignoring her very existence.

Ooh, but that burned. It annoyed the ever-loving *hell* out of her.

She whipped out her phone and dialed Mr. Quinn's private number. It went straight to voicemail and Iris gritted her teeth as she left her message.

"Mr. Quinn? Uhm... Hi, this is Iris Hughes. As I stated in my text message, Mr. Abbott was not expecting me. He's accused me of trespassing and has locked me in a—uhm—well, it's quite a nice suite of rooms actually. But I'm still his prisoner and this just isn't on. He's threatened to call the police. At this point I wish he would do it and that they'd get here soon because I'm going to have to report him for false imprisonment, or kidnapping, or something. The situation is really deteriorating quite badly and I'd appreciate it if you'd—y'know—call him to straighten this out? Please? Thank you ever so much. Uh... goodbye?"

She disconnected the call, annoyed with the deference she'd heard in her own voice during that call. She'd meant to sound tough, no-nonsense, not like some meek out-of-her-depth little lamb.

Ugh. Typical.

"Iris Hughes, legend in her own mind."

She started banging on the door.

"Mr. Abbott, let me out, please." Iris was proud of how level her voice was. How reasonable her tone. No sign of her incipient panic. "We need to talk."

She stopped to listen again and the low rumbly voice had gone silent.

A few seconds later she heard the scrabbling of huge paws on the wooden floors down the hall, the eager running steps came ever closer until she could her wet snuffling at the door, following by a scratch and whine.

At least *someone* was on her side.

"Hello Luna-puppy, can you please ask The Dickhead to let me out? I'll give you all the treats in the world if you could do me that solid."

"Bribing my dog isn't going to get you very far." The deep voice on the other side of the door caused her to squeak in alarm. *Shit*, how the hell had he managed to get to the door without making a sound? Was he some light-footed elf or something? "And calling me a dickhead isn't doing anything to ingratiate you to me either."

Iris glared at the door, wishing she could incinerate the solid wooden slab between them with the force of her fury.

"I'm done trying to ingratiate myself to you. I demand you let me out! This is proper kidnapping."

"As opposed to? Improper kidnapping?" There was absolutely zero inflection in his voice.

"Look, when are the police coming? I'm going to counter arrest your entitled superstar arse for kidnapping."

"Blackmail? Have we finally unearthed your real reason for coming all this way?"

"My *real* reason for coming all this way, you arrogant jerk, was to interview you, as per an arrangement made via your manager. An arrangement *you* allegedly agreed to, by the way."

"So you keep insisting."

"Well, I don't know what to tell you," Iris said in helpless frustration. "That was the arrangement. Maybe you should call him."

"Convenient for you that you showed up just as Quinny left for his annual spiritual retreat, isn't it?" Sarcasm was rife in his words and Iris clenched her fists.

"It's not convenient at *all*. Do you have the number of this retreat? This is urgent, we need to clear it up."

"*I* don't need to clear anything up. The burden of proof is on you."

"Well, then give me the number and *I'll* call him."

TDH made a snorting sound that, on anyone else, could be considered a laugh.

"Right, like you don't fucking know he's on silent retreat at a Buddhist monastery in Nepal."

"He's... what?"

"Un-a-vail-able right now," TDH emphasized each syllable in true dick-ish fashion, and with no lack of smug satisfaction.

Iris's mouth opened and closed in shock. Who the hell did shit like that? Real people didn't swan off to Nepal to meditate with silent monks, come *on*.

"B-but he *can't* be. I spoke to him on Thursday before I left for the airport. He assured me that everything had been arranged."

"*Suuure*, he did."

Iris's legs gave way and she slid down the door in a gelatinous, disbelieving puddle of despondency.

"Then open the door and I'll show you the emails and texts he sent me."

"Electronic correspondence can be faked," he said, sounding bored.

Iris's head dropped into her hands and she stifled a sob.

"You said the burden of proof is on me," she said, her voice hoarse with tears. "How can I prove anything to you when you won't even look at the evidence?"

He remained silent for a long while and she was just wondering if he was still there, when he spoke, "I prefer not to waste my time."

"Fine, you don't have to believe me, I'm happy to leave. Please, just open this door." Her voice was soft and pleading. "As soon as I've arranged a tow truck for my rental car, I'll leave and never darken your door again."

"Easier said than done, lady. The storm won't let up till tomorrow. You're lucky as hell you crossed the bridge from town before the rain started because the river broke its banks and swept the bridge and most of the road away. There are also felled trees blocking the roads. We're cut off for at least two weeks until they're able to fix the roads and repair the bridge. Repairs can only start after the storm passes and they're forecasting two more cutoff low-pressure fronts following in quick succession after this one. So, two weeks is an optimistic prediction."

"W-what?" Iris's voice shook as she considered her situation. To be stuck here—with *him*—for two weeks or more, was a horrific possibility. And—dear *God*—what if he chose to keep her locked up that entire time? Iris wasn't sure she'd stay sane if he did.

He was so fucking hateful she doubted he'd even share his food with her. Would he just leave her in this room to slowly starve to death? And when they finally came looking for her, would he justify his actions as self-defense?

So sorry, Your Honor, but she was an intruder. I feared for my life and privacy. I couldn't feed her because it meant opening the door and possibly exposing myself to her toxic presence.

"I don't want to die," she whimpered quietly.

"What?" She could hear the consternation in his voice and wondered if she'd misunderstood the implications of the news he'd just imparted.

"Are you going to keep me locked in this room until the roads are cleared?" It was hard to keep the nausea at bay at the mere thought of being trapped within these restrictive walls.

Silence.

"I-I need my bags."

More silence.

"I need my medication."

"What medication?" His voice was gruff and teeming with suspicion.

"Anti-anxiety medication." She offered the personal information reluctantly, but he needed to understand the urgency.

She didn't take it often, but kept the prescription filled just in case.

This situation definitely qualified as stressful, and if she was going to remain locked in here, she was going to need her meds.

"I have some in my jacket pocket," she explained. "I transferred them from my handbag—I didn't want to weigh myself down with too many things from the car—but the rest is in my big suitcase in the car."

"Anti-anxiety meds? What triggers the anxiety?" he asked. The question sounded like it was torn from him by a thousand hellhounds.

"*Stress*," she emphasized. "You know, like the stress that comes from being unjustifiably imprisoned when you suffer from a fear of being locked in?"

"That so?" He didn't sound at all sympathetic, or convinced. "What else?'

"Hunger—by the way there's no food in here."

"I see. Any other triggers?"

PMS—the fluctuating hormones could send her spiraling some months, while during others she would be perfectly fine but she wasn't about to disclose that information to Grumpasaurus sex—uhm—*rex* over there.

"This conversation is about to be a trigger if we don't change the subject," she muttered under her breath. She didn't often speak of her anxiety—she lived an active, normal life in spite of it. But she *did* need her meds in case of flare-ups. And she definitely needed it for what she recognized was going to be a *very* challenging few days, possibly weeks, in this man's company.

"Look, it doesn't matter what triggers the anxiety. With my meds I can keep it at bay."

She could almost feel the air from his loud, exasperated sigh through the door.

The lock turned in the door and it swung outward before she had a chance to react. Two seconds later, she was staring up at the tall, brooding, bearded Trystan Abbott, who was glowering down at her huddled form on the floor.

She wasn't sure—because of the bushy beard—but she was almost certain his lips thinned at the sight of her.

"You're a fucking weird chick," he said almost to himself, before turning away from her to haul her big, bright, pink hardshelled suitcase into the room. He lifted it clear over her head and dropped it on the floor by the kitchen counter.

Iris scrambled to her feet and stared at the open door, poised for flight, before his harsh voice stopped her in her tracks.

"You can run, sure, but you'll find yourself out in the storm again, with no way back to the nearest town. And rest assured, once you're out there, you won't be allowed back in here. So, what's it to be? You can make a run for it—and believe me, that's *my* personal favorite option—and wander around, in the rain and howling wind, with hundred-year-old trees being torn up all around you, flash floods, and mudslides, until *maybe* you make it to town alive. Or stay here in this room and out of my fucking way until the police can finally reach us and arrest your ass."

"If I could just get a tow truck for my car."

He sighed dramatically.

"Jesus Christ, you're a little slow on the uptake, aren't you?

No truck can get here, the road is gone. For that matter, so's your car. A tree totaled it during the night."

"What?" Iris felt the blood drain from her head at that bit of news.

"Your rental... it's toast. Luckily, just the roof and hood, which meant I could get into the trunk to retrieve this pink monstrosity." He indicated toward her suitcase. But Iris was too preoccupied to take offense at the slight against her beloved neon pink luggage.

"I was going to stay in the car last night, but thought I'd take my chances and walk here instead," she said, mostly speaking to herself.

"Well then, I guess you cheated death four times last night. First the river, then the car crushing and then the big bad wolf."

That diverted her train of thought enough to raise her eyes to his pitiless face.

"What was the fourth time?"

His eyes were shards of silver ice and his lips were pressed into a thin line before he said, voice quiet and intense, "Me, sugarplum... The last woman who thought she could manipulate me *died*, lady. So don't *fuck* with me."

What?

Was he referring to Trish Nesbitt? Iris had meant to ask him about Ms. Nesbitt's death during the interview. It had been an accident. Why would he imply that he'd had something to do with that?

"You mean Ms. Nesbitt? But that was an accident. Why—"

"No." That was it, just a single, implacable word. And it effectively shut her up.

"There will be no questions," he continued after a long pause. "No answers. No fucking interview. You will stay in this room. We will not speak. And when the time comes, you're to face criminal charges. That's it. End of."

He stalked to the door, all big, bristling male, and Iris noticed for the first time that he was wearing a pair of faded jeans paired with a red and black plaid flannel shirt.

She felt a nervous giggle rise up in her throat and clapped a hand over her mouth to suppress it. Too late. A soft, merry little chortle escaped, and he whirled around to pin her with a glare.

"What the fuck is so funny?"

She pressed her lips together and dropped her hand before shaking her head.

"N-nothing." But the word emerged on another traitorous burble of laughter. God, he looked *pissed* off. And Iris could have cursed her irreverent sense of humor for choosing this time to surface.

"It's just the hair"—*Oh God, Iris*, she begged herself. *Shut up!*—"and the b-beard and the whole lumberjack ensemble" —*Jesus please, strike me mute and spare me from this folly*— "You've really committed to this crazy hermit shit, haven't you?"

Gah, too late! Why did she have to have a chronic case of *foot-in-mouthitis?*

TDH's face froze, only the slight twitch below his left eye served as proof that he was still alive, as he continued to stare at her with zero expression on his face.

"You're here only because you've forced your way into my house and now somehow, by default, I've become responsible for your health and well-being. I'm trying—even though it goes against my own desires—to be a decent human being. But you're treading a *very* fine line. And it won't take much to remind me that I actually have fuck all responsibility toward you and kick you the hell out."

Iris clamped her lips together and nodded curtly. Right. Point made. No more hot takes from her then.

"Sorry," she muttered. "Thank you for taking me in."

Jeez, was she really thanking her jailer for imprisoning her right now? Talk about your classic gaslighting job.

His eyes narrowed on her face, as if he were trying to gauge her sincerity.

Apparently, he didn't like what he saw because he muttered something foul beneath his breath before he shook his head and strode toward the door.

"Please, don't lock the door." She directed her plea at his broad back, and he stopped in his tracks, his shoulders tensing.

"You have everything you need in here. There's no need for you to roam around the house. You stay in here, out of my way, out of my life, and out of my business. Trust me, we'll both be happier for it."

"I promise I'll stay in here, you don't have to lock the door."

"If you'll stay in here anyway, then me locking the door won't make a difference, will it?" The question was almost silky, despite the gruffness of his stupid lumberjack/Batman voice.

"It will make a difference to me," she countered, before adding in sheer desperation, "I have cleithrophobia. It's a fear of being confined."

"Bullshit. You just made that up."

With that, he closed the door and Iris remained tense,

breath bated until... the key turned in the lock. She swallowed back a sob, and her shoulders sank.

It wasn't a lie. She *was* cleithrophobic. Even though there was plenty of space in here, the thought of being trapped, of being unable to move about freely, or to leave anytime she wanted scraped at her nerve endings and left her feeling on edge and short of breath. The pills helped calm her, but if her situation didn't improve, her increasing fear and anxiety would override the medication.

This was her worst nightmare.

She didn't even want to consider how she'd react if he carried out his threat to have her arrested. She didn't think she could stand being kept in a jail cell.

Last night she'd been too tired to really think about it, and there'd been a sense of optimism, the absolute belief that everything would be sorted out in the morning. Today, there was only the prospect of two endless weeks imprisoned within just these walls. With nothing for company except her own thoughts. And God knew, her thoughts tended to veer toward histrionics and chaos rather than calm and logic.

She was about to descend into a chaotic whirlpool of worst-case scenarios when the lock clicked again. Her head whipped up and her heart leapt in the hope that he'd changed his mind. The door opened and a big, veined hand clutching her smaller carry-on suitcase appeared around the edge of the wood. The case was deposited on the floor, and nudged inward, before the door abruptly shut and locked again.

The hope in her chest shriveled and died, but she shoved it aside and focused on her case. It matched the big one. Neon pink and hard shelled. It looked none the worse for wear and for the first time Iris dared to hope that the interior had remained dry despite the deluge that had fallen—was still falling—from the skies over the course of the last twelve hours.

There was mud caked around the wheels and the bottom of the case, but it was still sealed.

Her laptop was in the case and Iris sent up a quick prayer to every deity she could think of before rolling the case to the small sitting room, sinking down onto the carpet, laying the small bag on its side, and unzipping it slowly.

She held her breath as she opened it, and then exhaled slowly as she cast an eye over the not-at-all wet—or even slightly damp—interior. Her laptop was in its protective lime green neoprene sleeve, the surface of which was dry to the touch.

She carefully unzipped the bag, and her laptop was nestled in there, looking just fine.

Iris exhaled slowly, thankful for this one good thing that had happened in the last forty-eight hours.

She considered the new title of her article.

How I Was Imprisoned by That Surly Bastard, Trystan Abbott.

Okay, that was a little rough... but it was only a working title. Still, if TDH wouldn't sit down to the agreed-upon interview with her, then she would have to write an honest account of her extremely negative experience with him. And he wouldn't be able to deny any of it. Because if he made good on his promise to have her arrested, then Iris would have her newly acquired future criminal record to back up the facts of her story.

She inhaled deeply, trying to center herself, and lay her big suitcase beside the smaller one. She eyed the cable tie for a moment, before grabbing a pair of kitchen scissors from the knife rack. She had her bag open in no time at all.

She spent the next half-hour pleasantly occupied with packing her clothes into the small closet and chest of drawers in the bedroom. It soothed her to have some familiar things around. Her laptop sat on the round dining table and her e-reader on the nightstand. Her toiletries and cosmetics were dotted around the bedroom and bathroom. She changed into her favorite jeans, and an oversized fluorescent yellow hoodie. She'd packed enough clothes to last for at least two weeks, and twice as many panties and bras.

Mr. Quinn had arranged for her to spend three weeks with his client, but Iris wasn't always the most organized of people and she'd been concerned that she may have under packed for the trip. But she was happy to note that she'd brought enough warm clothing and underwear to last for the duration of her stay. Hoodies, cardigans, jeans and sweatpants, lots of short-sleeved tees though—she rolled her eyes at the sight of those— and a flippin' *bikini*, of all things.

She'd also packed—thank the gods of small things—socks! So many, many warm pairs of thick socks. She immediately rolled a pair onto her cold, numb feet and spent a few minutes massaging some warmth back into her extremities.

Once she was fully unpacked, she tucked her suitcases into an out-of-the-way corner in the small living room and curled up with her laptop on the big easy chair facing away from the locked front door, hoping to find an email from Mr. Quinn. She didn't necessarily believe Trystan Abbott about his manager being uncontactable. It beggared belief that an important, busy man like Mr. Quinn wouldn't check his phone at least once a day.

She swore beneath her breath when she realized that she wasn't—of course—connected to the Wi-Fi, and picked up her phone instead.

"*Shit!*" Looked like her international roaming data plan had run out. Her own fault for cheaping out and getting a plan that was good for only twenty-four hours. She'd fully expected to have access to TDH's Wi-Fi after arrival and hadn't seen the need to switch out SIM cards or get a more comprehensive roaming plan. Now she was as cut off as she'd been when her battery had died.

She needed to remain in contact with family and friends, people who loved her—it was essential to her mental and emotional well-being—if she was to remain trapped in here.

She stared into space for a few moments, dreading yet another frustrating interaction with TDH, but knowing that she'd have to bow down to the inevitable and attempt to persuade him to share the Wi-Fi password with her. She was still considering her current predicament—choosing for the moment not to dwell on the bigger picture—when the key turned in the lock, catching her off-guard.

She didn't have time to react, before the door opened—without warning—and *he* stepped into the suite with a tray balanced on one brawny forearm.

She turned her head to follow his progress, but he didn't spare her so much as a glance, merely taking a few strides to the dining room table and placing the tray on it. Luna followed him into the room, and padded over to where Iris was sitting. The dog's head was the same height as Iris's and she booped her wet nose against Iris's cheek, clearly demanding an ear scratch.

For a moment, Iris forgot all her woes and giggled. She tucked her laptop between her bum and the side of the chair and used both hands to frame the dog's endearing face.

"You're such a sweetheart," she crooned into the dog's ear, before giving her the scratches she deserved.

"Luna, let's go," TDH called the dog in his most commanding Batman voice, and Luna spared him just one glance, before blatantly opting to ignore him in favor of Iris's scratches. "Come on, Luna."

"Please, can she stay with me for a while?" Iris asked, hating the beseeching note in her voice. But maybe, with Luna's companionship, the room would stop shrinking with every breath she took.

"No."

"I promise not to trick her into revealing any of your deepest darkest secrets."

He looked directly at her for the first time since entering the room and visibly flinched at the sight of her.

What the heck?

"Jesus, I didn't think I'd ever see a color more hideous than your luggage, but that hoodie has it beaten by miles."

Iris gasped.

"How *rude*," she spluttered. "We can't all walk around in mopey blacks, grays, and neutrals, like you."

"I'm literally wearing a red shirt right now," he pointed out. Iris blinked, nonplussed by that indisputable fact.

"Red and *black*," she eventually retorted with a disdainful little snort. "Besides, you're such a grumpy little storm cloud, you leech the color out of everything. So that red might as well be gray."

He was staring at her in that probing, intense way of his again, and Iris betrayed her unease by shifting her weight from foot to foot before continuing doggedly, "Anyway, my point is, some people happen to *like* color."

"There's color and then there's whatever the fuck that is," he said, pointing at her hoodie. He looked more animated than she'd seen him since arriving here. "You look like a glowstick."

"Just because I'm your prisoner doesn't give you license to relentlessly mock me."

His face tightened and his eyes went flat, as if her words had reminded him of exactly who she was and what she was doing there. Iris instantly regretted the loss of that bit of animation from his expression, and now wished she'd bantered with him instead of getting so offended. But she was exhausted, stressed, and quite honestly, petrified that she was going to wind up in jail at the end of all this. The uncertainty was eating at her, and the fear and vulnerability had her on the verge of a panic attack.

"Eat your breakfast," he snapped, jerking his head toward the tray on the table, and Iris registered the food for the first time. She wasn't sure exactly what it was he'd brought her to eat, but her eyes flooded with tears of gratitude.

He took a step back, appearing uncomfortable at the sight of her tears.

"Thank you so much," she whispered. Her words were punctuated by her growling stomach and his brow lowered at the sound. She swiped at her wet eyes, embarrassed by her weepiness. "I wasn't sure if you'd bring me any food and there's not much to eat in here."

His frown turned into a glower and he moved his shoulders in a jerky, awkward up-down motion.

"It's not my intention to starve you," he muttered. "I'll bring your lunch at one."

"Can Luna stay until then?"

"No."

"Please?"

"I said no. Luna, *come*." The dog gave Iris's knuckles a regretful lick and turned toward her owner. She walked, with almost defiant slowness, toward where he stood waiting at the door and gave a last little whine before vacating the room.

He turned to follow the dog, dragging the door shut behind him in the same movement.

"No, wait," she called, remembering something. She was shocked when he actually paused, not looking at her, merely waiting. "Can I have the Wi-Fi password? I need to stay in contact with my family, or they'll worry."

He didn't reply. Didn't acknowledge her request in any way at all. Instead, he shut the door with a quiet click and, a few long moments later, locked it.

Iris moaned. A quiet, despairing sound. Her entire body collapsed in on itself as the oppressive weight of the walls and ceilings closed in on her. She focused on her breathing, hoping it would tamp down the dread burgeoning in her chest.

When the panic didn't subside fast enough this time, she rushed to a window and slid it up until she was able to lean her upper body all the way out. She didn't care about the rain—from which the eaves provided some protection—or cold, instead she focused on the ground beneath the window. She could leave if she needed to, she could climb out of this window and be free. It wasn't so bad. She had options. She was fine.

It helped and as the panic subsided, she realized she was damp and actually shivering from the icy cold. She retreated inside, and—despite the plummeting temperature in the room—left the window partly open.

Chapter Four

Once she'd managed to get her panic attack under control, Iris tucked into the rapidly cooling breakfast. It wasn't anything fancy, two grilled cheese sandwiches and coffee. Nonetheless, she was grateful for such basic human courtesy from her jailer and scarfed down the meal like the starving woman she was.

She downed a couple of pills after the meal and—once she felt a little more in control—shut the window because it was freezing. She took solace in the fact that she could open it at any time. And that thought helped.

For now.

After that she wandered from bathroom to bedroom to living room to kitchen in an endless loop. She occasionally paused at the windows to glare out at the rain, willing it to stop. She knew she could climb out of one of the windows and make her way into the main part of the house, but she could pretty much predict TDH's reaction to any such move from her, and she didn't want to find herself out on her arse, trying to navigate her way—on foot—back to town in this relentless downpour.

She finally stopped her restless pacing because it didn't help —instead it heightened her anxiety and she had to remain calm. She collapsed onto the sofa and picked up the TV remote to flip through some channels, pausing every so often when something caught her interest. Eventually she stopped at what appeared to be a soap opera. They weren't speaking English—Iris couldn't quite place the language, it had a vaguely Germanic sound to it, so it was probably Afrikaans—but there were subtitles. Ooh, it looked like someone's baby had been kidnapped.

Iris grabbed up a scatter cushion and hugged it to her chest as she watched the drama unfold. It was a fascinating insight into South African society... well, the interaction between the characters was fascinating. She imagined that babies being kidnapped by jealous ex-lovers likely wasn't a common occurrence in everyday life here. It was fun to try and differentiate between the languages spoken. Iris had a good ear for languages and, so far, had picked up at least three separate dialects.

One twenty-five-minute installment flowed into the next, and before she knew it, Iris had watched five episodes. She was disappointed to realize that there were no other episodes forthcoming and assumed it was an omnibus of the week's quota.

It was a diverting way to spend a couple of hours, and had —*mostly*—kept her mind off the locked door. But now she was back to her dismal reality.

She switched off the TV and sighed, restlessness and boredom and prickling anxiety immediately setting in. She considered taking more pills, but tamped down the urge. She'd wait until after dinner. She was going to have to battle her way through this.

Iris wasn't used to having nothing to do—she lived an active life. Back home, when she wasn't occupied with her many freelance editing projects, she was helping her parents, or volunteering at various animal shelters. She rarely found herself at loose ends.

How she wished she had an editing project to sink her teeth into right now. But she'd finished up all her jobs after landing this dream assignment and had temporarily closed up shop to come here.

She'd hoped this would lead to bigger, better things. A career in entertainment journalism, maybe. She laughed bitterly at her naivete. All she'd be getting from this nightmare was a criminal record.

She buried her face in her hands, ready to give in to the ever-lurking tears, when she heard light scratching and sniffing at the door. Her head jerked up and she darted to the door to peek through the keyhole. All she could see was Luna's big, shiny black nose, and she smiled.

"Hey girl," she whispered, so thankful to have the dog there. "Thank you for visiting me. It makes me feel less lonely. I wish TDH would let you in to stay with me for a while." The last emerged on a wistful note and she sighed. She slid down the wall and sat flat on her bum, next to the door. She was reassured to hear Luna still snuffling at the keyhole, and continued talking to the dog.

"I wonder what my mum and dad are doing right now?

Probably run off their feet at the Bhandari wedding. They're catering for a thousand guests. Gosh, my parents were so excited to land that contract. But you can be damned sure Robbie will be bitching about working today, especially at an event that size. He'll moan even more than usual because I'm not there to help."

She smiled fondly—missing her family so much it ached—and picked at the cuticle on her thumb.

"He's ten years younger than me, you see. Only sixteen. He resents having to spend his weekends and spare time waiting tables at our parents' catering events. He wants to be like the rest of his mates. We don't have much in common, but that's one teenage resentment we share. I was the same. I was such an arsehole about it too. Even more so than Robbie."

She thought back to all the times she'd flared up at her parents about having to work on Fridays and Saturdays. She'd been such a bitch. And deliberately hurtful.

She shook off the thought. She was depressed enough right now without fueling that despondency with familial regrets.

She sat wrapped up in her memories for a long moment before a soft scratch at the door—followed by a quiet whine—jerked her from her thoughts.

"Sorry, Luna," she said, her voice barely above a whisper. "I got a bit bogged down there. I think I'm homesick. I'm not usually one to wallow in my own misery, but this situation is a little ridiculous, and I feel like I deserve at least a day of *what the fuckness* before I drag myself out of it."

She heard a sharp whistle, followed by a curt, "Let's go, girl!"

Luna's paws scrabbled on the floors and Iris heard her retreating without so much as a farewell sniff.

"Hey, where are you guys going?" she called, with no real hope of having her question acknowledged. "Can I come too?"

No response from either Luna or her horrible master, instead Iris heard a door slamming in the distance.

Did they really just go out in this shit weather? She hurried over to the window, hoping to catch a glimpse of them, even though the door had slammed on the other side of the house.

It was pelting down and the wind hadn't calmed at all. If anything, it seemed worse. Why would they venture out in this mess?

What if something happened to the damned fool man? Did she even care? If he got himself injured or killed, she'd be fine. Even better than she was now, really, because she'd be able to climb out of this very window and make her way into the main house where she'd have access to food and possibly a phone.

She was imagining a scenario whereby she heroically rescued him—with Luna's assistance—from the bottom of a steep hill when she heard the door opening again, immediately followed by fast, urgent footfalls heading her way. Seconds later the key rotated in the lock, and she turned from the window just as the door pushed inward.

Trystan Abbott stepped into the room. He was wearing a dark green heavy-duty oilskin rain jacket—the type fishermen on boats used—water was streaming off it in rivulets and leaving puddles on the floor. The man himself looked even bigger in the wet-weather gear and appeared to be bristling with agitation.

Immediately alarmed, Iris took a couple of steps toward him, before coming to an uncertain halt.

"What's wrong? Is Luna okay?"

No sooner had she asked the question than the big dog nosed her way into the room and Iris's shoulders dropped in relief.

"I need your help," TDH said, storming forward and grabbing her hand without any warning. Taken aback by the unsolicited contact—as well as by the iciness of his skin against hers—Iris didn't immediately protest. She was dragged halfway to the door before she dug her heels in and slowed down their progress. He stopped, his head whipped around, and he pinned her with an intimidating glare.

"My help with what?" Iris asked, matching his glare with one of her own.

"Laying sandbags in front of the garage doors to mitigate the effects of the flooding."

"What flooding?" she asked, alarmed. "Are we safe here?"

He sighed, the sound short and irritated and really bloody condescending.

"The house itself is pretty high, so the possibility of it flooding is minimal. The garage, however, is underground."

"Seems shortsighted," she couldn't help but retort, and he gave her another annoyed glower.

"Stop fucking mouthing off and get a move on."

"Maybe if you were less rude to me, I'd consider helping you save your millions of pounds worth of cars. Until then, I'm quite content to stay in my prison cell."

Only she wasn't. Iris was dying to get out, but she figured

she had some bargaining power here, which she ought to take advantage of.

He eyed her for a speculative moment, then shrugged in unconcern and dropped her hand.

"Fine, you'll probably slow me down anyway."

Shit, didn't the guy understand the fine art of negotiation?

"You're supposed to offer me something to sweeten the deal," she informed him, folding her arms over her chest.

"Don't be ridiculous. I don't need your help that desperately."

"Sure you do," she negated. "You came pounding in here reeking of panic and desperation. You're worried about your precious cars, aren't you?"

"Thought you'd jump at the opportunity to make yourself useful and get out of this room for a while. That prospect *should* have been enough of a deal sweetener."

Ugh... he was right about the latter. Why was she risking the possibility of him changing his mind?

Nonetheless, she needed to use the little leverage she had. "I'd help for the Wi-Fi password."

He crossed his beefy arms over his massive chest and his unkempt beard twitched as his top lip curled.

"Sure."

His easy acquiescence threw her, and she blinked up at him, her mouth slightly agape.

"What?"

"I said 'sure'," he repeated.

Iris's stomach sank and she gave him a dejected frown.

"You were going to give it to me anyway, weren't you?"

The wicked gleam in his eyes told her she was right, but he didn't admit as much out loud. Damn it, she should have asked for something else, like visitation rights with Luna... or leaving the door unlocked.

What a letdown. She'd been so certain she had the upper hand, but no, he held all the cards. She was so damned frantic to get out of this room that even if he'd refused to give her the password, she would still have conceded. And he knew it.

"Put on some shoes," he said, after a glance down at her socks.

He made no acknowledgment of, or apology for, the fact that he'd been about to drag her out into the wet and cold without shoes.

Iris grumbled under her breath as she went to the closet to drag out her hiking boots, which she'd nearly not brought because of how heavy they are. But she'd had some romantic notion of joining Trystan Abbott on long hikes, while they amicably chatted about his life, loves, and losses.

Such foolish, optimistic whimsy.

He eyed her boots when she rejoined him at the front door.

"Those are surprisingly practical," he acknowledged, almost begrudgingly, and Iris did her best to disguise her rolling eyes from him.

Unsuccessfully.

"What's with that expression?" he demanded to know, and she huffed an impatient sigh.

"I'm not sure why you're surprised by my choice of *practical* shoes when you know nothing about me." She used air quotes around the word practical just because she figured it would annoy him. Sure enough, his eyes flashed at the gesture.

"You don't strike me as a very practical person. You trekked across unknown terrain, in the dark and the rain, armed with nothing but a phone flashlight... thinking that your intrusion would be welcomed by someone who'd clearly sought the most isolated place he could find in order to avoid human contact. Not very practical or—y'know—clever."

"My decision to trek here through the dark, and *wind*—it only started raining after you tossed me out into the storm—was validated if what you said about the car being crushed is true."

He didn't respond, merely leveled a malevolent look at her before turning abruptly. "Do you have anything waterproof? A rain slicker? Jacket?"

Her lips thinned and her silence spoke for her. Same as his insufferable, smug, know-it-all snort spoke for him.

"Now, packing some kind of waterproof gear when traveling to an area infamous for its winter storms would definitely have been considered a practical, clever move."

Arrogant prick.

"I don't have anything that'll fit you," he said, running an assessing glance over her frame.

"I'll be fine. I can bear a little rain." Only it wasn't a little rain. There was a seriously scary amount of water falling from the sky right now.

"If you say so," he said with a disinterested shrug. "Follow me."

He led the way through the hallway back toward the kitchen. It was interesting to see the house in the gloomy light of a rainy day. Last night everything had been dark and a little terrifying but today she found herself astonished by how lovely this house was. The colors were bright and fresh—cream, sage, and the palest of pinks as an accent hue. It was unexpected and not at all what she would have pictured for Trystan Abbott's home.

They hastened past a wall of framed photos and Iris's steps slowed as she tried to take in the images. Clearly annoyed with her lingering, he backtracked a few steps and grabbed her hand to drag her along behind him.

The contact—like before—startled her. What the hell was up with these caveman tactics?

"Hey, *mister*, it's not okay to just grab a woman like that," she gasped, fighting to keep up, and simultaneously trying to pull her arm from his unrelenting grip.

"And it's not okay to snoop around people's private shit."

"They're photos. On display. There to be looked at. Why else go to the trouble of printing, framing and hanging them?"

"They're to be looked at by invited guests, which you are not." He didn't even bother to glance back at her as he said that, instead hauling her to the kitchen door leading outside.

She hesitated just inside the door, staring up at the gunmetal gray sky and the constant torrent of water streaming down from it. The man in front of her stopped as well and turned back to glower at her for a long moment before his shoulders lifted and fell in what looked like a heavy sigh.

Before she knew what his intention was he had dragged his raincoat off and draped it over her shoulders like a cape, fastening only the top two buttons at her throat and tugging the hood up over her head.

"It's hopeless trying to put your arms in the sleeves," he muttered, half to himself. "It's miles too big. And it'll be impossible to roll up, so this'll have to do until we get to the shed."

"You don't have to do this," she protested half-heartedly, but he ignored her and continued forward.

Iris followed him. The jacket helped, but the front of her hoodie and her jeans were still getting soaked. At least her shoulders and head remained dry, as long as she kept the hood from blowing back.

At that point—regretting every decision that had led to this miserable moment in her life—Iris was helpless to do anything other than keep her eyes trained on Trystan Abbott's broad shoulders and follow meekly.

Alarmingly, there was water flowing pretty rapidly over the toes of her boots, and the fast-running streams seemed to get deeper as they progressed further downhill into the garden.

He led her to the large-ish shed and she waited, shivering, while he unlocked the padlock on the doors. He turned to face her after swinging the doors open. Even though it was quieter inside the—blessedly dry—shed, the wind and rain were still a constant roar, and it was hard to hear him, but Iris kept her eyes glued to his face, afraid of missing some important instruction.

"There are two wheelbarrows," he all but shouted down at her. "We'll fill the first one together. I'll wheel it down to the garage where I'll offload and stack the bags. Meanwhile, you fill the empty wheelbarrow, and when I bring the other one back, I'll take the filled one back down. We can get an efficient production line type of system going like that."

Iris dubiously eyed the *very* many bright orange sandbags heaped against the back wall of the shed. They weren't very big, but they looked heavy as hell. Iris was of medium height and weight, and not particularly strong, and she wasn't sure she'd get the wheelbarrow loaded by the time he was done stacking the sandbags.

Still, since she'd managed to lug her twenty-five-kilogram suitcase around for short distances at a time, she could probably heave sandbags into a wheelbarrow if she had to. She just wouldn't be very fast at it.

"How heavy are those bags?" she asked, pushing the hood off her head when it kept slipping down over her eyes. In the meantime, she tried very hard not to notice how his flannel shirt was plastered to his muscular chest and shoulders, leaving not much to the imagination.

He gave her another once-over—again appearing unimpressed with what he saw—and lifted his shoulders.

"About fifteen kilograms. You look weak and soft as hell, but you'll probably be able to manage that."

"I'm not weak and soft," she retorted sharply.

"No?" Now it was his turn to look dubious.

"No, I can do this," she told him through chattering teeth. God, she was freezing. It felt like cold and wet had been pretty much her constant state of being since arriving in this godawful place. She turned toward the bags and fumbled with one, her frigid, numb fingers struggling to get a grip around the edges of the bag.

He made an impatient sound behind her and brushed by her to pick up two bags at once and load them into one of the empty wheelbarrows.

Show-off.

Iris was finally able to wedge her fingers beneath the bag and managed—with an embarrassing groan and a great deal of effort—to lift it. She couldn't quite straighten her back and did a humiliating crouched little crab walk to the wheelbarrow, where —with gargantuan effort—she heaved it a bit higher to dump it on top of the *six* bags he'd already put in there.

He didn't acknowledge her paltry contribution. Instead, he continued to steadily fill the wheelbarrow, six bags for every one of hers. She managed to double her pace after a couple of warm-up bags, but she was still much slower than he was.

She shrugged out of the raincoat, hoping she would move faster without having its cumbersome heaviness hamper her movements, but that didn't help.

The first wheelbarrow was filled within minutes—thanks to him—and he gave a pointed glare at the empty one, before leveling a critical look at her.

Yeah, message received.

Get your arse in gear, Iris!

"Wait," she called as he turned to leave. "Don't you want to put your raincoat back on?"

He shook his head.

"No point, I'm soaked through already. And it'll only slow me down."

He was gone before she could reply and she rolled her eyes at the tough-guy routine before getting to work.

She managed to get a good rhythm going and had the second wheelbarrow almost half-filled by the time he returned with his now-empty one.

He stood glowering at her hard work for a second.

"It's half-empty," he said. The impatience snapping around the edges of his words curled her hands into tight fists.

"It's half-full," she corrected. "And I'm going as fast as I can."

"Knew you'd be useless at this."

The unfair words snatched her breath from her chest as anger heated her from the inside out.

"I'm doing the best I can, you-you *prick*! You're twice my size. You can't expect me to have the same strength and speed as you."

"I get the feeling you've spent most of your life whining about how unfair life is and how you just can't seem to catch a break. Complaining seems to be your natural state."

"*Nothing* about these last few days has been normal, so excuse me for being vocal about how shit it's all been."

"Nobody to blame but yourself," he said with an unconcerned shrug, bypassing her to grab a couple of sandbags.

"And y'know..." she said, huffing and groaning as she lifted another bag herself. "*You.* And your clearly incompetent manager."

"Lift with your knees," he instructed, as he watched her bend at the waist to grab the corners of a bag and drag it to the wheelbarrow, where she lifted it the short distance into the barrow bed. "You'll fuck up your back if you keep doing it that way."

"This is the easiest way for me to do it," she argued, even though she was starting to feel the burn in her lower back already and her arms were in the process of turning to jelly.

"Try squatting when you grab the bag and then pushing up with your knees."

"I'm fine," she insisted stubbornly. She'd been lifting with her knees until the last few bags when her thighs had started to tremble with each squat. After nearly falling just before he'd returned, she'd started in on this less-practical method. It was getting the job done. She'd worry about the pain later.

She could feel disapproval oozing from his very pores, but refused to look at him. He struck her as the type of man who was used to being deferred to and obeyed. He wouldn't appreciate being blatantly ignored.

But she didn't care. It was clear the interview was a no-go, so she didn't have to suck up to him. She was his unwilling prisoner and she wasn't about to be pleasant to her jailer.

She deliberately avoided eye contact as she dragged bag after bag to the wheelbarrow, refusing to acknowledge her shaking arms and thighs, or the burning sensation in her back and chest.

He left with the filled wheelbarrow and she started on the empty one. When he next returned it was three-quarters full. He didn't say anything, merely filled the rest of it, while she switched her focus to the empty wheelbarrow. They worked silently, side by side, for another hour.

Iris's entire body was one massive ache by then and she was

going through the motions, moving like an unthinking automaton and barely registering his comings and goings while she worked.

When he returned with the wheelbarrow for the umpteenth time, Iris jerkily moved to retrieve another bag, but his hand on her elbow stayed the movement.

"We're out of bags," he said, and she blinked, gazing at the empty corner uncomprehendingly. "Why don't you sit over here while I stack these last few? I'll be right back."

He led her to a rickety wooden bench, probably stored in the shed because it had seen better days. She had zero control over her movements and was grateful to him for leading her to the bench as she wouldn't have been able to make it there under her own steam.

When she sat down, a silent scream of agony reverberated through her brain as her muscles protested the new movement after more than an hour of the same repetitive motions. Iris watched him disappear into the gloom and rain and knew that if he didn't return, she would be wholly incapable of going in search of him.

For the first time since they'd left the house, she found herself curious about Luna's whereabouts. The dog hadn't followed them outside and Iris wondered if it was because TDH had locked her in the house to prevent the canine from being underfoot while they worked.

Luna was a pleasant subject with which to occupy her wandering mind, and Iris wondered how old the dog was. Did she often travel with her owner? Iris hadn't really heard anything about him having a dog before. Usually celebrity-owned dogs achieved a degree of fame as well. And an oversized dog like Luna would surely have been noticed by the media.

Iris was idly mulling over the dog when Trystan Abbot reappeared, his hulking frame blocking out the sullen light in the doorway.

"Let's go," he commanded her in that no-nonsense, irritating way of his.

But, since Iris was incapable of moving, she attempted to deflect his attention. "What kind of dog is Luna?"

His head tilted as he watched at her. She couldn't read the expression on his face, not with the light behind him, but she sensed his curiosity.

He shocked the hell out of her when he deigned to reply. "Irish wolfhound."

"How old is she?"

"Two." Another easy reply. He propped a shoulder against the doorframe and folded his beefy arms over his chest, while he continued to stare at her. The rain had to be pelting against his back, but he gave no sign that it bothered him.

"And you've had her since she was a puppy?"

"Hmm."

"Does she often travel with you?"

"Hmm."

Not very forthcoming, but she took it to mean yes.

"Why an Irish wolfhound?"

His shoulders shifted. "Why not?"

"Why are you answering my questions?" The question was out before she even knew she was going to ask it, her brain as sluggish as her body.

"Because it's a very obvious delaying tactic," he said, pushing away from the doorframe and coming toward her. He moved with the sinuous flexibility of a man who knew his body —and its limitations—very well. She'd never seen anything quite as sexy as that intent prowling gait of his.

"Delaying tactic?" she repeated. Yet another delaying tactic. It was embarrassingly obvious, and she almost imagined she caught the fleeting glimpse of a grin beneath that beard.

"You can't move, can you?" he asked, lowering himself into a lithe squat in front of her. Crowding her with his heat and masculinity and bulk. His large hands were resting on the bench on either side of her hips and his face was inches away from hers.

The clean scent of fabric softener wafted up from his soaked clothing, combined with something woodsy—his shampoo or soap maybe. God, he smelled amazing. No expensive aftershave or cologne here. Just soap, and detergent, and outdoors, and *man*.

She swallowed past the painful lump that had lodged in her throat.

This was Trystan Abbot, hottest man on the planet according to several well-known publications, as well as the thousands of fan-run social media accounts dedicated to him. Not to mention the hundreds of millions of people scattered across the globe who flocked to see his movies every year.

The guy was undeniably charismatic, sexy, and a feast for the eyes. And—after the kidnapping and imprisonment and arseholery of the last twenty-four hours—Iris had lost sight of exactly who it was she was dealing with. But right now, despite his grumpiness and this whole lumberjack-hermit thing he had going on she was very conscious that the man in front of her was, in fact, a multiple-award-winning movie star.

"How bad is it?" he asked, an unfamiliar gentleness seeping into his voice.

"What?" She couldn't quite keep up with the conversation. Not when she was so exhausted and in pain and overwhelmingly aware of who he was.

"The pain? How bad is it?"

Oh.

She stared down at her hands, which were resting palm up on her lap, fingers curled into claws.

"Well, I don't think I can bend my fingers," she admitted. "And I'm not sure I can lift my arms. My thighs feel like jelly and I very much doubt my legs'll be able to support my weight. And my back…"

Her words faded into a moan as she finally acknowledged how bad her back was.

He sighed deeply, the exhalation emerging on a quiet grunt.

"C'mon, let's get you inside."

One of his arms encircled her waist, and the other slid beneath her thighs. And within seconds—in an impressive show of strength—he effortlessly went from a squat to standing upright, with her in his arms.

As if she hadn't been awed enough by his strength and stamina after all the heavy lifting she'd seen him do already today.

"You don't have to carry me," she protested, and he had the

nerve to laugh at her. It wasn't much of a laugh, just an incredulous little huff, but it was definitely mocking.

"What do you propose I do then? Load you into one of the wheelbarrows and push you uphill back to the house?"

"I'm heavy."

"You're certainly not light," he agreed. So rude. "But I'll manage."

Chapter Five

Iris knew there was no arguing with him over the matter. It was going to happen whether she wanted it to or not. And frankly, she was relieved. She really didn't think she was able to walk the distance back to the house without her legs giving way.

She was shivering—his body heat no match for the icy torrent of rain—and she curled one arm around his neck and lowered her cheek to his chest, covering her face with her free hand in a futile attempt to keep herself protected from the rain.

They'd foolishly left the oilskin behind.

She couldn't see where they were going, was just acutely cognizant of the steady, confident movements of the man who held her so securely in his arms.

In a matter of mere minutes, they were out of the rain and she lowered her hand and lifted her head to take in their surroundings. They were back in the kitchen, probably dripping all over the floor. Luna was making happy whining sounds of greeting.

Iris waited for him to put her down, but he didn't. After quietly commanding Luna to *stay*, he continued to walk through the kitchen, down the hall... back to her prison, she supposed. She was of no more use to him, no point keeping her around any longer than he had to. But he strode right past her door and continued down the hall before turning into a different room. It looked like a guest bedroom. Decorated in russets and browns.

"Wha—?"

He ignored her squawk of surprise and walked her directly into the en-suite bathroom.

"You don't have a tub in your suite. And I think you need a warm soak," he said, as he sat her down on the commode. He rolled up his sleeves, perched his butt on the bath's narrow rim, and opened the faucet, occasionally holding a hand beneath the stream of water to check the temperature, and adjusting accordingly.

Oh God, the massive soaker tub looked so damned appealing Iris actually moaned in longing at the sight of it.

He rummaged through the vanity cupboard while the tub filled with steaming hot water and made a soft sound of triumph when he found bath salts. He liberally sprinkled them into the water and agitated it with his hand. The scent of bergamot and jasmine immediately permeated the bathroom.

"Strip," he commanded her curtly and, for the first time since he took charge in the shed, Iris truly balked.

"Not with you here."

His eyes were incredulous as he turned to stare at her.

"Yes, with me here."

"No."

"It's nothing I haven't seen before, remember?"

Iris's cheeks lit with the fires of hell as she recalled the moment he'd slammed into the bathroom last night.

"Well, I don't *want* you to see me naked again."

"Do you think you're capable of getting out of your clothing without my assistance?"

Her lips thinned as she considered the question. And humiliatingly, the answer was a resounding *no*. The hoodie wouldn't be a problem, but the button fly of her boyfriend jeans would be a challenge. Well, not so much a challenge as an insurmountable obstacle. There was no way she'd be able to undo those buttons with her numb, aching fingers.

She shrugged out of her moisture-heavy hoodie—dropping it to the tiled floor with a wet *thwack*—leaving only the soaked-through black tank top she wore beneath it.

Thereafter she was at a loss, staring helplessly down at her double-knotted boots while trembling violently, her chattering teeth and shuddering breath the only noise in the room.

Trystan Abbott shocked the hell out of her, when—with a quiet grunt—he sank to his knees in front of her and made quick work of unlacing her boots, then he encircled her ankle in his large hand.

"Lift."

Incapable of doing anything other than obey, Iris dropped a hand to his broad shoulder for balance and lifted her foot while he tugged the boot off quickly and tossed it aside. He repeated the process with the other foot.

Then he remained kneeling there, at face level with her stomach. He said nothing and for a long moment he just sat there, staring at the soaked cotton tank top she wore. Thank God it was black or she'd be giving him quite the peep show—since she hadn't bothered with a bra.

"Let's do this," he finally spoke, raising his face to meet her eyes. She could see the grim determination in his expression and the steely resolve in those beautiful eyes.

Before she could register his words and the meaning behind them, he slipped his left hand between the waistband of her jeans and her goosefleshed abdomen.

Iris sucked in a shocked breath when she felt the cold backs of his long fingers brush against her sensitive flesh.

Oh, God! This was so humiliating.

He grasped the placket of her jeans between thumb and forefinger, his knuckles flexing against her tummy at the move. Iris gritted her teeth, refusing to react in any way. This was purely impersonal. He was doing it because it needed to be done. And as such, Iris needed to treat this intimate touch as nothing more than a clinical necessity. Like visiting her doctor's office. Yes, that was it! This was *exactly* the same as Dr. Herbert's touch.

Only... Dr. Herbert was seventy, wore ill-fitting dentures, sported the world's most unconvincing comb-over, and had known Iris since she was a baby. While the man kneeling at her feet was in his prime, gorgeous, and the world's biggest movie star. And *he* currently had a big, assertive hand tucked into the waistband of her jeans—the blunt tips of his fingers intimately close to the top of her bikini panties—while his other fingers undid the stubborn buttons of her jeans.

Iris couldn't help it—she moaned and covered her face with both hands.

"This is so embarrassing," she said, her voice muffled by her hands.

He didn't respond, merely peeled her wet jeans down her generous hips.

Iris squealed in horror when she realized her panties were starting to slide down with the denim.

"Oh, for the love of Jesus, *please* stop," she pleaded, and his hands stilled on her hips. Where before they'd gripped the top of her jeans, he now flattened them against her rounded hips and held them there, staring up at her quizzically.

"Think you can manage from here?" he asked after a beat of silence and she blinked, surprised by the question. No. Not surprised by the question, but by the odd tremble in his voice when he asked said question.

"I think so," she said on a whisper. He looked unconvinced and she nodded assertively. "Yes, I can."

He pushed lithely to his feet and towered above her once more, too damned close for comfort.

"Uhm, what about..." He made a vague gesture and Iris cocked her head as she tried to decipher what it could mean.

"What about *what*?"

He took a step back, waved his fingers at her chest before his eyes dropped to where he was pointing. They seemed to snag there and—baffled—Iris followed his gaze down before hastily folding her arms over her very, *very* hard nipples. She wished she could say the reaction was entirely due to the cold and wet, but... she disguised a little shudder as she remembered the feeling of his fingers sliding down her abdomen. Her frikking stupidly sensitive abdomen, which had always been one of her *wind me up and watch me pop* erogenous zones.

"Your bra," he stated after another weird little silence. "Can you—"

"Not wearing one," she said curtly, then immediately wished the words back. His lips curled into what looked like a full-on smirk and he opened his mouth to say something, but she hijacked his words before he could utter them.

"Don't say it," she bit out irritably, and this time he was the one to fold his arms over his chest as he waited for her to continue. Which she did, with a bitter note of self-deprecation in her voice. "I clearly don't need one, right? That *is* what you were going to say? Or some nasty variation of the same. Yes?"

He held up his hands in surrender and took another step back.

"Get into that tub before you turn into a papsicle—get it? —*papsicle* because you're a blood-sucking leech of a pap?"

She gritted her teeth so hard she felt something in her jaw pop. God, *ouch*, she wasn't going to be doing that again anytime soon.

"I'm not a pap," she snapped at him.

"You should own that shit. Even a rat doesn't deny that it's a rat and belongs with other rats."

"What a dumb analogy. You know, people are always raving about your intellect and emotional intelligence, but I confess, I haven't seen much—or *any*—of that on display since arriving here. All I've seen is a mean, bitter arsehole of a guy wallowing in his self-inflicted misery."

It was his turn to grit his teeth and Iris wondered if she'd actually hit a nerve.

"If I'm mean and bitter it's because I have an unwelcome intruder in my space. You're here on sufferance, lady"—as if she needed the reminder—"so tread fucking lightly. Hurry up and get warmed up so that I can get you out of my hair again."

He turned away from her and stalked out of the bathroom, leaving the door slightly ajar behind him, which was why she knew he hadn't gone any further than the attached guest bedroom.

"You're not going to give me more privacy than that?"

"Nope." His voice drifted back insouciantly. "You can shut the door, but I have the key, so you can't lock it."

Iris eyed the open door. She could see only a sliver of the bedroom and she doubted he was able to see much of anything through that small gap. Besides, she was terrified that if she *did* shut the door, he would lock it. And she didn't think she could stand it if he did that. She'd rather take her chances with the door ajar.

Decision made, she shrugged—eager to get into the bath—and clumsily shoved the jeans down her legs, before gingerly removing her tank top. She was sinking into the almost unbearably hot water mere moments later. She nearly added more cold water but she acclimatized quite quickly, despite the uncomfortable pins and needles skittering across her naked flesh.

Eventually, she was able to settle herself completely into the water with a blissful sigh. She lay there for a long time, allowing the heat to seep into her bones. Despite her shower last night, this was the first time she felt like she'd truly thawed since arriving here.

It was wonderful.

She hummed quietly to herself as she scooped water up over her arms, shoulders, and neck... allowing herself a moment of peace. Blocking her situation, and the awful man in the other room, out of her mind for a few precious minutes.

Just a few precious minutes, before...

"Hurry the fuck up, will you? I'd like to get warmed up as well."

She sighed regretfully and shook her head.

"Nobody's stopping you. Don't worry about me, I'll find my way back to my room."

Silence. There was a beat of blissful silence, during which Iris allowed herself to relax again.

Then, "If you're not done in five minutes I'm coming in there and hauling your ass out of that bathtub."

Of course he was.

Iris clicked her tongue and idly soaped herself before—after way too short a time—she reluctantly rinsed off, got up, and wrapped a towel around her comfortably warm body.

There was an oversized fluffy, white bathrobe hanging from a hook behind the door and—after toweling herself vigorously—Iris dropped the massive plush bath sheet into the laundry hamper and shrugged into the robe.

She threw her shoulders back and lifted her head before pushing the door open and stepping back into the bedroom.

He was waiting for her there. Well, it appeared that he'd left the room long enough to at least divest himself of his own wet clothes. He was now wearing a pair of clingy light gray sweat-pants—oh *mama*—and a form-fitting black T-shirt. He still looked pretty cold though. His hair was wet and she could see the gooseflesh pebbling his skin even with a couple of meters between them.

He was sitting on the edge of the large bed, his gaze trained on her face. His focus so intent, it was a little intimidating.

"You were in there for nearly fifteen minutes," he grouched.

"I could easily have stayed in there for another fifteen, if you hadn't been such a time tyrant."

His beard twitched—what was happening under there? Was he grinding his teeth, chewing the inside of his cheek, clenching his jaw? It was anybody's guess.

"The beard's a bit of overkill, no? Is it meant to be a disguise? Not like anybody will find you out here in the middle of nowhere."

"*You* did."

"Thanks to your manager."

"So you keep saying."

Iris made a disdainful sound in the back of her throat.

"I'm ready to be escorted back to my prison cell now," she informed him, with a haughty toss of her damp hair. *God*, she really wasn't—the thought of returning to that room made her skin crawl. Her bravado was a total bluff.

"Your Medusa-like curls seem to have multiplied." The observation was almost wrenched from him, and Iris raised a self-conscious hand to her hair. Usually she had highly control-lable, gentle waves, but her hair became a different creature when it got wet and was allowed to dry without any kind of intervention. The waves morphed into crazy spiral curls that sprouted in all directions, without any care or concern for structure and organization.

"It's not very polite to comment on my physical appearance."

He lifted an incredulous brow at her criticism. "You literally just commented on mine. Why are *you* allowed these licenses but not me?"

Iris blinked and then nodded slowly, acknowledging his point.

"You're right... I'm sorry. I think sometimes it's easy to lose sight of the fact that public figures deserve the same consideration as the rest of the population. I was being a hypocrite."

He stared at her, his probing gaze alit with a healthy dose of skepticism.

"I mean it," she insisted, not appreciating his blatant disbelief. Iris took pride in her honesty and rarely said what she didn't mean. That candor didn't always work in her favor but she was incapable of dissembling. And this man had accused her of being a liar from the get-go, which was *infuriating*.

"So, you don't think the beard is —what'd you call it?— overkill?"

"What?" *That* was his takeaway from her apology? Seriously, talking to him was like trying to communicate with an alien species. "No, I *meant* that. I just . . . shouldn't have said it. My brain-to-mouth filter sometimes malfunctions. I shouldn't have commented on your appearance. It was rude. I allowed myself to be provoked into saying something that was better left unsaid."

"So, you're blaming *me* for provoking you into speaking your mind? I did no such thing. I have to say, this is an extremely bizarre apology."

"It's an honest apology," she corrected him. "I'm sorry I said what I did about your beard. And that *crazy hermit* comment I made last night was uncalled for as well. And hurtful."

"I don't care enough about your opinions to be hurt by them," he told her stiffly.

Iris worried her plump lower lip with her teeth before lifting her shoulders in a minute shrug—hating that *she* cared enough about his opinion to actually be wounded by that stupid comment.

"Fair enough. I apologize regardless."

She swallowed painfully, while he stared at her again, a long, scraping regard that made her skin prickle and her nerve endings feel raw. Eventually he nodded—an acceptance of her apology perhaps?—and grasped her elbow in a firm, but loose grip. His hand so cold she could feel it through the thick fabric of the bathrobe.

Iris had to be getting used to his unsolicited touches because she barely reacted to it this time. In fact, she almost liked the proprietary hold. Ugh, maybe she was developing Stockholm syndrome or something.

He marched her back to her room without a word, and once there, he stood in the doorway and watched her for a moment before saying, "I'll bring you some lunch after I've had a shower."

"Thank you."

Another long stare and then he stepped back and slammed the door in her face. She held her breath for a few seconds, hoping… until she heard the key turn in the lock. Her breath escaped on a slow, dejected sigh and her shoulders dropped. Deep breaths… she could do this. She'd done it before.

She turned back to stare at her cell. It looked cozy. Spacious. Not prison-like at all, but it was fast becoming the equivalent of a dungeon to Iris. She *hated* it. Hated not being able to just open the door and leave anytime she wanted to.

She pushed down the panic that threatened to claw its way out of her throat in the form of a scream, and headed straight for the window. She shoved it up and inhaled deeply. So much for that warm bath… the frigid air immediately chilled her again. But she didn't care. She stood there for a long moment, staring at the ground just a meter below the windowsill. And after a few more deep breaths, stepped back and shut the window again, shivering but better.

She walked to the sofa and picked up her laptop. Maybe she could distract herself from obsessing over that locked door by writing. She also needed to update her journal. When Iris was a teenager and starting to exhibit her anxiety issues her school counsellor, Mrs. Crowley, had encouraged her to start a journal to keep track of her *events*—as the woman called them. The idea was to be as detailed as possible in her entries so that they could attempt to identify what specific interactions or incidents triggered her panic attacks.

Iris had found it to be therapeutic and had kept a journal ever since.

TDH still hadn't given her the Wi-Fi password as promised, but she didn't need Wi-Fi to write.

"Hey."

The deep, intrusive voice didn't register at first as Iris continued to tap industriously away at her keyboard.

"*Hey*, lady! I brought your lunch."

Her body jerked in fright and her eyes flew up to stare at the man hovering just inside the doorway. He was clutching yet another tray in his massive paws and had a dish towel slung over one broad shoulder, and...

She blinked a few times as she stared at his face uncomprehendingly. Specifically at the neatly trimmed beard.

It was still too long, but he'd definitely gone through some effort to tidy it up a bit. The bushiness had been somewhat tamed. There was a line of pale skin visible from his throat to the corner of his mouth where the hair didn't grow. It hadn't been as noticeable with the longer, bushier beard, but now it was obvious that he had a nasty scar hidden under the scruff. It must be as a result of his accident. Iris did her level best not to stare, but she knew she wasn't very successful when his jaw tightened and his brow lowered into an almost defensive glower.

His burning eyes bored into hers in unmistakable challenge and Iris pinched her lips between her teeth to refrain from commenting. The scar fueled her curiosity, but the trimmed beard was a surprise as well. Had he cut it because of her earlier comments? It didn't seem likely. Trystan Abbot surely didn't give one shit about her opinion. He'd even said as much. Yet... the timing was suspicious.

He put the tray down on the table with enough force to cause the dishes to rattle.

"Thank you," she said beneath her breath and the swift downward jerk of his head was the only indication that he'd heard her. "Where's Luna?"

"You're obsessed with my dog. Cut it out."

"I like dogs," she said, rolling her eyes. The man was pricklier, and more ill-tempered, than a rabid porcupine. "And Luna is a friendly face in enemy territory. I appreciate her. I wish you'd let her stay with me for a bit. She's good company."

He ignored her. So predictable.

Iris sighed and set aside her laptop—the writing had thankfully succeeded in distracting her from her circumstances—and rolled herself off the sofa, wincing with the movement. Her muscles were really starting to protest even the smallest of movements.

"Drink more fluids," Mr. Unsolicited Advice offered begrudgingly. "It'll help with the cramps."

"I have been," Iris said as she limped her way to the table where he still stood. He was as tense as a coiled spring and looked ready to bolt at any second. This was probably longer than he wanted to interact with her, which begged the question: *Why was he still here?*

Iris eyed the laden tray avariciously, her mouth flooding with saliva at the sight and smell of the generous portions of rustic meaty stew and home-baked bread.

"This looks and smells amazing," Iris said, and her stomach growled in agreement. "You made it yourself?"

"You see anyone else around?" The words were short, his tone impatient, but Iris gave him a sanguine look that she knew would probably annoy him.

"I haven't seen much of anything since I've been here. For all I know you could have a dozen guests and a full complement of house staff."

"Up until *you* crash-landed on our doorstep, Luna and I were blissfully and happily alone."

"Not even your bodyguard? That hot Aussie guy? That seems irresponsible."

"Yeah, trust me, I have regrets about leaving him behind. Chance wouldn't have let you come within a hundred yards of the house."

"Why *did* you leave him behind?" she asked, tilting her head curiously as she watched him closely to gauge his reaction. As expected, his eyes immediately shuttered and his body went rigid.

"This was supposed to be a safe space." The intense, resentful words spilled from his lips almost involuntarily. "A private place. But you fucking vultures keep tracking me down."

Stung, Iris retreated into silence, not sure how to respond to that. There were those who argued that public figures couldn't expect privacy, that they belonged to everyone, and—as such—their lives were diverting fodder for the greedy and entitled masses to feast on.

Iris had never been one of those people. She'd come here expecting a story, and admission into Trystan Abbott's private sanctum and inner circle. But she'd believed that she had his explicit consent to step into his life and his spotlight for a short period of time. She would never have come here otherwise. And she hated that he believed that she had such a wanton disregard for his right to privacy.

"If you'd be willing to look at them," she broached the subject tentatively, hoping he'd listen this time and not shut her down immediately as he had last time she'd brought up the subject. "Like I mentioned before, I do have correspondence between myself and Mr. Quinn."

His already furled brow furrowed even more, and it was hard not to scurry away from such an impressive display of masculine outrage. She stood her ground though, so close to him that she was getting a crick in her neck from the height difference between them as she tried to maintain eye contact.

Shockingly, *he* was the one who looked away first. He took a couple of steps backward.

"Eat your lunch."

Worrying at her lip with her teeth, Iris watched him retreat, disappointed that he hadn't responded to her suggestion about the correspondence between her and Hunter Quinn. She tried to ignore the sound of the key in the lock, hoping that if she didn't hear it she could trick herself into believing that it wasn't locked.

But the sound of the key turning reverberated through her brain like a bullet shattering a silent night. Her shoulders tensed and she tried to distract herself with thoughts of her jailer.

She wondered about that scar—it looked pretty bad. How severe had his injuries been? Newspapers had only reported that he was in a stable condition. A few horribly invasive pictures had surfaced of him in hospital immediately after the accident. There had been others as well, of Trish Nesbitt, that had turned Iris's stomach. She couldn't understand how someone could have taken pictures like that. Evan had pored over those images with morbid curiosity, often trying to show them to Iris—who had literally gagged after one quick glance at a picture of the—clearly dead—woman. Her friend had then mocked Iris for having the wrong constitution for this job.

She shook her head and dragged a chair out from underneath the dining table before sitting down to have the meal provided for her. She found a Post-it note with the Wi-Fi password scribbled on it beneath the bread basket, and quickly signed into the Wi-Fi while she scarfed down the delicious meal.

Trystan Abbott was a good cook.

Who knew?

She sent quick apologies to her parents and Evan—who'd finally surfaced from her hangover—explaining that she'd been without Wi-Fi for a while.

Evan threatened to *cut a bitch* if Iris didn't give immediate details about where she was and who she was interviewing. Iris grimaced, wishing she hadn't teased her friend about this big reveal. It didn't feel right to divulge any information until she'd cleared up this misunderstanding between herself and the two powerful men.

> I can't tell you anything yet, Ev. I'm
> sorry. Shit got a little complicated and
> I have to see if I've actually still got
> the interview before I can reveal
> anything more.

Her friend sent half a dozen poop emojis in response and Iris grinned.

> Tell me what you got up to last night?
> You get lucky?

> 'Course I did 😳

> That's my girl! Who was the lucky
> guy? Girl? Anyone I know?

> Hooked up with a hottie at that
> summer charity event I told you I was
> going to. Haven't seen her before.
> Doubt I'll see her again. But she
> was fun.

Iris grinned. It was hard to keep up with Evan sometimes, and she often wondered why her friend hung out with her. Evan was cool, edgy, interesting and she knew exactly what she wanted from life. She worked as a junior executive assistant to the editor of an up-and-coming gossip magazine. And she'd once told Iris that she meant to have the woman's job in two years, come hell or high water. Evan was such a driven and determined woman that Iris didn't for a second doubt that she'd achieve her goals with time to spare.

It was hard not to be envious of her friend, whom she'd met

at uni. They had the same dream, but Evan was miles ahead of Iris. Iris had spent so much time—during and after university—helping out with the catering business that, before she'd known it, four years had passed, and she was still in exactly the same place. Writing the occasional freelance article while working for her parents. Evan, in the meantime, had interned at *Vogue*, *GQ* and *Glamour*. Before landing this job at *Looker* magazine.

She was constantly regaling Iris with stories of glitzy celebrity parties, borrowed designer finery, dressing to the nines, and dating/sleeping with influential, beautiful people. Iris didn't envy any of that since she'd never been interested in being on trend and knowing the "right kind" of people. All she'd ever wanted to do was the work. She didn't care about the fast, glamorous life that came with it. She was—and always would be —a homebody. And while Evan had often inferred that Iris didn't have the right attitude or the cutthroat mentality required for this kind of work, Iris had always felt that all she needed was an opportunity to prove what she could do.

If Evan were here instead of Iris, she would have charmed—and quite possibly seduced—Trystan Abbott out of his foul mood by now. And she'd have convinced him of her credentials and legitimacy in no time flat. She would have become his pampered guest and he would never have asked pretty, petite Evan to hoist sandbags into a wheelbarrow.

Iris sighed wistfully. Annoyed that she was comparing herself to her best friend. Something she'd promised herself she would never do.

She was just going at a different pace. Evan didn't have the commitments Iris did. She was from a wealthy, influential family. She'd never been asked to sacrifice any of her needs or wants for the sake of the family business. That had been one of the many fundamental differences between them, and Iris had long ago accepted that comparing herself to Evan would only lead to grief and discontent. Instead, she celebrated her friend's wins and achievements and tried not to come down too hard on herself for being nowhere near the same level as Evan as far as career goals went.

This was supposed to be a great—if not equalizer then at least—step up for Iris. Her big break. And it was all falling apart around her.

She scrolled through the many pics Ev had sent and smiled a little wistfully at how perfect and happy her beautiful friend looked in each picture.

> It was a total celeb fest. A-listers everywhere. There was even a rumor that Trystan Abbott was coming, but he was a no-show.

Iris snorted at that text. Trystan Abbott had been too busy tormenting *her* last night to think about some fancy charity gala in London.

She sent a shocked emoji in response to Evan's text, not sure what else to say or do when she knew exactly where Trystan Abbott had been last night.

She replied to a couple of texts from her mom and dad and a random one from her brother:

> The fuck you do with my black sleeveless hoodie?!!!

Huh?

> 🖼 How should I know where your
> hoodie is? Ask Mum.

His only reply was a middle-finger emoji, which Iris stared at for a second before shrugging and moving on from the text. She didn't wear his clothes; they were all miles too big for her. And she shared a small flat with two other women, so she never had access to Robbie's clothing anyway. Sometimes he'd blame her for the most random shit. But Iris liked to believe it was because he missed her and accusing her of clothing theft was his way of staying in contact with her.

She finished her—now lukewarm—stew and got up with a pained groan, picking up the tray and hobbling to the sink to do the dishes.

That done, she tried to stretch for a few minutes hoping it would help, but it only seemed to make things worse, before giving up and heading back to the sofa and her laptop.

Chapter Six

The rest of the day was uneventful. TDH returned once more with her dinner—at about seven that evening—and said not one word to her. Luna remained conspicuous in her absence. And, despite being able to message family and friends, Iris felt crushingly alone.

After her reluctant host dropped the tray and escaped with ego-bruising swiftness, Iris picked at the meal of lemon and garlic butter basted fish fillets, with baked baby potatoes and a crunchy, fresh salad. Iris couldn't quite identify the light white-fleshed fish, but the meal was yet another winner from her warden. The fish was perfectly cooked and delicately seasoned but Iris lacked the appetite to do it justice.

She had messaged and tried calling Hunter Quinn several more times—no luck. She knew it was probably futile, he likely *was* on that bizarre-sounding silent retreat, but attempting to contact him made Iris feel somewhat in control. And maybe she was crazy for trying, but it was better than doing nothing at all.

She had also tried to do some research on the accident that had been the catalyst for Trystan fleeing the public eye, but there was nothing new to be found. A single-car accident, two victims, one fatality. The driver—Trish Nesbitt—had died, but was found to have had no narcotics and only a negligible amount of alcohol in her system. The only other person involved in the accident had remained tight-lipped about it and had eventually fallen off the face of the earth.

All of which she'd known before coming here, and all of which told her precisely nothing. Iris crawled into bed feeling unsettled, unhappy, and uncertain. This felt like a bigger story than she'd anticipated, like more responsibility than she knew what to do with. It felt grave, weighty, and like she could do serious damage if she fucked it up in any way.

As she lay in bed that night, she acknowledged to herself that she didn't feel that curl of excitement her biological father had often described when he was working on a big story. She didn't have that pressing need to find out everything there was to know about said story, every minute detail that could possibly lead to the biggest scoop of her life.

She didn't *want* to know. She wanted to leave it alone, undiscovered, buried with Trish Nesbitt and unspoken by Trystan Abbott. It felt like the worst kind of prying, and she didn't feel any driving instinct to uncover it.

This felt a long way off from the fun puff piece she'd imagined it would be. This was someone's life. Someone's *death*. And

Iris didn't think she had any right to trample all over Trish Nesbitt's grave.

"Worst time ever to discover that maybe this isn't what you want to do with your life, Iris, you dolt," she groaned into the darkness. The rain had abated somewhat, but the wind was still howling, whistling through the trees and the eaves of the big house.

She covered her face with her hands and prayed for sleep, but between the eerie whistling wind, the feeling of being helpless and trapped, and the clamoring thoughts in her brain, that blessed oblivion was a long way off.

WHEN TRYSTAN BROUGHT her breakfast the following morning, Iris remained seated on the sofa, miserably wrapped around the hot-water bottle she'd discovered in the bedroom closet.

Every muscle in her body hurt and her back was in spasm. She shifted to press the bag into the small of her back, muffling a groan as she watched him enter the room, without sparing her a glance.

Trystan. Somewhere between yesterday and this morning Iris had stopped thinking of him as TDH or by his full name. She wasn't sure how it had happened, or why, but she was uncomfortable with the fact that she now thought of him as just Trystan. It made him seem more human, approachable... which meant she had to tread carefully because she knew he'd hate it if he comprehended where her thoughts had roamed.

Trystan.

Grumpy, hot, reticent, aloof *Trystan.*

He remained silent as he lowered the tray to the table and turned to leave, not looking at her before hot-footing it back to the door. Once there, he hesitated. His jaw flexed beneath that now-short black beard. His profile was to her and Iris was inspecting the scar—but it was hard to see it clearly with the beard in the way—and fretting about the type of injury that would have caused it when he turned his head and caught her staring. He pinned her with an almost resentful glower.

She quickly averted her gaze and he actually *growled* in response to her evasion. The low, animalistic sound had her eyes snapping back up to his and there was a smoldering satisfaction in his stare when she met his eyes this time.

What the hell was going on with him this morning?

The silence stretched between them for an endless moment until, "You're not going to ask after Luna?"

"Why?" Iris asked, alarmed. "Is she hurt?"

"She's fine."

Iris stared at him in confusion, not sure what to say.

"You're always asking if she can stay with you."

Always, as if they already had some cozy little routine in place just two days into her imprisonment.

"What would be the point?" She fought—unsuccessfully— to keep the bitterness out of her voice. "You'd just say no."

"What's wrong with you?" he asked, his eyes raking over her crumpled form.

"Absolutely nothing. All sunshine and roses here," she said with a twist of her lips. She started to make a dismissive gesture with her arm, but aborted the movement halfway through. She grimaced and tucked the aching appendage close to her torso.

"You're in pain." He was crouched in front of her within seconds. How the hell did he move so fast? It wasn't normal. "How bad?"

"Pretty bad," she admitted in a miserable little voice.

"Where does it hurt the most?" His voice was neutral, unemotional but his gaze remained pinned to hers, following her eyes when she tried to evade that uncomfortable, probing molten silver stare.

"My back," she admitted with a shuddering sigh, her eyes burning as she fought to hold back her tears.

"Right. Okay." He dropped his hands on the sofa on either side of her hips and seemed to think for a moment before he nodded decisively. Just a fast, jerky up-down motion of his head.

"Do you have anything that can double as a swimsuit?"

"What?" His question baffled her and she stared at him like he'd grown an extra head. Was he crazy? A swimsuit? Why would she need a swimsuit? The rain had stopped during the night, but it was still gray and cold and windy out there.

"Humor me, okay?"

"I do have something," she conceded reluctantly, thinking of the ridiculous bikini she'd packed. "Why?"

"There's a hot tub in the natatorium."

"The *natatorium?*"

"A room containing an indoor swimming pool."

She glared at him, offended that he'd felt the need to explain.

"I *know* what a natatorium is, I was just surprised to learn that you had one."

"Why? You see what it's like in winter. And it's great to be able get a few laps in every day, regardless of the weather. I think an indoor swimming pool is essential in a place like this."

"Hmm... Your idea of essential and mine differ greatly." She knew she sounded tart and judgy, but seriously, an indoor pool? Nobody truly *needed* an indoor pool. Still, that hot tub he'd mentioned sounded like paradise round about now, so maybe she should get off her high horse and just be grateful he had a frikking *natatorium* tucked away in his holiday hideaway.

He didn't respond to her comment, merely continued to stare at her and they both simultaneously became aware of the fact that one of his long thumbs was absently stroking her thigh through the stretchy fabric of her sweatpants. Her mouth dropped open and his eyes widened as he jerked his hand away as if he'd been scalded.

Meanwhile, Iris felt as if she *had* been scalded. She could still feel the firm stroke of that thumb against her flesh, the heat from his hand seared into her skin like a brand.

He leaped to his feet and shoved his hands into his sweatpants pockets, lowering his head to glare down at her.

"Eat your breakfast and then get changed. I'll return for you in half an hour."

HE WAS as good as his word. Back in exactly thirty minutes, while Iris sat waiting—after having painfully struggled into the bright pink and white string bikini in record-breaking time—on the sofa. She felt outrageously exposed, despite the warm, thick bathrobe she wore over the scandalously tiny bikini.

She was just thinking that maybe a pair of boy shorts and a black bra would be a little more conservative when he stepped back into the room.

"You ready?" he asked, eyeing her modestly covered, huddled form skeptically. She nodded wordlessly, feeling tongue-tied, nervous, and ridiculous.

A slight movement behind him—in the open door—caught her eye, and her face lit up at the sight of Luna.

"*Luna*, I'm so happy to see you!" The dog ambled over to her and stoically accepted Iris's enthusiastic hug.

Shockingly, Trystan allowed the interaction without calling Luna away. He remained standing by the door, waiting with every appearance of patience.

Because of that seeming patience, Iris didn't feel the perverse need to make him wait longer than necessary and shakily pushed to her feet. To her surprise he moved toward her, covering the distance in a few short strides, until he was hovering right beside her, hands slightly outstretched as if to catch her if she fell.

She eyed those big, capable hands in horror and amusement, not at all sure what his intentions were right now.

"Do you need help?" The tight awkwardness in his voice told her that he wasn't certain of his next move either.

"I think I'm okay to walk," she said, taking one wobbly step before he made an impatient grunting sound and closed his hand around her elbow in support.

This time she didn't even bother calling him out on the grabbiness because she was actually grateful for the aid. And truthfully, she didn't really mind it, not even when she'd mentioned it to him before. She'd just felt the need to establish boundaries even if she hadn't felt truly threatened by his bossy touch.

She allowed him to steer her toward the door, though she hardly needed direction out of the room. Her phone beeped as they slowly made their way to the door and she pulled it out of her pocket with her free hand to check the incoming message.

He stopped walking abruptly and she lifted her head in confusion, to find him glaring down at the phone in her hand.

"Leave that behind."

"What? My *phone*? But..."

"No recording devices allowed in the rest of the house."

Was he joking? One look at his grim face told her what a ridiculous question that was. Despite evidence she'd seen to the contrary in the past, Trystan Abbott did not seem to possess much in the way of a sense of humor. Those interviews of an approachable and laughing Trystan Abbott had to have been staged.

"Recording device? It's my phone."

"It's a camera. And an audio recorder. It stays in the room."

"You're paranoid," she protested. As indictments went it was pretty weak, but it was all she could come up with right now in the face of this outrageousness.

"I don't think so. I'm cautious around someone who has

invaded my privacy and tried to feed me a pack of lies. You can use your phone in your own room..."

"My prison cell, you mean? And don't you *dare* call me a liar! I haven't lied to you, not once. I told you I have messages and texts from Mr. Quinn but you're being a dick about even looking at them. Here, I'll show you..."

She swiped at her phone, frantically looking for even *one* of those messages to shove into his face, but he calmly took the phone from her and held it behind his back.

"*Hey*, give that back!" she tried to grab it, but he lifted it above his head, flouting her attempts to take the device back from him.

She stopped reaching for her phone. It would be impossible to get it from him and she was merely making an idiot of herself in the process.

She'd never truly hated anyone in her life before, not even the people who had made her life a living hell back in school, but Iris was definitely leaning toward that emotion with this man.

"When you're alone," he continued doggedly, as if her outraged interruption hadn't even happened, which *infuriated* Iris even more. He disregarded the daggers flying at him from her eyes. "Call your family, laugh at cat memes, shop for more horrendous clothes... do whatever the fuck you want on that thing. But your phone doesn't leave this room. If it *ever* manages to find its way out, I'm confiscating it. And if I see anything on social media about where you are, or about me, I'm destroying it and moving your *prison cell* to the shed. We clear?"

Great. Just like that he'd gone back to being TDH. Iris was

grateful for that—she preferred TDH to Trystan. At least with TDH, what you saw was what you got.

But *Trystan* was dangerous. He had too much power and if he put his mind to it, he could destroy Iris *and* her family. And while she didn't care about her nonexistent professional reputation, she very much cared about her family and the business her parents had worked so hard to make a success of. If she got on the wrong side of this man, he could tear that all apart without even blinking.

He handed her phone back and Iris's lips tightened as she pointedly placed it on the small dining table on their way out of the door. She kept her focus on Luna, ignoring him as he led her from the room.

She hated that his grip was gentle on her arm, hated that he walked slowly out of consideration for the pain she was in. She hated the contradiction and wished he'd remain consistent in his arseholery. Because when he was considerate, it made him feel approachable, made her think they could talk, that she could be herself and joke and laugh with him.

Then, when he turned around and shut her down like she was less than human, it stung. It even hurt. And it shouldn't. Not when he meant nothing to her.

"Oh," Iris's gasp was soft, even reverent, as she took in the high vaulted glass ceilings of the natatorium with its gorgeous, golden exposed beams. The temperature-controlled room reminded her of a greenhouse, with three glass walls to complement the glass ceiling. They had a view of the forest and the lake from this room and the stonework was the color of beach sand. The pool was half-Olympic-sized at the very least. There was a round spa sunk into its far side. Wooden benches and huge, leafy plants added ambiance and comfort to the space, and there was a glass-fronted cedar-wood sauna on this side of the room.

"This is amazing," she whispered, her eyes huge as she looked around. She loved how lush and green it looked outside, despite the sullen gray clouds above.

"C'mon," he urged, leading her toward the opposite end of the massive dark blue pool. Before she knew it, she was standing at the side of the spa—which was a few shades darker than the pool—and she could see the mosaics highlighting the shelved seating that ran all-round the tub. "Climb in, I'll switch on the jets."

"I really appreciate this," she told him earnestly, ditching the robe without thinking, and then immediately regretting her rashness when he froze halfway through turning away.

Froze... and stared.

"That's very—uh—*bright*," he said, his words stumbling into one another like drunken sailors. He blinked at the two tiny pink and white triangles cupping her small boobs, before dropping his eyes to her gently rounded stomach, which—she regretted—had always had a bit of sag to it no matter how many crunches and sit-ups she did. She'd eventually given up on the dream of having an ab-tastic toned and taut tummy. She was happy enough with her curves to not stress the shit she couldn't change without some kind of surgical intervention.

His wandering eyes slid away from her stomach—and

dropped to her generous hips, then fell to the triangle at her crotch before jerking back up to her face.

"*This* is what you brought for swimming? In the Western Cape? In winter?" He finally managed to ask in hoarse incredulity, and Iris was rebelliously happy that she'd resisted the urge to fold her arms over her small boobs with their hard nipples. For a few seconds there, she'd mistakenly believed he was gawking at her body, when in fact, he'd been horrified by her choice of bathing apparel.

Please. As if the likes of Trystan Abbott would ever be gawking at someone the caliber of ordinary, curvy Iris Hughes.

She immediately berated herself for the appalling lack of self-esteem that thought had betrayed. She'd worked very hard on her body positivity, and on loving herself and the way she looked. She'd be damned if she'd let one scathing put-down from a man with unrealistic beauty standards undo years of hard work.

She frowned as she stared at him, with his stupid beard and his big body and his beautiful eyes and face, and acknowledged that—those beauty standards were unrealistic for 99% of humankind. *Trystan Abbott,* however, could date any of those otherworldly goddess-like creatures if he wanted. Well, he *had* dated very many of them. A gorgeous array of supermodels, actresses, athletes, even a frikking *princess*—the man's only real criteria seemed to be that his sexual partners be as beautiful as he.

"What's going through that complicated, crazy brain of yours right now?" he asked, and her eyes widened at the almost affectionate question.

"I was thinking that I'm happy I brought this bathing suit. No matter how unsuitable it may seem to you. Since it's coming in handy right now." She tilted her head defiantly and stepped into the blissfully warm water, and when she sat down she was submerged up to her neck. Her long sigh was filled with sheer contentment.

He watched her with an odd, indecipherable expression on his face before he turned to stride to a panel in the wall next to the sauna.

Iris made a delighted sound when the water bubbled to life, the jets exactly what she needed for her sore muscles.

She was shocked and a little horrified when Trystan—yes, he was back to *Trystan* again—joined her at the hot tub and shucked out of his clothes to reveal black board shorts beneath his sweatpants.

Iris tried not to gawk at the veritable feast of male perfection on display in front of her right now. Tight butt with long, strong, muscular legs and thighs combined with washboard abs, broad shoulders, chest and back. He had beautifully veined forearms and bulging biceps and triceps. There was zero fat on him. Everything was muscle, bone, and sinew.

She'd seen him wearing even less in movies, but nothing could prepare any human being for the reality of seeing Trystan Abbott in the flesh, so to speak. It was like seeing pictures of the painted ceiling of the Sistine Chapel in books and on the Internet all your life, and then finally witnessing the real deal with your own eyes. There was just no comparison.

Iris had *not* expected him to join her, but he sank into the water with his own version of a blissed-out sigh—a harsh, broken groan—and sat down across from her. He was far enough away for them to not even accidentally brush against each other, but it still felt too close. And too intimate. Way, way, *way* too intimate.

She studied him carefully, not sure what—if anything—to say. His head was tilted back and his eyes were shut, and she was happy to have a few moments of relative privacy to have a minor freak-out about her current bizarre reality.

She was in a hot tub with TRYSTAN ABBOTT! How was this her life right now?

All too soon, he lifted his head and opened his eyes, pinning her to the spot with his interrogative gaze. He'd caught her staring, but didn't seem to think anything of it. And Iris recognized that this was a man who was probably used to being gawked at on a daily basis. She was just being like everyone else on the planet.

The only people who wouldn't stare were those he worked with and those with whom he was intimately acquainted. Family, friends, familiars... Iris wasn't even an acquaintance. She didn't matter to him. And she never would.

"Are those aggressively pink splotches meant to be lips?" His question was confusing and unexpected, and she wasn't sure what the hell he meant.

"What?"

"On your bikini?"

Why was he asking about her bikini? In fact, why was he thinking about it at all?

"They're lipstick kisses."

"Right."

"They're cute."

"Right. Lipstick kisses all over your tits and ass. Cute. Got it."

She gritted her teeth—she *really* had to stop doing that—and refrained from asking him what that was supposed to mean.

Because his voice had been dripping with... *something*. Disdain? Sarcasm? Mockery? Whatever it was, it hadn't been anything positive.

"Thank you," she said instead, surprising and confusing him, if his expression was anything to go by.

"For what?"

"This," she said, idly waving her hand through the water. "It's heavenly."

He made a noncommittal grunting sound.

"So, I can't ask you anything because you'd lose your shit and accuse me of spying or some other unreasonable thing... but, I mean, you could ask *me* something. A few questions to ease your mind about who I am."

"I have absolutely no interest in finding out anything more than I already know about you."

"Oh."

She sank into wounded silence, while berating herself for allowing this man, who meant nothing to her, to once again hurt her dumb, sensitive feelings.

The awkward silence remained unbroken for a good few minutes before the man across from her sighed softly.

"Do you have a dog of your own at home to console you after your inevitable breakup with Luna?"

The unexpected question was silly and whimsical but Iris

recognized—and appreciated—it for the attempted olive branch that it was.

"No. I've never had a dog. I've always wanted one but my dad is allergic to animal dander. So, no pets at all."

"Your dad? Stanford Carter?"

"How do you know my father's name?" she asked, stunned. They didn't share a last name—obviously—and the only people who really knew of her familial relationship with the notorious Stanford Carter were her family and Evan.

"One phone call to my security team, some half-assed Internet searches, and I knew everything I needed to know about you."

"Everything except the fact that your manager arranged for me to be here."

He ignored that. "Your father was a first-class bastard. He destroyed marriages, careers, lives without blinking. All for the almighty buck. And you wonder why the fuck I would never consent to an interview with you? Even if Quinny had, for some fucked-up, brain fart of a reason, arranged this I would *never* have agreed to it. Not with your sleazy pedigree."

"My father was a great man... he was a wonderful journalist"—TDH scoffed at the word—"who enriched lives and kept the masses informed."

"He shoveled through shit to find the most sordid details about people's lives and laid them bare for public consumption. A real prince. Is that why you don't use his last name? Because you *know* nobody with any self-respect would ever agree to be interviewed by someone with such close ties to that bottom-feeding piece of filth?"

"I don't have to sit here and listen to this unprovoked defamation of both my character, and my father's," Iris said, her voice vibrating with indignation and humiliation. In truth, she was more affronted by his assassination of *her* character than she was by anything he'd said about her biological father.

Stanford Carter hadn't been a saint—he'd been ruthless in his pursuit of a story. To the exclusion of all else. He'd often neglected to show up for weekends, or visits, with Iris when he was on the trail of some scandalous story or the other. And Iris could understand why Trystan would feel that way about him. In fact, when Iris had seen those truly awful, invasive images of Trish Nesbitt and Trystan after their accident, it had struck her as something her father would have done. And that certainty had revolted her.

Despite her defense of him—which had been a knee-jerk reaction to Trystan's contempt—Iris had never truly aspired to emulate the man who'd fathered her by following exactly in his footsteps. She was seeking legitimacy, and if she did follow this path she wanted to be perceived as a journalist with ethics and integrity.

She pushed to her feet, but her heel skidded on the slick surface of the spa bottom and she lost her balance.

He went from sitting to standing in a second, his strong arms closing around her from behind before she even registered how close she'd come to falling and possibly striking her head on the side of the small heated pool.

His lightning-fast reflexes saved her and—while her brain played catch-up with what could have happened—her body reacted to all that sexy, hot, naked flesh pressed up against her back.

Her breath stuttered in her chest, and her already hard nipples contracted even more, while heat and moisture pooled between her legs. She instinctively clenched her thighs and arched closer to his hard heat.

But when her common sense *finally* caught up with her shameless body, a mere second later, she gasped in humiliation and attempted to extract herself from his tight hold. Hoping against hope he hadn't noticed her embarrassing reaction to his nearness.

He didn't let her go, though. His strong arms remained clamped around her upper body, pinning her own arms to her side, his chest plastered against her back, his groin pushed up against the small of her back.

He was panting in her ear, harsh, gasping breaths, as if he'd overexerted himself, which made no sense, since he'd gone completely still after the short, rapid burst of movement to catch her.

"Let go of me," she gritted out from between clenched teeth, but he remained silent while his hoarse breathing finally leveled out, becoming more even and quieter.

He relaxed his hold, releasing her arms, one large, capable hand drifting down to spread over her torso, while the other dropped to her waist.

"You okay?" he asked, his breath fluttering against the curls at her temple.

"I will be when you let me go." Her voice was husky, unconvincing, and she barely suppressed a moan when the hand at her torso stroked soothing circles over her sensitive flesh.

He was still pressed intimately close to her, so it was impossible to miss the stirring against the small of her back. Was he... getting *hard?*

Before she could figure it out, he released his grip and stepped away from her. She turned quickly, but he was already seated, and watching her with that focused, intent expression back on his face.

"Sit down."

Folding her arms defensively over her stupidly achy nipples, Iris refused to comply and glared down at him with a defiant tilt of her jaw.

"No. I'm ready to go back to my prison cell."

God, she couldn't think of anything she wanted less, but he'd touched a nerve. She was such a confused mess, following in the footsteps of a father she really did not respect at all, wanting to show him up, and prove to the world that she was a better person than he'd been. It was fucked up... *she* was fucked up. Out here trapped in the middle of nowhere, in pursuit of a dream she didn't believe in. And did not want.

She needed space to sort through her cluttered brain, and she needed to be *out* of Trystan Abbott's disturbing company. She couldn't think when he was around and actively antagonizing her.

His lips twitched and his eyes—still fixed on her face—flickered.

"I've read some of your work," he said, ignoring her demand. "What little there is of it."

His words surprised her as she had no body of work readily available on the Internet. In fact, she had nothing out there for public consumption that she could think of off the top of her head and wasn't sure to what he was referring.

"What work?"

"There's the poetry you wrote for your university paper."

"Oh my *God*." She sank back onto the seat and covered her face with her hands. She couldn't believe that any of those abysmal poems were actually available online. They were truly awful and dripping with teenaged angst and despair. "I thought they'd all been taken down."

"The Internet is forever, Miss Hughes." It was the first time he'd actually said her name. She'd honestly believed he'd forgotten it until he'd dropped those truth bombs about her father.

"So, it seems."

"For a budding journalist, you have surprisingly little content online, not a smart move. No blogs, vlogs, TikTok, Instagram. Other people your age are gagging to reveal their every shallow opinion to the world. Someone with your... *ambitions* should be even keener to share every puerile thought."

This was better—it felt like familiar territory. Iris relaxed marginally, slumping against the wall of the spa and allowing herself to enjoy the soothing jets once more. Maybe she should continue to nurse her outrage over what he'd said earlier, but Iris never could maintain a good mad. She was too cheerful and optimistic for that. Besides, it was hard to remain angry when she agreed with so much of what he'd said about her father.

"There's a mere five-year age gap between us so you don't

have to make yourself sound like Father Time in comparison to me," she told him with a sympathetic little moue. "Cut yourself some slack, you're only a little past your sell-by date."

"I'm in my fucking prime, you little witch. I'm not so shallow and vain that I'll be stricken with despair and doubt by the mere inference that I'm old. Back to my point, why don't you have more of an online presence?"

"Because I don't have time to sit around maintaining social media accounts. I work. I help my family, I..." she stopped. Nope. No! She was here to interview *him*, not vice versa. He didn't need to know about her life.

But there was *one* thing she needed to correct.

"My dad," she began, and watched his magnificent shoulders stiffen and his face go still. He looked like he couldn't quite believe that she'd dared bring up her father again. "The one allergic to animal dander? His name is Jason Hughes. He's my stepfather, and he's been my dad since I was seven years old. He raised me, nurtured me, loved me, and is the only father I've ever really known. I'm shocked your *extensive* research into my life didn't reveal that most basic fact about me. Jason Hughes is my dad while Stanford Carter is the man who blew into and out of my life once or twice a year for my first thirteen years. But I got my talent and love of writing from him and I owe it to myself, and to him, to explore that talent. This interview with you was my opportunity to do that. To honor my biological father in some way *and* make my real dad proud of me."

He stared at her, eyes narrowed, his straight, white teeth chewing at his bottom lip as he appeared to consider her words. He didn't say anything for a long time before his shoulders shifted. The play of muscles across that broad, tanned expanse captivated Iris and stole her breath away.

"Seems to me that the kind of man you describe your stepdad to be would already be proud of you, regardless of your achievements. While the type of man I *know* your biological father to have been wouldn't give an actual fuck about your achievements because he'd likely only ever seen you as an extension of himself. Emulating a fucker like that should be very low down on your list of priorities."

She hated that his words were a reflection of everything she'd believed herself, but never dared to acknowledge. Stanford Carter had showed little to no interest in her academic achievements, had never read any of her school essays, or poems, or stories. He'd glanced at them whenever she'd proudly handed them to him and patted her on the head, and said things like, "Like father, like daughter" or "That's my girl" or "Of course you got an A, you're a chip off the old block."

Her every achievement had been an opportunity for him to talk about himself. She'd known it, she'd seen it, but until now, until this awful man had laid that obvious truth bare with just a few cruel words, Iris had hoarded all of those non-compliments close and held them up as proof that her father had loved her and had been proud of her.

She dropped her gaze to the water, refusing to let him see how much the obvious truth had devastated her. She didn't say a word for a few long minutes, and he allowed the silence to simmer between them.

Chapter Seven

"Come on," Trystan said a while later. "We're turning into prunes. Some time in the sauna, stretches, and you'll feel much better."

"I already feel better, thank you," she said, the words stilted and overly polite. "The sauna might not be necessary."

His brow pleated and he shook his head.

"No, you'll likely stiffen up again once your muscles cool down. Trust me on this, I've had to deal with this type of pain enough times while bulking up for roles."

Iris hesitated for a few seconds before nodding and pushing to her feet. He helped her out of the pool and led her to the sauna, handing her a thick white towel at the entrance.

"You should strip out of the wet bikini," he said, his eyes flicking down over her body as he spoke. "Wrap yourself in this."

"But I'll be naked." She sounded like an outraged old maid, but she couldn't help herself.

His lips twitched with what looked suspiciously like humor and he lifted his closed fist to his mouth and coughed—laughed?—before speaking. "Not naked. You'll be wearing the towel."

"Are *you* coming in as well?"

"I am."

"But..." Her protest petered out beneath the weight of his penetrative stare.

"I assure you, you'll be perfectly safe with me, Miss Hughes."

God, she'd been here for two days and this man had already seen her fully—and near—naked three times. He might be quite at home with casual nudity, but that wasn't her. She'd never nonchalantly slip out of her clothing in front of someone who was essentially a stranger to her, and she didn't care if he found that gauche or naive. They inhabited very different universes and had very different ideas of what constituted normal.

And did he really have to keep reminding her that he had no interest in her? Okay, she was fair enough to acknowledge that *maybe* it was his way of reassuring her, since she tended to get all hysterical every time this naked shit happened. But couldn't he reassure her by saying stuff like, *"While I find you irresistible, Miss Hughes, I will manfully abstain from touching you! Even though it pains me to do so!"*?

She smothered a giggle at the preposterous thought but it was a welcome distraction from her current awkward reality.

"Fine," she blurted out, fighting back a blush as she

snatched the towel from him. "But you're going to have to turn around."

He folded his arms over his chest and turned, presenting her with a fine view of his gorgeous, muscular back and that famous *perfect* arse.

She allowed herself a hypocritical moment of gawking before hastily wrapping the towel around her body and attempting to slide out of her wet bikini. She made it harder on herself by trying to shimmy out of the wet costume from beneath the towel, but after a few minutes of struggling, and soft cursing, she was free of the bathing suit.

"Can I turn around?"

"Uh, yes. Okay." Her face was bright red from exertion and embarrassment and she was panting from the rigorous activity. He turned and gave her a leisurely inspection, forcing her to clutch the towel even tighter over her chest.

His stare dropped to the pink and white bits of wet fabric and string she held clutched in one hand.

"You can toss those in the laundry basket," he said, tilting his chin toward a bamboo hamper she hadn't noticed beside the sauna door.

"Thanks."

Her eyes didn't know where to focus—he had so much gleaming golden skin on display—and she didn't want to be caught staring. Not after making such a fuss about her own nudity. It had been easier in the spa when he'd been submerged up to his clavicles. Now that body, which had had millions of women swooning after a full-frontal nude scene in his last movie, was fully on display in all its ridiculous magnificence.

He grabbed another—smaller—towel from the shelves next to the hamper and—without warning—turned away from her, hooked his thumbs into the sides of his wet board shorts, and unceremoniously tugged them down over that perfectly sculpted butt. He bent at the waist as he dragged them down past his thighs to his knees before he stepped out of them and picked them up.

Iris, who'd made a choking sound as soon as she'd understood what was happening, had one hand clamped over her mouth, eyes glued to the man, willing herself to look away but quite unable to physically do so.

He turned toward her and a muffled squeak sounded from behind her hand. She squeezed her eyes shut, not sure if he was going to make use of that towel or not.

"You can look," he invited, laughter threaded through his voice.

Iris opened one eye cautiously and sighed in quiet relief, before opening the other. He'd fastened the towel around his hips, but the inadequate scrap of cloth only provided the barest nod to modesty. It was little bigger than a hand towel and gaped over one thickly muscled thigh. It was also very short, and only just covered his bits . . . although she couldn't be too sure of that because she didn't want to stare too long at the spot where he bulged against the front of the towel.

Iris wasn't a novice when it came to men, but the few guys she'd been with had been mere boys compared to this man. Trystan was bigger—all over—and more self-assured in his masculinity than any of her boyfriends had been. His magnetism and self-confidence were overwhelming and Iris found herself a little out of her depth around him. Especially when he was wearing nothing but a towel that seemed to be staying put through sheer force of will.

"Shall we?" he asked, holding the sauna door open for her. She ran her damp palms over the front of her fluffy towel and nodded, stepping past him into the hot and humid room that smelled faintly of cedar wood and eucalyptus—the latter of which she assumed was from essential oils.

She sat herself down on the lowest bench, tucking her knees and feet primly together and resting her palms on her thighs. She knew she probably resembled a schoolgirl posing for a class picture, but she couldn't help it. She was so tense. If he believed this would relax her, he was sorely mistaken. This was probably one of the tensest, most stressful situations in which she'd ever found herself.

He looked at her for a long moment, a smirk on his arrogant, handsome face, before he shook his head and sat diagonally across—and a level up—from her.

No, he didn't sit. He sprawled. Spreading himself out, arms stretched across the top of the bench, thighs apart, with the towel tucked between them. Every muscle bulging and gleaming and displayed to perfection.

It was annoying how he could look so goddamned flawless without even trying.

Iris folded her arms across her chest and purposely looked away from him, even though he'd quite intentionally placed himself right in her line of sight, perhaps out of some patholog-ical need to be stared at.

"I *did* enjoy your zombie apocalypse short story," he said a moment later, succeeding in dragging her eyes back up to him in horror.

"You *read* that? How? Where?"

"Found it on a random little website unimaginatively called *The Write Stuff*."

She barely concealed a grimace at that information. The now-defunct site had been operated by her ex-boyfriend Claude. He'd been her first serious boyfriend and they'd met during their first year of uni. He'd loved that dumb story and had tried to convince her to turn it into a weekly serial for his website.

"It was a unique take. Decently written, if a tad over-wrought in places. It would actually make a good movie if it were properly fleshed out and you spent more time on character development and less on the gory specifics. You're a bloodthirsty little thing, aren't you? Have you checked if it's even anatomically possible to suck someone's brains out through their eye sockets?"

"Surely you could? Your optic nerve connects to the brain, doesn't it?"

"So, the optic nerve would act as some kind of siphon?" he looked thoughtful as he considered that graphic and absurd thought.

What even *was* this conversation?

"I really thought that website no longer existed."

"Why are you so consistently appalled at the thought of having any of your work available online? It's a pretty bizarre reaction for someone hoping to make her mark in entertainment journalism. You can't be shy about having your work out there for the world to see. And praise. And rip to shreds."

He made a fair point.

Only...

"Only none of what you found actually showcases my capabilities," she said.

"I beg to differ. The poetry was shit, I'll give you that. But that zombie thing... confining the action to a space colony? The claustrophobic intensity? Brilliant. I wanted more. You should have serialized it."

"My boyfriend said the same thing," she admitted, not sure if he was mocking her or not.

"Boyfriend?"

Wow, Iris stared in bemusement as he leaned forward, every single muscle in his body tensing. She really wanted to touch him, stroke her hands and fingers over those hard slabs of flesh, gleaming with moisture from the pool and now from the steam. Would his skin feel as velvety smooth as it looked? Everything about him was so damned tempting, and Iris was shocked by how very much she wanted to stroke, and pet, and caress...

"What boyfriend?" His words barely penetrated the lustful haze which held Iris enthralled.

"What?" she asked, feeling sluggish, her body and brain unfamiliar to her.

"Tell me about the boyfriend."

"Boyfriend?"

"The one who said you should serialize your story."

"Claude? He's not my boyfriend. Not anymore, at least. Not for a long time."

"Do you have one?"

"One what?" This conversation was bizarre and Iris was having a really hard time following it.

"A boyfriend," he repeated with strained patience.

"No." Her brain cleared enough for her to add, "Why do you ask?"

His shoulders shifted, and the play of muscles across that broad expanse instantly distracted her.

"Just curious. Wondering what kind of boyfriend would let you roam around in the wilderness by yourself while you tracked down an international sex symbol with the intention of spending weeks alone with him."

"Did you just refer to yourself as an international sex symbol?"

"Merely repeating what others have said."

"Are you flattered by the label?"

His face closed up and his lips tightened.

"This isn't an interview."

Iris clamped her mouth shut and diverted her eyes once again.

"Right."

"How's your back?" he asked after a moment. Then, when she continued to mutinously stare at the condensation beaded on the glass door, "Don't be childish now, Hughes, look at me and answer the question."

"It's fine," she said, still not looking at him. He made a quiet sound of frustration.

"Why won't you look at me?"

"Why do you so desperately need to be looked at?" she

countered, angling her jaw upwards. "Do you miss having an audience?"

The silence seethed and—curious though she was to see his reaction—Iris maintained her stubborn focus on the door.

"I don't need an audience."

"Of course, you do. It's why you do what you do. You enjoy having the adulation of the masses, don't you?"

"Is that your best guess, Hughes? Some cheap, predictable psychobabble about what you think makes me tick? You know fuck all about me. You've seen me in a few movies, read or watched some interviews, and believe you know everything about me? You're a fucking child if you think everything you've seen and heard about me is true."

Iris finally gave him her eyes, which he then held trapped in his own furious, burning gaze.

"Why won't you enlighten me then?" she invited, her voice curt.

"Because you're nothing to me. Nobody. Why should I reveal any part of who I am to you? What the fuck makes you think you're so goddamned special? You're nothing but a little wannabe journalist with zero credentials and even less experience. Added to that, you're the spawn of one of the worst human beings to have ever befouled this planet with his existence. You're literally the last person on earth I'd ever confide in."

"Yes, I know this part," she told him with a bored yawn. Refusing to let him provoke her again. "My father's the devil, I'm Satan's spawn, blah, blah... You're getting repetitive. I heard the same boring rant not more than half an hour ago."

There was a gleam of—was that *appreciation?*—in his eyes and for the first time since she'd arrived, his lips stretched into that famous Abbott grin.

"Very well done, Hughes. You won't get very far with paper-thin skin in this industry."

His praise confused her and she glared at him warily, not sure what to make of it.

"I'm tired. I think I'd like to go back to my room now." Right now, even the oppressive hell that was her room seemed preferable to his disagreeable presence.

"Do you really prefer what you refer to as your prison cell over a sauna and my company?" His stare was contemplative, but his question without inflection, and Iris wasn't sure if she'd offended him.

Nor did she care.

"Yes."

God, that was such a *lie*. It was literally the second last place she'd rather be right now. But since *this* right here was the last place she wanted to be, she had no other choice than to return to her stifling, terrifying solitary confinement.

His eyebrows shot to his hairline.

"Very well. But you have to do some stretching when you get back to your room to prevent your back from seizing up again."

Iris nodded and pushed to her feet. The movement was easy and relatively painless.

Honesty compelled her to admit, "I really do feel a *lot* better. Thank you."

"You've already thanked me. Several times already, in fact.

But I should be the one to thank *you* . . ." His voice was gruff, as if the words tasted foreign on his tongue. "For your help yesterday."

"Like I had a choice," she muttered, still salty about the damned forced labor. His beard twitched as his jaw clenched and his lips thinned. Gosh, for an actor, he was terrible at hiding his emotions. Then again, he clearly didn't care if she knew he was pissed off with her or not. Probably preferred it if she did.

"You had a choice," he reminded her. "I was happy for you to stay in your room, but you wanted to negotiate for better conditions."

"All I got was a Wi-Fi password you were going to give me anyway."

"Not my fault you're a terrible negotiator." He got up and lithely descended the single step down. "Anyway, the sandbags did the trick, the flooding slowed down to a trickle."

"Glad to hear it," she said, a little distracted when he came to stand right beside her. Her nose was level with one flat brown nipple, and her eyes were riveted to those impressive pecs mere inches away. He was standing so close she could smell the faint hint of chlorine from the hot tub on his skin.

Her eyes tracked over the dark hair lightly sprinkled across his chest and abs... from where her rapt gaze helplessly followed the happy little trail wending its way down from his belly button—an innie, her favorite—to where it disappeared under the low-riding towel which looked in serious danger of slipping.

"For someone who accused me of needing an audience, you sure do seem to enjoy enabling my alleged thirst for attention by staring at me." His low voice rumbled almost directly into her ear, and startled her into jerking her head up.

"Fuuuck!" he yelled.

"*Ow!*" she yelped at the same time.

Her abrupt move had sent the top of her head straight into his jaw and they both felt the impact keenly. They stepped away from each other, Iris rubbing her throbbing crown, while Trystan had his palm cupped over his jaw.

"Jesus, you have a hard head."

"You have a harder jaw. You'd think that the beard would have provided some cushioning, but nope," she complained. "Is my head bleeding? I feel like it's bleeding."

His hand dropped from his jaw and he reached out to cup her face. Alarmed, Iris jerked away from his touch.

"What are you doing?"

"Let me look," he commanded with a scowl. Iris remained tense while he gingerly palmed her cheeks and angled her head downward. One of his hands continued to cradle her cheek, while the other parted the hair on her scalp. His touch was gentle, soothing, and seemed completely at odds with the abrupt man she knew him to be.

"It's not bleeding, but you're going to have a lump about the size of a goose egg."

"This entire trip has been nothing but hazardous to my health so far," she grumbled.

"Look at it this way," he said, his fingers still entangled in her hair, while his other hand continued to cradle her cheek, his long thumb now idly tracing the line of her cheekbone and sending shivers of sensation skittering over her skin. "You avoided being crushed to death by a falling tree on day one. That's a win."

Iris fought back a smile but couldn't disguise the betraying twitch of her lips. His eyes were drawn to the movement. His Adam's apple bobbed as he swallowed and his pupils dilated to the point where only a sliver of silver remained. His head lowered, until the merest breath separated his mouth from hers, and Iris choked back a moan.

"T-Trystan?" His name emerged on a whisper of uncertainty, and he shuddered—a full-body ripple that caused gooseflesh to visibly pebble his skin—then blinked, before shaking his head as if to clear it.

He dropped his hands and took a deliberate step away from her, leaving her feeling bereft, as if she'd lost something precious.

"I didn't realize we were on a first-name basis, Hughes," he said, that awful, detached coldness back in his voice, and Iris sucked in a pained breath. That one frigid statement hurting more than anything he'd said about her biological father earlier.

"I'm sorry, Mr. Abbott," she apologized, hating that the stiffness in her voice betrayed her hurt. So much for cultivating a thicker skin. "You're right, of course. I won't forget myself like that again."

He chose not to acknowledge her apology and instead opened the sauna door. He grabbed their robes from the hook outside the door and handed the smaller one to her.

"Put this on," he said while shrugging into his and thankfully—*tragically*—covering himself up and removing all that tempting flesh from her lascivious gaze. "Stay warm until you get back to your room, then get into some sweats, do those stretches, and spend the rest of the morning taking it easy. Okay?"

She was too busy shrugging into her robe, while keeping her towel from slipping, to do more than grunt in response to his bossiness.

"*Hughes!*"

His sharp tone immediately drew her attention.

"What?"

"Did you hear what I just said?"

"About the sweats and stretches and stuff? Yes."

He looked somewhat mollified as he nodded. "Good. Some acknowledgment next time."

She saluted him smartly, "Yes, oh lord and master!"

"Christ, you're annoying," he grumbled. "Let's go."

She meekly trailed behind him, her eyes happily exploring the house as they made their way from the natatorium back to her room. He must've been distracted because he didn't take hold of her elbow to hastily steer her along as he'd done the previous few times she'd been allowed out of her cell.

Her eyes snagged on a framed picture of a blissfully smiling couple in their wedding finery and Iris finally comprehended what people meant when they referred to a *lightbulb* moment, because it felt like someone had just flicked a switch in her brain.

"This isn't your house." The words were out before she could curtail them, and he stopped walking abruptly. Iris careened into his hard back, but it felt like bouncing off an immovable tree trunk for all the impact her momentum had made on his sturdy frame.

"Fuck." The soft word resonated with heartfelt regret. "You're just incapable of minding your own business, aren't you?"

"I didn't realize you knew Miles Hollingsworth," she said.

He turned toward her, clamping both hands onto her upper arms, and looming over her to glare down into her face.

She stared back at him unblinkingly, too accustomed to his bluster by now to be daunted.

"And you're going to forget that little factoid as soon as you're back in your room."

"But why? It's not like he's some kind of mafia kingpin. The man is a genius. How do you know him?"

"You think I can't hang out with geniuses?"

"Genii," she corrected, just to irritate him.

"You know damned well geniuses is the most commonly used plural," he ground out from between clenched teeth.

"Well, how do you know Miles Hollingsworth? Is he your financial advisor or something?"

"You know so much about him, you'd know he's not a fucking financial advisor."

No, he wasn't. Miles Hollingsworth was the former CEO of Hollingsworth Holdings Inc. A powerful, wealthy, self-made man who'd founded one of the largest holding companies in Europe. He'd caused a sensation a couple of years ago when he'd effectively retired at thirty-five, married his former house-keeper, and moved to... well to *here* apparently.

That explained the cars in the garage. MilesH for Miles

Hollingsworth. Which meant the Mini Cooper had to belong to his wife, Charity.

"Have you known him long?" Iris asked chattily, as he released one of her arms, but kept the other imprisoned to march her back to her room at twice the speed they'd been going earlier.

He didn't reply.

"You don't seem like you'd have much in common," she continued, starting to huff slightly as she practically ran to keep up with his long-legged stride. "Are you renting this house or something?"

That question broke his stride and he threw her an incredulous look before shaking his head and carrying on walking.

"Why'd you look at me like that?" she asked when they finally reached her door, which he opened impatiently.

"You're deluded if you think Miles Hollingsworth needs to rent out his home."

"Oh, yeah, that makes no sense," she acknowledged, chagrined.

A not-so-subtle shove between her shoulder blades caught her by surprise and sent her stumbling into the room.

"Hey, come on, man! Enough with the manhandling," she spluttered, furiously turning to face him with clenched fists. He looked shocked and contrite at the same time.

"Fuck, that was... shit. Hughes, I didn't realize..." A dull flush crept up his cheeks and he looked absolutely stricken. "There's no excuse, that was unforgivable. I'm sorry. Did I hurt you?"

What?

"Uhm, no, I lost my footing. But no more shoving, okay?"

"Honest to God, I meant to give you just the gentlest of nudges."

"No more nudging either." He lifted his hands in surrender.

"I promise."

"So... about Miles Hollingsworth."

Iris was curious by nature, one of the other reasons she'd believed journalism was the right career choice for her. But she now knew her curiosity wasn't fueled by the driving need to know all the facts—no, she was just nosy and loved a good gossip.

That nosiness, combined with boredom, along with a deep reluctance to be trapped in this room once again were only a few of the reasons she kept prodding Trystan about Miles Hollingsworth, despite his obvious reluctance to divulge any information to her. Iris purely hoped to keep him talking and to delay her inevitable imprisonment in this awful room.

"No."

The harshly spoken word foiled her sad—and obvious—delay tactic. He stepped back, slammed the door in her face, and a few seconds later the lock clicked in place.

"Thanks for lunch, you make a great tuna mayo toastie," Iris said, when Trystan collected the lunchtime tray four hours later. She was so eager for some conversation and companionship that even *his* company would be preferable to the increasingly horrific claustrophobic confines of this room.

Instead of nodding curtly and leaving, as was his habit, he stared down at the tray for a moment and then lifted his eyes to meet hers.

"My mom's recipe," he said, and Iris's eyebrows shot up at the reluctantly conceded personal information. "You didn't have to clean the dishes."

"I didn't mind," she said. "Besides, I was bored. It gave me something to do."

"Did you do those stretches this morning?"

Iris winced at the memory of those painful stretches. She was *not* as diligent with her daily stretching as she ought to be. She went to yoga only occasionally when Evan dragged her out to a class, but Iris would never be *that* girl. She was reasonably fit, she walked a lot, and worked out once or twice a week. She did the bare minimum to stay healthy and keep herself in acceptable shape, but she wasn't religious about it. And leading up to this trip, she'd been so distracted she'd skipped a few gym sessions.

And she'd felt it while stretching this morning. But she'd forced herself to do it, despite the pain, because Trystan had been right, it would help. It *had* helped, but God it had sucked.

"Yes."

"And how's your head?"

It took Iris a moment to figure out why he was asking her that, but when she remembered she rubbed the top of her head ruefully.

"There's barely even a lump, actually. It throbbed for a

while after I returned to the room, but the pain faded not too long after that."

"Good," he hovered awkwardly for a few moments, before saying, almost impulsively, "I'm taking Luna out for a walk soon. Would you like to join us? It may help with any residual stiffness you have."

Would she? What a dumb question.

Iris had spent the morning writing, then reading, then neatening up the already neat suite. Anything to keep it together. But nothing had been able to alleviate her frustration, restlessness, and the fear of losing all control of her emotional and mental stability. Her medication was barely helping her keep it together.

Calls home hadn't helped. Her parents kept pushing her for answers about where she was. And who could blame them? She'd built it up to be this huge thing, promising them a revelation that would blow their minds, and now she was being secretive about it.

Hunter Quinn had—unsurprisingly—still not responded to any of her messages. Iris had pretty much given up on that front.

Evan had been to yet another party last night and all she'd talked about was how *amazing* it had been. She'd spent a good deal of time name-dropping, talking about "some random hot guy" she'd "fucked", and then bitching about her boss for another half an hour after that.

She hadn't once asked Iris how she was doing. Which Iris wouldn't normally have noticed, only she'd really needed to talk about her increasing doubts about her career choice. That was when she'd recognized that most of their conversations centered around Evan and *her* life. Iris had picked up on this in the past but had always thought this was because her own life was so dull in comparison, but now that she had so much time with her thoughts, the disparity troubled her.

She set aside her disturbing contemplations about her friend and focused on Trystan's question.

"Oh, yes *please*," she replied, the words stumbling over each other in her panic that he would change his mind.

"It's not raining, but the wind is icy, so bundle up. And wear those boots from yesterday, the ground is muddy and a little treacherous."

"Okay."

"I'll be back for you in fifteen minutes."

"I'll be ready."

Chapter Eight

He was careful not to touch her. That was the first thing Iris noticed when he came for her exactly fifteen minutes later. He walked close beside her and she could practically feel his big hand hovering above the small of her back, but no contact was made. He walked slower than his usual breakneck pace as he shepherded her, with just his body, through a spacious living room toward the very same door he'd tricked her through her first night here.

"Why aren't you trying to shuffle me through here at your usual record-breaking pace? I mean I'm seeing *things*. Like those pics on the mantel." She nodded toward the framed images above a gorgeous stone hearth that looked like it would be heavenly when in use. "And that fireplace. Do you enjoy that fireplace every night while I'm huddled in front of a measly radiator heater?"

"There's no point in trying to hide our surroundings from you anymore, since you know whose house it is."

Iris honestly didn't know why it had been such a big secret in the first place. But she wasn't going to ask because she knew he wouldn't answer. Worse, he'd get pissed off with her for asking in the first place. And she couldn't risk him rescinding the offer of a walk. It would destroy her morale.

"And I haven't used the fireplace at all since I've been here."

"God, what a crime," she said with a disgusted click of her tongue. "What's wrong with you? It's there to be enjoyed."

"Seems like a lot of work for just one person."

"And a dog. Think about Luna, she'd *love* it."

Luna's tail swept indolently back and forth at the sound of her name.

Trystan's lips curled as he unlocked the front door and stepped aside to allow her through.

Iris cast the open door a jaundiced look before turning her narrowed eyes on him.

"You're not going to slam the door behind me as soon as I step through it, are you?"

The curl of his lips turned into a fully fledged grin before he ruthlessly curbed it and flattened his mouth. But the gleam of amusement was still evident in his eyes when he raised his brows at her in challenge.

"What do you think?" he asked, crossing his arms over his chest and leaning a shoulder against the doorframe while he waited for her next move.

Iris's eyes went from his smug face to the lush, wet, green landscape just beyond the front door and back again. The weather was gray and blustery, and the unwelcoming iciness was quickly seeping in through the front door, but the thought of getting some fresh air and, for *once*, not being drenched in the process, was too tempting to resist.

She threw back her shoulders, lifted her chin, and stepped over the threshold. She sucked in a breath at the shock of frigid air that hit the exposed skin of her face, and laughed in sheer exhilaration and joy when she exhaled an impressive cloud of steam seconds later.

"Oh my *God*," she squealed. "It's so cold. I didn't think it could get that cold here."

She was sure she heard him mutter, "That would explain the itsy-bitsy bikini."

But when she asked him what he'd said he gave her a wide-eyed innocent look and said, "I didn't say a damned thing."

Iris didn't call him out on the blatant lie—*or* the terrible acting—instead she eagerly took in her surroundings.

"It's so pretty out here," she exclaimed. They were standing in a courtyard surrounded by a neatly trimmed six-foot-high camellia hedge. She only recognized them because camellias were her mother's favorite flower, and the pale pink blooms prolifically dotted the entire length of the hedge. She hadn't known that the flowers *could* bloom in weather this cold, but how beautiful they looked in that verdant hedge, which surrounded a lovely natural pond. The space was alive with color thanks to the myriad of winter-blooming plants and shrubs dotted all around the garden.

"This is so different than I'd imagined it to be," she said with an incredulous laugh. "The other night it was so dark out here I couldn't see a thing. It was so creepy. All I could see was the outline of the hedges... and I stepped into the pond."

She shuddered at the unpleasant memory and her happy smile slipped.

Trystan was watching her closely, his hands shoved into his jacket pockets, while his breath clouded the air in front of him.

"You used Luna's tag to get inside, right?" he asked, and the question startled her. They hadn't talked about that night at all before now.

"Yes. She scared the bejesus out of me," Iris admitted with another laugh. This one was edged with remembered fear. "She approached from over there"—she pointed toward the far end of the garden—"And I took a step back, but my wet shoe skidded on some moss, I think, and I went down. Landed on my back. It's a miracle I didn't hit my head. And she came to stand right above me."

This time the sound that emerged from her throat—while still attempting to be a laugh—was choked.

"I was so certain I was going to die... Foolish, I know," she tried to lighten her tone and failed dismally. "Who could be scared of such a sweetheart, right? But it was pitch black and she was huge and I was terrified. But then she licked me."

This time her laugh was genuine and filled with warmth.

"I was screaming, and—grossly—got some dog tongue in my mouth. That shut me up really quickly. Luna and I became pals after that. And when it started raining, she led me inside."

He hadn't moved throughout her retelling, standing about a meter and a half away from her, hands still in his pockets, legs braced apart, eyes intent on her face. It was unnerving being pinned beneath that silvery gaze, especially when his expression remained stark and enigmatic.

"All that for a story." His voice lacked inflection but Iris couldn't help but bristle defensively at the comment.

"At that point the story was the last thing on my mind. I was cold and exhausted, confused by your lack of welcome, and terrified I'd be forced to try and find my way back to the car in the dark. I didn't even know which direction I'd have to go to get there.

"I didn't care about the story," she repeated, her voice small and getting that annoying telltale squeak it did when she was on the verge of tears. Worse, she felt her nose and the back of her throat start to burn as her eyes went blurry. "I was just *really* scared. And desperately wished I were back home."

Iris turned away from him, focusing her attention on Luna who was sniffing around the courtyard. She quickly pressed her burning eyes with the heels of her hands, willing the tears away while she tried to regain her composure.

Showing a great deal more tact and consideration than she'd come to expect from him, Trystan remained silent, but Iris was hyperaware of his presence just behind her.

"Do you—" His dark velvet voice sounded rough with gravel, and he paused to clear his throat before continuing. "Do you want to see the car?"

Once she was certain she had herself back under control, Iris turned to face him.

"Yes. I'd like to see it, and to see if the walk there is less harrowing by daylight. I kept expecting to plummet off a cliff, or something."

"No cliffs around here," he promised her gravely. "You were in more danger from the trees."

"I know that now."

"It's this way," he said, and turned to lead her out of the courtyard. Luna happily darted ahead, stopping to sniff at practically every shrub and tree en route.

There were smaller broken branches and even more enormous limbs littering the long, muddy drive leading up to the house, and Iris stared in horror at every progressively larger one they passed.

The road back to the car was a lot shorter than she remembered. Only about ten minutes. But in the dark, with the wind and low light, and so many ways for her to have wandered off the path and become lost, Iris was genuinely amazed that she'd made it to the house at all that night.

She grew quieter and quieter as their walk continued and when she reached the car, she stared—feeling lightheaded, and faintly nauseous—at the flattened piece of scrap metal with the gigantic dead oak tree sprawled across it.

"*Whoa*," Trystan exclaimed when she swayed slightly and—forgetting himself—he took her elbow to steady her. "You okay?"

"No. Part of me thought you were lying or exaggerating, but this is... I so very nearly chose to stay in the car that night."

"But you didn't," he told her in a fierce undertone. "You *didn't*, Iris. You bravely chose to head out in terrible weather, armed only with your phone's flashlight, and you made it to what should have been a safe haven. You're alive and well because you had the courage to do that. I don't know what *I* would have done. Stayed in the car probably. But *you* didn't.

You got out and you walked, while lugging that ridiculous pink case behind you. You confronted a beast, and despite how frightening and confusing that must have been, you still cleverly managed to find your way into a sheltered space."

"Luna's not a beast," she defended the dog fondly.

She was shocked when he responded with a quiet, "I wasn't referring to Luna."

"Oh."

For the first time since they'd arrived at the car she looked at him, and it was to find him staring down at her with fierce eyes. His face was grim, but those eyes, they were ablaze with a naked emotion that Iris was unable to decipher.

Instead, in her confusion, she latched onto the most minor detail among the many bewildering things he'd just said.

"You called me Iris."

"And you called me Trystan," he reminded her with a half-smile. "Guess than makes us even."

"I didn't think you knew my first name." She knew it was a silly thing to say.

"You literally told me when we first met. I even googled you, remember?"

Of course she did, but somehow hearing him use her first name was still a shock.

"You were so angry, I wasn't sure you even heard me."

"I heard you." He didn't elaborate, but inspected her face carefully. "Feeling better?"

She nodded, then immediately regretted it when he removed his warm hand from her elbow.

"Let's check out the lake," he suggested. "The water is

choppy, angry, and cloudy with silt but it's better than standing here staring at your pancaked rental."

She moaned.

"Ugh, it's a rental," she repeated, cringing at the reminder. She'd have to call the rental agency in the morning and attempt to explain this crazy situation.

"They'll have insurance against shit like this. Don't worry about it."

He started walking again. Luna led the way, a giant tree branch in her mouth. The dog didn't seem to expect either of them to throw it—good thing too because it was longer than Iris's arm and looked pretty heavy—she was just content to carry it around in her mouth.

"It's so beautiful here," Iris whispered in awe as they continued to walk. She could see the lake gleaming in the distance. She didn't have a very good view of it from her room, so this would be the first time she would get a proper look at it.

"Why are you whispering?" Trystan whispered back, a mocking edge in his hissed question.

She threw him an appreciative grin and shrugged.

"I don't know," she said in a normal, if still somewhat low, voice. "It feels like we're the only people in the world out here. Just us three. There's something reverential about it, like being in nature's cathedral. Part of me feels like we should show it an appropriate amount of wonderment and respect. It just lends itself to hushed tones, don't you think?"

"I get it."

The reply was quiet, simple, and none of the mocking tone of before lingered in the three words.

When they reached the lake, they simply stood there, side by side, close enough to almost brush arms, but not touching at all. The strong wind tore at Iris's clothes, sprayed a fine mist from the crests of the waves over her, stole her breath, and ruthlessly dallied with her riotous curls.

It was splendid.

"I love this," she yelled into the wind, but it tore her words away.

"What?" She heard his faint question and looked at him with a wide grin, before cupping her hands around her mouth and repeating the words.

His wild grin likely matched hers and he nodded. She saw his mouth form the words *me too*, but the wind whipped his voice away.

They stood there for a long time until the spray from the white caps started to mix with a moderate drizzle and they both began to shiver.

At that point Trystan reached for her again, only this time he didn't grab her upper arm or elbow, this time his hand closed around hers. The move was unconscious, as was Iris's easy acceptance of it, and they slowly walked back to the house hand in hand.

It was only when they reached the kitchen door that they simultaneously became aware of the intimacy of the gesture. Trystan quickly released her hand and Iris shoved the offending appendage into her jacket pocket, trying not to dwell on the warm, pleasant tingling on her flesh where his palm had kissed hers. She watched him fumble with the door handle for a few seconds before he allowed her to precede him through the door. Then he blocked Luna's way.

"No. Drop it," he commanded the dog, referring to the tree branch she'd lugged all the way back to the house with her. She'd put it down only to do her business and occasionally sniff around shrubs, but had picked it up every time they'd continued on their walk.

Now she was staring up at Trystan with pleading eyes as he refused her entry into the house with her new best friend.

"Luna, drop it. It's not coming into the house." Iris watched from around Trystan's arm as Luna whined plaintively. The dog finally heaved a long-suffering sigh and gently placed the branch on the welcome mat outside the door.

She affected an air of injured dignity as she trotted past Iris and Trystan with her head held high.

Trystan shut the door as soon as the dog was inside.

"You could have let her keep it for a while," Iris said, and Trystan snorted.

"Don't be fooled by those puppy-dog eyes. She couldn't give a fuck about the stick. If I allowed her to do that every time we came back from a walk, we'd have a fair to middling pile of discarded wet wood littered about the house. She loses interest in the damned things less than a minute after she gets her way. That's a lesson I learned the hard way."

Iris giggled and cast a fond glance at the dog who had settled into her basket and was contentedly licking herself.

Her smile faded and she idly traced her fingers along the edge of the faintly blue-veined waterfall white marble countertop.

"Thank you for allowing me to join you on your walk. I enjoyed it."

He nodded but said nothing, keeping his gaze fixed on her face. It was unnerving how often he just stared at her like she was some weird, exotic species of bug he'd picked up in the forest and he wasn't quite sure what to make of.

"I suppose I should be getting back to my room now," she offered, reluctance weighing down each word. After the lovely, carefree afternoon surrounded by so much beauty and open space the thought of returning to a confined area choked her up. But maybe he'd change his mind about locking her in this time. Maybe he'd recognize how cruel it was to keep her trapped.

"Yes." He didn't move.

"Okay," she said, also not moving.

Even though the island served as a barrier between them he still felt uncomfortably close, likely because of that probing stare, and Iris shifted her weight from foot to foot.

"You should change into some dry clothes," he said.

"That's nothing new," Iris said, as she plucked at her damp jacket. "Does it ever stop raining here?"

"Apparently it's been wetter than usual this year," he said, and Iris wondered at the inane conversation. "I've been to the Western Cape a few times before, but always in summer and usually for work. Never during winter. I was forewarned by Miles and Sam to prepare for some pretty extreme cold and rain, but this is even worse than I'd expected."

"Sam?" Iris shouldn't have asked—she knew she shouldn't have. Since Trystan wasn't likely to intentionally reveal any new information to her if he could help it. It had obviously been an unconscious slip of the tongue.

And that was confirmed when he once again went stone-faced and tensed.

"I'm sorry. None of my business," she backtracked hastily.

"I'm..." He paused, seeming to search for the right words. "Ever since the accident—Trish's death—every interaction with the press has been negative and intrusive. I don't want to talk to journalists. Not about her, or the accident, or anything really. Not yet. Maybe not ever. And every time I talk to you I can't lose sight of the fact that you're one of *them*."

"But—" Her brain was racing as she mulled over his unexpectedly candid confession. His eyes had darkened, his expression was moody, body language closed off. "You'll have to deal with them eventually. Press junkets for movies, promotional interviews and the like. You can't avoid the press forever. Not in your line of work."

"Then maybe it's time I find a new line of work." The words were spoken so quietly that Iris wasn't certain she'd heard him correctly. But one look into those roiling eyes told her she hadn't been mistaken and she gasped in shock.

"You can't be serious?" Why would he say something like this to her? Was it some kind of trick? Or test? He *had* to know that this was the kind of scoop that any journalist worth their salt would kill to have.

"As a heart attack."

Forgetting for a moment what this information could do for her career, Iris stared at him for a long, long moment and shook her head.

"That would be a shame, Trystan," she said. "You're extremely talented."

"You going to write about this?"

"As you have reminded me time and time again, you haven't consented to an interview with me," she reminded him. "Mr. Quinn's promises mean nothing in light of that fact."

"There are many who wouldn't let that stop them."

"I like to consider myself a woman of integrity. We were having a conversation, private and off the record."

He nodded again, a curt jerk of his jaw. Something sparked in his eyes—satisfaction? triumph?—Iris wasn't sure what. And once again she had the distinct feeling that she was being tested.

And she didn't like it. Was he toying with her? Of course he was. The naive, inexperienced wannabe journalist who was ridiculously eager to please the big movie star whom she had once borderline hero-worshipped.

He'd just admitted that he could never lose sight of the fact that she was one of *them*. The enemy. Why would he divulge such a secret to someone he clearly didn't trust and had no respect for?

"You're playing games with me. I don't like it." The statement was blunt, to the point, and his eyes reflected his surprise at the straightforward comment.

Trystan was clearly used to people who obfuscated, and played the same manipulative games he did, but Iris didn't pussyfoot around. She spoke her mind, regardless of the consequences. And while she was inexperienced in her field, she wasn't going to allow him to manipulate and walk all over her.

"Why would you think that?"

"Because until now you've been religiously cautious about what you say around me. You've done everything short of blindfolding me to prevent me seeing anything to do with the house before today—"

"Shit, blindfolding you would have been an ideal solution. Why didn't *I* think of that?" he interrupted her on a lazy drawl and she shot him an irritated glare.

"So, I don't buy this sudden about-face," she continued, ignoring his flippant question. "Why would you divulge such extremely personal information to *me* of all people? What game are you playing?"

"Let's get you back to your room," he said with a wicked grin. "It's time for your afternoon nap. You're getting cranky."

"I'm not a child," she snapped.

"You resemble one. With that mop of wild curls. And those ridiculously wide and innocent eyes. You look like a girl playing at being an adult. And it's hard to reconcile the innocence in those eyes with that *mouth*, and with those generous curves in that tiny, incendiary bikini. You're a fucking study in contradictions, and I'm starting to wonder if Quinny..." He clammed up abruptly, while Iris blinked up at him shock.

What did he mean about her mouth? And her curves? Were those compliments? He'd sounded extremely pissed off when he'd said them and it left Iris more confused than ever.

He made a sweeping *you first* gesture with his arm, and Iris —though keen to escape his frustrating presence—led the way back to her room with leaden, reluctant feet.

She tried not to dwell on the fact that she was now thinking of the cage as *her* room. This twisted situation was fast becoming normal and it made her uneasy. When she reached her door, she stopped and instead of opening it—unwilling to freely step into her own prison—she turned to face him. But she was taken aback by how closely he'd followed her. He was mere inches away, his big body sending off waves of heat, and even steam thanks to his wet clothes. She could smell his woodsy aftershave, feel his soft even breath ruffle the hair at the top of her head, hear the soft ticking coming from the old-fashioned platinum-and-leather-strapped wristwatch he wore.

"What's wrong?" he asked quietly, appearing confused by her abrupt stop.

"H-have you heard anything about when we can expect the roads to be passable again?" she asked, a little mortified by the unsteadiness of her voice.

"I called a friend in town this morning. Seems like the original estimate of two weeks is right. The road isn't a priority right now because this is the only house down here. If someone had been injured or if we were in dire need of supplies they would arrange a helicopter, but since neither of those scenarios is the case here, it would be a waste of much-needed emergency resources to dispatch any kind of airborne rescue vehicle to us."

"You can't arrange a private helicopter?"

"Why would I? I have food, clean drinking water, solar- and generator-powered electricity. I'm perfectly fine cut off from the world. In fact, I'm happy to be out of physical reach from the rest of humanity for now."

"What about me?"

"What about you?"

"You don't want me here."

"I don't. But I can deal for two weeks. Especially since I've found a way to keep you out of my way."

"So, you're just going to keep me locked up for the entire two weeks?" The notion was too unbearable for her brain to wrap around.

"I think I've been more than generous. You've had spa time, sauna time, free meals, and a hike. You have access to the Wi-Fi, and a television... think of it as a vacation."

"I told you before, I have cleithrophobia. It's kind of like claustrophobia but it's a fear of being trapped."

"Come *on*," he scoffed and the dismissive tone in his voice set her teeth on edge. "You expect me to believe that? It's entirely too conveniently specific to your situation. Anyway, you're hardly in a tiny prison cell. You have a kitchen, living room, bedroom, and bathroom. Beautiful views, windows that open and close. You're hardly trapped in a small enclosed space."

"But I can't leave," she said, trying to keep the panic she could hear edging its way into her voice at bay.

"You can't leave the room, no. But if you want to leave the house, I told you before, you're more than welcome to try and hoof it back to town. The weather has cleared up a bit, so maybe the river would have calmed down somewhat. Although if the lake this afternoon was any indication, I doubt the river would be much better. And there's more heavy rain forecast for

Wednesday. So, if you want to leave, it's best to do so within the next three days."

His eyes were glued to her face, head tilted, as he waited for her response. He was still way too close for comfort.

"That's not really a choice, is it? Stay locked in this room, or take my chances out there."

"It's only two weeks, Hughes. You'll be fine." He reached past her, his arm brushing against hers. The contact made her jump, but she immediately felt foolish when she grasped that he was only reaching for the door handle behind her. She heard the faint creak of the door as it swung open, and she dropped her gaze to the floor as she concentrated very hard on keeping her tears at bay.

When she felt like she had her emotions under control, she took a step back, then turned on her heel, and walked into the suite of rooms with stiff shoulders and her head held high. She fought to keep her nausea at bay, and bit back a scream.

"Iris?" She tensed at the sound of her name on his lips, but refused to turn and face him, not with tears welling in her eyes. "I'll bring in your dinner shortly."

She nodded, not trusting her voice, and waited for the door to shut.

Nothing.

What was he waiting for? The anticipation was torturous.

"Is there..." He paused, as if he were trying to gather his thoughts. "Do you have any requests? For dinner? I didn't think to ask before. Do you have any food allergies? Or maybe you're vegan or pescatarian, or something."

Iris swallowed thickly and shook her head again. Still, he didn't leave. Maybe he needed to hear it.

"I have no food allergies," she said, her voice subdued. "No preferences. Whatever you make is fine. Thank you."

"Okay."

She could feel him watching her, but refused to turn around and meet his eyes. Instead, she waited—every muscle tense and on edge—for the door to close and the key to turn.

Her phobia had always been mild before now. Controllable. But every day in this room made it worse, and knowing that she would have to endure this for two weeks was unbearable. Her skin felt too tight, her heart was racing, she fought back the shudders, but she was determined to keep her shit together until after he left.

She refused to let him see her break.

"I'll see you soon." God, *why* was he still here? And still talking?

In the end, she couldn't stand it anymore and she spoke, her voice hoarse with fear and panic.

"Please, Trystan. *Please* don't lock the door."

Her low, desperate plea was met with silence.

He didn't acknowledge her words in any way. *Finally*, interminable seconds later the door shut. Softly. Gently.

And—after another long moment—the lock clicked.

Iris exhaled the breath she'd unconsciously been holding. It emerged on a despairing sob. The trembling began seconds later.

Full-body shudders that she tried to control by wrapping her arms around her. It didn't work and she sank to the floor right where she stood, curling in on herself as she tried to keep the panic and fear at bay.

Her breath came in harsh gasps.

"You can do this, you can do this, you can do this." She repeated the soft, panicked mantra over and over and over again.

But no matter how often she repeated it, she could not bring herself to believe it.

Chapter Nine

The following three days were difficult for Iris. Every day was harder than the last. Trystan always came for her after breakfast, when she would join him and Luna on their daily walks. It was the highlight of her day, but it always made returning to her forced solitude and imprisonment that much harder. She had declined the walk the day before, citing exhaustion, but she'd sensed Trystan's confusion and concern.

He hadn't said anything though, instead he strove to remain impersonal with her and continued to discourage any questions. Conversation between them on their walks centered around Luna and their surroundings.

He'd also steadfastly refused to let Luna spend any time in the room with her, and once their walk was done, Iris had nothing but a long day of stark loneliness to look forward to, only occasionally broken by Luna's visits to her door.

It was wearing her down. There'd been no word from Hunter Quinn, and Trystan still refused to even look at Iris's emails from his manager. They were at an impasse and Iris, already worn down and depressed just from trying to maintain her mental health, could see no way forward for them from here.

"You didn't touch your food," Trystan said when he collected Iris's breakfast tray on Wednesday morning.

She was sitting on the sofa, her back to him, staring out of the window at yet another gray morning. She was beginning to actively hate this place where the sun never shone and the wind was always howling.

"Iris?" Trystan's sharp voice penetrated her funk and she gave him her profile.

"Yes?"

"I said you didn't eat your food."

"I'm not hungry."

"You have to be hungry, you didn't eat your dinner last night."

"I wasn't hungry then either."

Trystan made a gruff, annoyed sound and he was kneeling in front of her before she'd even registered that he'd moved. He was staring into her face, and she listlessly turned her head to avoid his eyes, but this time he caught her jaw in a firm but gentle grip and kept her face still for his probing gaze to thoroughly inspect.

"You've been crying."

Her lips quivered before she pinched them between her teeth.

"No." She still had *some* pride and it stung that he could so easily tell that she'd shed tears. "I just... I can't sleep. I'm tired."

"Okay. But you've also been crying."

She hated feeling so nakedly vulnerable in front of him and dragged her feet up onto the couch to hug her knees to her chest with one arm. She tugged her chin out of his grasp and buried her face in her knees. She curled her other arm over the top of her head, folding herself into a protective little ball, away from those silver eyes that missed no detail.

"Come on, Hughes," he whispered, and she felt the light touch of his fingers on her hair. "You've got more spunk than this."

"You don't know me," she whispered, her voice hoarse from the tears she'd already spilled.

"Of course I know you. You're the woman who walked away from the relative safety of her car in gale force winds, through dark, unfamiliar woods. You fought a wolf, bested a beast, broke into a house and fought your way to safety against all odds. You can brave anything."

Not this.

Iris had always believed she was brave. Despite not standing up to her high school bullies, or to her parents about working at the catering business. Despite her phobias, and her uneasy concern that her lifelong dream of pursuing a career in journalism was the wrong one for her, she'd always possessed an innate belief that she was a strong person. A woman of conviction.

But she'd never been tested like this before. So much for immersion therapy, because facing her worst fear day after day did not make it conquerable. It just made her weaker, more frightened, and unable to function.

Every day was a little worse than the last. And she wasn't sure how she was going to cling to her sanity. She'd tried writing, but couldn't concentrate. She spent hours staring blankly at the screen. She dreaded sleeping because the nightmares were terrifying. In the end all she could do was stay awake, staring into the dark, the locked door looming bigger and bigger in her mind until it was all she could think about. All she could focus on. Daylight brought no relief. She frequently opened the window and leaned out as far as she could, desperate for fresh air, until the cold drove her to close it again.

But she continued to open it every half hour—despite the iciness—just to breathe. It was the only thing keeping her sane right now. The knowledge that she could leave through that window if she became desperate enough. That she could walk away and maybe find her way to town.

It was mad, but it was fast becoming the only viable option available to her.

She was so wrapped up in her thoughts that she wasn't initially aware that Trystan was talking, but his voice gradually penetrated her self-imposed huddle of solitude.

"—raining, so we can't really go for a walk today, but I thought you might want to see the cinema room. We could watch a movie? Have some popcorn?"

His hand was buried in her curls by now, his fingers stroking her scalp. His other hand was flat on her back, moving in soothing circles.

"Iris? Would you like that?"

She lifted her head and his hand fell away, but the other one continued to rub her back gently.

"Why would you..." She wasn't sure how to finish the question. And in the end, stared at him mutely. He seemed to understand though, and his shoulders lifted.

"I don't like watching movies alone. So, what do you say? You wanna join Luna and me for a movie day?"

She nodded and his lips lifted.

"Good."

"What are you in the mood for?" Trystan asked after Iris had curled up on one of the massive recliners in the cinema room. She'd crept out of her melancholy enough to appreciate the sheer magnificence of this room.

It was decadence pure and simple. The screen took up an entire wall and there were two rows of six comfortable recliners, each with a fold-away tray and a cup holder. And in the third row were three reclining love seats for couples to share.

There was a popcorn machine, already filled with freshly popped kernels, the smell of which made Iris's mouth water. Now that she was out of that stifling locked room her appetite was returning with a vengeance.

Trystan was fussing around her for some reason, draping a plush blanket over her lap, bringing her a raspberry slushy and a carton of warm popcorn.

"It's lightly salted. Would you prefer butter or another flavor?'

"No, thank you, this is perfect."

Luna had sunk down to snooze directly in front of Iris's seat, and Iris occasionally ran her socked foot over the dog's flank.

"So, what would you like to watch? Miles has a great variety of movies and shows."

"I'm not fussy, you choose." She didn't care what they watched, as long as it kept her here.

He sat down in the recliner next to hers, kicking off his trainers and going full sprawl. He lifted what looked like a tablet from a small side table and swiped the screen a few times. He made a soft sound of approval before glancing over at Iris.

"You okay with scary movies?"

"I like scary movies."

He nodded and swiped again, before putting the tablet aside. The lights dimmed, and Iris curled her legs under her bum and snuggled cozily beneath the warm blanket as she stared at the screen.

She shoveled handfuls of popcorn at a time into her mouth, occasionally sharing with Luna, and happily washed it down with her slushy as she became invested in the story.

"Oh my God, she's a moron," she groaned out loud about forty minutes in when the female lead made the classic 'hello, is anybody there' blunder.

"Why do you say that?" Trystan—who'd been largely silent throughout the film—asked curiously.

"She lives alone. If you think someone is in your *empty* house, you don't ask if anybody is there. You get the hell out."

"Fair point. Although..." He left the word hanging, the sentence incomplete, and it was enough to distract her from the movie.

"Although what?"

"The other night when you snuck back into the house. I

heard an anomalous noise, and—I'm sorry to say—I asked if someone was there."

She clapped a hand over her mouth in horrified glee.

"You *didn't*."

"I totally did. I knew it wasn't Luna."

"How did you know that?"

"My dog is smart, but I'm pretty sure she can't turn door handles."

"I tried to be so quiet. How are your ears so crazy good? With the wind and rain and everything, it couldn't have been that noticeable."

"It wasn't. But I was already on alert after our initial meeting."

"And you really asked if someone was there?"

"I think it's instinctual."

"It's dumb. If I'd been an ax murderer, intent on slaughtering you, your question would have alerted me that you were aware of my presence."

"Luckily for me, your only intentions right then were getting naked and showering."

She fought back a furious blush, and lost. Fortunately, it was too dark in the room for him to see her crimson face.

"I was trying to get warm."

A discordant screech, echoing from the surround-sound speakers made them both jump, and they refocused on the screen where the character was clutching her chest in shock after having unearthed a body in the dumbwaiter.

"If you live alone and move into an ancient house with a

dumbwaiter, the house is *probably* too big for you," Iris observed caustically.

"Aah, you're one of those," Trystan said, taking a slurp of his slushy.

"One of what?" Iris prompted, when he didn't elaborate.

"A plot apart picker. Someone who tears apart the minutest details in a movie as they're watching it."

"I'm *not*," she protested indignantly. "I don't pick plots apart. Not usually. But scary movies bring out the worst in me. I think it's my way of coping with the tension and fear. If I can point out an implausibility, I'm better able to remember that none of it is real. Although it doesn't really work, since I always wind up checking cupboards and under the bed for monsters and boogeymen after watching a scary movie anyway."

"Seriously?" Now it was his turn to sound gleeful.

"Ssh, we're missing the film," she said, trying to divert his attention. His knowing chuckle told her he knew exactly what she was doing, but he let it go. Filching some of her popcorn, he settled back down in his seat to watch.

The rest of the movie was only occasionally interrupted by Iris's moans of disapproval and her squeaks of fear whenever something truly frightening happened.

Trystan immediately put on a lighthearted romantic comedy after the horror movie. A *palate cleanser*, he called it. Iris, who wasn't a big fan of romcoms—and exhausted after several nights of poor sleep—dozed through most of it. She startled awake when the end credits were rolling, and sat up in confusion.

"What happened?"

"Movie's over," Trystan said, after a jaw-popping yawn. "Don't blame you for snoring your way through it, it was godawful."

"Are you allowed to be that critical? I mean isn't there some kind of professional code that dictates that you say only nice or noncommittal things about other people's movies?"

He snort-laughed at that.

"I enjoy watching movies and I have opinions, same as everyone else. But I would *never* publicly slam a movie. I know how much work goes into making them. But this isn't a public space and, as such, I'm allowed to voice a private observation without fear that it'll be spread all over the gossip rags tomorrow."

Another test? Maybe. Maybe not. It was too exhausting analyzing every little thing he said for potential land mines and snares.

He stretched luxuriously and yawned, another huge yawn that triggered one of her own.

"I'm starving. Want to help me with lunch?" he asked, and Iris—keen to delay the return to her torture chamber—nodded eagerly.

"Yes, please."

"You any good in a kitchen?" he asked, as he got up and then held out a hand to help her up.

She stared at that big, capable hand for an uncertain moment, before taking it. His fingers closed around hers—strong and familiar—and he waited for her to unfold her legs before giving her a helpful tug up. She yelped and stumbled into his arms when her right ankle buckled.

His arms wrapped around her waist as he caught her.

"You okay?"

"My foot's asleep," she moaned, gingerly testing her weight on it before yelping again. "Ugh, pins and needles."

"That's the worst," he murmured into her ear. "Take your time, I've got you."

They stood like that for a few moments, while she gradually placed more weight on her foot as the tingling subsided. He held her comfortably, his arms loose around her waist, his big hands splayed in the small of her back, the tips just resting above the curve of her butt.

They were both wearing sweatpants and hoodies but even with all that fleecy fabric between them, she was still keenly aware of that large hard body pressed so close to hers.

She brought her hands up between them, flattening her palms against his chest.

"I'm okay now," she whispered, casting her eyes downward, uncomfortable with his piercing stare that seemed to miss nothing.

He held onto her for a beat longer, his hands moving upward to cup her waist.

"Hey, Iris?" His chest vibrated against her hands as he spoke.

"Yes?"

"I really, *really* hate it when you hide your eyes from me."

Her brow furrowed at the comment and she lifted her head

to stare at him in confusion. He made a deep, rumbling sound of approval when she met his gaze.

"That's better. I like seeing that defiant spark in them when you're pissed off with me. When you hide your eyes, I worry that you're on the verge of tears."

"Why would you care if I cried? At best I'm an unwelcome guest in your temporary home. At worst I'm an intruder who tried to lie her way into an interview with you."

"This is a... difficult situation. And I'm trying to be fair. I feel like I've found a workable solution for both of us, at least until this can be straightened out. I don't think that's so unreasonable."

It wasn't unreasonable. Not at all. Iris was the one with the problem and no matter how much she tried to explain it to him, she doubted he'd ever truly grasp how distressing it was for her to be locked in that room.

"You're not being unreasonable, or unfair. But my phobia isn't rational. I can't reason my way out of it. I wish I could."

His arms fell away from her waist and he stepped back, leaving Iris cold and bereft. She wrapped her own arms around her body in an attempt to keep that dreadful, lonely coldness at bay.

"I don't know you, Iris. I can't trust you. You understand that, don't you? I can't allow you to roam freely around my space. I can't afford to be so blindly foolish. You're asking me to believe that you suffer from a phobia that very opportunely means you can't stay in a locked room? You see how highly suspicious that is, right? How could you even board a plane to come here in the first place, if that were the case?"

She nearly hadn't, but a combination of medication, an aisle seat, deep-breathing exercises, as well as the excitement at the prospect of meeting and interviewing Trystan Abbott had helped her fight through her debilitating fear.

About halfway through the flight, when she'd realized that she was well on her way to South Africa and that she hadn't lost her shit even a little, she'd felt so damned powerful and triumphant and proud. It had been a huge boost to her self-esteem. The flight hadn't been easy by any means, but once she'd understood that she could do it—that she *was* doing it—Iris had felt almost invincible.

Only to find herself here, and right back to square one with her phobia.

"I don't understand why Mr. Quinn didn't message or email you about my arrival," she said wearily, tired of having the same dead-end conversation with him. "If you would allow me to, I could show you my correspondence with him."

"I told you before, electronic correspondence is easily faked," he said with a dismissive wave of his hand.

"Of course it is," Iris said with a dejected sigh, really not in the mood for this conversation again either. This wasn't even a misunderstanding anymore—it was the willful stubborn insistence of one party not to believe a single word the other said. There was no arguing with that. No reasoning. He didn't want to believe her and so—no matter what proof she offered to support her argument—he wouldn't.

"You asked if I was any good in the kitchen," she said, changing the subject. She ignored the astonishment in his usually enigmatic gaze, knowing he'd expected her to continue arguing her case. Iris felt a swell of satisfaction that she'd managed to surprise him. He was too smug in his belief that he knew everything there was to know about her and what motivated her.

"My parents own a catering and events company. They started off as caterers and I grew up knowing my way around a kitchen. I'm a pretty decent cook, nowhere near as good as my dad, of course. He's a genius in the kitchen. My mum's better with the admin."

"Well, I'm happy for you to recreate one of your dad's recipes for lunch. I'm pretty fed up of cooking. As you may have noticed, I'm not the most creative of cooks."

"You do okay," she said and he grinned.

"If that's not damning someone with faint praise, I don't know what is." He chuckled in genuine amusement.

"Are you sure you trust me to cook. Not afraid I'll drug you and snoop around your house while you're unconscious?"

His smile broadened, lively amusement still lingering in his eyes.

"Well, I *wasn't* until you asked me that question," he said, his tone mocking. "Come on, time to dazzle me with your culinary abilities."

It was a pleasure to cook in the massive state-of-the-art kitchen. It was truly a chef's space, with everything she could possibly need right at her fingertips. She'd been honest when she'd boasted about being a decent cook. She happily whipped up a chicken korma—one of her dad's specialties—from scratch, with butter naan and raita as sides.

Trystan proved an able sous chef, happily chopping and dicing anything she needed him to. He remained largely silent, while Iris regaled him with stories of her family's business and some of the more outlandish events they'd planned and catered.

"I'm actually a little sorry I missed the Bhandari wedding this past weekend. It's one of the biggest events we've ever catered. Over a thousand guests. Dad was really chuffed we got the contract.

"I went to school with the bride, Shruti. She and I were never really friends, she was more popular than me. In the beginning, I hero worshipped her a bit. She's so beautiful, perfect hair and body. Super intelligent and athletic. She was everything I thought I wanted to be. I didn't have many friends at school, I always had my head stuck in a book or I'd be staring into space thinking up crazy stories. The other kids thought I was a bit weird."

"Did they bully you?" It was the first time he'd spoken in ages, and it made her aware of how long she'd been prattling on inanely.

"Sorry, you must be bored to tears. I do tend to go on a bit when given free rein to talk."

"If I were bored to tears I wouldn't be asking questions, now would I?"

Fair point.

"What was the question?" she asked, prevaricating.

"Were you bullied?"

"A little," she admitted. She ignored his annoyed hiss when she deliberately looked away from him to "check" on the curry simmering away on the gas stove top for the second time in under a minute.

"A little?" he repeated and she inhaled shakily, before forcing herself to meet that all-seeing gaze.

"Okay, a lot. Usually small things, like name-calling and taking or breaking my stuff. They made fun of my braces, my hair, my body. My parents being in the service industry. Nothing was off limits to them.

"I didn't want a phone, and I had no social media accounts because I knew the online bullying would be relentless if I did. And it became yet another thing for them to mock me about.

"Then one Friday afternoon, just after the final bell, Shruti —the ringleader—and her cohorts shoved me into a supply room and locked the door. The teachers were all in a staff meeting and the other kids had mostly gone home already. Any student who did hear my panicked screams dared not go against Shruti and her minions. It felt like I was locked in there, in the dark, for hours. But in reality it was only forty minutes or so. That's how long it took for my form teacher to return to the classroom and find me there. I was a wreck. I'd..."

She stopped talking, not sure she wanted to tell him anymore, her face blossoming with color.

"What?" His voice quiet, reassuring, and interested. His eyes were gentle.

She breathed out a shuddering sigh and shrugged. Her fingers tracing the veins in the marble-top counter.

"I'd wet myself. No other students were there to witness it, but… I was so scared they'd find out. That it would be another thing for them to mock me about."

"How old were you?"

She'd been so absorbed in the memories that she'd mostly put behind her that the question, uttered in that dark, brooding voice, startled her. She jumped and looked at him. She was getting so used to being in his company every day that it no longer seemed surreal that she was standing here in Trystan Abbott's presence.

"It started when I was fourteen and didn't stop until I started my A-levels at seventeen. They were the longest three years of my life. I was fifteen at the time of that particular incident."

"So, you were sorry to miss the wedding because you planned to spit in the champagne fountain, right?" he asked and —after the meander down shitty memory lane—his dry wit was very welcome. Iris burst into laughter and he watched her for a moment, his eyes alight with an indefinable emotion, before he joined in on the laughter.

"Not gonna lie, the thought definitely occurred to me," she admitted with a chuckle. "But honestly? I wanted to witness the spectacle. All the gorgeous saris, the colors, the food. I fully intended to remain out of the bride's sight, though. I wanted to avoid the inevitable snarky comments. She really is *such* a bitch. And going by the few times I'd encountered her over the past few years, the last decade has done nothing to improve her disposition at all."

"Do you work for your parents full time?" he asked, while removing a couple of plates from a kitchen cabinet.

"No. I help out most weekends, and when they're short-staffed, but I'm a freelance editor. I work mostly with indie authors, and have a decent—and growing—client base."

He set the table, while she turned off the gas cooker to give the curry a few minutes to cool down.

"Sounds like a thriving business."

"It is. I earn good money and enjoy the work. But..."

"You want to write your own stories," he completed for her, and she blinked at him in surprise.

"I—no... I mean, I want to be a journalist. I have a level 3 diploma in multimedia journalism, I've just never had the opportunity to—"

"Iris, you seem like a determined woman. Someone who usually achieves what she sets out to do. You're what? Twenty-six? And you've been faffing around editing, working for your parents, doing anything except what you say you so desperately want to do. I'd think that by now you would have at least worked or interned at any number of publications or news agencies. But you haven't. Why not?"

"The time was never right. My dad went through a bad spell with his health a few years ago and I needed to help out more with the business." Even to her own ears, her excuses sounded flimsy. Because, quite honestly, she'd had numerous solid opportunities to work as a junior reporter at several local newspapers, and she'd turned down internships at two national news broadcasters. She'd always used family commitments as a convenient excuse not to grab those chances, and now she could clearly see how much she'd been bullshitting herself.

"If I didn't want to be a journalist, I wouldn't be stuck in this godforsaken place with you, now would I?" she asked, throwing the question down like a gauntlet between them. Instead of bristling like she'd expected him to do, he canted his head as he leisurely perused her hot, agitated face.

"You make a valid point, Hughes. I clearly don't know what the fuck I'm talking about." Infuriatingly, he sounded like he was humoring her and that rubbed Iris up the wrong way.

"You don't," she told him, anger making her voice quiver. "You have no idea what motivates me."

"Oh, I think I do."

"No, you don't," she denied, her voice heated and her words curt.

His eyes argued with her, but he chose not to verbalize what he was thinking.

"Wine?" he asked instead, reaching for a pair of long-stemmed glasses.

She stared at him, hating to let this go, needing to convince him of her commitment to her chosen career path. But knowing she couldn't make a solid case when she, herself, doubted her choices.

"Iris?" He prompted and she inhaled deeply, hating how much she loved the sound of her name on his lips.

"Red please," she said in response to his earlier question, and turned to retrieve the raita from the fridge.

They sat down to lunch at the quaint, cozy banquette in the kitchen and ate silently for a while, soft jazzy music playing in the background and alleviating the strained silence between them.

"Sam Brand is my security advisor," Trystan volunteered

unexpectedly after he was about halfway through his meal. Up until that point he'd only complimented her on the food, before they'd lapsed into silence.

It was odd that he'd choose this moment to refer to the name he'd mentioned three days ago.

"Oh? I thought that Australian guy, Chance, was." The big, blond Australian bodyguard—Chance Griffin—had caused a minor sensation in the gossip magazines when he'd first started shadowing Trystan about a year ago. People had been sighing over his good looks, rhapsodizing over his brawny body, and the sight of him with Trystan had soon become common. There was even rampant speculation that the two men were hot for each other. Which had resulted in a lot of erotic fan fiction centered around Trystan and his bodyguard.

"Chance works for Sam. One of the reasons I chose not to have Chance here was because Sam lives in town, and he was reasonably confident that I'd be perfectly safe here. Chance is staying with Sam while I'm here, on call in case I choose to venture out into the world. But I wanted—needed—to be alone.

"In fact, Sam and Miles Hollingsworth are good friends. Miles is merely a passing acquaintance of mine. We'd met at a few charity functions and he seems like a decent guy, but we're not what I'd call intimates.

"Sam knew I needed someplace private to stay and—since Miles and his wife are in London for the next six months—Sam asked Miles if I could stay here while he and his wife are out of the country. So, no... Miles Hollingsworth is *not* my financial advisor." The last was offered with a faint smile but Iris was baffled by this sudden flood of previously withheld information, and was unable to return the gesture.

"I see," she said, not really seeing at all. "Why are you telling me all of this?"

"You asked." His answer was both simple and immensely complicated at the same time.

Why had he suddenly decided to start answering her questions? Or more specifically why that one?

And would he answer another question if she merely *asked.*

Only one way to find out.

"Speaking of Australians," she began. "Are you aware that your fancy American accent has been slipping steadily by the day?"

He surprised her by looking not one whit offended by that question, and then shocked her even further by laughing.

"I tried so fucking hard to get rid of my native accent when I was starting out because Quinny believed that it would limit my opportunities. It became almost second nature to disguise it.

"By the time I was big enough for it to no longer matter, it had become commonplace to speak in that godawful hybrid accent. But when I'm back in Oz, or spending time with my family, or away from the US, my natural accent starts to reassert itself. In fact, I'm hoping to shed the American one completely. It was the worst advice Quinny ever gave me. And that's saying a lot, since he is partially responsible for one of my biggest flops. Although, to be fair, we've been together from the start, and we were young and inexperienced with a lot to learn back then."

"Your biggest flop? You mean *Eagle-Man?*" Iris asked, with a sympathetic wince, even though she was trying hard not to laugh at the memory of that embarrassment of a movie. It had been one of his earlier films and it would have been a death knell to the career of any less-talented and—let's be honest here—less *hot* actor.

He glared at her.

"Do you *mind*? I like to pretend that atrocity does not exist."

"I don't blame you. But it's really not as bad as *Night of the Killer Wētās*. Although, I have to admit, I really loved that one."

"That was an indie. Come on, I was doing a favor for a friend. I was young and stupid, how the hell was I supposed to know those wētās would come back to bite me in the arse?" Iris loved how his accent had reverted back to Aussie so much that he no longer said *ass*. "No matter, I stand by my decision to make that one. It has a certain charm. And it has a devout, hard-core fandom. But fucking *Eagle-Man*? Jesus, it had a decent budget and had no business turning out as dire as it did."

Iris laughed—the sound joyful and contagious—and after a while he let go of his feigned indignation to join her.

It was a pleasant way to spend the afternoon, and after lunch he brought out a deck of cards and they played a few games of gin rummy.

It was heading into early evening, and getting dark, when he finally put the cards away. They cleaned the kitchen together and he fed Luna.

"I have a couple of phone calls to make," he told her once the kitchen was restored to neatness.

She stared at him blankly, not sure why he was telling her that. She wasn't stopping him from making his calls.

"Iris, I'll need you to return to your room," he elaborated, and her heart sank to the soles of her feet. She'd been having such a great time; they'd been getting along so well—he'd felt almost like a friend—that she hadn't for a second contemplated the reality that he'd go back to being her jailer once he was done entertaining himself with her.

"I could stay in the kitchen with Luna," she suggested, misery lending a wobble to her voice.

Why was he doing this to her? Somehow this felt worse than before.

Yesterday and the days before, despite their companionable —mostly silent—walks, she hadn't enjoyed his company as much and therefore hadn't fooled herself into believing that maybe he was starting to like and trust her. He'd remained at an emotional distance and she'd been okay with that. It kept her from liking and trusting *him*.

He'd been an adversary, an enemy, and that had made his actions understandable.

But this... *this* was cruel.

"Are you going to lock the door?" she asked him, lifting her chin and straightening her shoulders in an effort to hide her panic from him.

"I have to. But I promise you, I'm just down the hall. You're not alone. Tomorrow we'll walk Luna together. Would you like that?"

She hated the achingly gentle tone of voice he was using, hated how he was speaking to her like she was a child in need of coddling. Hated that he had no clue, not one single fucking idea of how bad things got for her in that room. He thought she was exaggerating, that she was being childish, that she was making up some ridiculous excuse to avoid being imprisoned in her room. How could he *still* believe that after what she'd revealed about being locked in the supply room?

His hand was in the small of her back and he was exerting only the slightest of pressure—not shoving, not *nudging*—to get her to walk. Her feet moved. Leaden, reluctant, but they moved... carrying her back to that awful place.

The walk back felt interminable but was over in the blink of an eye. Before she knew it, she was standing in the room, staring at him, as he loomed in the doorway—a large, dark and threatening figure—with the light from the hallway streaming in behind him.

She stood there on shaking legs, her eyes pleading with him when her voice failed.

"I'll bring your dinner later," he said.

I'm not hungry, the words wouldn't emerge from her locked throat.

"Iris," he whispered, his voice sounding as despairing as she felt. "Stop looking at me like that, I can't..."

He shook his head, swallowing down whatever he'd been about to say.

He stepped into the room and cupped her face with his hands.

"I'll be back soon, okay?" He dropped his forehead to hers and—in a move that *finally* shocked her out of her numbness— dropped a hard, almost angry, kiss on her lips.

She gasped, and when her lips parted, his tongue slid into her mouth—just a brief foray—leaving a trail of slick fire in its wake.

The kiss was over before it even properly began and he stepped back an instant later.

"I'm sorry, I shouldn't have—" He swallowed thickly and shook his head in frustration, while she continued to stare at him in mute shock. "Christ, this is such a fucking mess."

He scrubbed a hand over his face and retreated, slamming the door in his wake.

She jumped at the harsh sound and then—when the door locked—she sobbed. A quiet, despairing, hopeless sound.

Chapter Ten

Sleep eluded him.

Trystan tossed and turned all night, haunted by the memory of Iris's face. She hadn't touched the leftover curry he'd taken to her room after his failed attempt to reach Quinny.

She'd barely seemed to register his presence in her room, remaining curled up in that defensive little ball on the sofa. He'd tried to convince himself that it wasn't his problem, that *she* wasn't his problem. If she didn't want to eat, then he didn't—*shouldn't*—fucking care...

Only, something about the way she'd sat there, silently rocking herself in what he assumed was an attempt at self-soothing had made him want to scoop her up and cradle her in his lap.

Another part of him had resented her histrionics. She was being dramatic, she had plenty of space, plenty of diversions, she was fine. It wasn't a tiny, dark supply room, for fuck's sake. Even though he'd asked about the bullying, Trystan recognized that she must have shared that story in an attempt to manipulate him into giving her, her way. But Trystan had been burned too many times by the paparazzi. They went to fucking extremes to get to him.

After the accident one of them had literally cut himself to get into the same emergency room as Trystan. From there he'd managed to get pictures of Trystan, bloodied and unconscious, as well as Trish in the morgue. There'd been others as well, posing as doctors and nurses. One had even brought her infant daughter in with a feigned emergency.

It had been a losing battle keeping those images out of the gutter press. In the end, a few of them had inevitably oozed their way into the less reputable gossip rags. And it had been impossible to keep the pictures of Trish's body in the car off the Internet. Trystan's face had been blurred out because they'd known he would sue their asses, but Trish had been fair game. And her family had to live with the knowledge that images of their loved one's dead body were littered across the web for anybody to gawk at.

So, this shit Iris was trying to pull was fucking amateur hour.

That hadn't been terror in her eyes—she was just a more skilled actress than he'd given her credit for.

He sat up in bed with a groan, scrubbing his hands over his face, disliking the feel of his beard on his palms. He was tempted to shave the damned thing off, but the thought of fully revealing his scar prevented him from doing so.

He shouldn't have kissed her.

What the fuck had he been thinking? He was making one ridiculous mistake after the other with this woman. She wasn't the sweet, innocent thing she pretended to be. She was cold, calculating, her father's daughter. No matter what stories she told about the *real* father who'd raised her, blood would always tell.

But she came in a refreshingly cute package, and that was proving to be his undoing. He didn't go for cute, never had. He didn't go for sweet or innocent either, so her act should in no way appeal to him and yet ...

That mop of adorable dark brown curls, combined with her silky smooth skin, a pouty mouth that resembled a deep pink rosebud on the verge of blooming, and *God*, those killer curves.

The memory of her generously proportioned body in that tiny pink and white bikini drove him fucking insane. He didn't know how the hell he'd managed to keep his hands off her that day by the pool when all that tempting gold-tinged tawny skin had been right there for the stroking.

He hadn't realized that small and curvy could rev his engine like this until Iris had barreled her unwelcome way into his life.

He groaned again as he belatedly registered the erection throbbing between his thighs. Not his first since she'd shown up at his doorstep, and he very much doubted it would be his last.

He picked up his phone to check the time. Just after six-thirty in the morning. It was still pitch black out, but Trystan knew there was little point in trying to get any sleep now. He got out of bed and pulled on a pair of sweatpants, ignoring his persistent hard-on.

The rain had started up again about half an hour ago—for the first time in three days—initially just a few hard drops, but now it was a steady downpour. They'd never get that damned bridge fixed at this rate.

He padded his way barefoot and shirtless in the dark toward the kitchen, but stopped abruptly at the sight of Luna silhouetted in the dim light.

Shit, no wonder she had terrified Iris so badly that first night. In the dark she *did* resemble a wolf.

The dog was standing outside Iris's room. Her tail and ears were down, and she was whining slightly.

"What's wrong, girl?" he asked softly, coming to a stop beside his dog. He put a hand on her ruff, and was alarmed to note that she was quivering. "What's going on?"

The dog whined and pawed at Iris's door.

Trystan stared at the door, a feeling of deep unease unfurling in his gut.

He knocked quietly.

No answer.

Of course there'd be no answer—she was asleep.

"Iris?" he called, knocking a little louder.

No response.

She was sleeping, like he and Luna should be. It was way too early and too cold to be standing in hallways knocking and pawing at people's doors.

He hesitated, but when Luna whimpered and scratched the wood again, he shook his head and swore silently at himself.

He'd just take a look to reassure himself, and his dog, that she was okay. She was asleep—she'd never know that he'd snuck in like some creepy stalker while she was at her most vulnerable.

He unlocked the door with a quiet *snick* and stepped into the room.

The first thing that struck him was the frigid cold.

"Christ Almighty," he muttered to himself, as the iciness hit his naked skin. Why the hell was it so cold in here?

He flicked on the living room light and immediately spotted the open window.

"For fuck's sake, Iris," he swore underneath his breath. "How could you leave the window open in this weather?"

He hurried over to close it, and then glanced around the empty room.

Something about the eerie stillness wasn't right. Even if Iris was asleep in the bedroom, it was just too oppressively silent in here.

"Iris?" He could hear panic creeping into his voice as he made his way to the bedroom. The door wasn't closed, and it didn't take him long to realize that she wasn't in bed. He hurried to the bathroom, but that room was dark and empty as well.

"Shit, shit... oh *fuck*, Iris. What did you do?" He surged back to the window and yanked it back up to peer out into the absolute darkness out there.

He was aware of his breath coming in short, panicky gulps as he desperately stared into the blackness hoping to spot her. He'd never expected her to call his bluff. Not in weather like this. He recalled his flippant invitation that she try to *hoof it back to town* if she really didn't want to stay in a locked room.

Well, apparently, she'd decided that risking her life out in this mess was better than remaining locked up in this room.

And he'd driven her to it. Driven her out in this weather, in the dark, because he wouldn't listen to her, wouldn't believe that her extreme terror of being trapped was so huge, so irrational, that she would do literally anything to escape it.

When had she left? How long had she been out in this? The rain had started only half an hour ago but before that it had been relatively calm, even the wind had died down.

Trystan ran to his room and yanked on his clothes and boots.

She didn't have any waterproof clothes. She'd be soaked by now. And cold. She'd be so cold. He couldn't stand the thought of it.

His breath came in desperate gasps as he made his way to the back door. He had to believe she'd head back to her car and follow the road from there. Because it was the only logical course of action for her to take. The route was familiar and she would know the general direction back to town. But in the dark, she could trip, get disoriented, turned around. She could find herself lost in the blink of an eye.

And even if she did somehow manage to head in the right direction, that fucking river was impassible. She'd never be able to safely cross it.

He dragged on his oil slicker and grabbed his heavy-duty flashlight.

Luna had been following him on his mad dash through the house, and she whined in disapproval when he told her to stay. He eyed the unhappy dog for a moment.

"Would you be able to find her if I can't, girl?" he asked. "Can you find our Iris?"

The dog chuffed softly. She had never really shown any kind of aptitude for scent games, but—despite the rain—she might well be his best chance of finding Iris fast.

Mind made up, he put on her collar and leash, and they both headed out into the rapidly building storm.

"*Iris!*" His voice was instantly swallowed up by the dull roar of the rain and wind. But it didn't stop him from calling her name every few meters in the hopes that somehow she would hear him.

Luna had been pulling at the leash since the moment they'd left the yard, and Trystan let her lead, hoping against hope that she was actually taking him toward Iris and not chasing some small animal.

The dog *was* heading in the direction of Iris's car, which gave him hope. The rain was getting so bad he could barely see five feet in front of him, and he worried that they could walk right past her and not catch so much as a glimpse of her.

"*Iris!*"

He would never forgive himself if something happened to her. She could die out here. Get lost never to be found again. He couldn't live with that.

They'd been walking for nearly half an hour and the pre-dawn sky was starting to lighten. It was, thankfully, becoming easier to see. Luna abruptly veered away from the path that would take them to the car and headed in the direction of the river instead.

The river which had been little more than a stream when

Trystan had first arrived, but was now a raging, roiling, furious force of nature.

Trystan heard it before he saw it, the whooshing roar of the turbulent waters. But when he took the turn that would bring the river in sight, his blood froze in his veins.

There she stood, right on the verge of that murky, gray, fast-moving, angry beast. God, she looked so tiny standing there, a fragile little thing wearing too few layers, and a jacket that was nowhere near waterproof enough for this weather.

She was too close to the water—the bank was muddy, unstable—all it would take was one misstep to send her tumbling into that mess of tree trunks, branches, and other debris. She would be swallowed up, and she would disappear immediately and be forever lost.

All that vibrant energy. That wide, beautiful, slightly naughty smile, that delightful high-pitched giggle, the irreverent sense of humor. Her annoying, insatiable curiosity. Her talent, her beauty, her pure, bright light—it would all be snuffed out in one terrible instant.

"*Iris, please!*" he shouted, his voice hoarse with fear. "*Get back!*"

She didn't—couldn't—hear him above the noise of the river. She shifted from foot to foot and even from this distance he could see her anxiety.

She wanted to cross—she was clearly desperate to cross—and he worried that the same illogical fear that had sent her fleeing into the darkness and the storm would drive her to attempt it.

"Iris, baby, *please*, step back. Oh *God...*" The last emerged on a terrified whimper. If she decided to go, he'd never get to her in time. Horror and fear, like living panicked things, clawed at his throat, setting off his gag reflex.

Images of Trish Nesbitt's cold, bloodied, and lifeless face moments after the accident that had claimed her life flashed through his head.

Not Iris. Never iris. He couldn't fucking stand it.

"Luna. Sit. Stay." He didn't check to see if the dog obeyed, but he was confident enough in her training to believe that she would sit and wait for them.

He zigzagged down the embankment, half-stumbling, half-running and losing his balance in the mud several times to land on his hands and knees. Each time, he pushed himself back up and continued resolutely forward. He was desperate to reach her, and get her back to warmth and safety.

It felt like forever, during which he prayed to every god he could think of to keep her safe for him. Just until he could reach her and take over the job from them.

He sobbed in relief when he finally got near enough to close his hands around her elbows and wrench her back from the river.

He felt her body tensing in shock at his unexpected touch and—once he'd dragged her a safe distance from the water's edge—he whirled her around and closed his arms around her trembling body.

He couldn't speak, couldn't do anything more than hold her close, one hand tightly fisted in her wet curls, and the other clamped around her waist.

"You're okay, you're okay," he gasped when he finally found his voice. "I've got you. You're okay, Iris."

She was shaking violently, her small hands fisted against his chest. He lifted his head to peer into her pale, terrified face.

"Trystan. N-No! *Please*. I can't... I can't go back. Please don't make me go back—" The abject terror in her eyes broke him. How had he not seen this before? How could he have been so blind and indifferent to such absolute, raw fear.

"It's okay, sweet." His voice was hoarse with emotion, and shaking in reaction to her severe distress. His hand left her hair to palm her cheek and she flinched away from him, which just about tore his heart from his chest. "You don't have to be afraid, okay? I swear to God, Iris, you never have to be afraid again. I promise you that. But we *have* to go back. We need to get you home and warm, understand? We'll talk later."

He wasn't sure she could hear him above the noise from the river and the rain, and even if she had heard him, he wasn't entirely certain she was able to understand him right now. She looked like she was in shock, her mental and emotional state altered. He doubted very much she was able to form a coherent thought.

Trystan was consumed by the urgent need to get her out of the rain, warm, dry, safe... her well-being was inextricably linked to his right now.

She pushed at his chest, straining her body toward the river.

"I have to go. Please, let me go. I have to leave. I'll go to town, I'll be fine."

That she actively fought him in her desperation to cross that deadly river, rather than return to a locked room, spoke volumes. There was no faking this level of fear. Trystan had effectively been torturing this sweet, vibrant woman every time he'd turned the key in that door. And he wasn't sure how to cope with that knowledge. He didn't know if he'd ever be able to forgive himself for that.

He lifted her struggling body into his arms. She was weak with cold and offered little real resistance, yet Trystan staggered beneath her slight weight, as the long, panicked walk in the driving rain and the urgent stumbling sprint down the embankment to reach her caught up with him.

He planted his legs apart and inhaled deeply, searching for the last remnants of his strength. He refused to let her walk back since she clearly didn't have much more left in the tank. This was Trystan's fault and getting Iris and Luna back to safety was on him and no one else.

He secured his hold around her violently shivering body and started the slow trudge back up the slippery embankment.

It was tough going—he slid back a few paces for every few feet he advanced—exhaustion soon slumped his shoulders and had his lungs bellowing.

Iris—after her initial burst of defiant energy—appeared barely aware of her surroundings, and that, combined with her obvious exhaustion and weakness, frightened Trystan.

He gritted his teeth and dug deep, fighting through the pain and fear and fatigue, finding reserves he hadn't even known he possessed as he battled his way to the top of that damned slope to where Luna sat patiently waiting for them.

The dog leaped to her feet when he finally reached her, her

tail wagging happily as she circled Trystan and Iris to sniff and lick whatever skin she could find.

Trystan allowed himself a moment to catch his breath, while his eyes searched Iris's cold, pale face. Her eyes were shut, and she'd gone limp in his arms. The fact that she hadn't uttered so much as a token protest while he'd battled his way up that hill told him how very out of it she was. And now, one look at her face in the sullen morning light confirmed that she'd lost consciousness.

He panicked, juggling her in his arms as he bent his leg and frantically shifted her weight partially to his knee, freeing up his hand somewhat to search her wrist for a pulse. He nearly wept in relief when he felt it strong, and little too fast, beneath his fingers.

"Thank God. Okay, sweetheart," he murmured, as he readjusted her weight, uncaring that she couldn't hear him. "Let's get you home."

THE WALK back to the house was interminable. Trystan nearly dropped to his knees beneath the mantle of utter exhaustion several times, but—fueled by his determination to get Iris warm and safe again—he persevered. By the time he reached the back door, Iris was beginning to stir in his arms.

"Wha—what's happen...?"

"Ssh, relax," he whispered soothingly, as he eased through the kitchen door and out of the rain. He stopped only to awkwardly shut the door behind them, refusing to let go of his charge while he took care of the task. The closed door instantly muffled the relentless racket of the pounding rain, and Trystan heaved a sigh of relief at the cessation of noise.

He walked her straight to his bedroom, calling Luna to follow. He impatiently kicked his way through the closed door, and went directly to the bathroom, where he gingerly deposited his precious cargo on the toilet seat before reaching for a thick, fluffy bath sheet and making short work of drying Luna with it.

"Go lie down," he commanded the still-damp dog, and Luna instantly obeyed, retreating to his room to find her spot by the heater. Trystan immediately refocused on Iris, who appeared to be listing to one side as she seemed to float in and out of consciousness.

"Shit," he muttered, closing the distance between himself and her in an instant. "Iris, stand up, help me get you out of these wet things, okay?"

With a combination of coaxing and minor bullying he managed to get her up, and started maneuvering her uncooperative, heavy limbs through sleeves and trouser legs, until she was clad in just a tiny pair of silky blue panties and a wispy lacy pink push-up bra that left very little to the imagination.

He glared down at the woefully inadequate pile of wet clothing at their feet. She'd been wearing only a long-sleeved T-shirt under a thicker flannel shirt and the black puffer jacket she was so fond of. Combined with a pair of now-sodden jeans. Her only remotely suitable attire for the weather was her hiking boots.

She was soaked to the bone and as he stared at her wet, goosefleshed, shivering body, he choked back a distraught sob.

He peeled off his own clothes, keeping on his boxers, and lifted her into his arms to carry her into the huge shower.

She made a weak sound of protest at his actions, showing some signs of life as she feebly batted at his hands when he set her on her feet in the glass cubicle.

"I'm sorry, but these have to come off, sweetheart. I need to get you warm, okay?" He quickly and efficiently divested her of her bra and panties, and this time she didn't even protest. Her listlessness frightened him and his hands shook with a combination of panic and cold as he turned on the faucet, starting with a gentle, lukewarm spray and gradually turning the heat up, in an effort to avoid shocking her system.

Hypothermia was a real concern, and he rubbed her limp arms briskly before gathering her close and wrapping his arms around her still-shuddering body. His hands felt like enormous, clumsy paws as he stroked her back in rough circular motions.

Her trembling gradually subsided and he felt the warmth start to creep back into her skin. Her small, pert breasts with their dark cold-hardened nipples were pressed against his chest, but there was nothing remotely sexual about this embrace.

Her vulnerability set off every protective instinct Trystan had. She seemed so fucking fragile that Trystan was finally willing to battle the very demons that had driven him to this cold, isolated place, if it meant keeping her safe. Those same demons had turned him into a monster who couldn't recognize genuine fear in someone else when he saw it.

Day after day he'd locked her in that fucking room, ignoring her pleas, blind to her terror and ignorant to her building desperation. Always so fucking convinced of his blamelessness, and so dismissive of her attempts to explain what she was feeling.

When her trembling finally stopped, he turned off the shower.

"Don't move," he whispered, not sure if she heard or understood him. He stepped out to grab several towels from the warming rack. He was back with her seconds later and enfolded a large bath sheet around her small body.

He stepped out of his wet shorts as unobtrusively as he could, keeping his movements slow and deliberate, not wanting to alarm her or have her question his intentions. He wrapped a smaller towel around his waist in no time, and used the last towel he'd grabbed to clumsily wrap her hair.

"I'm sorry, this probably won't dry the way you want it to," he said, keeping his voice low, calm, and gentle, in an effort to keep her from panicking, even though she barely seemed aware of her surroundings "But I don't think you should sleep with a wet head, especially not after the ordeal you've just been through, so I want to get your hair as dry as possible."

Her silent acquiescence to everything he was doing was alarming him. Earlier he could dismiss it as shock and cold—now her passivity was starting to really concern him.

He led her back to the room and sat her down on the edge of the bed.

"Feeling better? Warmer?"

Her gaze was cast downward and she didn't seem to hear him.

"Iris?" He sat down beside her and used his thumb and forefinger to nudge her head upward. She still wouldn't meet his gaze, her pretty eyes—pupils blown—focused on the wall behind him.

He'd intended to make her a hot drink, warm up her insides now that the immediate danger of hypothermia had passed, but that wide, unfixed stare alarmed him.

"Iris, look at me, c'mon," he coaxed. She was slow to react but her eyes eventually swung toward him and he heaved a sigh of relief. "Are you still cold?"

"Sleepy," she muttered from between lips that barely moved.

"I know, baby," he whispered. "Let's get you to bed."

He got up and tugged her to her feet and pulled back the covers to usher her into the bed. He wasted a few precious seconds to don a pair of boxer briefs, and climbed in behind her to spoon against her much smaller body.

She didn't protest because she was out as soon as her head hit her pillow, while Trystan was left awake with his own tumultuous thoughts.

He switched off the bedside lamp, and thankfully his block-out curtains managed to keep out the gray morning light.

He listened to the rain, gentler now, but ever-present. How long had she been out there? The thought of her stumbling her way around in the dark, wet, and cold brought a fresh surge of nauseating guilt and remorse. If she'd lost her footing, taken a wrong turn...

Jesus, it didn't bear contemplation. And yet, he couldn't stop his mind from going there. And he shuddered as he considered the fact that she could have slipped, fallen, and disappeared into that river, and he would never have known. Never have found her. She would be gone.

The worst of it was Trystan had never harbored any real concern that she would snoop around or find any personal information to turn against him. It wasn't even his *house*, for God's sake! He had no personal effects lying around. He'd kept her in that room out of sheer perverse stubbornness. He'd imprisoned her to teach her a lesson, punishing her for the sins of her father —and every other pap of similar ilk. And most egregious of all, he'd locked her away because he'd relished his punishing self-imposed isolation, and had resented Iris because of how much he'd begun to enjoy her company and her refreshing irreverence. And also because he'd known that the more time he spent with her, the less likely he was to keep his hands to himself. It had felt safer to keep her tucked away, out of sight—even though she was never really out of mind.

He sighed heavily, his arms tightening around her small body. Her head wrap was coming loose and he reluctantly moved one arm from her waist to tug the towel off and toss it to the floor. Her hair—soft and fragrant—had exploded into a mass of adorable curls, and he allowed himself an undeserved moment of sheer indulgence as he buried his face in that soft cloud and inhaled her addictive scent deep into his lungs.

He held it for a beat before exhaling softly, trying to release all his fear and tension in that single breath. It didn't quite work, but he felt calmer, more centered.

Iris was okay. She was safe, alive... *warm.* Trystan didn't deserve to take comfort and feel peace at her presence in his bed, but—call him a selfish fucking bastard if you wanted—he did. He had a lot to make up for, but she was here, in his arms, and Trystan would fight the devil himself to keep her there.

Chapter Eleven

I ris opened her eyes to an unfamiliar wall. It was gloomy, but despite the poor light she could tell that the wall was dark blue and not the creamy off-white to which she'd become accustomed these last few days.

She *should* have felt refreshed after what had to have been her first real sleep since her arrival but instead she felt exhausted... and anxious.

Although the anxiety was nothing new, not when every day brought with it seeping dread and building panic at the stark reality of being trapped in a room where the walls felt like they were closing in more and more every day.

But today's anxiety felt different, and as she became aware of the heavy male body spooned behind her, she began to get an inclination as to where the dread and anxiety stemmed from.

She was confused. This man—who was giving off enough heat to power a furnace—was pressed so close to her, it was hard to figure out where he ended and she began. His bent knee was thrust between her thighs and his other leg was thrown across hers. One of his long arms was under her neck, while the other was draped over her waist, his hand pressed between her—*naked*—breasts.

Yes, she was naked. And he was very close to naked. Hard to miss that fact with the amount of hot, bare flesh plastered against her back.

Oh, and he had an erection. The fabric of whatever underwear he was wearing did very little to conceal that fact. He wasn't grinding it against her or anything like that, but it was tapping insistently—almost politely—against the small of her back.

Please ma'am, would you let me in?

The absurd notion had her snorting and she felt him tense behind her.

"Iris." The instantly familiar voice was gravelly with sleep and despite the placating tone in that single word, Iris went still as a statue. Even her breathing stalled.

Of course she'd known that it was Trystan Abbott in bed with her. Who the hell else could it have been? But the confirmation still shook her.

What the hell was going on here?

She tried to remember what had happened last night, but—while attempting to remember sent feelings of breathless panic, desperate fear, and pulsating anxiety threading through her veins—the memory remained elusive.

She didn't try *too* hard though, the negative feelings

convincing her not to prod too much right now. It would come back soon enough.

"Are you okay?" Trystan asked into her hair and... did he just drop a kiss onto her head? "How do you feel?"

Iris didn't *think* they'd had sex. She was certain she'd remember that. And her body would definitely know. But what other explanation could there be for this level of intimacy?

"I'm not sure," she admitted. "Why am I here? And why are we in bed together?"

He laughed quietly, but the sound was almost despairing.

"I like how you always get straight to the point."

He did? That was news to her. She'd always thought her bluntness annoyed him.

"What do you remember about last night?" he asked, somber now, all trace of laughter gone from his voice.

Iris searched her memory. They'd watched movies all afternoon, talked, joked, laughed and then he'd—he'd...

Her breathing came faster as remembered fear and panic flooded her brain. She began trembling, teeth chattering with the intense vibrations of her shaking.

"You locked me in again," she said in a small, broken voice that would have embarrassed her if she hadn't been so very distraught at the memory that brought her fear surging back as if she were locked in right now.

She was aware of him talking, his hold on her tighter, his voice urgent, but soothing.

"—open. Do you hear me, Iris? The door is unlocked. And open. You're safe, you're okay. You can leave anytime you want to."

"W-what?"

"Look," he instructed her, pointing toward the door, which looked wrong. It was crookedly hanging off the hinges. "It's open. You're fine."

"It's broken," she pointed out nonsensically, and he chuckled, a rusty, relieved sound.

"Yeah, I had to get in here in a hurry and my hands weren't free."

"You kicked the door in," she remembered. It was all a bit vague, but she did remember that. "You could have hurt yourself. Broken your foot, or sprained your ankle, or something. That was really reckless."

"You scolding me right now, Hughes?" he asked, no heat in his voice at all.

"You should be more careful. Why did you do that?"

"At the time I was a little preoccupied with trying to get you warm."

"Oh God," she whispered in horror and humiliation as the events of last night finally came flooding back. "Oh my God, Trystan. I'm so sorry. I don't know what I was thinking."

"You weren't thinking, sweet. You were reacting," he said, his voice achingly gentle, no reprimand in those words. His chest heaved as he sighed again, and he turned her around with tender hands until she was facing him, her breasts brushing again his hard chest. His erection prodding against her thigh.

But he was ignoring that and so would she. Despite her screaming awareness of the impudent damned thing.

"I put us both in so much danger," she moaned, covering her

face with her hands. "All *three* of us. Luna was there too, wasn't she?"

"She's the one who found you."

Iris sobbed, the sound despairing and broken. Another one followed.

"No, Iris, sweetheart, please don't cry."

But she couldn't help it. The floodgates opened and she wept. Days of ever-increasing fear, followed by the illogical terror that had shut down the rational parts of her brain until all that was left was an overpowering need to escape, to flee...

In her mind, self-preservation had meant getting out of that room, despite the fact that it was the absolute worst thing she could have done. There had been no rhyme or reason to her fear. Her overwhelming instinct was to get out and she'd stared out into the cold, black night and had convinced herself that—because it wasn't raining or windy--it was safe and she would be fine.

And once she was out, she'd kept going... no thought in her mind other than, if she could just get to town, everything would be fine. She'd be safe.

"I don't know why I did that," she said, her voice muffled against his chest. "I was so *scared*. I can't even explain it, I just know that I've never felt such terror in my life before."

"It was cold and wet and dark, nobody can blame you for being scared, Iris. I was pretty fucking terrified too. When I saw you standing there. Right next to that river. *Jesus*."

He shuddered at the recollection.

"No," she shook her head in denial, aware that his beautiful chest was slick with her tears. "That's not what I meant. Being in that room. Locked in. Trapped. *That's* what scared me. I wanted out so desperately, I didn't even consider the consequences of leaving through that window. And that's what really scares me now. I had no thought of self-preservation. I nearly killed myself—*and* you—because of what I *know* is a stupid, irrational fear."

"It's not stupid and irrational to you, Iris. And I don't blame you for what happened. Phobias aren't rational. You tried to tell me that, and I refused to listen. Worse, I refused to believe you. That's *my* fault, okay?"

She nodded, and swiped at her face.

"I got your chest all wet," she pointed out mournfully.

"It'll dry."

He was stroking her back and Iris was once again reminded of their nudity. And now, after the initial storm of regret, fear and despair had passed, it was all she could think about.

"I'm naked," she blurted the obvious fact without preamble. His hand paused its stroking for a moment before he continued.

"I needed to get you warmed up as fast as possible. That meant a hot shower."

"You're nearly naked too." Gosh she sounded like a complete idiot, but her brain seemed to have malfunctioned and she wasn't entirely sure what to do with this information, or about the situation right now.

"Skin on skin is the quick and dirty method of getting, and staying, warm."

"Oh, I'm sure it was completely necessary, only... it's a little weird now, no?"

"Are you uncomfortable?"

God, no... she was so comfortable and relaxed, she felt like she was on the verge of melting into a pool of gooey liquid. But there was the *other* matter to consider.

She tried to find a delicate way of phrasing it, but in the end her candidness won out, as always.

"You have an erection."

"Yes. Can't really help that, though. Hashtag-woke-up-like-this. But don't worry, it's over here, minding its own business. And not worthy of your concern, or your attention."

His words startled a delighted laugh out of her and she looked up to see his lips curve into a smile.

"You've had a traumatic, draining experience, Iris. Get some more sleep. I'll be here if you need me."

She felt like she should protest, like she should at least insist on going to her own bed, but she felt so warm and snug and safe that she really didn't want to. Instead, she snuggled closer, trying not to notice how that extremely persistent hard-on of his briefly slid between her thighs as she wriggled against him.

He muffled a groan and she went still at the sound.

"I'm sorry," she murmured and he inhaled deeply before releasing the breath slowly.

"It's all good. I'm just..." He went silent and she waited for him to complete the sentence, but he left it hanging.

"Just what?" she asked after nearly a full minute had passed.

"Nothing. Don't worry about it. About me. I'm fine." His strained voice made a liar of him, but Iris's lids were growing heavier and her brain was fogging over. She wanted to pursue the matter but she was asleep before her mind could formulate a response.

WHEN NEXT SHE AWOKE, Iris found herself alone in Trystan's bed. She was sprawled on her stomach in the middle of the mattress and she yawned as she pushed herself up.

The room was dark. And something told her it was very late at night, or possibly very early in the morning. God, how long had she slept? And where was Trystan? Had her restless movements while sleeping sent him in search of a different bed? Who could blame him? She tended to hog the bed and covers because she was unused to sharing.

She reached over to the nightstand and found the switch for the lamp. Half of the room flooded with warm light, and Iris was gratified to note that one of her oversized hoodies—a lime green one—had been draped at the foot of the bed. Silently thanking Trystan for his thoughtfulness, she tugged the warm, fleecy garment over her head and padded to the bathroom.

After taking care of her immediate needs, she checked herself out in the mirror and nearly screamed at the sight. God, what had he done to her *hair*? It was a tangled, frizzy mess of unruly curls. It was going to take forever to detangle it.

Ugh, that was a problem for later. Right now, her stomach was actively trying to eat her spine, and she needed food. She padded to the door, which was still crookedly hanging from the hinges, and thankfully *unlocked*. She eyed the damage for a moment, remembering the moment he'd kicked it in.

It had been an extreme action, but—now that her memory was less hazy—Iris could recall his panic and desperation.

It had confused her, that urgency. It still did. Yes, she'd been cold, in shock, but she meant nothing to him. And he'd mentioned on several occasions that his preference would be for her to try and head back to town.

Granted, he wouldn't have expected her to do it in pitch black, stormy weather, but she still found his level of concern surprising.

She made her way to the kitchen, shuddering when she passed the closed door to her room on the way. Nausea surged to her throat at the thought of returning to it, but she knew she'd eventually have to go back in there. Her one consolation was that it was unlikely that Trystan would lock her in again.

She heard talking before she got to the kitchen and she smiled in anticipation, certain that it was Trystan speaking to Luna... but something in his tone of voice gave her pause and she stopped just outside the door.

"What were you thinking? Why did you send her out here? Was it some twisted game? I..." There was a pause as whomever he was on the line with—and it wasn't hard to guess it was Mr. Quinn—interrupted him. "What the fuck do you mean you thought she'd get me out my rut? You mean she was a sacrificial lamb you thought I'd have fun toying with, don't you? That's twisted, Quinny. I didn't need to be shaken out of my rut... I'm not in a rut. I'm re-evaluating. And I need you to respect my space and allow me to do that in privacy. I didn't fucking *want* her here. She lacks experience and even before I knew who her father was, I told you to cancel it."

Iris gasped, her hand going to her mouth, and Trystan abruptly stopped speaking, obviously hearing the faint sound.

Aware that the jig was up and that she'd been caught eavesdropping, Iris stepped into the kitchen where Trystan stood facing the door, his mobile phone still plastered to his ear. His eyes were wide as he stared at her, face pale, lips thinned.

"I'll call you back," he barked into the phone, before swiping at the screen and tossing it to the counter.

"How're you feeling, Iris?" he asked, his voice dark and intent.

"That was Mr. Quinn, wasn't it?" she asked, pointing a shaky finger at the phone on the counter. He gave the device an impatient glare before closing the distance between them in a few short strides.

"How are you?" he repeated the question, cupping her face and tilting it upward to stare into her eyes.

"You knew who I was when I first arrived, didn't you?" she demanded to know, her sluggish brain finally making sense of his words. "You told him to cancel the interview, only he didn't, and when I showed up you were angry with him *and* with me. Then you accused me of being an intruder when you knew *full well* that I was exactly who I said I was."

"We'll discuss that later," he murmured, his hands still gentle on her face, his thumbs stroking her cheeks.

Furious, Iris yanked her head out of his grasp and shoved at his stupidly big, immovable chest with the heels of her hands for good measure. Naturally, he didn't budge.

"We'll discuss it *now*," she insisted, stepping away from him and planting her hands on her hips as she glared up at him. "You knew who I was, you *knew* I had a legitimate reason for being here, but you left me out in the rain and the cold! And then when I *did* get into the house, you accused me of trespassing, threatened me with arrest, and kept me locked in that awful fucking room for days on end. I've been here for a week, and not once in that time did you think to set my mind at ease and admit that you'd known about the interview all along. Instead, I was left for hours at a time, worrying about what would happen when the police finally came for me. Imagining being locked in a prison cell, exacerbating the terror I already felt of being trapped in that room."

His throat moved as he swallowed, his face even paler than before, his silvery eyes stormy and troubled.

"I-I was furious with Quinny for ignoring my wishes. And I was pissed off with you as well, for being here, for distracting me from my—"

"Your what?" she interrupted him shortly. "From your melodramatic moping? Because that's what you were doing, hiding here, away from the world, with a major case of the sads. Something terrible happened to you, and I'm sorry about that, but that doesn't mean you get to treat the rest of humanity like shit. It doesn't mean you get to treat *me* like I'm somehow awful for having ambition, and for being excited about an interview that more seasoned journalists would be creaming over."

"You're right."

"And I don't think that—" she stopped as his words sank in,

and tilted her head as she eyed him speculatively. "What did you say?"

"I said you're right. I was being a fucking dick. And I'm—" He shoved his hands into his hoodie pocket as he glared fiercely into her face. Always so damned intense. "I made a lot of mistakes with you, Iris. I treated you badly. And I regret that. I wish... I hope..."

He was really struggling to verbalize whatever was going on in that clever brain of his and Iris remained silent, waiting, not sure if prompting him would send him skittering back into his brittle shell again.

"I know that I've said and done some truly shitty and unforgivable things, and I hope that we could possibly start over?"

"Oh, just a clean slate, you mean? Forget everything you did, move on, and pretend it never happened?" Must be great to be a guy like Trystan Abbott. How often did this work for him? Just wave the magic Zero Consequences wand and start over.

She shook her head, and gave a short, incredulous bark of laughter.

"I can't simply forget what you did to me, Trystan. And right now, I'm not sure I'll ever be able to forgive it, not after everything that has happened. But what I *can* do is set it aside for the duration of my stay here, if only to make life more tolerable for both of us. We don't have to be friends, we don't have to be anything. We just have to get through however long we have left here together and then move on with our lives. That would be simplest, I think."

"What about the interview?"

"You don't want to do it, I respect your decision."

"And that's it?"

"Frankly, I don't care anymore. I just want this ordeal to end so that I can go home."

He dipped his head and for once *he* was the one avoiding her eyes.

"Are you hungry?" he asked.

Thrown by the abrupt switch in topics, Iris blinked in confusion.

"What?"

"It's only four in the morning, but you've slept for nearly twenty-four hours. You must be starving."

It was ridiculously prosaic after the intensity of the last few minutes, but she *was* hungry and she did need to eat. And since she'd—only moments before—resolved to set the matter aside for now, she might as well focus on something she had some control over. Sulking and not talking to him would achieve nothing and exacerbate an already complicated situation.

"I am, yes."

"I'll whip up some breakfast," he said. "Have a seat."

"I could help," she offered, and he eyed her for a moment, as if he were evaluating her condition. Eventually, he nodded.

"I'm making omelets. Why don't you fix the coffee and toast and set the table?"

Happy to have something to do, she sprang into action.

They didn't speak much while they each went about their individual tasks, but the silence between them was surprisingly companionable. Luna was asleep in her basket close to the back door, clearly disdainful of so much activity this early in the morning.

"Do you live with your family?" The question, coming as it did off the back of a nearly ten-minute-long silence between them, surprised Iris. She looked up from the mug of coffee she was pouring, but his back was to her as he fried the omelets.

"No. I share a flat with two women in Wandsworth. I'm shocked your *comprehensive* background check on me didn't tell you that." She couldn't resist the barb.

"If it had, I wouldn't be asking," he responded evenly, before continuing. "Sharing for how long now?"

"Nearly three years."

"And you get along with them?"

"For the most part. Nobody's ever late with the rent, we're respectful of each other's space, we don't nick one another's stuff. It has worked out better than any of us imagined it would. Especially considering we were total strangers when we moved in together."

"I shared an apartment with my mates Dazza—Darryl—and Quinny during and after college," he volunteered the information freely, as he slid the omelets onto a couple of waiting plates on the counter next to the stove top. He carried the plates to the banquette, while Iris brought over the coffee and toast. "Those were some of the best years of my life."

Once they were seated, he smiled fondly and continued speaking while he buttered a slice of toast. "Dazza's the one who wrote and directed *Night of the Killer Wētās*. He went on to do some pretty amazing shit after that."

"Are you talking about Darryl Constanza?" New Zealander Darryl Constanza was one of the most acclaimed directors in the world right now—three of his last eight movies had won best picture awards. Everybody knew that the two men were friends, and had been since childhood—when they'd met shortly after Darryl's family had moved to Australia—Iris just hadn't realized that Constanza had directed that terrible movie.

"Yeah, he's a good mate."

"He directed *Wētās*?"

"He went by the name Daz Stanza back then. He had aspirations of being an actor and thought it would be a cool stage name. Thank God he eventually listened to Quinny and me when we convinced him it was terrible. But the bastard is lucky, I will be forever associated with that movie, while he got off scot-free."

"I didn't realize you and Mr. Quinn went so far back," Iris said, sipping her coffee.

"Yeah, he and Dazza are my best mates. They have been since we were kids. Quinny has a good head for business, and he managed both Dazza and me when we were starting out."

"I feel like that's something I should have known."

"Not many people know. Quinny kept it on the down-low. He had his reasons back when we were up and coming, and after all these years there's no point in revealing how close we really are."

Iris mulled over his words, while Trystan watched her in that unnerving way of his. This time she called him out on it. "Why do you keep staring at me like that?"

"Like what?"

"I don't know, like you're mentally taking me apart to see what makes me tick, before very methodically putting me back together again."

He cleared his throat and lifted his shoulders, his cheeks going red, and this time Iris was the one who stared as she tried to figure out what had triggered that reaction. He replied before she could work it out.

"I-I like looking at you."

She gaped at him, jaw going slack, eyes popping, head tilted.

"I don't understand," she admitted, and he grinned.

"Nothing *to* understand, Hughes," Trystan said. He sliced off a piece of omelet with the side of his fork and popped it into his mouth. He chewed slowly and deliberately, while Iris waited impatiently for him to elaborate. "I just *like* looking at you. You have a very interesting face, and I'm mesmerized by the way your individual features fit together."

"And that's why you keep staring at me?"

"Why else would I be doing it?"

"I don't know... to unsettle me?"

He chuckled and took another bite of his omelet.

"From day one, I found you—I don't know—*enjoyable* to look at. Your face is so expressive, with those doe eyes that project your every thought and feeling, and that mobile mouth that looks like a furled rose on the brink of blossoming, and I'm quite *helpless* to do anything but stare in absolute wonder."

"I have a question," she announced, choosing to ignore the inflammatory comments that had sent butterflies aflutter in her stomach. "I presume I'm allowed to ask questions without you immediately assuming I'm in interview mode?"

His lips twitched at her dramatic announcement and he waved a hand in her direction, inviting her to continue.

"Have you been able to contact Mr. Quinn this entire time?"

"The other evening—after movies—was the first time I'd tried. I didn't reach him then," he admitted. "He really is on a retreat. But he does periodically check his phone. Today, he answered immediately when I called—he'd been trying to return my call, but I've been a little distracted, as you know. I think he was hoping to hear I was ready to go back to work. He's been pushing for this big publicity tour to promote *Cryo Cop*."

Cryo Cop was Trystan's upcoming movie—his and Trish Nesbitt's—and it was premiering in a couple of months. Iris had had every intention of questioning him about the lack of publicity around the much-anticipated release in her now never-to-be interview. But it was Trish Nesbitt's last movie and that, along with Trystan's apparent disappearance, had already created a lot of buzz around the film.

Iris mulled over his words for a moment—they rang with sincerity—and she found herself believing him.

"I heard you accuse Mr. Quinn of using me to get you out of a rut," she said. "Why would he do that?"

"Because he's a meddling bastard who thinks that I just need to be shaken out of my funk before I'll be ready to start working again."

"And he thought *I* could do that?" Jeez, how deluded was Mr. Quinn? And why Iris? She was a perfectly ordinary woman, possessing none of the charms of the other women toward whom Trystan regularly seemed to gravitate. Then again, maybe she was looking at this the wrong way. Maybe that wasn't the kind of diversion he meant— maybe he'd always intended for Iris to antagonize Trystan. Especially if he'd known who her father had been.

"To be fair," Trystan said slowly, as he lifted his cup and took a long sip, leaving her hanging. He lowered the cup and eyed her squarely. "You've already done it. Have been doing it, *are* doing it right now. You've dragged me kicking and screaming out of—how did you put it?—out of the sads. And, for a gloriously satisfying instant, straight into the mads. With you here, all I've been able to think of was how much you annoy me, amuse me, entertain me. And I resented the hell out of you for that because I'm supposed to be here to wallow in my guilt and grief and misery. Not come up with flimsy excuses to keep spending time with you. And certainly *not* spend hours fantasizing about what it would be like to shut you up by kissing that perfect mouth."

Uh, *what?*

"But…" How did she even respond to that? This was not something the Iris Hugheses of the world ever expected to hear from the Trystan Abbottses. In the end all she could come up with was a single-word question, "*Why?*"

"Why what?"

"Why me? Is it because you've been so alone and bored these last few months that you were ripe for a distraction?"

"Hardly," he said, finishing off the last of his omelet. "You must know that you're not the first person to have approached Quinny for an interview since the accident? He could have picked anyone else, if that were the case."

"So, to Mr. Quinn, I was only some court jester to amuse his prized client out of the doldrums? What about the interview?

He knew you didn't want to do it, but he sent me here regardless. Where would that have left me? Professionally?" The magnitude of Hunter Quinn's manipulation was staggering and infuriating.

"I don't know how Quinny expected this to go. I don't believe he thought it all the way through. But it *is* telling that he arranged for it to take place right when he was uncontactable," Trystan said, but Iris wasn't sure if she could trust him to tell the truth right now.

"Is this what rich and powerful men do for kicks?" she asked, her voice bitter. "Manipulate ordinary people like puppets?"

"Iris, if you're referring to yourself as *ordinary*, I beg to differ."

"You know nothing about me, Trystan," she pushed her half-eaten plate of food aside and surged to her feet. "You're so far removed from the real world and real people that I'm some kind of novelty to you. But that will quickly wear off and you'll get bored. I'd sooner skip ahead to that part, if you don't mind... it'll save us both a whole lot of awkwardness. Thanks for breakfast. Now if you'll excuse me, I'd like to be alone."

Chapter Twelve

Iris didn't wait for Trystan's reply instead she turned and left the kitchen. It was still dark outside, but for once it was silent. No wind and no rain. The quiet was so unfamiliar that it was eerie, and gooseflesh skittered up and down Iris's spine as she retreated to her room.

She had no intention of staying there—the traumatic memories of the last few days were still too fresh in her mind for that—but she needed her laptop, some underwear, and leggings. She'd been walking around in just the thigh-length hoodie, and no underwear. She'd tried not to think about it, even though she couldn't help feeling awkward as hell since she knew that Trystan had to have been aware of her lack of panties. After all, *he* was the one who'd omitted her underwear when he'd brought her the hoodie.

Then again, maybe he'd been reluctant to sift through her

undies. Some men were squeamish when it came to things like that.

She hastily dragged on a pair of panties and some thick leggings, before grabbing her headphones, laptop, and charger, and fleeing from the room again.

It was only as she settled into what looked like a solarium that she thought about her phone.

She'd taken it with her last night but hadn't seen it since. She had a sinking feeling that she'd lost it somewhere in her mad dash toward the river. She'd have to email her parents to let them know she would be out of touch for a while.

She did that and shot one off to Evan too. She hadn't heard from her friend in a couple of days, and wondered if she was okay. The other woman liked to regale Iris with the minutia of her life, and it was unusual for her to remain out of touch, especially during the week when she was bored at work and not distracted by her social life.

Correspondence done, she updated her journal, bitching about Trystan's duplicity as well as Mr. Quinn's manipulation. She didn't hold back since she could be as brutal as she liked in the privacy of her journal and her entries were filled with vitriol.

As she read through the entry she'd written just hours before fleeing into the cold, wet night, it was clear from her language that she'd been spiraling.

She'd written about Trystan, spending time with him, enjoying his company, feeling optimistic that maybe he was starting to like and trust her, and then the feeling of utter betrayal when he'd locked her in that room.

I don't know how to feel. I can't breathe, I can't think, I'm suffocating, choking on my fear, my skin is too tight on my body and I know it's just a matter of time before I burst out of it. I'm scared, terrified, I have to get out of here before that happens. Before I lose myself.

Jesus. She stopped reading, shaking her head at the sheer irrationality of her thought processes. She'd been perfectly safe in that room, she'd nearly died out there in the dark, and yet she'd chosen *out there* as the lesser of two evils.

It scared her. She'd never endangered herself like that before. But then, she'd never found herself in a situation like this before either. She'd never before had to deal with being locked in day after day after day. And what had started as a controllable condition had rapidly escalated through the roof.

She shook her head and saved and closed her journal before opening her manuscript. The silly story she was working on was just for fun, but it was diverting and kept her mind occupied.

"WHAT ARE YOU WORKING ON?" The deep voice dragged Iris back to the present with a jolt and she looked up from her laptop to stare blankly at the tall man who was sitting in the chair opposite the sofa where she'd set up office.

She blinked a few times, her mind still swimming with plot lines and bits of snatched dialogue between characters.

"How long have you been sitting there?" she finally asked, her voice thick from disuse... for that matter how long had *she* been sitting there? She'd lost all track of time—it was fully daylight now—and she felt stiff from being seated in one position for so long.

"I've been here, reading, for nearly forty minutes. I didn't want to disturb you, but I thought maybe you needed a break."

"What's the time?" She set her laptop aside and got up to stretch her legs, wincing a bit when her limbs protested the movement.

"About eight-thirty."

Which meant Iris had been sitting there, wholly absorbed in her writing, for nearly two-and-a-half hours. She couldn't remember the last time she'd done that. It excited her, and all she could think of was getting back to it.

"So, what are you working on?" he asked again.

She ambled over to the window and looked out. It wasn't raining and—wonder of wonders— patches of blue were peeking through the clouds.

"A story." She tossed the words nonchalantly over her shoulder.

"About?"

"Don't worry, it's not about you," she sniped, turning back to face him.

He didn't respond to that, merely stared, his beautiful eyes filled with gentle censure, and that annoyed Iris because it made her feel irrationally guilty. Which, in turn, made her feel defensive because if anyone should feel guilty here it should be Trystan.

"I need a new room," she muttered, and the expression in his gaze morphed into concern.

"Of course," he said. "Pick one and I'll move your bags."

"That's fine, I'll move my own bags."

"Don't be silly, Iris, I'm happy to do it."

She nodded and picked up her laptop. As she headed toward the door, she was aware of him getting up as well, and her gaze flew up to meet his in alarm.

"What are you doing? Are you following me?"

"If I'm to bring your bags, I'll need to know which room you're moving to." His tone of voice was so reasonable it made her feel immediately churlish and paranoid.

She didn't say anything in response, but as she exited the very pretty light- and plant-filled solarium he ushered her to the left.

"The spare bedrooms are down this way," he told her. She mutely turned in the direction he'd indicated and was utterly unsurprised to discover that the two spare bedrooms were on either side of *his* room.

Because, *of course*, they were.

"There are only two spare bedrooms in this gigantic house?" she asked skeptically.

"There are four other bedrooms, excluding the suite you were staying in, but they're in the Hollingsworths' private living quarters. They've requested that I—and any of my guests—make use of this wing of the house only."

"Oh. I'm not your guest though."

"Neither are you theirs."

Fair enough.

"In that case, this room is fine," Iris said, picking the smaller of the two. The one Trystan had led her to—God, had it really only been five days ago?—after they'd spent the morning hauling sandbags. A comfortable space dressed in russets and browns, with a queen-sized bed and a small en suite bathroom.

Trystan nodded and turned to leave.

Iris ventured into the lovely room. Whomever had decorated this house had amazing taste, everything had definitely been designed with comfort in mind.

Trystan returned shortly with her handbag slung over one shoulder and her suitcases rolling behind him. Luna ambled lazily along behind him, curious about the activity.

"Thank you," Iris said.

He nodded, dropping her handbag on the bed and standing in the middle of the room with his hands thrust into the pockets of the black dropped-crotch fleecy joggers he was wearing. He stared at her moodily from beneath the fall of pitch-black hair that had flopped to his forehead.

"Iris, it occurs to me that I haven't—*uhm*—I haven't apologized." His voice was gruff, filled with awkward self-consciousness.

"Hmm," she hummed noncommittally. "That had occurred to me as well."

His shoulders hunched defensively and his brow lowered. His lips tightened and his beard bristled as his jaw clenched.

Iris waited. Wondering if he would follow through.

"I'm sorry."

"For?"

"Every goddamned thing."

"I think," she mused, shoving her hands into her hoodie's front pocket. "I'm going to need specifics."

"Fuck." The word emerged on a sigh, and he stepped

toward her, crowding her. But Iris refused to back down, standing her ground, and waiting.

"I'm sorry for sending you back out into the storm that first night," he said. "And I'm so fucking sorry for locking you in that room when I knew full well who you were. I was being a bastard and I had no excuse, other than I didn't want to deal with a nosy reporter in my space. And I'm sorry for continuing to do so, even after discovering that I enjoyed your company and that you weren't what I thought you would be.

"I was wrong. I was a fucking prick. And I'm ashamed of myself for not believing you when you told me about your phobia. I'll never forget the horror I felt when I realized what I'd driven you to. You scared fucking years off my life and I never want to feel like that again."

As apologies went it was pretty good and a lot more comprehensive than she'd been expecting.

"I know you said you'd be unable to forgive me for all that I've done, but you deserve an apology regardless. I fucked up. I know I did. And if I had it to do all over again, knowing what I now know, I'd change so fucking much."

"What do you now know?" Her question was a whisper and he shifted infinitesimally closer to her, leaving mere inches between his big body and hers.

"I know that I look at you and I fucking *ache* to do this," he admitted hoarsely, lifting his hands to cup her face. She loved it when he did that—it made her feel cared for, cherished... *Weak* with longing. His tongue darted out to wet his lips, and his blazing eyes fell to her lips. "And this..."

The last word was muffled as he lowered his lips to hers, capturing her soft *oh* in the sweetest, gentlest of kisses.

It was exploratory, uncertain, not at all the type of kiss she would've expected from a confident, sexy man like Trystan Abbott, but she appreciated it because she recognized the question in the embrace. He was waiting for her permission to take it further.

And Iris, curious to discover more, parted her lips slightly, and flicked her tongue over the sensual curve of his lower lip.

He groaned, the small gesture from her emboldening him. One of his hands dropped to her waist and he tugged her closer, until she was pressed against him, his erection throbbing against her stomach. His tongue surged into her mouth, a living flame, setting everything in its path on fire.

The bristles of his beard abraded her face, and Iris wasn't sure if she liked it or not. It wasn't unpleasant, just unfamiliar, and as he deepened the kiss she forgot about the curious sensation, and went up onto her toes and wrapped her arms around his neck.

He made an urgent, muffled sound against her mouth and, before she knew it, his other hand was at her waist as well and he'd hoisted her off her feet.

She wrapped her legs around his waist and he made a deep sound of satisfaction before carrying her to the bed. He propped a hand on the mattress before planting a knee on the bed and lowering Iris onto her back.

He was braced above her, his weight supported by that one hand and knee, his mouth still devouring hers with the single-minded focus of a man who'd been starving for weeks.

Her legs remained wrapped around his waist and when he brought his other knee up onto the bed, he lowered himself until his hardness was grinding against her aching core.

Iris couldn't find her breath and her hands moved from where they'd been entangled in the long, silky hair at the nape of his neck, downward toward his hard thrusting behind. Her fingers dug into the taut muscles she found there as she tried to guide his movements, frantically pulling him against her as she pushed her aching pussy up against his hard, hot cock.

She dragged her mouth away from his, uttering wordless, incoherent little pleas.

A small rational part of her brain was reeling in shock. This was too fast. It usually took Iris a while to even get close to an orgasm, but here she was, on the brink of coming after one kiss and some frantic dry humping. And that with a man with whom she was mostly still pissed off. She didn't understand what was going on with her. This was completely uncharacteristic behavior for her.

If she'd been capable of rational thought perhaps she'd be embarrassed, but right now she didn't care about how she *should* feel, not when she was so entirely focused on how she *was* feeling.

"Fuck... *Iris*," Trystan's voice was breathless and he sounded shaken to his core, as he continued to thrust against her.

It wasn't satisfying either of them. The position was wrong, they weren't getting enough traction, and they had way too many layers between them.

He fumbled with his pants, dragging them down past his

narrow hips, and she helped him, pushing at them until his cock was free, stiff and throbbing between them.

He went to work on her leggings next, dragging them and her panties down to her knees.

"Is this okay? Are you okay?" he asked urgently. Breathlessly.

"Okay. It's okay," she assured, and—because she couldn't part her thighs thanks to the leggings that were now bunched around her knees—he lifted her legs and draped them over one of his shoulders. He leaned forward—hands braced on either side of her torso—positioning his penis between her thighs and sawing his shaft between her pussy lips, the thick column of flesh dragging over the hard knot of her clit and ringing a cry of relief from Iris's lips.

"*Oh,*" she whimpered. "That feels so good."

She was helpless in this position with her knees pushed to her chest, and was wholly reliant on him to give her the pleasure she craved.

He did not disappoint.

He continued to slide against her, using his cock head to scoop the creamy wetness flowing from her entrance to ease his path.

Iris was a wreck by now and his relentless stroking of her clitoris soon sent her crashing into a powerful orgasm. But he didn't let up, instead he continued to thrust himself against her spasming flesh, his eyes boring into hers with a feverish intensity that she found herself unable to look away from.

"You're so fucking gorgeous," he gritted out from between

clenched teeth, dropping a hard kiss on her lips, before bringing his head up to stare at her again.

"Oh, oh... *oh*, Trystan," she wept, as she came again, and this time was even more overwhelming than the last. Her eyes drifted shut as she mindlessly humped against his hot cock.

"Don't close your eyes, Iris. Look at me," he demanded gruffly and she forced herself to refocus, punch drunk and reeling. She was barely able to see straight, but he grunted in satisfaction when she met his eyes again. She lifted a palm to cup his grim, intense, beautiful face reverently... and was fascinated when he fell apart completely at her gentle touch.

His face clenched; it was the only word she could think of to describe the violent jolt of emotion that flickered across that handsome face. And his body went tense and still, as his mouth opened on a silent cry.

He throbbed wildly between her thighs, and Iris felt his cum land in hot streams on her belly, and probably on the hoodie that he'd pushed up to beneath her breasts.

His climax seemed to last for ages, and when his arms finally gave in and he fell to the side, her mound and belly were slick with his seed.

He dragged her hoodie off and tossed it aside. He made an appreciative sound at the sight of her bare breasts and simply stared at them for a long time, before dropping a reverent kiss on each contracted tip. He lifted his head with clear reluctance and tugged his own T-shirt over his head before bunching the garment in his fist and roughly cleaning his cum off her abdomen with it.

"Sorry. I made a huge fucking mess," he muttered, sounding self-conscious.

"S'fine," Iris said, her eyes starting to drift shut. The unfamiliar position, along with the intensity of two powerful orgasms, had left her wrung out and as limp as a noodle.

He tossed his T-shirt in the same direction as her hoodie, and hastily dragged her into his arms, as if he were afraid she'd protest his touch if he left her to think about it for too long. But Iris was incapable of rational thought right now. She kicked her leggings and underwear off, snuggled close to his warm, hard body, and instantly fell asleep.

When Iris next opened her eyes, it was to find herself staring straight into a pair of familiar molten silver ones.

"You okay?" he asked gruffly and she smiled, stretching lazily beneath the covers that he must have dragged over them while she was sleeping.

"You going to ask me that every time I wake up next to you?"

"I don't know," he countered. "Are you planning to wake up next to me a lot in the future?"

She sighed and her smile slipped. "Now *that* is what I would call a loaded question."

"I didn't mean for this to happen," he said with a sigh of his own. "I mean, I don't regret it or anything, but it was really just meant to be a kiss."

"Some kiss."

"Tell me about it," he muttered. "I don't know what happened. I've never lost control like that before."

"I mean, as first kisses go, it was... explosive."

"I like the sound of that," he said, with a warm smile. "A first kiss implies that more will follow."

Iris chewed on her lip, not sure how to respond to that. Not like she didn't want to kiss him again and again and again, but she wasn't sure it would be good for her mental or emotional health.

His smile faded when the silence went on for too long, and a frown flickered across his forehead. He made an awkward little humming sound in the back of his throat before asking, "How do you feel?"

"Sated."

"I mean about what happened."

"I enjoyed it. It doesn't really have to be any more than that, does it?"

He didn't look pleased with her response and Iris sat up, clutching the duvet to her chest.

"Trystan, we're both adults with healthy sexual appetites. We'd just been through a traumatic experience and I think this was merely a way for us to work through some of that extreme emotional distress."

"Right." His eyes were troubled as they ran over her face, but he didn't say anything more. He frowned and propped himself up on an elbow to cup her cheek, his thumb gently stroked her cheekbone.

"Your skin didn't react well to my beard," he muttered. "Does it hurt?"

She shook her head, only now becoming aware of a slight tingle on her cheeks and in her neck.

"It looks uncomfortable." He seemed unhappy as he inspected her face carefully, his fingers tender against her abraded skin. "I'm sorry."

"You've said and done plenty of things to apologize for, Trystan," she told him, a small smile on her lips. "But this isn't one of them."

He sat up next to her, the duvet slipping to his hips, leaving that impressive upper body on display, and Iris greedily looked her fill. He'd kept his shirt on earlier, which had been a crying shame. Now her hands longed to explore that beautiful expanse of tanned, muscled flesh, but she wasn't sure where they went from here.

"I think it's time for a shower," she said and he quirked an eyebrow at her.

"Together?"

She laughed at the optimistic question.

"Nice try, mister," she said, snatching up a pillow to cover her nudity as she climbed out of bed. She stood next to the bed and stared down at Trystan, who remained propped up against the headboard. The duvet had slid an inch further south, but Iris kept her gaze determinedly on his face and continued to speak. "But maybe we both need some time to think about what just happened."

"It'll be impossible for me to do anything *but* that," he said with a little grimace. "Look, I know this is all a bit much and you're justifiably angry with me. I get it, I really do. I behaved reprehensibly but, Iris, I really fucking want you. I have practically since day one, which is why I've been so damned hell-bent on keeping you at a distance."

"What just happened was lovely, Trystan," she paused, choosing her next words very carefully. "But that's probably as far as it goes for us."

"Why?" His question was edged with frustration.

"Because I think you see me as some kind of challenge, a prize to be won. Someone taboo and off limits to you. I don't belong in your world. And judging from the way you've cut yourself off here, isolated yourself from your charmed life and your glamorous friends, my ordinariness is appealing and different—and what you believe you want right now. You *think* you crave normality, but what you *really* need is to go back to your reality and face whatever demons drove you away in the first place."

"You need to stop psychoanalyzing me, Iris. Why I'm here is none of your fucking business."

"Trystan, you've run away from your life and your responsibilities to hide in this godforsaken place like a big old chicken. You need to stop behaving like a two-year-old having a tantrum and, together with your shitty manager, figure out what you're going to do about your future.

"Because while what he did to me was wrong, it was also an act of desperation. The bastard is so damned keen to get your attention and snatch you back to the real world that he dragged my unwitting arse straight into your mess. So, *excuse* me if you think I'm out of line, but this became my business when your manager tricked me into coming here and *you* chose to deny knowing about my reasons for being here."

She turned away from him, heading toward the bathroom, trying not to care that her bare butt was on display. After all, he'd seen pretty much all there was to see of her by now and she knew that her self-consciousness was a little absurd under the circumstances.

He remained silent after her impassioned rebuke, and Iris was almost convinced he would allow her to have the last say, until she reached the en suite door.

"Iris?"

She paused in the doorway, shoulders tensed and back braced, as she waited for whatever he had to say. She refused to turn and face him, even though she knew by now how crazy it drove him when she wouldn't look at him.

She could sense his aggravation and frustration in the long pause before he finally spoke again. "Your most ridiculous assumption lies in your belief that I think you're ordinary. I think I may have mentioned before that nothing could be further from the truth."

She couldn't help it, his words—spoken with such passionate sincerity—forced her to turn and face him. She needed to see for herself if the feeling she'd heard in his voice was visible in his eyes, or on his face.

But disappointingly, his expression revealed not a single emotion. His eyes seared into hers and she actually found herself flinching beneath the scorching ferocity of that gaze.

She remained silent in the wake of his astonishing proclamation, not entirely sure what to make of it. In the end, she turned away and stepped into the bathroom, shutting the door behind her with quiet deliberation.

Chapter Thirteen

ris remained in her room for the rest of that day and most of the following one. Luna had come scratching at the bedroom door about an hour after Iris's awkward, silent breakfast with Trystan.

Iris had let the dog in and Luna was now stretched out on the bed—taking up pretty much all of the mattress space—and snoring away contentedly. Iris had retreated to the comfortable easy chair in the corner and, after updating her journal, had tried writing a few chapters. But her concentration was shot, and she couldn't stop thinking about Trystan, and the things they had done to each other yesterday.

Worse, she couldn't stop fantasizing about doing it, and so much more, again. Was she being foolish in denying them both what they so desperately wanted? Probably, but she couldn't allow herself to be vulnerable around a man like Trystan Abbott. He would soon come to his senses and realize that everything she'd said was true. He didn't really want her, he wanted what he thought she represented. And Iris didn't think she'd be able to survive being carelessly discarded by him. He'd become too real to her.

Iris shook herself as she realized that she'd been staring into space for a good five minutes. She sighed and set aside her laptop, curling up in the chair with her knees tucked against her chest.

She was so caught up in her thoughts that she didn't hear the quiet knock on her door at first. Luna's gentle *woof* snatched her back to reality and her head jerked up when the knock sounded again.

"Yes?" she called hoarsely. "Come in."

The door opened and Trystan stepped into the room. Iris stared at him unblinkingly for a long, blank moment. He had shaved, and her stomach did a horrible flip-flop as she stared into that very familiar face. This was *THE* Trystan Abbott. And for a second, she felt a pang of loss that *her* Trystan had disappeared so completely... and then she finally saw it, the scar bisecting the clean line of his jaw. Without the beard it was more noticeable, a physical reminder of the accident that had killed Trish Nesbitt.

She dragged her eyes away from that still pink, slightly raised thin keloid. It sliced diagonally up from just below his Adam's apple to the left corner of his mouth and Iris swallowed, her fingers literally twitching as she ached to touch him there, to soothe the wound that had almost completely healed, but for the physical reminder it had left behind. It did not detract one bit from his good looks. Where before his features had been perfect, Iris found that the scar simply added to his undeniable charismatic sex appeal.

"Iris?" He prompted, and she was snatched from her mooning, to meet his eyes. He looked self-conscious and achingly vulnerable; his eyes filled with naked fear.

"Trystan, it's—"

"It's Quinny," he interrupted, his voice harsh. "For you. He says he can't reach you on your phone." She noticed only then that he held his mobile phone out to her.

"I lost my phone. That night." She didn't have to elaborate—he'd know exactly which night she meant. She was confused and out of sorts, still distracted by the scar. She took the phone from him and he immediately retreated, slamming out of the room.

She sighed. Well, that was something that would need to be resolved quickly. He clearly had the wrong idea about why she'd been staring.

She lifted the phone and was surprised to see Hunter Quinn's face on screen. She hadn't expected a video call.

She schooled her features into neutrality, even though her face wanted to default into a pissed-off scowl.

"Yes?" she barked, unable to keep the annoyance from her voice.

"Miss Hughes, I see you've been trying to reach me and—"

"You *knew* I would be trying to reach you once your client discovered that I'd shown up on his doorstep unannounced and you *chose* to go on some stupid silent retreat right when I was due to arrive here. I'm pretty sure that the timing wasn't a coincidence."

He stared at her, clearly taken aback by her immediate offensive. Before now, she'd been nothing but polite and professional toward him.

"This entire situation has been sorely lacking in professionalism, and I must say I'm *very* disappointed in you, Mr. Quinn. You allowed me to walk into this situation like a lamb into the wolf's den. Do you even *know* what hell I've been through since arriving here?"

"Trystan has informed me, yes." His voice and demeanor were surprisingly subdued and that disconcerted Iris. She'd expected suave apologies, schmoozing, spin-doctoring, but what she got was, "I'm so sorry, Miss Hughes, I was out of line. So was Trystan. I should never have put you in this position. It was unconscionable. And you're right, it was unprofessional. I was just—" He swallowed and shook his head almost helplessly. "I mean, you've seen him. I don't know... I'm not sure how to fix it."

"What did you think sending *me* here would accomplish?"

He scrubbed a hand over his mouth.

"You have a sincerity, an earnestness that I thought would appeal to him."

"Did you think I'd fall into bed with him, and somehow seduce him out of his depression?"

"What?" He looked genuinely shocked. "No. Nothing like that. I simply hoped that he'd respond to your—well, there's no easy way to put it— you appeared to hero-worship him. It was sweet, so fucking pure and innocent and I wanted to remind him that there were people like you out there, people who enjoyed his work. I hoped he'd remember everything he used to love about his job."

"The adulation, you mean?" she asked cynically, and he shook his head.

"No, in the beginning, he took real joy in what he did. He hasn't in a long time, since before the accident. You seem to carry that joy with you. And I'd hoped he would recognize it, respond to it... and—yeah—it was fucking stupid. I used you. And it was wrong. Rest assured, Trystan has already torn me a new one and . . ." His deep blue eyes shadowed and a flicker of sadness crossed his face. "Well, there will be consequences for my actions. I just wanted to sincerely apologize to you. Whatever story you decide to write—"

"There won't be a story."

"What?"

"Trystan refused to do the interview, and I won't write about him if he doesn't want me to."

"You could still write about your stay with—"

"No. I can't. I won't. If he wants privacy, that's what he'll be getting from me. That's what he *should* have gotten from you."

He had the grace to look ashamed, and his eyes were downcast as he nodded. When he lifted his gaze again, he had the tiniest of smiles on his lips.

"I was right about you, though," he said. "You're good for him. This is the first time in a long time I've seen him so passionate about anything. And even though it meant him ripping me a new asshole and firing me, it was worth it just for that. Because, regardless of what you may think of me, Miss

Hughes, I love him. He's one of my best friends, and I'm glad to see some of that spark back in him."

"Wait, he *fired* you? But—"

He smiled again. "Goodbye, Miss Hughes."

The screen went blank before she could say anything in response to that. She stared at the phone for a long moment before shaking her head and swearing beneath her breath.

She surged to her feet and stalked out of the room in search of Trystan.

She found him in the solarium, hands in the pockets of yet another pair of obscenely butt-hugging gray sweatpants, staring out at the lake.

"You idiot," she launched into him as soon as she caught sight of him, and he turned to face her in surprise. She marched right up to him and thrust the phone against his chest.

He took it automatically and stared at her in consternation as she planted her hands on her hips and glared up at him.

"You fired your best friend? *Why?*"

"Why?" he repeated, his voice incredulous. "You're seriously asking me that?"

"Of course I am. He has your best interests at heart, he cares about you. Yes, he's an idiot, but that's no reason to fire him."

"Iris, you nearly died the other night!"

"I'm well aware of that," she retorted. "But Mr. Quinn isn't the reason I was out in that storm."

"He might not be directly responsible, and ninety-nine-point nine percent of the blame lies on my shoulders. I know that, but that one percent falls on him, and that's unacceptable to me."

"Trystan, he's your friend."

"And *you're* my—" He cut himself off, staring at her in mute frustration, clearly not sure how to end that sentence.

"I'm your nothing," she finished it for him. "No, that's not right, I'm your unwanted guest. A complete stranger to you and as such, you had no way of knowing I'd react the way I did."

"You tried to tell me."

"To be honest"—and Iris was always honest to a fault. It would be so easy to keep blaming and punishing him, he might even deserve it, but that wasn't who she was—"It had never been that bad before. Even *I* didn't know I'd react like that."

"But you did react like that, sweetheart. And that's on me. And on Quinny for sending you here in the first place. He knew I wasn't myself, knew I was irritable and unreasonable. Before coming here I'd been unfairly ripping into—and snapping and snarling at—everyone around me. He had no reason to believe I'd behave any differently with you. I can't trust his judgment anymore. Not after Trish and now this."

She sighed and her gaze roamed over his face, coming to rest on that scar on his jaw. He lifted a self-conscious hand to it and she shook her head, her own hand intercepting his and pulling it away from his face.

"Don't," she implored and he stood there, raw dread and insecurity in his eyes, as he allowed her to look at him. After a long moment, she ran trembling fingertips over the raised flesh and he leaned helplessly into her touch. "I knew this was there, I saw it after you trimmed the beard. I didn't recognize the extent of the damage until you shaved though."

He swallowed, his Adam's apple bobbing convulsively and betraying his apprehension.

"Are you going to have it surgically removed?" she asked and his eyes flickered, before he shook his head.

"Why not?"

"Trish can't get her life back, why the fuck should I get my face back?"

Iris sucked her lower lip into her mouth and kept her gaze locked onto his before she sighed and took his hand again.

"Come," she urged, tugging him toward a sofa. "Sit with me."

He followed almost passively and sat down next to her. She turned to face him, her eyes probing his troubled gaze again.

"Did you love her?" She held her breath, not really wanting to know and yet needing to.

"Love her?" he repeated. "Trish, you mean?"

"Yes."

His eyes darkened and he shook his head resolutely. His denouncement was immediate and unequivocal "No. Absolutely not."

Well, denials didn't get more vehement than that, and Iris felt a heady sense of relief, which didn't last long when he continued with, "But maybe I should've and that's the problem."

"Explain." He hesitated and she squeezed his hand. "Please, Trystan, I want to understand what's going on with you."

"Why?"

"Because you're hurting and I want to know how to make it better."

His mouth trembled and shockingly his eyes flooded with moisture. He blinked rapidly, looking self-conscious about the moment of vulnerability.

"In light of everything that has happened between us and everything that I've done to you, Iris, you might have difficulty believing this," he said, his voice choked. "But you make it better just by being here."

Oh God, how the hell was she supposed to resist this man when he said things like that?

"Please tell me what happened with Trish." She wasn't sure he would, and so was surprised and relieved when he started speaking without even the slightest of hesitations.

"We met while working on *Cryo Cop*." Iris nodded. This was common knowledge; the press had been abuzz about the apparent chemistry between two of Hollywood's brightest and most beautiful stars. And then, when they'd started dating just a few short months later everyone had been speculating about secret weddings and possible pregnancies. The rumor mill had been agog, the paparazzi had stalked them and their star appeal had gone through the roof.

"Trish and I got along, we enjoyed each other's company, we had fun and had some great on-screen chemistry... then her manager and Quinny decided a good way to generate buzz for the movie would be to fabricate a behind-the-scenes romance between us. That was all it was at first, a little light flirtation in public, a few dinners, being seen out together, attending functions as a couple. Nothing serious, just enough to fuel public interest. One night, it got physical. I drove her home, and we fell into bed together." Iris nodded, swallowing down a wave of nausea at the thought of him with the beautiful Trish Nesbitt, which was ridiculous since she'd known about their relationship. "I immediately knew that it was a mistake. We were colleagues, friends. And I didn't want sex muddling that up. It felt wrong, and very uncomfortable. I was on autopilot, y'know? Insert tab A into slot B type of shit, just going through the motions. But she seemed so into it. I kept asking her if it was okay, if she was sure because *I* didn't feel like it was okay and I absolutely wasn't sure about it. And... *fuck*, I should have called a halt to it. I don't know why I didn't.

"Safe to say it was the world's most mediocre sex, for both of us. From beginning to end I just wanted it to be over and I couldn't understand why I felt that way. Afterward, we had an awkward discussion about our relationship boundaries. And we agreed that it could never happen again. Well, I *thought* she agreed with me. But after that she was—I don't know—more physical in public, more brazen with her hands and mouth. I was surprised. Shocked. So fucking uncomfortable. And I felt like I couldn't openly rebuff her without hurting her especially after we'd been together. That would have been a dick move. She was such a great woman, she appeared so grounded and stable. But—" His head moved, a short jerk of denial, as if he were still trying to wrap his head around these memories.

"The night of the accident we were at a premiere party, and as we pulled up she told me she was in love with me." His brow lowered and his eyes went distant, as if he were so immersed in his memories that he no longer saw Iris. "It came out of left field. I was shocked and, as a result, I wasn't as kind as I should have been. At that point, I'd been trying to ease out of the agreement with her for weeks. I'd spoken to Quinny about how we could end it. I knew she was getting too emotionally invested. And I tried to be sensitive of her feelings, but then she started showing up at my home, and once she even crawled into my *bed* while I was asleep, for fuck's sake!

"We'd made the commitment to go to the party together months before, and I didn't want to humiliate her by not showing up. But by then, the situation had escalated so badly, I knew it had to be our last social event together. I'd told Quinny and her manager beforehand, told them I was ready for a public break-up. They could paint me as the bad guy, I didn't fucking care. I was done."

He made a quiet, despairing sound in the back of his throat, his hand tightening around hers almost to the point of pain, but Iris said nothing, not wanting to distract him.

"The night of the party, after she told me she loved me, that was it for me. The end of a very long tether. I slammed out of the car and dragged her to a private room. Once there, I told her I didn't feel the same way, that I never would. That she was delusional if she thought what we'd had was in any way real. I was . . . cruel. But I was frantic by then. I didn't know how to handle the situation any longer. She was a colleague. I tried to respect that, but her behavior frightened me. I felt stalked. Hunted.

"She went eerily calm after I exploded. She apologized for misunderstanding the situation and I was so relieved. I thought, 'Finally, she gets it. Thank God.' I thought that was that. We left the room and spent the party doing separate things. We'd gone in my car, and I felt obligated to drive her home. When we were both ready to leave, she offered to drive because I'd had a couple of drinks. I agreed because I wasn't in the mood for another confrontation. But once we were in the car her demeanor changed.

"She went from relatively pleasant to almost catatonic and, I don't know, I can't describe it. I'd never seen anything like that in my life before. She was lifeless, almost robotic. And she was speeding. I wasn't drunk, I wasn't even slightly buzzed. I was sober, but like I said, I'd agreed to let her drive because she was insistent and I didn't want another argument. I just wanted to get the evening over and done with and move on with my life.

"I told her to slow down. It was about three in the morning. The roads were empty..."

He stopped speaking, again getting that faraway blank look in his eyes.

"Trystan?" Iris whispered. Her voice jerked him from wherever he'd gone and his eyes were tormented as they swept over her face.

He gulped in a breath of air like a man deprived of oxygen, and when he spoke again his voice was shaky, almost reedy.

"I haven't told anyone else," he admitted. "Not even Quinny or Dazza. It was just... so—" His words failed him and his lips thinned as he retreated into silence again. Not for long though and this time she didn't have to prompt him. He continued as though compelled to. "She told me she loved me. That I belonged to her. That if she couldn't have me n-no one else could, then she jerked the steering wheel and drove the car straight into a tree."

The silence was broken only by his harsh gasping breaths.

Iris, however, found herself quite unable to breathe as the shock of his words stole the air from her lungs and left her reeling in horror.

She desperately cast about for something—*anything*—to say, but he spoke before she could, "It wasn't at all how I'd imagined something like that would be. Like the movies"—his mouth twisted in irony—"make it seem. I was fully aware throughout it all. I was in pain, bleeding, I knew something was wrong with my face, but the shock kept me from recognizing the full extent of my injury."

His fingers absently brushed over his scar. "They told me the shard of glass that caused this missed my carotid by half an inch. But I didn't know that at the time, of course. I didn't care about me right then. I was more concerned about Trish and she was—" His face spasmed in grief and horror, and Iris's hands went up to cup his jaw, her thumb tracing the ridge of his scar. "Trish was groaning, her face and head were..." He shook his head and made a low, despairing sound, as if he were reliving the moment. "I couldn't help her, my arms felt like lead. I tried to reach for her, to stem the bleeding, but she was gone seconds later. And even then, I didn't pass out. I wish I had, but I remained conscious, trapped with her corpse until the rescue services arrived. I was told it was under five minutes. It felt like five hours. The first person to arrive was a pap..." Now it was Iris's turn to moan in horror. "He took pictures while I begged him to call an ambulance. To this day I'm not sure if he was the one who called 911 or not. The rest you know. Trish died. And I lived. But there were times"—his voice was bleak and Iris wanted to stop him from saying what she knew he would say next. Only, her throat had seized up and her eyes were blurry with tears and when he said the inevitable, her horror emerged on a broken sob—"there were times I desperately wished I hadn't lived. Because having her death on my conscience is eating away at my soul."

"Trystan, no," she moaned, her face wet with tears. She leaned toward him and pressed her lips to his for a brief, heartfelt kiss. "Please, don't say that. You didn't kill her, her death does *not* belong on your conscience."

"I knew she was troubled, Iris, I should have helped her. But all I could think of was getting her the hell away from me. I should have left her alone. I should never have slept with her when she was so broken."

"You didn't know. How could you have?"

"I can't forgive myself for not seeing it until it was too late. I felt like the worst kind of abuser. She was vulnerable and I used her."

"You had consensual sex, there was no coercion or manipulation involved. Did you make any promises to her when you got together?"

His eyes flickered uncertainly. "What do you mean?"

"I mean did you talk about having a long-term or permanent relationship with her?"

"No, from the very beginning we were clear on it being a promotional stunt. When it got intimate, we both agreed afterwards that it shouldn't have happened," he tilted his head as if he was remembering something. "In fact, Trish was the one who instigated the sex. When I protested beforehand that we were making a mistake, she kissed me and said something along the lines of, 'If only all mistakes could be such harmless fun.' That's what she called it, *harmless fun*." His lips twisted at the memory. "I came here to try and make sense of it all, get my head straight, think about where I go from here."

"You didn't come here to do *more* than that, did you?" she asked because it needed to be asked, but his look of shock and horror gave her the answer before he could verbalize it.

"No, sweet, of course not. I was angry at myself, the world, at Quinny for coming up with the idea of faking a relationship with her in the first place. And I dreaded anything to do with *Cryo Cop*. All interviews would center around Trish, the accident, my relationship with her. Her manager wanted me to claim that we were engaged. Can you fucking believe that? Quinny told him to fuck off and threatened to sue him if he leaked the lie. I was grateful for that at least because at the time I just wanted to be left the fuck alone. I still do."

"And then I came along and disturbed your peace," Iris murmured, absolutely appalled. It was so much worse than she'd ever believed.

"No, Iris, then you came along and I finally started to feel alive again. And yeah, I'm not gonna lie, it pissed me the hell off. I'd gotten so used to walking around feeling half-dead, that when this wet, bedraggled little dynamo showed up at my door, screaming about wolves and cliffs and dying phone batteries, I was unprepared for the fucking jolt of electricity straight to my heart. You woke me up, and I didn't like it. And to my eternal shame, I treated you dreadfully as a result. Suddenly I was starting to feel things again. Things like irritation, amusement, curiosity, desire, and fear. And that unsettled me. It fucking terrified me.

"When you ran off into the storm, I knew that I'd failed you as well. Once again, I'd missed the signs... no, this time I'd *willfully* ignored them. I could have gotten you killed too and that fucking destroys me, Iris. It felt like that night with Trish all over again. Only *so* much worse because you're someone I've come to care for a great deal in an absurdly short span of time. I know you think I'm making that shit up, or that I'm craving normalcy or whatever the fuck bullshit you said earlier, but it's more than that, Iris. You make me feel—" He paused as if he were searching for the correct word, then he smiled, a small, beautiful smile and repeated it, this time with a period at the end, "You make me feel."

She sobbed, and her replying smile was a tearful, trembling mess.

"Trystan," she whispered. "I'm not Trish Nesbitt, I'm nothing like her. I allowed my phobia to get the better of me, and responded in an irrational manner. I didn't go out into that storm to kill myself; on the contrary, it was an illogical act of self-preservation. I'm *so* sorry it triggered memories of that awful night for you."

"No, sweet, you don't ever apologize to me for that night. Never, you hear me? It wasn't your fault."

"Oh, Trystan," she murmured, her lips curling into a sweet smile. He leaned forward and then stayed the movement, his mouth a breath away from hers.

He waited and Iris closed the gap, her lips making contact

with his in a soft, hungry kiss. His hands tunneled into her hair as he pulled her head closer to feast on her mouth.

When they came up for air again, she was straddling his lap and his lips were suckling at the sensitive skin of her neck.

"Iris, baby," he groaned against her skin. "I want to fuck you."

She moaned helplessly and thrust herself against him.

"No," he whispered, tugging at her hair to pull her head back, exposing more of her neck to his hungry lips. "I want to do much more than that. I want to love you. Will you let me do that, Iris? Will you let me love you?"

"Yes," she breathed, while his lips explored the sensitive skin of her throat.

"Thank Christ because I fucking *ache* for you," he whispered to Iris, who was enthusiastically grinding herself up against his big, thick shaft.

"Show me how much you ache for me, Trystan," she encouraged and he growled deep in his throat, before getting up and lifting her in the process. It was yet another thrilling show of strength that reminded her of the time he'd picked her up in the shed—what felt like months ago—and she squealed in delight, wrapping her arms tightly around his neck and her legs around his waist as he carried her toward his bedroom.

Luna, who'd been sleeping in the kitchen, got up to follow them, but Trystan commanded her to stay, as he very quickly made his way to the bedroom and gently deposited Iris onto his king-sized bed.

"God, the colors you wear are seriously blinding," he said

with a half-laugh, taking in her electric blue long-sleeved T-shirt, which she'd combined with a pair of fluorescent pink leggings and neon yellow leg warmers. "You're an '80s throwback."

"Keep it up, mate, and you'll be getting no nookie." She stretched voluptuously on his bed, parting her thighs slightly in invitation.

He laughed, the sound lighthearted and filled with joy.

"You always look beautiful, no matter how brightly adorned you are," he told her, settling between her thighs, his erection hot and heavy against the crotch seam of her leggings.

He kissed her and she sighed in contentment, opening her mouth for his tongue and languidly returning his kiss, stroke for stroke. Her hands burrowed beneath his black Nirvana T-shirt, finding the smooth, taut skin beneath and exploring the perfect musculature of his back and chest.

"You're beautiful too," she whispered after he let her up for a breath. She ran her lips over his freshly shaved jaw, and sighed as his stubble scraped against the sensitive skin around her mouth.

"Why'd you shave?" she asked and he lifted his head at the question, his gaze probing.

"Don't you like it?" He sounded genuinely dismayed at the prospect and she laughed softly.

"Trystan, you have to know you're gorgeous with or without the beard. I'd just grown used to it, and I felt like it was a version of you only *I* got to see. *This* Trystan is instantly recognizable and beloved by millions—"

"Fuck the millions," he interrupted harshly. "I'd rather be beloved by one."

"But that's not your reality."

"It *is* if that one is the only one who truly matters to *me*."

Chapter Fourteen

Trystan's words confused her, maybe even scared her a little, and she ran her fingers through his silky hair, still much longer than he usually wore it—at least that was still hers alone. She kissed his beautiful, stubborn jaw, and ran her tongue up the line of his scar.

He tensed.

"Every part of you is beautiful, Trystan," she murmured against his mouth. "Inside and out."

He exhaled, a soft, shuddering sound that resembled a sob, and his kiss was filled with reverence.

"I adore you," he whispered, peppering her neck with gentle, lingering kisses. He unhurriedly dragged her T-shirt up, and those same kisses followed the trail of exposed skin, starting at her belly button and moving up over her torso, skirting around her bra, just skimming over the skin above the lacy cups before he whisked her shirt up and away.

Then he knelt between her legs and simply stared at her for a long, long time. His eyes falling to her balconette bra, where her dark nipples were beaded and visible through the white lace. He swallowed loudly, his chest starting to visibly heave as his large hands moved to completely engulf those small mounds. Her nipples scraped against the lace of her bra as the weight of his large hands settled on her breasts and she cried out at the unbearable sensation.

His lips quirked wickedly as he thumbed aside the lace of one cup and exposed her breast to his lascivious gaze.

"Fuck me, you're gorgeous," he groaned, lowering his head until she could feel his warm breath on the puckered tip of that breast. "You have the prettiest little tits. I need to taste them, to suck these tempting dark brown peaks into my mouth. I want to swallow them down, scrape them with my teeth, bite them, suck them, fucking devour them..."

God, if words could make her come, those ones would... she was panting by now, thrusting her chest toward that achingly close mouth, *needing* him to do what he said he wanted to do.

"Please," she begged, her hands trying to tug his head down toward her chest. "Trystan, please, *please*... do that."

"Do what, baby?" he asked sweetly, and she glowered at him.

"The kissing and biting and devouring," she said, and he chuckled before lowering his mouth to her breast and sucking her nipple into his mouth.

It was so wonderful that Iris nearly came out of her skin.

"Aah, my God, please, *more*." She felt his lips widening into a smile, before he increased the suction, adding the smallest scrape of his teeth to the sensation. The top of Iris's head just about blew off, her back bowed as she tried to push herself closer, and she frantically rubbed her clit against his hardness, wanting so much more than this, while at the same time finding *just* this to be exactly the right amount of stimulation to set off a bone melting orgasm.

Her breath caught and held in her chest for a long fraught moment as her climax washed over her in a tsunami of sensation.

Trystan groaned when he recognized what was happening to her and he shuddered while she came against his cock with his mouth clamped over her nipple. When she finally went limp, he lifted his lips from the distended nub and removed her bra wordlessly, chucking it aside before tugging her leggings and sodden panties down her limp legs.

He quickly removed his own shirt and sweatpants and his cock landed, hot and heavy and naked against her thigh.

That was when he froze.

"*Fuck*," he said, along with a few other things that turned the air blue, and Iris blinked up at him in hazy confusion.

"What's wrong?"

"I don't have condoms. I didn't think I'd be having sex on this trip, it—"

"Oh," she blinked as she struggled to think. No condoms. That was bad but... "Wait, I have one. In my handbag."

"Your handbag?" he repeated, his eyes immediately sparking with hope. "Where?"

"Room, hurry up," she urged, slapping his taut arse to get him moving. He laughed and leaped from the bed naked and magnificent, his angry-looking cock swaying as it led the way out of the room. He was back thirty seconds later with her tote in hand.

"Christ, it's cold out there," he said with a shudder, tossing her bag at her. She sat up lethargically, annoyed at being forced to move while in the middle of her glorious post-orgasmic haze, and rummaged around until she found the one sad little condom that had been in her bag for nearly a year.

"This is the only one," she said. "So, you'd better make it count, mister."

He grinned.

"Miles might have some stocked around here somewhere. I'll dig them out later. But for now..." He took the brightly colored square from her and eyed it dubiously. "Please tell me this isn't going to give me a flourescent green glow-in-the-dark cock."

She giggled at the heartfelt plea, while he tore off the corner of the packaging with his strong white teeth. He removed the prophylactic and heaved a dramatic sigh of relief at the sight of the colourless condom which he efficiently donned. He then knelt between her splayed thighs, cock twitching while he stared down at her wet, pulsing femininity with an appreciative gleam in his eyes.

"Damn it, I wanted to taste that pretty pussy," he muttered regretfully, then perked right up. "But it'll be my little treat for later."

He lifted one of her legs to his shoulder and leaned over and into her.

"You ready to come on my cock, sweetheart?"

"Confident bastard, aren't you?" she laughed and he gave her an unrepentant grin, which faded when he pushed into her. It was a snug fit as he was bigger than she'd expected, and it verged on discomfort as the broad head of his penis wedged itself into her tight channel.

"You okay?" he asked, beads of sweat popping up on his forehead, as he focused on her face, seeming attuned to the minutest change in her expression.

"Hmm," she moaned, not quite capable of speech.

"If you need me to stop or slow down, tell me, okay? I don't want to hurt you."

"Don't stop," she said quickly, immediately worried that he'd withdraw.

"Only if you tell me to."

"I won't."

He smiled. "Okay, then I won't."

He worked his way into her, slowly, as gently as he could. His thumb was on her clit, while his mouth alternated between her nipples, making her wriggle in reaction to the overstimulation. Her hips were moving, tiny micro thrusts that sent him deeper and deeper into her body until—at *last*—he was there, fully buried inside of her.

He grunted in satisfaction and she sighed, as she adapted to his magnificent size.

"You feel *so* good," she whispered and he gave her a strained smile.

"Iris, you..." He didn't seem able to complete what he wanted to say and merely shook his head.

Iris would have pushed him to say whatever it was he

wanted to, but she was so immersed in sensation, she couldn't form a coherent thought of her own. He dragged his length all the way out of her slick, sensitive channel and she sucked in a harsh breath, which she released when he slammed his way back in.

Her free leg bent at the knee and she planted her foot on the mattress to give herself purchase as she raised her hips to meet his hard, demanding thrusts. Her hands were exploring his chest, back, and butt, while her mouth licked and sucked at his nipples, neck, and mouth.

She was in bliss, orgasm followed orgasm and she never wanted it to end, but shortly after her third climax, Trystan shuddered in her arms, his head dropped to her shoulder, and his thrusts lost all rhythm. He plowed into her one last time and kept his throbbing length buried deep inside of her as he came with a low, helpless cry that Iris only barely recognized as her name.

TRYSTAN WOKE to the wet heat of Iris's soft mouth on his cock. Her small hand was encircled around the base, while she suckled on his glans like it was the sweetest of lollipops. Her tongue snaked around the corona, sending him arching off the bed with a helpless groan. His hands went to her hair, his fingers twining themselves into the soft, bouncy curls.

"Iris," he murmured, reverently, his eyes fixated on that plump, suctioning rosebud of a mouth as it drove him to distraction. "I swear to Christ, you're killing me, baby. Murdering me with that perfect mouth of yours."

She lifted her eyes to his and grinned, a huge, satisfied shit-eating grin, before she quite deliberately snaked her tongue over the weeping slit of his dick.

A shudder worked its way up his spine and he made a sound that would have embarrassed him at any other time. A helpless, weak, almost keening sound.

"This isn't fair," he groused. "If you get to feast, I should too. Slide that pussy on over here and plant it on my mouth, I'm starving for you."

She made a little sound of denial and to his utter devastation lifted her lips from his pulsating penis to say the most absurd thing, "I haven't showered yet."

"Neither have I. What the fuck does that matter? I guarantee you'll still taste as sweet as sugar. Now stop saying ridiculous shit and shimmy on over."

She hesitated for a split second longer, before thankfully complying. Trystan made a deep sound of satisfaction, when he finally had access to the mauve and pink perfection of her pretty little pussy, and immediately went to work. Using his tongue, lips, and teeth to devour her tender, sensitive flesh.

He kept her on the edge, making it last, taking her to the brink and then bringing her back down. He lost track of how long he worked on her. He was so wholly engrossed in giving her pleasure, he almost forgot about his own.

She moaned, her hips pistoning wildly whenever he did something that she really enjoyed and he lingered in those spots longer, driving her to distraction. She gamely tried to keep sucking his painfully hard, throbbing cock, but she kept losing concentration, and Trystan figured if he ever wanted to get off, he'd have to finish her first.

He relentlessly consumed her spasming, delicious flesh, suckling her distended clit while plunging his fingers into her dripping, hot pussy. He felt her clench around him and hooked his fingers upward, finding the spot his cock had discovered last night, and sending her tumbling wildly over the edge.

She was screaming his name, forming incoherent pleas for mercy, while simultaneously begging God to release her. She was wild and beautiful, and he was fucking awed by her.

When she finally came down from what had—to all intents and purposes—looked, and felt, like an epic orgasm to Trystan, she dropped her head on his thigh, her small body shuddering, while her soft flesh quivered gently against his lips. He continued to kiss her and lap at her, loving the taste of her creamy spend, as he eased her out of it.

She lifted her head and looked back at him.

"I think you literally killed me for a few seconds there," she said breathlessly, and he grinned. Her hand was still possessively curled around his hard shaft, and she murmured a soft *oh* as if she'd only just remembered what she'd been doing before.

"Did you forget about my poor, neglected cock, baby?" he asked with a laugh. "I don't know if my ego can stand that."

"Please, I'm sure your ego will survive," she said with a scoffing little laugh. "If your insufferable little smirk is anything to go by, you *know* that you just rocked my world."

"Only fair, since you've been rocking mine from the moment you showed up on my doorstep, so—" She shut him up by taking him deep into her mouth and he groaned in helpless pleasure, his head dropping back on the pillow.

She was as ruthless and relentless as he'd been and by the time she *eventually* swallowed down every last drop he had to offer, Trystan was a wreck who barely knew his own name. Afterwards, as he gathered her close, he knew he was so far gone for this woman he would never be able to let her go.

FOUR DAYS LATER, Iris was writing in the solarium, her feet propped on Trystan's lap while he read a John Grisham novel. His free hand was idly playing with her toes while he read. Luna was sprawled on the floor next to the couch, contentedly snoring away.

It was a comfortable and domestic routine that they'd fallen into these last few days. They made love every night—Trystan had thankfully found a box of condoms in one of the rooms in the Hollingsworths' private section—they made breakfast together in the mornings and walked Luna after the meal, exploring their beautiful surroundings. It hadn't rained since the night she'd fled into the storm, and every day—while still cold, and often blustery—revealed more and more of the beauty and appeal of this place.

After their walk they usually retreated to the solarium where she would write and he would read. They often sat close to each other, petting, touching, stroking... as if it was unbearable to be apart and without physical contact for too long.

Trystan's phone rang. Sadly they'd never found Iris's, even though they looked for it every day on their walks. The sound of the ringing phone was so rare—he usually only received texts or emails—and so intrusive that Iris's head shot up in surprise.

Trystan set the book face down on his lap and picked his device up from the side table. He stared at the screen then his face lit up with a grin as he swiped to answer.

"Dazza, mate! How the fuck have you been?"

"Tryst, nice to see you're still alive, you wanker." The voice coming from the speaker had a broad Australian accent. "I thought we'd lost you to the wilds of South Africa. I heard the weather has been fucking dire in your part of the world."

"Yeah, we've had some major storms, been cut off, spotty Wi-Fi, y'know the deal." Interestingly, Trystan's accent thickened while he spoke to his friend. He looked up from the screen and noticed Iris's attentive expression and his grin widened. "Hey, Daz, you wanna meet my girl?"

Iris's eyes widened and she frantically shook her head and mouthed *no*. She was wearing one of his hoodies, which was miles too big for her, and her hair was a mess as usual. She self-consciously patted at her curls and shook her head again, more adamantly this time.

"Girl? What fucking girl, Tryst? You went up there alone and you've been cut off. Have you lost your marbles out there in the isolated wild, mate?" There was genuine concern in the man's voice.

"Iris, say hi to Dazza," Trystan said, his grin huge and beautiful, and Iris narrowed her eyes at him, promising him swift retribution, before plastering a smile onto her own lips just moments before he swung the phone around to face her. She stared into the startled face of an attractive brown haired man about Trystan's age, his jaw covered in light brown scruff, his blue eyes wide in surprise.

"Oh *hey*, so you're an actual woman."

Iris burst into laughter at the mundane observation.

"Hi, yes, my name's Iris. I'm happy to meet you."

"Yeah, I'm Darryl... how the fuck are you there? When I spoke to that wanker last he was all alone, with a storm bearing down on him."

"I showed up in the middle of that storm. I've been stuck here with his grumpy arse since then."

"Hey," Trystan exclaimed in mock outrage, and she threw him a happy smile.

"But how? Why?" Darryl looked confused and justifiably suspicious. Iris couldn't blame him. If her emotionally fragile, vulnerable—not to mention *world* famous—friend suddenly introduced her to an utter stranger who seemed to have appeared out of thin air under questionable circumstances, she'd be wary as well.

"I'll let Trystan explain," she said softly. "I really am happy to meet you. Trystan talks about you a lot. And I have to confess, I kind of harbor a secret love for *Night of the Killer Wētās*."

He still looked wary but said, "Aah, so you're one of that lot."

She laughed at his disgruntled response and handed the phone back to Trystan. She closed her laptop, swung her legs from Trystan's lap, and got up. He caught her hand as she passed him and brought it to his lips to plant a tender kiss on her knuckles.

She reciprocated by ruffling his hair affectionately and leaving the room.

But not before she heard, "What the fuck, Trystan? Who is she? You can't simply let—"

She winced and shut the door behind her, knowing her presence here would take a lot of explaining from both Trystan *and* Hunter Quinn. And even then, Darryl Constanza would probably still doubt that she and Trystan shared anything real.

Iris sighed as she put her laptop on the kitchen table and stared out at the immense yellowwood tree in the backyard. Not that she could blame the man for his suspicion and doubt, when Iris herself harbored similar doubts about this thing between her and Trystan.

She found herself falling deeper and deeper for him every day, but how could it possibly be real? She hesitated to call it love. Just days ago, he'd been imprisoning her in her room. Now she was entertaining notions of love. It was laughable, it was incongruous... but oh *God*, it felt so real.

They were in each other's company twenty-four hours a day. And such propinquity could well be responsible for amplifying every emotion. It was hard to trust your feelings in a situation like this.

And yet when she looked at him, Iris wanted to believe that what they had could work, that what they had could survive the skepticism of family and friends. And worse still, the close scrutiny of the public and press. Iris didn't think she could handle the publicity of being seen on Trystan Abbott's arm. She was an innately private person, and she didn't respond well to being the center of attention.

But that was part and parcel of who and what he was.

Trystan's strong arms wrapped around her waist and his warm, hard body slotted against her back. She hadn't heard him come in, but she welcomed his embrace, leaning back against him while he bent down to notch his jaw in the nook between her shoulder and neck.

"I'm sorry about that. Quinny and Dazza have been protective since the accident."

She smiled and turned her head to plant a kiss on his stubbled cheek. He'd stuck to being clean-shaven, and part of Iris still missed the wild man who had met her at the door that first night.

"I don't blame him. He doesn't know me. I'm just a random stranger you're suddenly introducing as *your* girl. If you were my friend, I'd find that totally sus too. Besides, you're *you* and I'm me. It would be hard for anyone to reconcile the idea of the two of us together."

He made an impatient sound at the back of his throat and turned her around to face him. His arms remained loosely wrapped around her waist.

"The fuck does that mean?" he demanded to know once he was able to glower down into her eyes.

"Trystan, your friend's reaction is just a sample of how it would be in the real world. We don't make sense together."

"We make sense to *me*," he said vehemently. "You make me happy, Iris."

"Yes, I make you happy *here*. Now. In this place. Out there,

I feel like I'd hold you back. I don't want your life, Trystan. I don't want the limelight, the glamor, the premiere parties, the press, the invasive questions about myself, my family, and friends. I can't do that. Not even for you."

"Iris, I'm falling for you. No, that's not true. I've already fallen for you. *Hard.* I don't want to consider a life without you. I refuse to."

"How can you say that? You barely know me. You don't know my family, my friends. You don't know if I like sushi."

His lips quirked at the last one.

"What? Why sushi?" he asked, momentarily diverted. And she shrugged irritably.

"It feels like the type of thing that could make or break a couple. You have two types of people, those who love sushi and those who don't. There's no in between."

He laughed and the sound rang with pleasure.

"You're full of enchanting surprises, sweet, I can't remember the last time I laughed as much as when I'm with you. And you wonder why I love you?"

She went silent at his words, and his eyes darkened at the question he saw in hers.

"What did you think I *meant* when I said I've fallen for you, Iris? I'm in love with you."

She stared up at him, wanting to believe, not knowing how it could possibly be real. "You can't be, it's too fast."

"It's been ten days. My parents fell in love after two dates, they were married a month after their first meeting. Nobody thought it would last. They celebrated their thirty-fourth wedding anniversary this year. They've had three kids and are sickeningly happy together."

"See? I didn't know that about you, about your family. There's so much we don't know about each other."

"Well, you know now because I told you. These are things we'll learn as we go along. I just want you to give us a fair shot, Iris. Don't give up because you think the obstacles are insurmountable. They're there to be overcome and we can do that together."

"You're a romantic, Trystan Abbott. Who knew?" she said, her words laced with affection. "Let's not talk about this now, okay? Let's just enjoy each other and our time together."

He dropped his forehead on hers, his warm breath washing over her lips.

"We'll have to talk about it sometime, sweet, but I'm happy to put the conversation on hold for a while." He hooked his hands beneath her armpits and lifted her onto the counter so they were, happily, at the same eye level. "Now, how about you tell me more about this sushi theory of yours?"

"Sam says they've started working on the road and bridge," Trystan told Iris a couple of days later over breakfast. She'd been reading an email from her parents filled with news of work, Mum's arthritis, and Robbie's crush on one of the new waitstaff her dad had hired.

"What?" she asked, still focused on the email.

"Looks like the road and bridge will be fixed soon," he repeated, and her stomach dropped as the specter of what she now thought of as The Real World loomed ever closer.

"Oh."

"I was wondering," he began, sounding tentative, which was unusual for him.

When he didn't continue, she bumped his shin with her toe, "What, Trystan? Spit it out."

"I was wondering if you'd let me read what you've been working on," he muttered, and her lips quirked at the almost shy request.

"Why?"

"Because you look so engrossed when you're busy with it, and so excited at times. I don't know if you realize how often you smile when you're writing. And it's a part of you I want to know more about."

She chewed at the inside of her lip as she considered it.

"I mean, it's rough. And incomplete... and it needs editing."

"I'll bear all of that in mind."

She swallowed and stared into those earnest eyes. And then she sighed.

"Do you have an e-reader?" She'd only ever seen him read physical books borrowed from the Hollingsworths' extensive collection.

"I do."

"I'll email it to you and you can send it to your e-reader." His lips stretched into a broad grin.

"I can't wait to read it."

Chapter Fifteen

Trystan lay horizontally across the bed, his head resting on Iris's stomach while he held his e-reader aloft, reading her manuscript.

She was stroking her fingers through his hair, trying not to freak out too much at the thought of him reading her silly story. It was all well and good when she was writing it just for her own amusement, but having someone whose opinion she actually valued read it was a little terrifying.

He made a sound in the back of his throat and her hand paused.

"What?" she asked.

"Huh?"

"You grunted, why?"

"Iris, kindly shut the fuck up, will you? I'm trying to read here."

She muttered beneath her breath and went back to sifting

her fingers through his silky hair, tensing every time he made any kind of sound. He appeared wholly absorbed and soon—despite her tension—Iris got bored, and her mind drifted. Before long, she was fast asleep.

The familiar weight of his body settling over hers, and the soft press of his lips on her cheek woke her.

"Whazzappening?" she mumbled, and Trystan's mouth moved to her neck to drop another kiss against the sensitive flesh there. He was familiar with all of her erogenous zones by now and knew exactly how to take her from quietly and pleasantly aroused, to wild and screaming in seconds. Fortunately, he appeared focused on soft and tender this time, pressing gentle open-mouthed kisses up her neck toward the spot beneath her ear that always made her moan.

"Finished reading," he whispered, nipping her earlobe and she snapped out of the sexual haze in an instant, slamming her palms against his chest to push his heavy, uncooperative body away from hers.

"You did?" He groaned when she wriggled her way out from under him, and he rolled onto his back and covered his eyes with one brawny forearm. "Well? What did you think?"

His sensual lips curled up at the corners.

"I think that I'm in love with a genius." He shifted his arm until it was curled around the top of his head and stared at her in awe and admiration.

"Shut up," she laughed, shoving at his shoulder playfully. She was becoming more and more comfortable with his freely offered declarations of love and was reacting to the *genius* part of his statement.

"It's true, you're brilliant. And I'm not sure why you're so goddamned insecure about your talent. You've been hiding your light under a bushel, sweetheart. Why are you editing when you should be writing?"

"It's a big leap, putting my work out there. You're right, I should have more of an online presence. I should belong to writing groups, and be on forums and just be trying harder, but it's so much easier to write for my own pleasure. And after so many years of being bullied and ridiculed I worry that I have a thin skin, that I won't be able to handle the criticism."

"You're the most contrary woman I know. You came all the way out here to interview a recluse and tell *his* sad story. How is telling one of your own any different?"

"Because mine are fiction. Telling someone else's story, telling the truth... that feels easier. Safer. I wouldn't be spotlighting myself. I would be directing the attention firmly onto another person. This..." She gestured toward his e-reader on the nightstand. "It's personal. It comes from me."

"And like you, it's amazing."

"It's a frivolous, gory tale about a werewolf. It's nothing serious."

"Don't get me wrong, Iris . . . It does need work. It's rough, a little clunky in places. Your protagonist is mopey as fuck, but God, it's compelling. And it's different. Werewolves have been done to death across all genres but this feels fresh. Using her newfound instincts to help with her police work, keeping her secret from her partner and her family. Then there's her pregnancy and how her lycanthropy could possibly affect her fetus. I want more."

She smiled shyly and he hooked a hand around her head to drag her down for a hard kiss.

"And there are *definitely* some familiar aspects to the story. She got lost in a storm, huh? Stalked by a large animal?"

"Nowhere near as sweet as Luna."

He dragged her onto him and she happily straddled his waist, her hands braced on his chest.

"You should be writing fiction full time, sweet. Not dallying in journalism, not editing, not waiting tables for your parents."

"I have to pay the bills somehow," she laughed.

"Hmm." The hum was noncommittal as he closed his arms around her and tugged her down to lay on his chest. She rested her cheek on a well-defined pec, listening to the comforting, steady beat of his heart. The fingers of one of his hands idly played with her curls, while the other rested on her bum, kneading the flesh there almost absently.

They stayed like that for a while. Neither of them speaking, just enjoying each other's closeness.

"When I said that I thought maybe it was time for a new line of work I was serious," Trystan said into the silence. "I don't think I can do this anymore. I don't *want* to do it anymore. Even before Trish's death I've been feeling apathetic about it. I find myself loathing it. Despising everything that goes with it. The lack of privacy, the people constantly vying for my attention, men and women throwing themselves at me. But that's not the worst of it, Iris. I used to love what I do and now I absolutely despise it. Every role I play is a variation of the same character and I'm bored and just so fucking *tired* of it. That's one of the reasons I believe in us, Iris. I could be just a regular guy, and you wouldn't have to worry about all the other shit that goes along with dating someone like the man I was before. No invasive press, or screaming fans, or long periods apart while I'm on location."

She propped her chin on the back of her hand to look into his face. He had to know that this was just a lovely dream, that he couldn't just take a step back and be forgotten. He had one of the most recognizable faces in the world and that wasn't going to change anytime soon. She didn't point that out to him and instead she watched him thoughtfully.

"What would you do?" she asked.

His shoulders shifted and he shook his head, the gesture almost helpless.

"I mean, I wouldn't have to do anything, really. I've made enough money for several lifetimes and I'll be earning a fortune off residuals for the rest of my life."

"You'd be bored out of your mind in no time," she scoffed.

"I kind of like carpentry, I could make high-end furniture."

"Like a reverse Harrison Ford," she mused. "I could see it. These gorgeous hands were practically made for artisanal work —you'd create beautiful furniture. I still don't think it's quite you though."

"What do *you* think I should do?"

She smiled and kissed his jaw, her mouth landing on his scar. She liked kissing him there—it made her feel like she was healing it a little more with every affectionate peck. It was stupidly whimsical, but she was prone to occasional—okay, more like frequent—flights of fantasy.

"I need to give it a little more consideration, but for now I think you should help me fix dinner after which, we should cuddle up in the cinema room and watch a movie. My choice."

He laughed and palmed her face to give her a long, sweet kiss before rolling her off him and swinging his legs over the side of the bed.

"Maybe I should be a chef," he suggested, smothering a yawn.

"You're a good cook, but you don't have enough imagination in the kitchen, I'm afraid," she told him, her voice filled with feigned regret, and she giggled when he swatted her arse on their way out of the room.

"Christ Almighty," Trystan groaned when Iris gleefully pushed the start button on her chosen movie. "Where the fuck did you dig this old thing out from?"

"I rented it off one of the streaming services," she said as she crept under his arm, nestling her head in the crook between his shoulder and armpit, huddling beneath the fleecy blanket as she settled in to watch the movie.

"Fuck, Iris, why would you want to torture me like this?"

"Ssh," she hissed as the title shimmered onto the screen in a drippy, creepy red font: *Night of The Killer Wētās.* "It's starting." He swore beneath his breath and dug a fistful of popcorn out of their large shared carton.

She squealed in delight when a *painfully* young Trystan Abbott appeared on the screen in his debut role. He'd been just twenty-one at the time of filming, not yet as big and muscular as he was now. He'd been a tall, skinny, attractive young man, with striking eyes and moody dark good looks. There were hints of the beauty to come, glimpses of his talent in the earnest delivery of every terrible line, and it was clear that he—and every other cast member—were having the time of their lives.

Trystan hooted beside her when Hunter Quinn—the boom operator—appeared in shot, gave the camera a deer-in-the-headlights look and awkwardly edged his way back out of sight. And laughed uproariously when his friend Darryl—who'd cast himself as the hero's self-sacrificing best friend—died dramatically after having his face gorily chewed off by a gigantic, obviously fake wētā.

The production values were appalling, the special effects horrendous, the acting mostly subpar, but some of the writing was brilliant. Trystan's talent shone through though, as did Darryl Constanza's directing skills. There was a reason this train smash of a movie was a cult classic. And it lay in the occasional witty one-liner, the obvious innate acting ability of a future leading man, and the hilarious on-and off-screen gaffes of the inexperienced cast and crew. It was endearing, and it was entertaining from beginning to end.

When the end credits rolled, Trystan remained silent and Iris, who was idly stroking his arm, murmured, "*That* is what you should be doing, Trystan. What you love. I don't mean the *Cryo Cops* and the super-hero big-budget stuff, I mean passion projects alongside people you enjoy working with. As you so smugly boasted earlier, you have enough wealth for several lifetimes. You don't need the money, so why not work on movies you'd enjoy doing? Quirky, off-the-wall arthouse ventures that showcase your talent more than they do your outstanding body."

"How do you see me so clearly?" he asked, his voice wobbling. "It's bothered me. So much. Being typecast, always playing the action hero, flexing abs and arse, spouting catchy one-liners. Don't get me wrong, I've had fun... but the last few. I've been so bored. I've hated it. And I forgot how rewarding I once found this work. But the roles I truly enjoyed, the dramatic roles, with meat to them have all been box office failures, with critics mocking my efforts and urging me to stay in my *wheel-house*. It made me doubt myself. I felt ridiculous, started thinking that all I was capable of doing were movies like *Cryo Cop* and *Max Velocity*. I've always wanted to test my acting chops, try comedy, do more drama. But I've been shoved into this box and I feel trapped."

"You need to rediscover the love you once had for your craft. Maybe re-hire your idiot manager so that he can help you find these roles you love. He knows you better than most people. He'd know what to look for."

Trystan was staring at her with something like reverence in his eyes. He blinked rapidly for a few moments before speaking, his voice hoarse with emotion, "I'm beginning to think my manager's not quite an idiot. Because he certainly knew what the fuck he was doing when he sent you to me, Iris."

"Do *not* remind me of what that duplicitous bastard did, Trystan, or I'll want to punch his pretty face all over again."

"You think he's pretty?" Trystan asked with a glower, looking seriously aggravated at the notion that she might find one of his best friends attractive.

"Don't worry, darling, he's not as cute as you."

He looked momentarily appeased before his brow lowered again. "What about Dazza?"

"He's too surfer boy-ish for me," she placated. "I like my men dark and glowery, and moody as fuck."

"And don't you forget it," he warned in a dark, moody voice and she laughed happily.

"So are you still going to throw in the towel on your acting?" she asked, the laughter fading from her eyes, hoping he would consider her words.

"I've been unhappy for so long," he admitted, lifting her hand to toy with her fingers, avoiding her eyes as he focused on his task. "It's been hard to remember what I loved about my work. Tonight has helped. It'll be a long road, and I'll need to speak with Quinny and my PR manager, Bee, to see how feasible restructuring my career will be. I'm committed to four more projects—two sequels, a super hero thing and heist flick—I can't get out of those. But you're right, I need a change. A palate cleanser. I'll take on fewer projects and only ones that I truly love. I've always wanted to try my hand at directing as well, but I had that dream tucked so far out of sight I'd almost forgotten it existed. It's something to consider." She could hear the rising excitement brewing beneath the even—almost distant and disinterested—tone of his voice. He was desperately trying to keep his cool, but she could tell, he wanted this, he was enthused about it and couldn't wait to mull it over with Hunter Quinn.

He lifted the hand he'd been stroking to his lips and planted a soft kiss on her palm, finally meeting her eyes and revealing the boyish enthusiasm in his gleaming gray gaze.

"Thank you... it's not always easy to see the simplest of solutions right in front of your nose. I needed this. I'm so fucking excited to try it, to do only what I want to and to hell with what the public and the critics think."

"I'm very happy to have helped. And I can't even begin to tell you how hot I'm finding this steely resolve of yours," she teased, fanning herself. "Now are you going to take me to bed, mister? Or am I going to have to seduce you on this uncomfortable love seat?"

He growled and picked her up caveman style. She squealed, laughing uncontrollably all the way back to the bedroom.

"CAN I BORROW YOUR PHONE?" Iris asked Trystan two days later after they'd returned from their post-breakfast walk. It was a glorious day, with blue skies and moderate temperatures ranging in the mid-teens. They were back in the kitchen now, facing each other across the island. "I want to call my parents. I haven't spoken to them in a week and I think they need to hear my voice. They like to pretend they're cool, but I know they've been concerned about me. More so since I lost my phone. They probably think I've been kidnapped or something, despite my constant messages and emails. I think it would be good for them to see that I'm okay."

"You don't have to explain, Iris," he said with a chuckle, handing his device over. "Of course you can call them. I'm sorry; I should have offered sooner. If you want to catch up with your friend, Evan, afterward, you can call her too."

Iris had told Trystan she was concerned about Evan's

silence. Her friend had only responded to one of her emails, and it had been a curt two-line message.

"I'll give you some privacy," he said, turning to go and Iris hesitated. She'd spoken to both of his best friends, and had self-consciously participated in a group call with his parents and older brother, Dan, the night before. While *her* parents and best friend still had no clue why she was here and who she was with.

"No, stay. I think it's time I tell my parents why I'm here, but be warned, they won't be cool about it."

"I don't blame them. Their daughter has been trapped and alone with a strange man. It would make any parent uncomfortable."

She stared at him for a beat and then burst into laughter.

"Oh my God, it's so cute that you're actually serious right now," she said, clutching her sides after nearly busting a gut laughing. He looked confused and that set her off again.

"Trystan, sweetheart." God, he really was adorable at times. His eyes sparked in pleasure at the endearment, and she vowed to call him that more often. "When I say my parents aren't going to be cool about it, I mean they're going to lose their collective shit when they realize that I'm with *you*. Dad's a massive fan, he's watched every one of your movies. And mum—" she grimaced. "I think she has a wee crush on you, actually. Which could get awkward."

"Is she as hot as you?" Trystan asked with a wicked grin and Iris gasped in horror.

"Don't you even dare... Just shut *up* about my mum's potential hotness! *Ew!*"

He laughed. "I'll be on my best behavior, I swear. I'm fucking great with parents."

"Fine, but stay out of sight until I've explained the situation to them." She sat down at the banquette and he squeezed in next to her. He unlocked his phone and she quickly dialed her mother's number before she could change her mind.

"How do you know the number? I haven't got a single number memorized."

"Mum made me recite it over and over again when I was a kid. It hasn't changed since. She was paranoid about—" The phone was answered abruptly and her mother's ear and graying brown hair appeared on-screen.

"Hello? Hello? Who's this?"

"Mum? *Mum*, it's me! Move the phone away from your ear, for God's sake, Mum. It's a video call."

"Hello? *Iris*? Is that you? Jason, it's Iris! Whose number is this? Are you okay?"

Iris cast her eyes heavenward and prayed for strength before trying again.

"Mum, it's a video call, move the phone away from your ear."

She heard Trystan smother a chuckle and glared at him.

Her mother finally moved the phone but the image was a bit blurry thanks to her having rubbed her ear against the camera lens.

"Oh, there you are. You look warm and healthy. We've been so worried about you... *Jason*, Iris is on the phone."

"Is that Iris?" her father called, before he appeared on screen beside her mother. Iris smiled at the sight of their endearing faces. Her mother so pretty, with her graying brunette hair and pale brown skin, her father so dapper in his bow tie, his blond head balding, his eyes a faded gray. She'd missed them so much.

"Hello, my darling," her father said, his voice warm with love and affection. "We've missed you. When will you finish up this top-secret job and come home?"

"About that... I need to explain about the job," Iris said, happy he'd given her the opening. "I came here to interview Trystan Abbott."

"What?" Her father looked blank and her mother's jaw literally dropped.

"Who?" her mother asked in a faint voice.

"Uhm, Trystan Abbott, but the interview was cancelled. I'm sorry I didn't tell you sooner. It just didn't feel right to divulge the information when I knew the interview wasn't happening any longer and the situation was a little volatile."

"Volatile? What does that mean?" Her father sounded concerned. "Are you in danger?"

"God, no, Dad, of course not. I just meant that—"

"If I may," Trystan murmured, and she cast a helpless look his way and sighed before nodding. He scooched over into view and her mother actually yelped.

"Oh, sweet Jesus, he's sitting right there," she muttered, then actually crossed herself as if he were Satan himself. Trystan's lips twitched.

"Hello Mr. and Mrs. Hughes. I'm afraid when Iris says the situation was volatile, she means that I was behaving like a—and please do excuse my language—a total dick toward her. I didn't want to be interviewed and wasn't very pleasant about it, I'm afraid."

Her parents still looked a little shell-shocked to see him, but her father rallied faster than her mother.

"Have you been treating my daughter poorly, Mr. Abbott?" His voice was thick with displeasure, and it was a little disconcerting to see her usually mild-mannered father narrow his eyes intimidatingly at a man she knew he admired.

"Call me Trystan, please, and in answer to your question, I wasn't very kind to her at first. But you know Iris, it's impossible to continue being an asshole around her. And let me tell you, I tried my damnedest. I wanted to meet you both so that I could inform you that your daughter has changed my life. And to thank you in person for raising such an amazing woman."

Iris found it hard to swallow past the lump in her throat as she stared at this man who had *undoubtedly* changed her life as well. She would never be the same after this. And she damned sure knew that she didn't want to face the rest of her life without him.

Her parents looked confused, even alarmed, and Iris leaped in to do some damage control.

"Long story short, my reason for being here no longer exists, but until they fix the roads I can't leave. Trystan has been kind enough to host me, despite my showing up pretty much unannounced on his doorstep."

"Best thing that ever happened to me," Trystan inserted happily and Iris facepalmed before facing her parents again with a determined smile.

"So, as you can see, I'm fine. Nothing at all for you to worry about and hopefully I'll be home soon. Now what's been happening with Robbie? And how's business? Any interesting events coming up?"

"You want us to talk about that with *Trystan Abbott* sitting there?" her mother asked in horror.

"Just pretend he's not here," Iris waved her concern off with a breezy hand gesture.

"But he's *right* there," her mother pointed out unnecessarily.

Trystan snorted again, and when Iris slanted him a glance he was suspiciously straight-faced.

Her parents somewhat hesitantly began to tell her about Robbie's crush, about a few new interesting upcoming events. The geyser at home had burst. Mrs. Desmond next door had fallen and broken her hip.

They soon grew comfortable with Trystan's quiet presence, and conversation flowed freely between Iris and her parents.

Until...

"So, Mr. Abbott, why won't you let my daughter interview you?" Rosa Hughes abruptly shifted topic, and both Trystan and Iris froze. "She's ever so good at what she does. She once interviewed Mrs. O'Malley down the road for her primary school newspaper. And everybody said she was the cutest little reporter, with her earnest questions about Mrs. O'Malley's missing rabbit. The rabbit was found not two days after the story ran."

"*Mum*, please ..." Iris groaned, writhing in embarrassment. Her mother always whipped out the rabbit story when she spoke about Iris's journalism career. That, to the older woman, was the pinnacle of Iris's achievements. Then again, Iris hadn't given them much else to brag about after that when it came to her chosen career.

"It's not about Iris, Mrs. Hughes. I agree that your daughter is extremely talented. It's about me. I'm not in the best place right now. I have a lot of decisions to make about my future and I'd rather not talk to any reporters until after I've made them."

Her mother's face contorted in sympathy, and she nodded. Iris tensed, knowing what would come next.

"Is it because of that accident? I'm so sorry that happened to you."

To his credit, Trystan merely nodded curtly in response to her words.

"Thank you, and yes, it's partly about that and partly because I have to make changes. I have to create a safe space in my life for someone vitally important to me," Iris's head swung sharply toward him, but he kept his gaze fixed on the screen.

"I wish you luck with that. It was ever so nice meeting you. Jason would agree, but I think he's a little starstruck right now. He's never this quiet."

"I'm quiet because I can't get a word in edgewise, woman," her father grumbled, and Trystan chuckled. "Now if you're done embarrassing our daughter, I have something to say to Mr. Abbott."

"Of course," Trystan nodded with a smile, which her father didn't return.

"If you break my little girl's heart, young man, I'll break your legs. And don't think I can't, I know three different types of martial arts."

"*Dad...*"

"Jason, what—"

Trystan ignored the shocked exclamations from both women and nodded solemnly at the thin, balding fifty-something-year-old man glaring daggers at him through the screen.

"If she'd give me her heart, sir, it would be my greatest treasure and I would keep it safe for the rest of my life. But until the day she entrusts it to me, it's not mine to break."

Her father seemed satisfied with that answer, and once again Iris felt herself on the verge of tears at Trystan's words.

Her parents rang off shortly after that. Her mother—who appeared deep in thought—said goodbye with an absent *I love you.*

After the called ended, Iris and Trystan sat side by side in silence. She fidgeted with his phone, turning it over and over again in her hands. She wasn't sure what to say to him and, to his credit, he allowed her the space to process.

"I'll leave you to speak to your friend in privacy," he said after a long while and she nodded in gratitude, not sure she could go through the same thing with Evan.

Chapter Sixteen

"You're where? With whom?"

"I can't tell you where exactly, Ev, but my interview was supposed to be with Trystan Abbott."

"Trystan Abbott? *The* Trystan Abbott? Seriously? Oh my God, you lucky bitch! How the hell did *you* manage that? I would give my eye teeth and my left tit to land a plum assignment like that. Tell me everything . . . Is he really that fucking hot in real life? Who are you selling the story to? I have first dibs, right? Jesus, my boss is going to wee herself with envy, and I'll finally get the promotion I deserve. Maybe I'll even get *her* job!"

"I'm not doing the story." Iris was frowning. Evan's instantly avaricious response bothered her.

"What? Why not?"

"He didn't consent to the interview. His agent was mistaken." She chose her words carefully, a little wary after the other woman's initial giddy reaction. It had been all about *Evan* and how this interview would impact *her* career.

What the hell?

It reminded Iris of how her father had often used her achievements to prop himself up. In fact, Evan was more like Stanford Carter than Iris could ever be. She made no secret of the fact that she admired Iris's father greatly. Evan had always spoken about how lucky Iris had been to have a mentor like Stanford Carter, and Iris had never corrected her, choosing to let the other woman believe that her father had cared enough to guide Iris in some way. When it couldn't be further from the truth.

Now, when she reflected on her years of friendship with Evan, she comprehended how often the other woman had spoken of Stanford Carter, how she'd always asked questions about him, researched his career, and had even made a scrapbook with clippings of all his stories to *share* with Iris. Not give, merely share.

Now, Iris wondered if Evan had befriended her because of who Iris's father had been. If the other woman had believed that it would help her get ahead somehow.

"But you've been there with him, alone, for two weeks... You have a story, Iris. Even without the interview."

"No. I don't. I refuse to write about him without his explicit consent."

"Oh my God, you're so soft. The fucking opportunity of a lifetime and you're wasting it. You don't deserve this chance; you don't have a clue what to do with it. Do you want to be a journalist or not? Because let me tell you, this is getting fucking embarrassing. Your dad is probably rolling over in his grave right now at what a wimp his daughter is."

Iris blinked at her friend's face in horror—Evan's expression had twisted in disgust and contempt and Iris barely recognized her.

"Uhm, Evan, I have to go. The connection is bad and—"

"Wait, so you're calling me from *his* number, right?" Iris's stomach plummeted at the question. How could she have been so stupid? "If you won't do the interview, do you think he'd mind if I WhatsApped him? Asked him a few questions? See if he'd be open to having a chat with me?

"Please don't do that," Iris whispered in horror.

"Iris, I'm more experienced than you. Maybe he's reluctant to be interviewed by a complete novice, but I have some credentials at least. I'll even share the byline with you."

Iris hated that it had taken her this long to recognize that the person she'd considered her best friend was just another bully, and had *always* been a bully. Only she'd been slyer about it, with her subtle little put-downs, her gentle concern about how Iris just wasn't tough enough for the industry. Everything she'd ever said and done had been to make herself look and feel more important by making Iris feel small.

Now, as Evan continued to plot and plan and ponder ways to snatch Iris's so-called big fish right out from under her nose, her callous disregard of Trystan's wishes infuriated Iris and stirred up her protective instinct. Evan was never getting her greedy hooks into Trystan. Not if Iris had anything to do with it.

"Evan, back the fuck off!" Iris snapped, shutting the other woman up, and Evan's mouth dropped open. "As soon as I hang up this phone, I'll be blocking your number. There will be no contacting him with unsolicited requests for interviews. *Ever.* Am I making myself clear."

"Jesus, when the fuck did you get so selfish, Iris? You're the one who doesn't want the interview, why not give it to someone who does?"

"Goodbye, Evan," Iris disconnected the call without another word and instantly blocked and deleted the woman's number from Trystan's phone. She then had a moment's panic that Evan could somehow track down the phone's GPS location and went into his location services, which she discovered were already switched off.

She heaved a sigh of relief and then shuddered in reaction. The thought of the ugliness of the real world intruding here, in this safe haven Trystan had found for himself, was disturbing and she hated that she'd been the one to nearly ruin it for him.

Of course, there was no guarantee that Evan wouldn't just try to contact him from a different number. Nausea surged in the pit of her stomach and Iris actually retched at the thought, and her hand flew to her mouth as she fought back the urge to vomit.

Trystan sauntered back into the kitchen and when he saw her sitting there, pale and trembling, rushed toward her.

"What's wrong? Iris?" She stared at him, panic and sorrow rendering her temporarily mute. Her silence alarmed Trystan. "C'mon, sweetness, talk to me. Tell me what happened."

"I th-think I messed up," she whispered. "Evan, she..." she tried to explain but everything came out in an incoherent, jumbled mess. He seemed to get the gist of it though and made soothing noises while she spoke.

"It's okay, baby, my number isn't traceable, and no unsolicited messages from strange numbers will ever make it past the firewall. Don't worry about it. I'm so sorry about your friend, though."

"Time to make better friends, I guess," she whispered shakily, trying to hide her grief from him. But he knew her well enough by now to see straight through her facade, and he tugged her to her feet to enfold her in a hug.

"So, it's official," Trystan told her the following morning at breakfast, after checking his messages. "The road and bridge will be fully repaired by tomorrow morning. They estimate that it'll be done by about nine a.m."

Iris didn't know how to react to that. What was supposed to happen now?

"I should probably contact the rental company about getting a new car," she finally said.

Her proclamation was met with utter silence and she lifted her head to find him staring mutely at her, his eyes blazing with emotion.

"Trystan, don't look at me like that," she admonished. "I have to go home at some point. I can't stay here forever."

"You don't *have* to do anything, Iris. Of course you can stay here, with me... for as long as you fucking want."

"*You* have to go home at some point too. And what then? Do I just travel from place to place with you like some—I don't know—some good luck talisman?"

"I don't see why not." He tried to play it off as a joke, but it fell flat.

"Trystan, I am *not*—nor will I ever be—an extension of you! I'm my own person, you don't get to cart me around like a personal possession."

"Fuck, Iris, I don't want that. I want you to live with me, *be* with me. Write, edit, do whatever you want, but do it with *me* by your side. As my partner, my lover... even my *wife*. I'll take you any way I can get you because I don't want to lose you."

"That wouldn't work," she said and he swore, the expletive loud and violent, startling Luna into lifting her head to stare at him quizzically.

"How do you *know* it won't work when you won't even give us a chance? You're running scared about us. You're a lot of things, Iris Hughes, but you're not a coward... so don't chicken out over this."

"Trystan, what I meant by that is *your* vision of what a life together would be for us is flawed, and it's doomed to fail—" She tried to reason with him, but he interrupted her.

"No, we can make it work. Iris and Trystan's world, the two of us and no one else. I told you—I don't have to go back to my old life. I want a new one with you. But I need you to be brave, Iris. For us. I need you to be that woman who faced a wolf and a beast in the same night and survived. No, *thrived*. I can't be the only one willing to fight for what we have and for what we could build."

She swallowed down a sob but couldn't prevent the tear from slipping down her cheek. His tormented gaze tracked its path and he reached out to catch it on his thumb.

"I love you, Iris," he whispered, his voice taut with pain. "And I want you to stay with me."

Iris's eyes memorized each beautiful feature individually, lovingly brushing over the hills and valleys of that gorgeous face. Her gaze snagged on the scar. This man. This beautiful, terrified man, who was still here hiding from his ghosts, afraid to face his future. He wasn't even aware of what he was asking of her, what he was asking of himself, and if they were ever going to stand a chance Iris had to make him understand.

"I love *you*, Trystan, and I want you to come away with me."

His breath stuttered in his lungs and halted completely. His hand crept up to the center of his chest and absently rubbed at the spot just above his heart.

"You're hiding, Trystan," she whispered. "You're still hiding from the ghost of who you were. And you're asking me to hide with you. I *do* want to be with you, but I refuse to hide here—or anywhere else—with you. If you want a life with me then you've got to be prepared to *live* it with me. You've got to forgive yourself for Trish Nesbitt. You have to fix your life and your career. And I don't mean by becoming a carpenter, or whatever the hell else. That's not who you are. Telling *me* to be brave, while you're using me as an excuse to live a life of obscurity because *you're* afraid to face your demons, is just the height of hypocrisy.

"You told my parents you have to find a way to create a safe space in your life for me. But you can't do that while you're hiding in places like this. It's amazing here, it's beautiful, private, and it feels like we're the only two people left on the face of the earth, but it's not home. And if we're going to be together, we need to figure out where home will be. Because it's *not* here, or any place similar to here. For us to truly know if we'll work, we can't be the only people on earth. We need to be out there, in the real world. Where everybody thinks they own a part of you.

"It'll test us, but it'll also make us stronger and if we survive all the tough times ahead, we'll know that we're made for each other. I *do* want to fight for us. But the fight is out there. Not here."

She pushed herself up from the table and gave him a bittersweet smile.

"So no, I won't stay with you, Trystan. But I do hope you'll come with me."

She didn't give him a chance to reply, knowing he would need time to ruminate over her words, and she turned on her heel to walk out of the room.

Iris was pretty busy for the rest of the day. She booked a flight home in two days' time and made a reservation at a hotel in George, close to the airport, for the next night. She also emailed the rental company about a new car and arranged for a taxi to pick her up and take her to the rental shop in town. She sent her parents and flatmates the news that she'd be home soon. She didn't see Trystan at all. She'd missed the walk with him and Luna and felt a pang of loss at the thought of this possibly having been her last opportunity to walk with them. She blinked back tears at the thought, and refocused on packing her bags. She had so much crap scattered all over the house.

She and Trystan had been sharing a room since the first night they'd made love and that's where most of her stuff was. After she packed her bags, she moved them to the guest room that she hadn't occupied in nearly ten days. Something told her she'd be sleeping there tonight.

Trystan remained elusive, but Luna started following her around, as if sensing that she was going somewhere. In the end, Iris simply curled up on the sofa in the solarium while Luna rested her heavy head on Iris's lap.

She stroked the dog's big, shaggy head, crying silently as she did so.

"I'm going to miss you so much, girl. You've been the best, goodest girl. Take care of your dad for me when I'm gone, okay? Keep him out of the sads. That's your job, okay?"

She wrapped her arms around the dog's neck and hugged her close, taking comfort in her solid strength and lovely doggy smell.

Eventually Iris got hungry and padded toward the kitchen, hoping to find him there, ready for dinner. But the kitchen was empty and cold. Iris made herself a quick sandwich and ate it standing at the counter.

It was nearly nine when she walked toward his bedroom door. It was closed and there was no light shining from beneath it. Iris exhaled on a shuddering sigh and with slumped shoulders walked toward her own room.

That night was the first in a long time that she spent alone, and she wept into her pillow before finally falling asleep.

"GOOD MORNING," Trystan greeted the following day when Iris walked into the kitchen at nine a.m. Her taxi would be there in an hour, and she had time for a quick bite and one last stroll to the lake before she had to leave.

"Morning," she muttered, avoiding his eyes. Hers were swollen from the tears she'd shed last night, and she'd rather he not see that.

"Iris." His tone was admonishing, and she knew it was because she refused to look at him, but she didn't give a damn. He'd put her through hell last night with his cold-shoulder treatment just because she'd had the gall to lay out her own terms for their relationship, and now he wanted to play nice again?

She shoved a couple of slices of bread in the toaster and tapped her nails impatiently against the marble countertop while she waited for it to pop. She buttered it and smeared it with strawberry jam before grabbing a mug of coffee and sitting at the island to eat, instead of at the banquette with him, as she'd done on so many other mornings.

She heard his deep sigh from behind her, but ignored him.

"You're mad at me."

"Ya think?" she muttered beneath her breath.

"I know." His deep voice came from directly behind her and she yelped in shock and nearly choked on her toast.

"God, you scared me! Was it necessary to sneak up on me?" she seethed, turning toward him to blister him with a look.

"I didn't sneak You were so focused on ignoring me, you simply didn't notice me coming up behind you."

"I have to finish my breakfast. My taxi will be here in forty minutes."

"It won't. I cancelled it," he said, and she gaped at him.

"What? How could you even do that? How did you know which taxi company I contacted."

"There's only one in town."

"But why would you... Is this your way of trying to keep me here against my will?"

"Jesus, no, not at all. I made other arrangements. A taxi wasn't needed."

"I don't need you to make my arrangements for me."

"Iris, I was making the arrangements for *us*."

"Wait. What?"

"Well, you did ask me to come away with you, didn't you? I couldn't just up and leave. I needed to arrange our flight, contact Chance to come and fetch us, make sure Luna's travel documents are still in order, pack, rehire Quinny, then set him to work getting my apartment in London livable for us. Then I also had to contact Miles about shutting down this place. Thankfully, he said to just lock up and go. His mother and stepdad live close by and will sort it out. All in all, it was fucking exhausting. I fell into bed at eight then woke up this morning only to discover that *you* didn't come to bed last night. What the fuck, Iris?"

"Wait, so you're coming with me?"

"Of course I am. Was there ever a doubt?"

"Well... yes," she said. "When you made no effort to talk to me after our initial discussion yesterday, I assumed you needed more time to think. Then when you simply disappeared for the rest of the day, I thought I had my answer."

"Woman, you threw all of this at me yesterday with very little warning. You just said you were leaving and I could either come with you or lose you. I needed a minute to process. And plan."

Iris wrinkled her nose in acknowledgment. She *had* sprung it on him, she knew that, but once she'd heard the road was fixed, she'd simply jumped into *got to get home* mode. She didn't even know why she'd reacted that way. Hearing the road was open had set off all kinds of alarm bells in her and an urgent need to leave.

"I'm sorry," she said. "It just felt like, with the road open, there was no reason for me to be here any longer. I didn't feel like I had a place—or a right to be—here. This isn't my home, Trystan. I've missed my family and my life. I wanted to get back to them and I guess, a small part of me still believed I should get out before you kicked me out."

"Oh, Iris." The disappointment she heard in his voice gutted her and she nodded.

"I know. It was an unfair, baseless assumption. And I really shouldn't have flung all those ultimatums at you. It was wrong."

His lips twitched and his eyes gentled.

"It certainly lit a fire under my arse. Here I was thinking, we'd spend a few days exploring the area, maybe staying in the next town over for a couple of nights..."

She winced. "That *does* sound lovely. But I can't afford to just lounge around here indefinitely on vacation, y'know? Maybe some other time?"

"So you're really coming with me?" she asked, her happiness and excitement giving the question a joyful cadence that she couldn't quite control.

"You actually thought I could say no to you? That I'd choose staying here, in this lonely place, without you? Iris, did you miss the part where I said I love you?"

Her lips spread into a wide smile and she launched herself into his arms.

"Oh my God, so we're really going to do this?" she said in a voice that quavered in disbelief and her hand went to her stomach as she was hit by a sudden bout of queasiness.

"Hey, don't go getting cold feet on me now," Trystan chastised, and she gulped and shook her head.

"No, I'm fine. We're doing this. We're going out there and people will know I kissed Trystan Abbott—famous movie star." He rolled his eyes and teasingly tugged at one of her curls.

"People will know I kissed Iris Hughes—talented, future bestselling author."

"It's a little intimidating," she admitted, and he looped an arm around her neck and kissed the top of her head.

"Storm in a teacup," he predicted.

"And what was that you said about a flat in London? I *have* a flat."

"Iris, sweetheart, I love you, but I'm not sharing a flat with you and your two flatmates. On this one, I'm afraid I can't compromise."

"Where's the flat?"

"Knightsbridge."

"Oh, *of course*, he has a flat in Knightsbridge," she muttered sarcastically to herself, rolling her eyes. "When did your life get so fucking surreal, Iris?"

He grinned and kissed the tip of her nose.

"Eat your toast. Chance will be here shortly. I'll bring out the bags and do last checks."

It was all happening so fast; it was hard to believe they were leaving. She truly loved it here—the place had really grown on her—and she hoped they'd be able to return sometime... preferably in summer.

She ate while he collected their bags and went down into the basement garage to fiddle around with a few things. He returned to pilfer a slice of her toast.

"There's a ton of food in the fridge," he said, between bites. "So I'll leave the electricity on. I assume Miles's family will know what to do with it."

He wandered off again, cheekily stealing her cup of coffee, on his way out of the kitchen.

Before too long, she'd finished her breakfast and cleaned the dishes, which gave her some time to wander from room to room, ostensibly to see if she'd left anything behind, but really to say goodbye.

When she came to the suite of rooms that had been her prison for those first few terrible nights she paused and sucked in a deep breath before stepping inside. She'd expected... *something*. But all she felt was mild surprise that she'd built it up to be this dreadful place, when in reality it was really just a pleasant little living area for a teen, or perhaps a housekeeper.

Iris laughed quietly underneath her breath and exited the room without a backward glance. The events that had led to that horrible night had taken place a lifetime ago. And the two people caught up in the middle of all that drama had changed because of each other, *for* each other, and they were both the better for of it.

She walked to the front of the house where Trystan stood waiting, Luna on a leash beside him. He held out his hand to her and she took it without hesitation.

"Ready?" he asked, and she smiled at him and nodded.

"As I'll ever be," she said, inhaling deeply, trying to keep her nervousness and doubts at bay. It was hard to do so as she watched the black Mercedes-Benz 4X4 with heavily tinted windows slowly make its way up the drive toward them, the first sign of The Real World they'd seen in weeks.

Trystan took a step toward the vehicle as it slid to a stop in front of them.

Both front-passenger and driver-side doors opened, and two fair-haired men stepped out.

Iris hung back, her one hand on Luna's head, as Trystan released her other.

"Sam, good to see you," he greeted warmly, shaking hands with the shorter of the two.

He had to be Sam Brand. Iris ran a speculative gaze over the man with the close-cropped medium-blond hair and piercing ice-blue eyes. He was about five-ten or -eleven—a couple of inches shorter than Trystan—with a lean, muscular build. He was pretty good-looking, in a rugged way.

The other guy was recognizable from the press he'd been getting since his first appearance as Trystan's bodyguard. Chance Griffin was huge, at least six -foot-four or -five with sandy hair, also kept military short like his boss's. He was a silent behemoth, his face unsmiling, his eyes concealed by dark glasses. She sensed him sizing her up before his head moved slightly as he checked out the rest of their surroundings. Very much On Duty... and a pit formed in Iris's stomach as she understood that this was Trystan's reality.

Hers too, now.

It was the first indication of how much her life was about to change and she was already having misgivings. That didn't bode too well for the longevity of this relationship.

She shook herself, and shifted her gaze toward Trystan and immediately felt calmer, more centered, as she was reminded of why she was doing this. What was at stake. He was laughing at something Sam had said when his gaze drifted toward her, and his expression softened.

"Sam, I'd like you to meet Iris," he said, voice warm and smile affectionate. He reached for her hand again and tugged her forward.

The other man ran an assessing, unsmiling glance over her person.

"So you're the intruder, huh?"

Iris shot Trystan an unimpressed glare.

"Is that what he called me? He knew full well who I was."

The man merely raised a brow, before spoiling the whole stern thing he had going by grinning.

"I gather all's well that ends well?" he said and Trystan threw an arm around her shoulders and tugged her to his side. She put up a token resistance but melted against him after a few seconds.

"Never been so happy to have an unannounced visitor," Trystan drawled.

"Again," Iris grumbled. "*Not* unannounced."

He lowered a kiss on top of her head.

"Just playing, sugarplum," he dropped the words in her ear, before nuzzling the sensitive skin just beneath her ear lobe. He lifted his head to address Sam again. "So'd you bring the thing?"

"Yep." Sam tugged a flat box out of his pocket and handed it to Iris. She stared at it in consternation, not taking it from him.

"What's this?" she asked even though she could see full well what it was.

"Your new phone," Trystan replied. "It's my fault you lost the old one, so please accept this one."

"But..."

"Iris."

She rolled her eyes and took the box from Sam. It was pointless arguing over such a small thing and she needed a phone anyway. She'd figure out a way to pay him back later.

"So the plane's all prepped?" Trysan asked. "As per my specifications?"

"It is."

"*The* plane?" Iris squeaked, phone instantly forgotten. "As in a specific plane?"

Well, that was unexpected.

"Hmm."

She supposed it was to be accepted that a man of his celebrity and status would travel by private jet, but it hadn't once occurred to her that it would be their mode of transportation home. Did he own it? Or was he just renting it? Regardless, the staggering display of wealth was daunting and made her uncomfortable.

Before she had a chance to mull it over, he moved his hand to the small of her back and urged her toward the car.

"Time to go, sweetheart."

Iris took one last look at the beautiful house that had sheltered them these past few weeks and took her first step into an unknown future.

Chapter Seventeen

"You okay?" Trystan asked once they were seated aboard the luxurious private jet. He had steered Iris to two comfortable side-by-side seats and was now turned toward her, both of her hands clasped in his, keeping his gaze trained on hers. Chance discreetly moved to the front of the plane—taking Luna with him—and after stowing his tog bag in a tucked-away storage compartment, moved toward the cockpit where he had a brief conversation with the pilot.

"I think so." She wasn't sure what else to say in response to his question, her eyes nervously scanning the gorgeous interior of the outrageously luxe plane. Everything was tastefully decorated in muted cream and burgundy, with burled wood finishes. It felt like she was sitting in an easy chair and it in no way resembled the discomfort of the plane seat she'd endured during her inbound journey—her first flight ever. It was a lot to take in, but she couldn't enjoy the experience when her entire being was focused on the still-open door.

Their cabin attendant was amiably chatting with a member of the ground crew, her hand on the interior handle of the door, which she was clearly ready to close once her conversation concluded.

"Iris? Hey, Iris. Eyes on me, yeah?" Trystan murmured, his index finger and thumb grasping her chin and turning her head toward him. "Do you need to take your pills?"

She nodded and fumbled through her massive bag as she hunted for the plastic tube.

"They're not in here," she whispered, hysteria and panic edging their way into her voice.

"Let me have a look," he said, his voice still low and soothing. She handed her bag to him and he rooted around for a few seconds before producing the bottle of pills.

"They were buried beneath the heaps of receipts and the half-dozen packets of travel tissues you have stowed in there," he teased when she grabbed hold of the small container gratefully. He handed her a glass bottle of water, which he'd magically produced seemingly out of thin air, and she gratefully gulped down a couple of pills.

His warm hand burrowed beneath her curls where he palmed the nape of her neck which he gently massaged.

Iris focused on her deep-breathing techniques and was vaguely aware of a female voice asking if they needed anything. Trystan's voice was curt when he responded, but Iris didn't hear what he said. She was fighting hard to keep her nausea at bay.

"What do you need to do to make this easier?"

"I just need to breathe," she told him shakily. "I'm sorry. I'll be okay. It's a little harder after everything that happened."

TRYSTAN WINCED. *Harder* after he'd exacerbated an under-control phobia by imprisoning her, she meant. He could feel the fine tremors racking through her body, and wasn't entirely sure what to do for her. He'd known this wouldn't be easy and had been dreading it, but had hoped the private jet would be an exciting enough experience to distract her from her fear.

"I'm sorry. I'll be fine," she said again, and his heart just about broke as he understood that despite her terror, she was trying to comfort him. When he didn't fucking deserve it. "I just need a minute."

She was bent nearly double, her face almost to her knees and his hand left her nape to stroke gentle circles on her narrow back.

"Take your time, baby," he murmured, leaning toward her, trying to offer her his heat and strength as a bolster. He began to regale her with facts about the Bombadier Global 7500 they were on.

It wasn't his jet. It belonged to their generous host, Miles Hollingsworth.

The man used it often for business, since he shuttled between South Africa and London regularly. The plane had just dropped off several of his executives a few days ago—for meetings—and when Miles had learned that Trystan was on his way back he'd generously offered him use of the jet.

Trystan, thinking this would be better for Iris, had happily accepted. The stranded executives would probably have to make their way back to London on a commercial airline.

Trystan regularly rented private jets, but that would have been difficult with the timeframe he'd had to work with. He'd been about to book a couple of first-class seats with his favorite airline when Miles had made the offer.

The pilot's genial voice welcomed them aboard and informed them that they would be taking off soon and that they could expect turbulence for the first hour or so of their journey before enjoying clear skies for the rest of it.

The cabin attendant, a blonde with a flirtatious smile—who'd introduced herself as Piper when they'd boarded—once again came over to ask if he needed anything before take-off. Trystan shot her an irritated look at her blatant exclusion of the clearly distressed Iris.

"Tea," he commanded shortly. "With plenty of honey. For Miss Hughes."

The smile faded from the woman's lips and a more professional, no-nonsense expression settled on her face.

"Of course. I'll be right back." She retreated to the galley, which was situated between the seating area and the lounge, bedroom and bathroom in the back.

"Is it closed?" Iris's small voice asked from the general vicinity of her knees.

"Yes." He didn't bother asking what she meant, knowing she was hyper-focused on that door. "How do I make this better, baby?"

She lifted her head cautiously. Her pretty features were strained, her eyes wild, and her lush lips were quivering.

"I'm not sure," she admitted on a whisper.

He cradled her face in both hands and did the only thing he could think of. He kissed her.

Iris moaned and leaned into the kiss, her own hands going up to cover his as she opened her mouth to his searching tongue. Trystan was more than happy to acquiesce to her every demand and he deepened the kiss, his tongue seeking refuge in her warm, inviting mouth.

They lost themselves in each other for a few long, satisfying moments and it was only when Trystan eased them both out of the embrace that he became aware of the fact that they were taking off.

Iris came to a simultaneous realization, if her quiet *oh* was anything to go by, and her bewildered gaze flew, first to the securely shut hatch, then to his eyes.

"How're you feeling?" Trystan asked and her cheeks darkened. God, she was sweet. She didn't belong in his world and he had a moment's misgiving about how it would affect her, terrified that it would ruin her. Eat her up alive and destroy her. If Trish Nesbitt—who'd been an inhabitant of his world—couldn't survive it, then what the hell chance did someone like Iris have?

But then she smiled and that familiar mischievous spark lit up her gaze.

"No turning back now, huh?" she murmured, and he knew she meant more than just the plane.

"Nope, we're in this for the long haul," he said and her lips tilted at the corners.

"Okay."

"Better?"

"More and more so with every passing moment." This time she graced him with a full smile and as always, it robbed him of his breath. How the fuck did she do that? One slightly naughty, off-center grin and Trystan was ready to slay dragons for her. It was maddening. Confusing. Fucking exhilarating.

He gradually became aware of someone hovering beside his seat and swung his head to meet Piper's gaze.

"Tea for Miss Hughes," she said with an impersonal smile, and Iris's eyes dropped to the proffered tray in confusion.

"I thought you could use some sweet tea," Trystan told her and she smiled again, this time gracing the attendant with all that glorious sunshine.

"Thank you so much," she said, as the woman placed the tray on the table in front of their seats.

"If you need anything else, please don't hesitate to ask," Piper told Iris, her voice a little warmer. "And if you're still feeling under the weather and would like a lie-down, let me know and I'll turn down the bed for you."

Iris's eyes nearly popped out of her head.

"The *bed*?"

"In the back," the attendant elaborated with a kind smile.

"There's an actual bed on this plane?" Iris asked, her attention on Trystan now, and he grinned at the combination of shock and glee in her voice.

Piper's smile widened and she tactfully retreated, but Trystan was so laser-focused on Iris's expressive face he barely registered the woman's departure.

"Yes, in the bedroom next to the lounge. The captain has

turned off the *fasten seatbelts* sign, so you're free to have a look around."

"God, who has a bedroom and lounge on their plane?"

"Miles Hollingsworth," Trystan told her with a laugh.

"This isn't yours?"

"God, no." She looked a little relieved at his answer until he continued. "*My* plane has a game room and a home-theatre system on board."

Her hand flew to her mouth in actual horror and he hooted with laughter.

"You should see your face," he teased. "I don't have a private jet, sugarplum. I rent them for long-haul flights, but buying one is a little too extravagant for my taste."

She looked somewhat appeased by the explanation, until he went on to say, "I *do* have a 100-foot luxury yacht though. But I've been working so much these last few years, I've barely had time to enjoy it."

"That's a lot of boat for just one man," she said and he took hold of her free hand and entwined his long fingers with her small, slender ones. His thumb traced the soft underside of her thumb and then skimmed up the delicate line of her index finger before he lifted her hand to his mouth and dropped a kiss on the back of it.

"I'm happy to share it with you."

She looked appalled at the notion and he swallowed down his smile in the face of her transparent horror. He liked that she wasn't enthralled by his wealth and possessions. Trystan recalled the faint mockery in her tone whenever she'd referred to Miles's fleet of luxury and sports cars, back when she'd assumed they belonged to him. She didn't give a shit about his money and the lifestyle that went along with it. In fact, she seemed to find it all a little repugnant. Which, while not ideal—since it was a fact of his life with which she'd have to get comfortable, fast—was refreshing.

"I'm not sure I'm a boat person," she said and he squeezed her fingers reassuringly.

"You'll love it."

"This is all a little overwhelming," she muttered beneath her breath.

"We'll ease into it, okay? Baby steps," he said. He kept his voice gentle, not wanting her anxiety to flare up again.

She wriggled her hand out of his, and he reluctantly ceded it back to her. Her bright eyes swept around the cabin's interior with a little more interest and enthusiasm than before, when she'd been too wrapped up in her anxiety to pay attention to her surroundings.

"This *is* pretty lush," she said, running a reverent hand over the buttery leather seats. She unbuckled her seatbelt and toed her trainers off, before tucking her feet under her butt and reaching for her tea.

She sipped the hot drink quietly for a few moments, while soaking in her surroundings, and then sat up again abruptly. "Where's Luna?"

"Sitting with Chance," Trystan said, twisting a strand of her soft hair around his index finger, hopelessly unable to stop himself from touching her.

"Ooh, I haven't met Chance yet," she said, uncurling her legs. "So rude of me not to have properly introduced myself."

"Of course you met him. He drove us here."

"Your friend Sam dominated the conversation. I didn't get a chance to speak to the hot Aussie at *all*," she said with a sulky little pout that made him want to suck that lush lower lip into his mouth.

"Hey now," he warned. "I'm the only hot Aussie you need to be concerning yourself with."

She rather offensively dismissed his comment with an amused snort and a nonchalant wave and pushed to her feet. "He's a *bodyguard*, Trystan. That's next level in the hotness stakes."

"I can be a bodyguard," he said, fighting hard—and losing badly—to keep the sullen grumble out of his voice.

She paused to stare down at him with a speculative tilt to her head. "And a marine, and an air force pilot, and a..."

The confusion on her face cleared up instantly, as she understood what he meant, and she laughed. "That's pretend, babe. Now leave me to chat with the nice big protector guy, will you? I'll be back in a jiffy."

She appeased him by bending down to drop a quick kiss on his mouth. In retaliation for her sass, he swatted her butt as she passed his seat.

She rubbed her tush and threw him a blatantly sultry look over her shoulder, promising him all kinds of sexy retribution in that one stare. He shifted in his seat and surreptitiously adjusted himself as he watched the sway of that gorgeous, pert arse as she strolled away from him.

He didn't really mind her fascination with Chance. Her unquenchable thirst for knowledge was what prompted her to seek the man out and she would likely question him relentlessly about the ins and outs of his job. Trystan grinned a little at the thought. She was like a dog with a bone when she wanted to know something. He could personally attest to that fact. And he felt a little sorry for Chance, who rarely spoke and was always the epitome of discretion and professionalism.

Forty minutes later, Trystan was glaring at those two unlikeliest of compatriots and wondered what the fuck was so funny. Iris and Trystan's previously reticent close-protection officer were chortling like a pair of fucking teenaged girls at a sleepover, and Trystan was starting to feel seriously aggrieved that his company had been so easily thrown aside.

Granted, Iris was probably happy for someone new to talk to after so many weeks of just Trystan's surly arse for company. But—since Trystan was nowhere near sick of *her* company—he couldn't quite curb the disturbing sting of jealousy and resentment he felt at suddenly having to share her with others.

The emotions were unfamiliar and disturbing. He'd never felt this chest-thumping possessiveness over any woman before, and he told himself it had to be because of how long he'd had her wholly to himself. Out in the real world, she'd have other men with whom to compare him, people vying for her attention and time, a whole life to get back to.

They'd been so focused on *his* life and the demands thereof that he hadn't spared much thought to her family and friends.

People whom she trusted, would go to for advice, and whose opinions she valued. People who might not approve of their relationship, who would hold sway in her decision-making processes. And he was suddenly terrified that the worst obstacles they had to face may not be found in the overwhelming reality of *his* life... but rather in the quiet appeal of hers.

"Trystan," Iris's voice from across the cabin jerked him from his troubling, invasive thoughts.

He lifted his head to meet her warm, smiling eyes and found himself helpless to do anything other than return her smile like a lovesick puppy.

"Have you ever been to Humpy Dunes?" she asked and Trystan's brows lowered in confusion.

"What?" He watched through narrowed eyes as Chance caught her attention by quietly muttering her name. She refocused her attention to the still-seated man and tilted her head as she listened to whatever he had to say. Her face lit up in a broad self-effacing grin and she lifted her sparkling eyes back to Trystan's face.

"Oops, sorry. My bad... *Humpty Doo.* Have you ever been to Humpty Doo? Home of Bite Tyson, the world's biggest boxing saltwater croc?"

Trystan levered himself up and made his way toward the trio seated at a cluster of four seats, facing one another across a coffee table. Luna and Chance were in the two seats facing forward and Iris was facing aft, curled up, her feet tucked under her butt, looking as comfortable as she would in her own living room.

Trystan stood beside the empty seat next to Iris's, one hand braced on the headrest as he awkwardly met his close-protection officer's eyes. The man looked as uncomfortable as Trystan felt. They rarely spoke, really, and had never exchanged small talk.

"You from the Northern Territory, mate?" Trystan asked after clearing his throat. He was never awkward, but this was damned weird.

"Yeah." Aah. The taciturn bastard was back, no trace left of the chuckling buffoon who'd comfortably exchanged pleasantries with Iris just a few minutes ago.

Trystan sat down next to Iris, and she lifted the rest to snuggle under his arm. Gratified by her easy affection, Trystan felt the tense knot that had settled in his chest start to ease up slightly and he placed an arm around her shoulders and tugged her even closer.

"Never spent much time up in the Northern Territory myself," he expounded. Feeling a lot more confident now that he was holding Iris close again, he dismissed his former uncertainty and doubt as a mere aberration. Nothing to be overly concerned about. "A few flying visits for promotional purposes. D'ya get back often?"

"Nah, little reason to," Chance said with a nonchalant lift of his shoulders, his hand dropped to Luna's ruff and he stroked the sleeping dog almost absently. "Not a lot of family or friends left there. My life and home are in London now."

"London? I didn't know that. Where?"

"Hammersmith."

"You must be looking forward to getting home, then," Iris said, her fingers delicately stroking over the veins on the back of

Trystan's hand. Her touch was sweet and distracting, but he fought to remain focused on the conversation. It wasn't easy when Chance was so damned reticent in his responses.

"I am. I have the week off, so it'll be nice to sleep in my own bed again." The man's direct gaze landed on Trystan's face. "They will have someone filling in for me, of course."

"Of course," Trystan nodded, not having the slightest concern about that. "I *did* speak with Sam about a detail for Iris, though."

He sensed Iris tensing beside him, but kept this gaze on Chance's face.

"What?" she squeaked in protest. "Why? I don't want or need anything like that."

He sighed and redirected his gaze to her outraged face. "Because as soon as the press gets wind of you, they're going to be relentless and I'd like to keep you protected from the worst of that."

"But..."

"Iris, I'd feel better if you have some security, okay? This is..." He shook his head, hating that the restrictions of his life would inevitably have to spill over into hers. "It's necessary. For your safety and my peace of mind. I'm sorry it has to be like this."

Her teeth worried her plump lower lip and she graced him with a small smile.

"I suppose it was naïve of me not to consider this inevitability."

"It's not too late to turn back and live in our little stormy getaway for the rest of our days."

"I think the Hollingsworths would want their house back at some point."

"I'd buy it from Miles. Or better yet, build us one in the same area. A nice hidey-hole just for us."

Her smile was bittersweet as she wove her much smaller fingers through his. "No more hiding, remember?"

Trystan glanced over at Chance, but the man was a master of discretion. He was fully focused on his phone screen with his headphones firmly in place, giving them the privacy, if not the space, Trystan craved.

Trystan lifted their entwined fingers to his lips and dropped a kiss on her knuckles.

"I want to fucking show you off to the world, Iris, but I worry that it'll all be too overwhelming for you."

"I can face anything with you by my side, Trystan."

God, he really hoped that was true.

Piper chose that moment to interrupt and ask them about their meals.

"I DON'T THINK I'll ever be able to travel any other way now," Iris moaned the following morning, stretching out on the bed beside Trystan. She'd just had the best sleep, spooned by Trystan, who'd kept her wrapped in his strong arms all night. There'd been some turbulence, but the flight had been smooth and comfortable for the most part.

The pilot had just announced that they would be landing in two hours—at a private airfield outside of London—which gave them enough time to freshen up and have breakfast.

Trystan's hold tightened around her for a few seconds and she turned in his arms to face him. She still hadn't grown accustomed to waking up next to him, and lovingly tracked her gaze over his familiar features—his eyes still bleary with sleep, his overly long hair mussed, and stubble darkening his jaw.

She cupped that bristled jaw, running her thumb over his scar, and once again feeling a pang of loss as she remembered his unkempt beard. She marveled at how far they'd come since then.

He didn't say anything, merely stared at her with his usual single-minded focus. She smiled as she recollected his words when she'd called him out on it: *I like looking at you.* Such a simple sentiment and, yet, it had shaken her to the very foundation of her being. This beautiful man *liked* looking at her. She still didn't quite know how to feel about that... all she knew was that she preened a little every time he looked at her now.

He lifted a hand and smoothed it over her untamable hair, sweeping her wild curls back from her forehead and dropping a chaste kiss just above her left brow. If the erection straining against her stomach was any indication, he was feeling anything *but* chaste, and she couldn't blame him for that. Not after the way they'd left things last night. They'd had a hot-and-heavy make-out session after falling into bed, which had only ended in mutual frustration. Iris suspected that Trystan would've had no scruples about making her a card-carrying member of the Mile High Club, but she'd remained maddeningly aware of Chance and Piper on the other side of the flimsy wall.

Trystan had dialed it down and eventually had spooned behind her, wrapping her in his arms and cuddling her close to his chest—until she'd relaxed enough to fall asleep. And now here they were, both still so damned turned on Iris was tempted to just throw caution and discretion to the wind and give the man what he so desperately needed. Well... not just the man. She really wouldn't mind taking the edge off either.

His other hand, the one at her waist, crept down and gave her bum a cheeky squeeze before he groaned and with clear reluctance removed his hands from her body and sat up, leaving her feeling cold and lonely.

He threw back the covers—ignoring her outraged *hey*—and leaped agilely to his feet. His beautiful hard cock tented the front of his boxers—his only clothing—as he stretched with unashamed abandon, enviably comfortable in his skin. He yawned and then stared down at her with a wicked little grin, his eyes raking over her body which was curled up defensively against the chill of the air-conditioning after he'd so thoughtlessly tossed aside the warm bedding. She was wearing nothing but a camisole and a pair of skimpy bikini panties, and she blushed at the naked appreciation she saw in his smoldering silver eyes.

He shook his head, his grin downgrading to a self-deprecating smirk, and lifted the corner of the comforter to toss it back over her huddled body.

"I always believed I had a decent amount of willpower, but you're constantly proving me wrong just by being your fucking perfect self."

"Shut up," she said with an amused snort and sat up. Her dark areolas and cold-hardened nipples were clearly visible to his voracious gaze through her white top, and he groaned and adjusted himself uncomfortably before screwing his eyes shut.

"Begone, devil woman," he said before whirling around and heading to the en-suite bathroom. There was a smaller bathroom upfront for the flight staff and Chance, but this one was ridiculous. It had a large shower and even a little doggy area where Luna could relieve herself (apparently the Hollingsworths had a spoiled pupper who travelled everywhere with them).

He paused in the doorway and turned to face her again, that naughty grin back.

"Wanna share a shower? It's a little more soundproof in here."

Iris gazed at him in open-mouthed wonder.

"Seriously? It is?"

"I kid you not," he intoned solemnly, holding one hand over his heart. "In fact, I don't know why I didn't think of this last —*oomph*."

The last as Iris launched herself out of bed and straight into his arms, climbing him like a tree until she had her legs wrapped around his waist, her arms around his neck, and her lips nuzzled behind his ear.

He laughed, the sound warm and filled with unabashed joy, as his hands clamped over her arse to hold her up.

"I take it that's a *yes*?"

Iris watched as Trystan and Chance conferred several feet from where she was seated. Chance had approached them a few moments ago, with an apologetic glance at Iris, before muttering a curt, *We have a problem*, at Trystan. They'd just finished breakfast and were estimated to land in about half an hour.

Whatever Chance was telling him had left a thunderous expression on Trystan's face, and he raked his hand through his hair, before settling his palm in the nape of his neck as he glowered at the floor while Chance continued to speak in urgent undertones. Trystan was nodding curtly in response to the man's words, and his shoulders heaved as he lifted his eyes to meet hers across the cabin. Alarmed, Iris went from a relaxed slouch to upright. He looked furious. She hadn't seen him this pissed off since the early days of their acquaintance.

He shook his head and his lips formed a terse *fuck*, before he nodded once again, turning to say something to Chance, before making his way back to her. He sat down and refastened his seatbelt in grim silence, leaving her in suspense as he focused on that task.

"What's wrong?" she finally asked, unable to stand the tension any longer, sharply aware of the fury coming off him in hot waves.

"Who did you tell that we were flying back today?"

"What? Nobody." She was taken aback by his frigid voice. He hadn't spoken to her in that tone in weeks, and the return of that iciness sent a shudder of dread down her spine.

"Nobody? Not even your parents?"

"Well, of course, my p-parents," she spluttered, her nerves

causing her to trip over her words. "But nobody else. W-what's happening, Trystan? You're frightening me."

"The press *somehow* got wind of our arrival. They're lying in wait at the airport."

"Oh no," she gasped, lifting a hand to her mouth. "How?"

"That's what *I'd* like to know," he said. The snideness lurking beneath those words gave her pause and her hand dropped to her lap as she stared at him in hurt confusion.

"Wait, do you think *I* had something to do with this?"

He lifted his shoulders. "*My* people know better."

"And my people are what? Greedy bastards who would sell me out for a story?"

He didn't so much as flinch at her frigid question, meeting her eyes with his steady gaze.

"You're not in touch with any of your dad's pap cronies?"

"My *dad* is a caterer."

"You know what I meant."

"Go to hell, Trystan." She fumbled with her seatbelt and, after managing to get it unbuckled, she pushed to her feet.

"Where are you going?" he asked, something close to panic in his voice.

"To sit with Luna and Chance. They're better company."

"Iris—" She held her palm up and halted whatever he'd been about to say.

"No. I'd rather not hear whatever insult you have lined up next and I have nothing else to say to you right now."

Chapter Eighteen

Trystan sighed explosively, muttered a few choice expletives beneath his breath and grabbed Iris's hand as she attempted to walk away.

"Let me go," she commanded, her voice rigid with the pain she was ineptly trying to hide from him.

"Iris, I'm not used to trusting—"

"Strangers?" She completed for him, tugging her hand out of his. "That's what I am to you, right?"

He found himself at a loss as to how to respond to that and his brow furrowed as he stared at the angry woman standing in front of him, her arms folded defensively over her pert chest.

Fuck.

"Iris," he began, weighing his words carefully before he spoke. "It's not easy for me to let people into my inner circle. The people I trust the most have been in my life for years, decades even. Allowing you in means making myself vulnerable and that's never been easy for me to do."

Her eyes were watchful and she opened and closed her mouth a few times—clearly picking her words—before, voice subdued, she said, "We haven't even landed yet and you already have these doubts. That doesn't bode well for us, Trystan."

An icy chill settled in the pit of his stomach as he acknowledged her words with a regretful nod. "We're adjusting. We'll figure it out."

"And what does *figuring it out* entail? You unjustifiably accusing me and mine every time something like this happens? Because that'll get old very fast. I can't be the scapegoat whenever you have some breach in security, Trystan. I *won't*."

"It won't be like that, Iris."

"How do you know that?"

"Because I love you."

"Not enough to trust me."

Trystan wasn't sure how to defend against that assertion when he'd literally just demonstrated that supposed lack of trust.

"It was a knee-jerk reaction and it was stupid. We've had breaches before, tips from eagle-eyed airport staff to the press. I should have taken that into account."

"But I was right here and convenient."

"Iris, please sit down," he implored and tugged on her hand again. She resisted for a moment before relenting and sitting down. She remained tense and perched at the very edge of the seat, looking for all the world like she would bolt at the slightest provocation.

"We're going to experience these—" He hunted for the correct words. "I suppose we could call them growing pains, yeah? That's normal. And we may inadvertently hurt each other in the process but we have to believe that our relationship is strong enough to overcome these hurdles. I overreacted. It was a stupid mistake."

"And what if it wasn't a mistake?" she asked through stiff lips and he frowned.

"What do you mean?"

"What if one of my people *did* let it slip? What then?"

He didn't hesitate before replying. "It would still be unfair to blame *you* for that, since you can't control what they do. And they can't possibly understand yet what damage a careless slip of the tongue can cause. This is as new to them as it is to you. And to me."

"You wouldn't blame them?"

"No. We can have a discussion with them about the need for privacy and discretion."

Her back unbent a fraction.

"Forgive me?" he asked with an exaggerated pout designed to make her laugh, and her lips trembled in response. He doubled down on the sad face. "Please?"

"Oh my God, stop that," she said, covering her face with both hands. "You look like Puss in Boots."

Pleased that he'd managed to coax a smile from her, he took her hands in his and tugged them down to her lap, where he continued to hold them, stroking his thumbs over the soft skin of her palms. He kept his eyes on hers for a long moment, wanting her to recognize his sincerity.

"I hurt you. I'm so sorry."

"Don't do it again, okay?"

He lifted one of her hands and planted a kiss on the back of it, before tenderly cradling it to his cheek.

"I promise."

IN THE END, their flight was rerouted to an airport in Luton. They were met by two big men—more of Sam Brand's people—who'd been waiting for them next to a couple of black Mercedes-Benzes, one sedan and one Maybach SUV with heavily tinted windows.

Suddenly this felt all too real and Iris's stomach flipped and twisted like she was on a roller-coaster ride as Chance went into ultra-serious bodyguard mode. The affable man from the flight disappeared completely, and he moved with menace and purpose as he expertly shepherded them through the airport and ushered them into the waiting SUV.

The second car seemed like a needless extravagance, but Iris guessed it was there to provide additional security.

Chance took the front passenger seat, and raised the sound-proof divider between Iris, Trystan and Luna, and himself and the driver. Iris sat beside Trystan feeling tense and out of sorts, especially when he immediately picked up his phone and started tapping rapidly at the screen. The phone rang a few seconds after he'd sent the text.

"I'm sorry, baby, I have to take this." Trystan slanted her an apologetic look before thumbing the green answer button and lifting the device to his ear. He kept a comforting hand on her knee as he spoke to—she soon deduced—Hunter Quinn.

Not entirely sure what to do with herself now that she'd been left to her own devices, Iris belatedly checked her new phone which she'd spent time setting up on the plane. It had come with a generous amount of data. Thankfully most of her contacts and information had been safely stored in the cloud. Trystan had, of course, insisted she add his details first.

She was shocked to find a ridiculous number of missed calls and texts waiting for her.

She checked the messages first. Her parents, brother, flat-mates, Evan, and so many others had sent her texts. Some of them messages from people she hadn't spoken to, or heard from, in years.

What the hell?

She checked her mother's messages first.

> Don't come round the house. It's chaos here. I don't know how this happened, but the press has been saying the most ridiculous things, Iris. Call me as soon as you get this.

What was going on? This was—

"*What?*" Trystan suddenly exploded, his entire body tensing as an intimidating glower settled on his face. His eyes darted toward her, and pinned her to the spot. He spoke again, his lips thin, voice tight, "No. No way in hell. It must be a mistake."

Whatever his manager was telling him clearly wasn't the

answer he'd been hoping for and, if possible, he went even more rigid. "No, you're wrong. *Well, check it again!*" Iris startled at the sudden increase in volume and sharpness in his voice. "No. I don't think so, Quinny. She wouldn't. It's not possible."

Oh God, was he talking about her? She wouldn't what? What was going on? Could this have something to do with her mother's text? She wanted to call her mum to find out, but found herself unable to drag her eyes away from his. He looked fierce, resolute, but as he listened to whatever Hunter Quinn was telling him, something in his eyes flickered and she saw the doubt begin to creep in.

"Trystan?" she whispered, her hand covering his where it still rested on her knee. His grip had tightened to the point of pain, but to her horror and panic, he flinched at her touch and instantly moved his hand to his own knee. "What's happening?"

"Yeah... yeah." He nodded as he spoke, his eyes going distant as he focused on his friend's words. "I agree. Do what you think is best. Yeah. I'll take care of it. I'll text Brand. Yes. I fucking *know*, alright? It's done. Okay. Right."

He ended the call and Iris reached for his arm, but he shook her off and retreated to the bench seat across from her—where Luna was lying stretched out and sleeping—putting as much distance between them as was possible within the confines of the car. The dog, momentarily disturbed by the movement, opened her eyes for a few seconds before drifting off to sleep again, her head resting against Trystan's thigh.

He tapped on his phone again, sending another text, his focus trained on the screen while the suffocating silence between them festered and became an almost living entity, strangling Iris's words in her throat.

His phone *pinged* and he grunted in satisfaction before lowering the privacy window between them and the driver and Chance. He handed his phone to Chance and then shut the divider again, clasping his hands between his spread knees and leaning toward her to stare into her face for a long, brutal moment. His eyes like ice, his features frigid, his demeanor frosty.

"May I have your laptop for a second please?" he asked. Iris wasn't sure what frightened her more, his brittle voice or the ridiculous formality in his words.

"Why?" she asked, not liking the way her own voice quavered in confusion.

"I need the internet and Chance has my phone."

"Th-the internet?"

"You are connected, right?"

"Yes. Uhm... through the phone." What a ridiculous exchange. "Please tell me what's happening, Trystan. You're scaring me."

He held out a steady hand and, hoping it would be the fastest way to get the answers she needed, Iris unzipped her laptop bag and handed her slim pink laptop to him. He opened it and then sighed impatiently.

"It's password protected."

"Oh, right. It's IrisHApril—my birth month—all one word," she told him. "The first I is uppercase as are the H and the A." He gave her a fleeting, censorious frown—probably because of the ludicrously easy password—before typing it in.

She watched, chewing her cuticle pensively, as he tapped away at the keyboard and then went still as he seemed to find what he was looking for. She watched the muscles in his jaw bunch as he clenched his teeth, but his face remained impassive, even though she could tell that he was livid.

"Trystan?" She hated how tremulous her voice sounded, hated even more that it was an accurate indication of how she was feeling right now.

He swiped at the track pad with his index finger, the movement filled with restrained violence, and then perused the screen for a few seconds. He seemed to blanch, going pale as he traced his finger over the track pad again and then clicked.

His throat moved as he swallowed, and he seemed to go even paler.

"What..." His voice emerged on a thready whisper and he cleared his throat before starting again. "What the fuck is this, Iris?"

"What?"

"*I hate him,*" he intoned, his eyes moving as he read from the screen. "*I don't think I've ever been able to say that about anyone before, but this man is cruel, he's odious, he's an utter bastard. People idolize him—the* great *Trystan Abbott—with his beauty and charisma and charm. But they haven't seen this side of him. This twisted, brutal side of—*"

"No! Oh my God, Trystan. *Stop!*" It was Iris's turn to pale as she recognized what he was reading.

He'd found her journal. Of *course* he had. It was right there on her desktop. Iris made no effort to hide it. It was *her* laptop after all. And while the thoughts were private, it wasn't a big secret that she kept a journal. Except that... *Trystan* didn't know about it. She hadn't ever told him.

"Those are my private thoughts. It's my journal, Trystan. And it's not a big deal. I've kept one since I was a teenager. My therapist recommended it as a way to keep track of my triggers. I wrote that the night we met." She attempted a laugh, which fell miserably flat. "I'm sure *you* had similar feelings toward me in those early days."

"Only *my* feelings weren't published in a tell-all *exposé* in *Looker* magazine an hour ago."

She stared at him in dazed confusion, not quite comprehending those tight, furious words.

"I don't understand," she whispered, a surge of horror clawing up from her stomach into her throat, bringing with it the taste of bitter bile.

He sighed, the sound taut with impatience, and swiped at the trackpad again before tossing the laptop onto the seat beside her, the gesture fill with contempt.

Iris stared in dismay and disbelief as she saw images of herself and Trystan splashed across the screen. There were other images, pictures she'd taken while at the house. Candid shots of Trystan playing with Luna, a selfie of her and Trystan cuddled on the sofa together, a picture Trystan had taken of her after wrestling her phone from her grasp. Her gaze snagged on that photo. Her hair was a windswept mess, but she looked so happy as she stared back at him. Her cheeks were flushed and the love, joy and warmth in her eyes and her wide smile were unmistakable.

Her bewildered eyes swept across the private images that

had somehow found their way onto a very public website and only then did the accompanying words start to sink in.

They were *her* words. Sometimes taken directly from her journal, other times altered slightly to fit the prose, but they were her private thoughts on display for the world to see.

Worse... they—

"Oh God..." she whimpered faintly and her hand went to her mouth as she comprehended everything else the article exposed. About Trystan. And Trish Nesbitt. Things he had told her in confidence, which she'd then faithfully, foolishly, *stupidly*, transcribed into her journal for no good reason other than habit.

"No, no, no," she whimpered. "I don't understand how—"

Her eyes leaped up to Trystan's face. He was staring out of the window, his emotions reined in tight, his eyes staring off into the distance.

"Trystan, I didn't do this." How could this be? She didn't understand how this could possibly have happened. It felt like a waking nightmare... maybe it was. Maybe she was still asleep on the plane. Surely this could not be real?

He turned his head slowly and the expression in his eyes destroyed her. Such bleak desolation, battling with fury, betrayal, and something that looked like hatred.

"Yeah? If your plan was to lie to me about your role in this, then you probably shouldn't have put your name in the fucking byline."

Her eyes drifted back to the article, tracking to the very top.

The lurid title screamed at her *How Trystan Abbott Imprisoned Me*, followed by *Story by Iris Hughes and Evan Brooks.*

Iris's stomach dropped when she saw the second name. *Evan?* Why would she do something so malicious? Was she really so keen on making her mark that she'd carelessly toss away their friendship like this? Then again, Iris's biological father would probably happily have sold one of his daughter's kidneys for a story like this, so why did this even surprise her? When Evan had shown every indication of being of the exact same ilk as Stanford Carter.

But how could she have accessed Iris's private files? The pictures?

As she stared at Trystan's averted profile, she realized that none of that mattered now.

"I don't know how this happened, Trystan. I swear to God, I would *never* do something like this. You know that. You know me."

"Do I?" Those two words, delivered in a devastatingly cutting monotone silenced her and she swallowed down the pained protest swelling in her throat. "Fuck me, I should have known better. This is my own fault. I can't even blame you that much. I served myself up on a motherfucking platter and made it painfully easy for you to do this. Maybe part of me knew you would, maybe that's why I so inexplicably laid my soul bare to you. Of *all* people. Maybe I'm relieved that my role in Trish's death is finally out there. No more secrets, right?"

He rubbed his hands over his face, looking tired, defeated, and resigned. He didn't even look particularly angry, and that—more than anything else—was what terrified Iris the most. He'd given up. On her. On *them*.

"I was a fool," he laughed softly, the sound self-deprecating, the words almost absent as if he was speaking more to himself than to her. "You're a shark... and when you bleed in front of a predator, you get eaten. But I allowed myself to be lulled into a false sense of security, while stupidly ignoring the fact that blood will tell and a predator's instincts will *always* win out in the end."

"No, Trystan. I don't know how this happ—"

"Give it up, Iris! Your sick little game is over. You've won. Okay?"

The car slowed down and pulled onto the shoulder of the road, where it came to a complete stop and Trystan rapped on the privacy window.

"Now would you kindly get the fuck out of my car?" he said, his voice cordial as he gestured toward the door, which Chance had opened.

Iris's eyes darted to the door, then back to Trystan, who was inspecting his nails with studied disinterest.

"Trystan, no... please don't do this to us. I didn't write that article. I swear to God, I didn't. You can't leave me stranded on the side of the road."

He laughed at that, a horrible, scornful sound. "And give you even *more* dirt to bury me with? I would never. Just get out of my car and out of my life, Iris. I never want to see you again."

At that moment Iris realized that the driver had also exited the car and was removing her luggage from the boot. He was transferring cases to the second car, which was parked slightly in front of theirs.

"I love you," she reminded him desperately. "You love me. You said we'd make this work. You said—"

"Yeah, I said a lot of things, most of which are probably in that article somewhere... but the woman I thought I loved doesn't exist. She never existed. She was someone you made up. And I'll grieve for her and miss her. You? Not so much. I fucking hate *you* for preying on the weakness you found in me. I don't think I'll ever be able to forgive you for that."

BEFORE SHE WAS able to properly comprehend what was happening, Iris found herself curled up on the back seat of the smaller black Mercedes-Benz sedan. Her thoughts a whirl, her emotions chaotic, and her heart racing. She was shaking so much that some distant, detached part of her brain recognized that she was exhibiting all the symptoms of shock.

The car started moving and she scrambled upright, desperately searching for the other vehicle. It was two or three cars ahead of this one. She pressed her palms against the window, her breath misting the glass as she hoped for a glimpse of Trystan, wanting to see him, wanting him to recognize the mistake he was making. But the heavily tinted windows of the SUV gave no hint as to the occupant inside of the vehicle. And as she watched, the car slipped further and further away, until it was lost in the sea of vehicles around them.

A quiet, despairing sob slipped out as she finally lost sight of the Maybach. Her eyes continued to restlessly search the traffic around them, hoping to spot the car again, but it was no use. It —*he*—was gone.

Forever.

At some point Iris became aware that her face was wet with the tears seeping from her eyes. She hadn't even known that she was crying. It wasn't a violent storm of tears but a slow, constant flow. It was as if her eyes had somehow sprung a leak that was impossible to stem or repair.

Trystan's easy dismissal of her protests and denials had ripped open a catastrophic wound in her chest. The pain was brutal, and the consequences fatal to her heart and soul. She wanted to curl up in a ball, claw at her chest, and weep. But all she could do was sit here with hot, salty tears dripping silently down her cheeks while the shards of her shattered heart sliced her to pieces.

It was only when the car slowed down and slid to a stop that she was dragged from her all-encompassing sorrow, and was reminded that she wasn't alone in the car. That there was a witness to her humiliation and devastation. The privacy shield wasn't even in place and her eyes lifted to meet a pair of concerned green eyes in the rearview mirror.

Chance.

Iris hadn't even noticed that he'd stayed with her. She'd assumed that she'd been bundled over to a stranger. That Chance would remain with Trystan who was, after all, his principal and thus his priority. The original driver of this car must have traded spots with Chance because the Australian was the only person in the vehicle with her.

She shifted her eyes away from his, reaching for the door handle, wanting to get out of this car and away from the memory of these few brief weeks with Trystan when she comprehended that they weren't anywhere near her home.

"Where are we?"

"Gunnersbury Park." His reply was succinct and baffling.

"What? Why?"

"I wasn't sure where you wanted me to take you." He extended a blue linen square toward her, and she blinked at the handkerchief for a moment before taking it from him with a muttered *thanks* and dabbing at her wet cheeks self-consciously.

"There now. Give your nose a good blow, and take a deep breath. You'll feel better," he said, his low and sympathetic voice merely causing her tears to well again. He had turned in his seat to look at her and she hated the gleam of pity she was sure she'd spotted in his eyes.

"I'm sorry," she whispered, taking that deep breath, and was even more embarrassed when it hitched on a sob.

"That's okay. You're having a day."

"I didn't do it. I know you don't know me, but I didn't write that article." It was pathetic, this need she had to justify herself, to clear her name.

She knew she was blameless, and the knowledge of her own lack of wrongdoing should be enough for her. But Trystan's instant rejection of her truth had sparked this deep sense of injustice, outrage and betrayal in her. Along with this patholog-ical overwhelming *need* to convince the world of her innocence.

"It's not my place to comment, ma'am. I'm just the driver."

Her chin quivered and she pursed her lips as she fought to scrape together some semblance of pride and self-control. She nodded, and blew her nose. Her face felt hot and swollen from the tears, her throat raw from the suppressed sobs. Her stomach was in turmoil and her head pounding.

"Right. Of course," she whispered. "You need my address."

"I have your address," he corrected. "Your parents' address as well, in Southfields. I'm not sure if you want to be with your family, or if you prefer to return to your flat."

How thoughtful of him.

"I'm an absolute mess. I don't want my parents to see me like this," she said, twisting the now-damp handkerchief in her hands.

"The flat then?"

She nodded.

He hesitated and looked conflicted for a second before saying, "I live in Hammersmith—Baron's Court—and I'm headed home straight after dropping you. I have a few days off after my extended stay out of the country."

Iris studied his rugged face in confusion, not sure why he was telling her this.

His broad shoulders shifted uncomfortably and his cheeks went ruddy.

"You could stay with me."

The offer flabbergasted her. She wasn't sure what to make of it, at all. She'd literally just met this man. Why on Earth would he invite her to stay with him? She didn't think he was attracted to her. That wasn't the vibe she was getting at all. But why else would he—

"They won't find you there." His words jerked her from her thoughts, confusing her even further.

"They?"

"Miss Hughes—"

"Iris."

"Uhm... *Iris*, I don't think you quite comprehend the shit-storm that's waiting for you. And he retracted your protection. So you won't have any kind of buffer to help you through this."

"*He...* Trystan, you mean?"

He nodded curtly, his jaw tensing as if he were biting back his words.

"As you know, before we left Cape Town, he arranged with Brand to have a protective detail assigned to you. He cancelled that arrangement after learning about the article. After I drop you at home, I'm afraid you're on your own."

"I see." The words were a choked whisper and Iris averted her eyes to her lap, staring at her restless hands, which were still twisting and twisting the damp blue handkerchief. "Thank you so much for the offer, Chance. But I'd really rather go home. They won't be interested in me for long. Trystan is the big fish. He's the one whose reputation is at risk. That's why he feels so betrayed."

She was making excuses for Trystan. She knew it. And felt pathetic because of it. But she also recognized just how bad this could—and likely *would*—get for him. He'd been wrong to instantly believe the worst about her. But she could under-stand his point of view. She hadn't read the article in its entirety but she'd seen enough to comprehend just how damaging it was.

Everything—all of their most private and intimate moments —had been in that journal. She bit back an agonized, humiliated moan. How much of that had Evan included in her vile article?

Iris could open up her laptop. Read it. But she wasn't ready to do that yet.

Her eyes lifted back to Chance's. He was still staring at her, concern in his eyes. It hurt to acknowledge that this total stranger seemed to care more about her well-being than the man she loved.

Then again, if she were Trystan, she would probably hate her right now as well.

She felt sick to her stomach, her conflicting emotions tearing her apart. The love, hate, resentment, fury, and empathy she felt for Trystan warring inside of her and worsening her headache. She needed privacy. The safe haven of home.

She barely had a hold on her sanity. Her anxiety was a living thing, clawing its way to the surface, threatening to bury her beneath the rubble of her crumbling life.

Chance sighed. He reached into the inner chest pocket of his jacket and withdrew a card. He handed it to her. She stared at the dark blue business card with the embossed silver *Brand EPS—Executive Protection Services—*insignia.

"I'll take you home, but if you change your mind"—he nodded at the card in her hand—"give me a call. My offer stands. Okay?"

She nodded, too emotionally overwrought to meet his eyes, knowing it would start up that slow, relentless stream of hot tears again.

"Thank you."

He dipped his chin in acknowledgement and turned to face front and get them underway again.

"OH MY GOD." Iris moaned, her hand going up to her mouth in horror, when the Mercedes parked across the road from her building. There appeared to be at least a dozen to twenty journalist-looking types milling around on the sidewalk outside the entrance.

"You still want to do this?" Chance asked in a grim voice.

"Maybe my parents—"

"It's about the same there. Also at your family's business premises."

"Oh no." Her eyes flooded again. She hated that she'd brought this trouble to her parents' doorstep.

"Iris," he said, his voice achingly kind. "You can stay with me until this blows over."

She was tempted. Oh God, she was so tempted, but she wasn't going to be driven from her home. She'd done nothing wrong, had nothing to hide. The vultures would move on as soon as they realized that she was the most boring person on the face of the Earth. And that Trystan was done with her already. Everything would be fine.

She squared her shoulders and shook her head.

"I truly adore you for making that offer, Chance. Thank you. But I'm going home. And as soon as the initial excitement and interest has died down, I'm going to fix this. This has all been one massive misunderstanding."

Even as she said it, Iris knew there was no possible way to fix this. Not really. It was a brave, brash sentiment, with zero basis in reality. There was no unringing this bell, no mitigating this disaster. It was out there and it was unstoppable. And that reality terrified her.

She caught a flash of admiration and respect in Chance's eyes—combined with warmth and sympathy—before he put on his sunglasses. His voice was grim when he said, "Whatever you want, Iris. But never let these bastards see you cry or doubt yourself. You give them nothing of yourself. Okay?"

She nodded and exhaled gustily before fishing around in her handbag for her own sunglasses. Once she had them on, she took one more look at the intimidating crowd lying in wait.

"I'm ready."

Chapter Nineteen

"Iris, you can't stay cooped up in that flat all day, every day. It's not healthy. Why don't you come home for the weekend? Your dad and I would love to have you round."

Iris smiled tiredly at her mother's face on the phone screen, and shook her head. "I can't this weekend, Mum. I have a deadline. And you guys have the 'OMalley wedding tomorrow night, don't you?"

"Your dad and Robbie can handle that. You and I can have a nice girls' night in."

It was tempting, so tempting. Iris would do anything to escape the prison her flat had become these past two weeks. Her anxiety levels were constantly spiking, she had her therapist on speed dial, and she just wasn't coping. Her work was the only thing keeping her from spiraling into a deep depressive episode. The constant gnawing guilt at the trouble she'd caused her family, her flatmates… Trystan, added to the inability to leave her building without being accosted in some way by the gutter press, were taking their toll. And Iris wasn't sure how much longer she'd be able to cope with this.

"Mum, you know I can't do that," she whispered, her voice taut with pain. "They'll follow me. They'll start harassing you and Dad again. And eventually it *will* affect the business. Clients won't want to hire you if it means being accosted in the streets by so-called journalists trying to pump them for information about me."

"I don't care, luv. We haven't seen you in weeks. We can handle this. We can handle anything as a family. Just trust us."

Iris's eyes welled with those ever-present tears and her lips quivered, before she brutally bit down on the inside of her cheek as punishment for her emotional reaction. She tasted blood but it worked. The shock of pain jerked her out of the downward spiral into self-pity.

"Let's do something next week, okay?" she said with a closed-mouth smile. "I just have to finish this edit and I'll be free to spend some time with you."

"That's what you said last time, Iris. Look, this—"

"Oh, sorry, Mum," she interrupted quickly. "I have to go—my pizza delivery is here. Chat soon, right? I love you."

She disconnected the call before her mother could protest and tossed the phone aside to bury her face in her hands.

Things weren't getting better. Iris had believed they would. Had hoped the situation would blow over. But the press wouldn't leave her alone. She thought back to the conversation she'd had with Evan the day after she'd returned home. She'd tried to force her former friend to print a retraction, but the other woman had point blank refused to even contemplate it.

"Why should I?" she'd asked with an insufferable smirk on her face. "None of it is a lie."

"You stole my words. My private, innermost thoughts. You ruined my life, Evan, and laid my soul bare for the world to gawk at."

"God, you're always so fucking dramatic. And I didn't steal shit. You gave me your password. Maybe next time don't leave your *private thoughts* in an easily accessible folder in the cloud. Lesson learned, right?"

Iris cringed at the reminder of her stupidity. Her blind trust in her "friend" who'd never really been a friend. She'd given Evan her password years ago, when the woman had needed to use her laptop after her own had died just before a deadline. Iris had used variations of that same password on the laptop since then. It wouldn't have taken Evan long to figure it out.

"Why are you doing this to me?"

"Why? Maybe because you've *never* bothered to capitalize on the many advantages you were given. Stanford Carter was your father and mentor for fuck's sake. This damned interview with Trystan Abbott falls in your lap. But you're too—*what?* Principled? Good? Better than the rest of us mortal beings?—to take advantage of that fact. I did you a favor. You're not that special, Iris. He'd have dumped you anyway. At least this way you'll be remembered. Maybe even get ahead in your stagnating journalism career. And if I happen to reap a few benefits from it too, why not? We're friends, aren't we?"

"No. We're not friends, Evan," Iris had responded with

absolute certainty. It was the only thing she felt sure of lately. "I *thought* we were. But it's clear that I was wrong. We've never been friends, have we? You've been using me all along. You're no better than a vile piece of shit stuck to the bottom of my shoe and it's way past time I scraped you off. You ruined a man's life, Evan. How can you be okay with that?"

Evan had actually *laughed* at her words. Iris cringed even now, a fortnight later, as she recalled the mockery in the woman's laughter.

"That's so precious. Little Iris trying to be a hard arse. I didn't ruin his life. Far from it. Trystan Abbott is a movie star. Everybody loves him. And once the shock wears off, people will start to sympathize with him. Nobody will blame him for what happened to Trish Nesbitt. It wasn't his fault, after all. She borderline stalked him.

"*You*, however, will always be remembered as the girl Trystan Abbott fucked in a moment of weakness and vulnerability. The woman who took advantage of his grief. It won't take long for someone to point out that you're not pretty or talented, and if he hadn't been hurt and in mourning, he wouldn't have looked at you twice. What do you think will happen then, Iris?"

Iris shivered at the memory of that taunting question. It had chilled her to the bone. The recognition that the public and press would inevitably turn against her, if they hadn't already. That it didn't matter how the story had got out, hers was the name in the story and in the byline. And she was the one who'd seemingly betrayed Trystan's confidence. Nobody believed her protestations to the contrary. Nobody cared about the truth. Least of all Trystan. Everybody already believed the worst of her, and they would continue to do so. No matter what she said or did. And it had been unbelievably naïve of her to believe any differently.

Iris had known then that she'd never see remorse, regret, an apology, or a retraction from Evan. And it was hopeless even trying to appeal to her conscience on the matter. She was riding high on the success of this article. She'd received the promotion she'd been after. Her boss had been fired. She'd done a shitty thing and had been rewarded for it. Why the hell should she feel any regret about that?

And it had all unfolded pretty much as Evan had predicted. A few days of rabid interest in Iris and her side of the story had quickly morphed into something else. Something darker. The questions yelled at her the few times she'd dared to venture out of her building had been overly intrusive and lurid queries about sex with Trystan:

Is Trystan a good shag, Iris? How many orgasms in one session? – that particularly unsavory gem had come from a leering old man with whom Iris had been acquainted her entire life. One of her biological father's cronies. He'd proceeded to shout out questions about length and girth and preferred sexual positions. It had made her sick to her stomach and as soon as she'd fought her way back into the building and up to the flat, she'd lost her lunch. The questions had only become more profane and personal.

Trystan, meanwhile, had stopped hiding from the limelight. He was back with a bang. As Evan had predicted, the public had reacted extremely sympathetically to the Trish Nesbitt revelations. When approached for a comment about Trish's death, he'd gone on the record to state that he had valued her as a colleague and as a friend, and deeply regretted her death and his role in the circumstances leading up to it.

Like an addict needing her fix, Iris picked up her phone—ignoring the hundreds of unread emails, texts, and voicemail notifications—to find the bookmarked interview Trystan had done just last week, with a well-known late-night television host.

He'd looked tired, his features thin and drawn. Her hungry eyes ran over those features with which she'd become so intimately acquainted and she felt that familiar pang of loss at the sight of his brutally shorn black hair. He'd gone for a military-style buzzcut. It suited him, of course—everything suited Trystan—but every last remnant of the man she'd fallen for was now gone.

Iris felt equal amounts of regret and resentment toward him, each emotion vying for superiority in her chest. It confused and frustrated her, these warring factions of hatred and love that had taken up residence in her heart and mind.

"Trish's loss was a profound one to the industry and to me personally," he said in reply to a question from the host. "My paramount regret about the resurgence of interest around the circumstances of her death is that it has undoubtedly reopened barely healed wounds for her family."

Iris gnawed at the skin around her thumb-nail and hissed in pain, before tucking the digit into her palm. She'd torn the cuticle days ago and it couldn't properly heal because she kept worrying at it.

The legendary talk-show host—Michael Holmes—was

making sympathetic noises in response to Trystan's words, his face contorted in an exaggerated expression of somber concern before he asked the question Iris knew—from repeated viewings—was coming.

"And this woman—this so-called reporter—Iris Hughes..." The man grimaced, as if the mere taste of Iris's name on his lips was repulsive. "Have you spoken with her, or seen her, since your return?"

"I'd prefer not to discuss her," Trystan's voice had gone cold, and she could see the familiar frigid warning in his eyes and knew the man must have strayed off script.

"What she did was unconscionable," the man persisted, despite the clear warning in Trystan's voice. "An ethical breach. Will you be pursuing legal action against her?"

"Are you certain you want to continue this line of questioning, Mike?" Trystan asked with a thin sharklike smile. "You don't want to ask me anything about *Cryo Cop*?"

"I have plenty of questions about your upcoming release, of course," the host said with a wide smile and in an agreeable tone of voice, before continuing. "But before we get to that, I was wondering if you'd read the most recent leaked excerpts from Iris Hughes's journal? It's clear she has a host of psychological problems. Did her neuroses and anxiety issues remind you in some way of the problems you'd faced with Trish Nesbitt? It must have been traumatic, being trapped with someone like her. Traumatic and undoubtedly triggering. Since you *did* lock her in her room for a while, you must have felt threatened by her. Did she—wait, what are you doing?"

The last question, following the barrage of others, was

panicked and high-pitched and came as Trystan pushed himself up from the iconic blue sofa that he'd been sprawling on like a relaxed cat just minutes earlier.

"I'm done." Trystan said with an easy shrug, not an ounce of emotion in his level voice.

"But—" Mike Holmes slanted a panicked glance at the camera and then off to the right. "C'mon, Trystan, we haven't finished yet."

"*I* have." He was tugging at the mic pack, before tossing an exasperated glare off to the side and asking, almost politely, "Can someone get this"—the next word was bleeped out—"thing off me please?"

He strode off stage, ignoring Mike Holmes's repeated protests, while the camera tracked his progress until he disappeared backstage. They switched back to Mike, who stared blankly directly into the lens for a few seconds before blinking, and smiling with the practiced ease of a consummate professional. He smoothly apologized for the disrupted schedule with a forced chuckle and moved on to their next guest.

It had been Trystan's only televised interview. He'd made a few red-carpet appearances before and after that—always stag—ignoring all of the inevitable questions about Trish or Iris.

After that disastrous interview, interest in Iris had ratcheted up from rabid curiosity to slanderous and sordid insults. Nothing was exempt from public scrutiny, excerpts from her journal—her private thoughts and insecurities, her innermost secrets, her sexual fantasies, everything that had happened between her and Trystan—had been released on an entertainment blog just hours before that interview. Iris wasn't sure how, likely Evan, probably at the behest of Mike Holmes's team.

How it had happened was moot. The fact was it *had* happened and Iris felt like she'd been stripped naked and flayed alive before a jeering, unsympathetic crowd. Especially since Trystan's outraged fans had started the *teamtrystan* hashtag, demanding that Iris be canceled, while labeling her everything from a money-hungry slut, to an obsessive psychopathic stalker, who many believed posed an actual physical threat toward Trystan. It was around then that the death threats had begun too.

Iris felt increasingly isolated from her family, from the few people she'd considered her friends. Her flatmates had been curious and supportive at first but after those first snippets of the journal had been leaked, they'd begun to avoid her. As if they were afraid that the public ridicule was somehow contagious.

The requests—then near demands—for interviews were becoming overwhelming, with some of the more notorious gossip rags offering obscene amounts of money for her "side" of the story. She was pretty certain her steadfast refusal to engage with any of them was one of the reasons the gutter press had turned hostile so quickly. Why she was now being vilified, mocked, and straight-up lied about. She didn't have the energy or the desire—quite frankly—to fight some of the libelous things being printed about her. And she felt like she was free-falling into a dark abyss, no bottom in sight.

All she had right now to keep her sane was her work. And

her writing. The writing gave her an escape from her intolerable reality.

She sighed and tucked her phone under her desk chair's cushion. Even though the device was on silent, the screen lit up with every new notification. It was distracting and, worse, she would often see the opening lines of whatever horrible message had been sent to her, which—when they came continuously—could send her into a terrible funk.

She was between editing jobs right now. A few of her clients had jumped on the *#cancelirishughes* bandwagon and dropped her like a hot potato, but her more long-term regulars had stuck with her. It did mean she had less work to focus on and she was concerned she would start feeling the financial pinch soon. In all likelihood, she'd have to move back in with her parents at some point until the world forgot about her, but for now she was only just managing to keep her head above water.

She opened up her manuscript, and reread the last chapter. This was the one thing that brought her any joy at the moment. She loved how the story and characters were developing. Her pregnant werewolf detective would be going into labor soon. And Iris had submerged herself in a happy little research bubble, reading anything she could find on lycanthropy, with materials ranging from serious psychological tomes, to myths and folklore, as well as sexy, fun paranormal romances.

She was watching a fascinating documentary about European lycanthropic mythology when a quiet knock sounded on her bedroom door. She paused and tilted her head, wondering if she'd imagined the sound.

When the timid knock came again, she swiveled her chair to face the door.

"Come in."

"Hey, Iris" her flatmate Hilary said quietly. "We need to talk."

Hilary and their other flatmate, Nora, stood framed in Iris's bedroom doorway, and Iris froze at the sight of them. The women wore matching expressions of apology and both looked supremely uncomfortable. Iris immediately knew what they wanted to discuss with her.

She fought to keep the wobble out of her voice, but couldn't quite hold back the hot press of tears welling up in her eyes as she asked, "When do you want me out?"

———✿———

"You HAVE TO, Trystan. Seriously, the studio is threatening us with breach of contract if you don't do at least one more interview." Bianca, Trystan's PR guru, glared at him over the rims of her cat's-eye glasses. It was her signature *I mean business, Mister!* glower. A look she'd used more on Trystan these past two weeks than she'd done in the entirety of their decade-long business relationship. "Quinn, talk some sense into him. He's being unreasonable."

Quinny slanted Trystan a helpless look. He was usually a hardass when it came to shit like this, but he was still treading on eggshells around Trystan after everything that had happened with—

His brain skittered away from her name. He tried not to consciously form that name in his mind, on his lips, but he couldn't fucking escape it in his dreams. And that made uninterrupted sleep an impossibility.

"After the shit Holmes pulled at the last one, I'm not inclined to do another fucking interview, Bee," Trystan told the woman, hoping his tone brooked no argument.

Bee could be stubborn about these things but who could blame her? That was what he paid her for after all. He chugged down his protein shake in one go and slammed the shaker on the marble countertop when he was done. He swiped his forearm across his upper lip afterward—he hated the vile stuff—but after eating pretty much whatever the fuck he wanted over the past few months, and not maintaining his strict workout schedule, he needed to get back into shape.

Bee and Quinny had ambushed him first thing this morning. It wasn't even five-thirty yet, for Christ's sake. They'd made sure to show up before Trystan's morning workout.

"What about a compromise?" Quinny offered, stepping forward with his palms up in surrender. He looked incongruous in Trystan's kitchen, wearing a three-piece navy-blue pin-striped suit, while Trystan himself only wore gray sweatpants and a navy-blue tank top.

Bee—a petite sixty-something-year-old flower child—was dressed in her usual bohemian flighty style, wearing a flowy caftan-esque chiffon thing. Her hair was up in a messy chignon, bottle-blonde wisps trailing down around her face. Her make-up was caked on as always, with clumpy mascara—that was already smearing despite the early hour—and bright red lipstick, which had left a stain on her incisors. She folded her arms across her chest, and the many bracelets and beads she wore on her wrists, clacked together at the movement.

"What kind of compromise?" she asked, squinting at Quinny suspiciously. Her glasses would be a lot more effective if she actually looked through them, instead of over them, every once in a while.

"Why not let Trystan choose the journalist, the venue, and the medium?"

"Trystan would choose a high school blogger just to fuck with me," Bee protested, and Trystan grinned wickedly.

"Brilliant idea, Bee! This is why I pay you the big bucks, baby."

"Shut up, you massive man child," she said, reluctant affection nipping at the edges of her words.

Trystan braced his palms on the countertop and stared unseeingly down at the grayish-green veins in the white marble between his hands.

"I don't mind Quinny's idea. Let me think about it, okay?"

"I'll need an answer by tonight, Trystan," Bee implored.

"Yeah, okay," he said with a careless shrug, not really interested, but knowing he'd pick someone just to get her and Quinny off his back. Better to just get this shit over and done with. He lifted his gaze to Chance, who stood quietly in the furthest corner of the kitchen. He nodded at the man, "You ready?"

Chance's expression didn't change. "If you are."

"Let's go."

Trystan had a home gym, and since he'd learned that

Chance was proficient in mixed martial arts and Krav Maga, he'd been working out and training with the guy. Trystan was a pretty decent MMA fighter—nothing *close* to Chance's level of course—but Krav Maga was new to him and he was enjoying the training sessions with his bodyguard.

He used to go running every day, but since his return it was impossible to leave the building without a crowd of journalists dogging his every step and screaming questions at him. He still did a few kilometers on the treadmill, but his heart wasn't in it—he missed his outdoor runs too much. Instead, he channeled his excess energy into weight training and martial arts with Chance.

He waved insouciantly at his manager and PR agent as Chance preceded him from the kitchen, ignoring their outraged faces.

"Lock up on your way out," he told them as he left the room.

"Great workout," he huffed, an hour and a half later as he lay flat on his back on a workout mat. Chance nodded in response.

"You're getting better," the man said, as he prodded the inside of his cheek with his tongue, wincing a little as he found the spot that had split open after Trystan had broken through his defenses to sneak in a punch. His cheek was swollen and would likely bruise.

"Sorry about your face there, mate," Trystan said.

"That's fine. Better this ugly mug taking some damage than those fine porcelain features of yours," Chance said with a rare grin. Laugh lines fanned out from the corners of his eyes which told Trystan that the man's features probably settled into a smile more often when he wasn't at work.

Chance had pulled his punches in the beginning and when Trystan had called him out on it, he'd laughed and muttered something about not wanting to mess up Trystan's pretty profile. But after Trystan had told him to cut it out, Chance had been less solicitous, landing body blows, while still staying away from Trystan's face.

Trystan pushed to his feet with a pained groan, and limped, barefoot, from the room toward the kitchen.

The penthouse apartment was blessedly quiet, Bee and Quinny long gone. His cleaning staff had also been and gone if the lemon-fresh scent in the air was anything to go by. He usually kept a chef and housekeeper in-house, but had wanted solitude after his return from South Africa and all that had followed it. And so Trystan had dispatched the spluttering Frenchman and his equally outraged wife—the housekeeper—to his home in Malibu, where his brother, Dan, was currently staying with his wife and kids on a short family vacation.

Chance was tolerated because he was a necessity. Especially now.

Trystan withdrew two bottles of water from the fridge and handed one to Chance, who'd followed him into the kitchen.

The man rarely spoke, which usually suited Trystan fine, but this morning he felt the need to speak to someone. Someone who didn't really give a fuck about his fame or infamy.

"So... know any good journalists I can contact for this godforsaken interview?" he asked, half-jokingly, but honestly not sure who the hell he was going to approach. "*Good journalist*, what a fucking oxymoron that is."

Chance unscrewed his bottle top, took a thirsty drink and then eased his bulk onto a tall bar stool, the bottle loosely grasped between his hands on the counter.

"Only the one you introduced me to," the big Aussie said in such quiet tones that for a second Trystan wasn't sure he'd heard him correctly. But when the words sank in, he staggered slightly and sat down on one of the stools as well, swiveling to face Chance.

Nobody within his inner circle had dared to refer to her even obliquely since his return and he wasn't quite sure how to deal with Chance's statement.

He toyed with his bottle cap, screwing and unscrewing it as he considered how to respond to that quiet statement.

"Iris—" If he hadn't been sitting down, his knees would have buckled at the sound and feel of her name on his lips. Jesus... fuck, he'd missed saying it. Missed hearing it. He swallowed past the arid dryness of his throat before continuing. "Iris isn't a journalist. She never really wanted to be one."

"Yeah? Fucked up that she wrote that article then, isn't it? Why would she do such a thing?"

"For the money most likely. The fame. The attention." Every word he uttered felt wrong, bulky and out of place in his mouth.

"For someone who wanted money, fame and attention, she definitely isn't courting it much now, is she? Hasn't consented to a single interview, hides out in her flat all day long."

"What do you mean? How do you know this?" Trystan

knew he should shut this down. Chance was being borderline insubordinate—he was pushing buttons, testing boundaries. And yet, Trystan couldn't bring himself to stop the man. He hadn't dared think of her over the past two weeks. In his dreams he made love to her every night. In his nightmares, she laughed at him and cruelly mocked his vulnerability and stupidity for trusting her and confiding in her. And yet, in reality, he hadn't once dared to find out how much she was enjoying all of her fame and notoriety at his expense.

"It's my job to know things. She's a potential threat to your safety—"

"*Iris?*" Trystan scoffed, genuinely shocked at Chance's statement. "She wouldn't hurt a fly."

"Someone who wouldn't hurt a fly would never have written all of those personal things about you."

"What are you doing?" Trystan asked through stiff lips, leveling a frigid glare at the man. "This is none of your fucking business."

Chance shrugged, taking another sip of water.

"You asked. And I thought we were just talking."

Trystan was clenching his jaw so hard, he could hear his teeth grinding.

"What do you mean she hides out in her flat all day long?" he heard himself asking, his tone of voice intense, as if the words were being spoken by another iteration of himself. One who cared very much about the answer to that question.

"Well, she can't leave without being accosted by the press. She's shut down all her social media accounts—not that she was very active on them before, mind you... terribly negligent for an attention hog to not post every detail of her life on social media. Anyway, shut them all down because of the harassment."

"*What* harassment?" Trystan asked tautly and Chance's gaze sharpened on his face.

"The usual unimaginative bullshit, people calling her a whore, slut, cunt..."

"Jesus," Trystan muttered, running a shaky hand over his face. The thought of the sweet, gentle Iris he believed he'd known confronted by such hatred and ugliness was sickening.

"Well, they think it serves her right for the way she treated you. And then all that stuff in her journal about her anxiety and phobias. Fucking weird shit to reveal about yourself to an unforgiving public, if you ask me. Don't know why she'd do that."

Trystan glared at the man, knowing what Chance was doing, recognizing that he had a point to prove, but unable to stop him from doing so. Because he wanted to—*needed to*—hear this.

"Those are the randos on the street. The paps are worse. Because she's refused to grant any interviews, they've gone feral on her. All the pseudo-psychological articles about her so-called clinical depression, pathological stalking tendencies. I think she was described as psychotic and psychopathic in a single article."

"She's staying with her family, right?"

"She didn't want to bring the shitstorm to their doorstep. That was a little naïve of her... because, of *course* it affected them. They've lost business, been harassed, had to change their numbers. The kid brother has been in several fights already."

Chance said naïve, while Trystan called it innocent. She was so damned innocent. Despite what and who her father had been, despite what she had aspired to be, she had no real concept of how ugly people could get. After all, she'd once confronted a near-rabid beast with sweet optimism and confidence and the belief that he would never really hurt her.

"And Iris is where?"

"Trapped. In her flat."

Trystan swallowed back a moan at those words.

Trapped. God. She would hate that. She had to be terrified. With no freedom of movement, it was her worst nightmare.

"She checked her messages for the first time last night. Thousands of them. Dozens were threats of bodily harm or death."

Trystan's head shot up and his stomach churned.

"*What?*"

"You had to know this would happen," Chance said, his voice even—almost affable—and his green eyes somber. "You're *you*. She's a little nobody from Southfields with no weight behind her name. And when you left her unprotected to face the wolves by herself you sent out a very clear message to all the sickos and fuckin' crazies out there: open season on Iris Hughes."

Chapter Twenty

pen season on Iris Hughes.

The five words rattled around in Trystan's brain for the rest of the day. He couldn't get it out of his mind. Along with the fucking horror he felt at the knowledge of everything she'd been subjected to these past few weeks.

Chance had clammed up after that last statement, going back to his usual monosyllabic, taciturn self. Although Trystan was starting to believe that the usual that Chance showed Trystan was not the usual he presented to everyone else.

The other man had politely deferred from answering any further questions about Iris and had excused himself to take a quick shower. The rest of the day he'd spent lurking and hovering, occasionally playing with Luna, and vetting any of Trystan's unscheduled drop-ins—from the pizza-delivery guy to Trystan's PA. He'd left at six-thirty, when Caleb had arrived to take over babysitting/bodyguarding duties.

After picking at the pepperoni pizza he'd ordered for dinner, Trystan eventually retreated to his den with Luna, leaving Caleb in the living room with a thick book. Trystan didn't usually have a round-the-clock in-house protective detail, but Sam felt the extra precautionary measure was necessary for the next few months or weeks, at least. And Trystan found it easier to acquiesce than argue with the man.

Luna settled down on the sofa next to him and immediately fell asleep. Trystan envied her that easy descent into oblivion. He scratched behind her ears, and she moaned in contentment without opening her eyes.

He reached for his laptop on the coffee table, hiked an ankle onto the opposite knee and rested the lightweight device on his thigh. He stared at the closed computer for a second before swallowing thickly and opening it.

He hadn't looked her up. Hadn't asked anyone for any information about her. Had shied away from following up on what had happened to her after that last day. Instead, he'd read that initial fucked-up article in the car en route from the airport—after his security team had so unceremoniously hustled her into the other car—and had resented her. Fucking loathed her. The seething sense of betrayal had fueled his fury and he'd clung to it. Had needed it because without the betrayal, without the fury, all he had was his overwhelming grief.

He ran a search on her name and read—with increasing horror—the articles, the social media clips showing her literally fleeing from journalists, the outraged rants on his behalf calling her a psycho stalker, a bitch, an ugly whore, a greedy slut...

It went on and on, every damned—sometimes blatantly libelous—article making outrageous accusations against her.

Then, just before his ill-fated interview with Mike Holmes five days ago, more excerpts from her journal had found their way online. Divulging painfully personal details about her phobias, her anxiety, her coping mechanisms, and the therapy she needed to keep it under control.

It was hard to read, and the mocking responses to those revelations from an unsympathetic public which added *#teamtrystan* to every repulsive, nearly-impossible-to-watch social media clip... That they would use his name to fucking torment her sickened him. And why wouldn't they?

Chance was right. Trystan had thrown her to the wolves. He had abandoned her. And that very abandonment had validated this cruel, relentless public haranguing. Trystan had left Iris to face this hatred and vitriol alone, without even the physical comfort and support of her family. Despite that article being the death knell to their short-lived relationship, he should've protected her from this. Should've kept a security detail on her. But he'd wanted her to hurt, wanted her to suffer. And now... faced with the proof of that torment he found himself unable to stomach the reality of it.

He opened up the original article—wanting to remind himself of what she had done, of why he'd left her exposed to all of this invective—then sucked in a deep breath and released it on a slow, controlled exhalation. He then forced himself to reread the article she'd coauthored with her friend.

A quick scan at first, like ripping off a Band-Aid, then slower and with more consideration. After the fifth time, his

horror and outrage—which had intensified with each consecu-
tive reread—had him so choked up he found it hard to breathe.

His motor functions felt sluggish, his brain foggy... and—
after he once again forced himself to read those leaked excerpts
from her journal—he knew exactly what to do.

He needed a moment to curb his fury, desperation and
panic, before picking up his phone to call Bee. He anticipated
resistance, but this was a matter of life and death and he would
not be swayed from his current course of action.

"THANK you so much for this, Chance." Iris was emotionally
and physically exhausted and on the verge of tears. All of which
could be heard in her quavering voice as she effusively thanked
Chance while he led her into the guest room of the quaint house
that he shared with a—as-yet-unknown to Iris—colleague.

"Don't mention it. I wish you'd called me sooner," he said,
placing her suitcases beside the bed.

"It won't be for long. Just until they lose my scent and I can
sneak home."

"Stay as long as you like. I don't mind. Colby won't either."

"And your friend knows I'll be staying, right?"

"I haven't had the opportunity to tell her yet, but she's not
one to turn her back on someone in need."

It was truly grating to be described as someone in need. Iris
was usually ferociously independent, and she hated being

reliant on relative strangers at a time like this. She'd never felt more alone...

"Are you sure?"

"Definitely. Don't worry about it. And make yourself at home. You'll have the house to yourself during the day. I'm on days at the moment, leave at four-thirty am, usually home after seven, unless, uh, he needs me to accompany him somewhere, or I go out with my mates. Colby leaves at seven and is home by five-thirty. She doesn't go out too much. But she may have some friends over occasionally."

Iris nodded politely, but doubted that she'd be here long enough to get too familiar with their patterns. She did briefly allow her mind to linger over Chance's hours. He was still Trystan's primary close-protection office and she wondered why Trystan would need Chance that early in the morning. He hadn't struck her as an extreme early bird... then again, he'd practically been on vacation when she'd met him. No schedule, no responsibilities, and a fake little holiday romance to help him pass the time.

She shoved aside that last thought. It was getting harder and harder to keep her anger and bitterness toward him at bay. The worse things got for her, the more she found herself resenting Trystan. She'd known her life would change once her relationship with him became public knowledge, but she would've been able to handle anything with him by her side. Without his support, she was left with nothing but chaos and loneliness. She missed her quiet old life, missed being anonymous, missed spending time with her parents and brother. God, she even missed lending a hand at their catering events a couple of times a month.

But right now, she was stuck in this colorless, featureless purgatory, with no end in sight. An easy target for some truly unhinged and frightening people to mock and threaten. Her anxiety levels were through the roof. She was hypervigilant, paranoid and jumping at her own shadow. She'd already had several panic attacks—one so severe it had actually felt like she was dying.

"Iris?" Chance's voice interrupted her churning thoughts, thankfully dragging her back into the present. He was still standing beside her luggage, his hands on his hips as his concerned green gaze ran over her face. "You okay?"

"I'm—yes—I'm fine." Her voice was weak and scratchy and she sounded far from fine, but he nodded, taking her words at face value.

"I have to go. I'm on duty this morning."

"Oh?" Her eyes drifted to the quaint cuckoo clock on the wall—everything about this room was a little twee, not at all what she'd expected from Chance's home—it was a little after eight in the morning. He'd collected her from her flat at seven-thirty, and strong-armed their way through the ever-present crowd of reporters already lurking outside her building. There were always a few milling about on the sidewalk, no matter what the hour. One could *almost* admire their dedication.

"A bit of a late start for you this morning then, isn't it?" she observed, not wanting to look like she was fishing for information.

Chance made a noncommittal sound before lifting his big

shoulders. "I asked the night guy, Caleb, to stay a few hours longer so that I could help you move. But he'll be pissed if I don't relieve him soon."

"Yes, of course. You should go. I'll be fine."

"Right. See you this evening then." He strode toward the bedroom door, throwing words back over his shoulder on his way out. "The fridge and pantry are fully stocked. Help yourself. But stay well away from the chocolate chip ice cream, and —if you value your life—do *not* touch any Jaffa cakes or custard creams you may find lurking in the pantry. Colby has a sweet tooth and she can be irrationally mean if any of her snacks disappear."

He was definitely speaking from experience if the pained expression on his handsome face was any indication.

"Noted," Iris said with a weak smile. "Thanks for the warning."

"See ya later."

He was gone moments later, leaving Iris alone with a sinking feeling of dread settling in the pit of her stomach. She poked around her—incongruously—pretty and frilly temporary room.

It wasn't to her taste, all delicate pinks and lace and doilies. And it made her wonder about Chance's housemate. Despite the expensive, tailored suits he wore on the job, Chance couldn't quite disguise the roughness beneath his urbane exterior. He seemed wholly out of place in this pretty little dollhouse overly adorned with fragile knickknacks and keepsakes.

The pale pink, cream, and white quilt on the guest bed alone appeared to be a family heirloom and—afraid of somehow ruining it—Iris carefully stripped it from the bed and folded it neatly. She placed it in the large antique cedar kist at the foot of the bed.

Iris called her mother first, needing to reassure her parents that she was fine.

"I don't see why you couldn't stay with us, Iris. We can't let these horrible people dictate how we live our lives."

"I know that, Mum. But it's too hard right now... They've already targeted you. If they knew I was there, it would be much worse."

"Iris..."

"Mum," she interrupted quickly, not wanting to hear another variation of the same plea. "Chance and his housemate both work for one of the biggest security firms in the world. I'm safe as houses here. Better, nobody knows I'm here, which makes me breathe easier. I can actually go outside, sit in the garden, get some fresh air without people constantly vying for my attention, asking me intrusive questions, or straight up screaming insults at me."

"I'm so angry at that man for dragging you into this mess. And for then up and leaving you high and dry to deal with it alone."

"Evan did this, Mum. Not Trystan. He's protecting himself."

"You're allowed to be angry with him, Iris. God knows, your father and I am. I will never ever watch one of his films again!"

Oh, Iris *was* angry. She was a seething mass of fury, but there wasn't any point in rehashing all of those negative emotions with her mother. It wouldn't achieve anything. She didn't even think it would be particularly cathartic. The best thing for Iris right now would be to just forget any of this ever happened. Which was difficult when everybody was so determined to remind her of it.

"I'd prefer to just forget I ever knew him, Mum. And move on with my life. I'll work through the negative emotions in therapy." Just add it to the long list of other shit she needed to work through.

It was hard not to curl up into a ball of self-pitying misery. Not to howl *why me* at the unsympathetic sky. She'd been a target for bullies her entire life. Only to discover that even her best friend had been subtly bullying and manipulating her for years, and then she'd gone and fallen in love with one too.

She felt like a fool and like the years-long progress she'd made in dealing with her anxiety and self-doubt had all been lost beneath this landslide of betrayal from two people in whom she'd mistakenly placed so much trust.

Her mother wisely dropped the subject and after talking for a few more minutes, they rang off with heartfelt *I love yous*.

Iris was unpacking an hour later when she heard the front door open. Startled and a little concerned at the unexpected sound, she cautiously poked her head around the bedroom door, just in time to see a small, curvy woman wearily trudge into the hallway.

The woman looked up, and her eyes widened in shock.

"*Oh.*"

"Hi," Iris greeted, her voice tentative as she stepped fully into the hallway, and walked toward where the woman was still standing staring at her in confusion. She held out her hand.

"You must be Colby. I'm Iris Hughes. I'm not sure if Chance had the opportunity to tell you that I'd be staying here for a few days. Uh... only if you're okay with that, of course."

"I know who you are." The other woman said, not reaching for her hand, and Iris let it drop limply to her side. "Chance didn't tell me about you being here."

"Oh..." Iris swallowed thickly, trying to keep her breathing steady and her anxiety under control. What would she do now? Where would she go? "I'm sorry. I thought... I'll just get my stuff and call an Uber. I—"

"No." The woman, who was wearing a blue pencil skirt, crisp white blouse and a matching blue jacket, shook her head. "I'm sorry. You must think I'm terribly rude. I just wasn't expecting to find anyone here. Least of all someone who's been dominating the entertainment news lately. Not that I'm really that interested in gossip, mind you. I just need to stay abreast of things because of our client list, you know?"

Iris nodded automatically. Not at all sure what to make of this pretty woman with the Betty Boop figure, the doll-like face and the earnest wide, round blue eyes. She was cute as a button, while simultaneously appearing to be as serious as a heart attack.

"I'm Colby Campbell, Chance's housemate. And, of course you're welcome to stay for as long as you need to. What's happening to you is very unfair, and I'm sorry."

The sincerity in her voice brought tears to Iris's eyes, and the other woman's already large eyes widened even further at the sight of them.

"Oh God, please don't cry. I didn't mean to upset you."

"I'm not upset. It's just that… people haven't been very kind recently."

"I can imagine." Colby placed her briefcase neatly—in a slot obviously for that exact purpose—next to the shoe rack in the entrance hall, and kicked up her heels one at a time to unbuckle and peel off her neat black and white Mary Jane pumps. The shoes also very tidily went into an empty spot on the shoe rack.

Without the heels she was a good four inches shorter than Iris. Probably only barely scraping in at five-foot-one.

"Have you settled in yet?" she asked Iris, as she padded past her on stockinged feet.

"I'm unpacking now. I only arrived about an hour ago. Chance dropped me off, but I wasn't expecting either of you back for hours."

"I have a migraine coming on," Colby murmured, heading toward the kitchen. "Nothing I can do to stop it really."

"Oh gosh, I'm so sorry."

"I sometimes get them when I have my period. Like women don't suffer enough, right? I need a cup of chamomile tea, some ibuprofen, my heated beanbag, and a dark room."

"Of course. Why don't you get changed, and I'll sort out the tea and beanbag?" Iris offered, happy to be of some use to the woman who was being so kind despite the shock of finding an unexpected intruder in her home.

"Do you mind terribly?" Colby asked, looking pale and strained. "The beanbag is in my knitting basket in the living room. You'll find the tea in the cupboard above the kettle."

"Not at all."

The other woman gave Iris a weak smile "Thank you so

much. I'm going to be useless soon. I've been seeing bright spots for half an hour already, which is why I left the office. I didn't sleep well last night. That's usually a sign of an imminent migraine for me, but it's such a vague symptom staying home felt like overkill, especially considering how rarely I get migraines."

"How long does it usually last?"

"It varies, but my average is seven hours. I try to sleep through it, but that doesn't always help."

"You go on up to bed. I'll be there shortly with your tea and beanbag."

"We'll talk later, okay?" Colby muttered apologetically, her words slurring ever so slightly. She stumbled a little as she turned and headed toward the staircase.

Colby and Chance's bedrooms were upstairs. Chance had taken Iris on a quick tour of the place when they'd first arrived. The two larger upstairs bedrooms shared a Jack and Jill bathroom, which now seemed odd to Iris since they clearly weren't a couple and neither appeared to be using the smaller downstairs bathroom. Which had to mean they shared the one upstairs. It was an intimate arrangement for two people who barely communicated enough for one to convey to the other that he'd invited a guest to stay at their house.

Oh well. It felt rude to speculate when these two strangers had been so kind to her already.

She got busy with the tea and the beanbag and took the items upstairs less than ten minutes later. Iris found Colby curled up in a king-sized four-poster bed—one of those romantic ones with a gauzy canopy. The bed dominated the medium-sized room, and the rest of the oversized pieces of furniture looked stuffed in, with barely any room for movement between them.

"Colby?" Iris whispered, as she stepped into the darkened room. "I have your tea. I'll leave it on the bedside table, okay?"

She did so and placed the beanbag on the bed beside the small huddled figure. Colby gave a pained little grunt of acknowledgement and Iris tiptoed out of the room and shut the door carefully behind her.

"I NEED TO SPEAK WITH IRIS," Trystan told Chance one morning, four days after his unscheduled meeting with Bee and Quinny. The close-protection officer slanted a narrow-eyed look at Trystan in response to the comment, but his face remained inscrutable while he waited for Trystan to continue. "She's not taking my calls and her mailbox is full."

"She probably blocked or deleted your number," Chance said with a noncommittal shrug. For some reason—despite the guy's poker face—Trystan had the feeling the big blond bastard relished pointing that out. And he hated that the man was likely correct in that assumption.

"Yes. That's highly probable. But be that as it may, I still need to have a conversation with her, and I want you to make that happen."

"How?" Chance asked. He was perched on a barstool in the kitchen, doing a crossword puzzle with a *pen*, which he lowered to the page of his puzzle book as his gaze intensified on Trystan's face.

"I don't fucking know," Trystan responded, frustration creeping into his voice. "That's the type of shit you guys do, right?"

"Kidnapping?"

"*What?* No... what the fuck? Of course not, I meant facilitate safe meetings between parties."

"I don't think she'd be amenable to a meeting with you right now, sir. Kidnapping would be the only way to get her in the same room with you. Also, we're not a dating or matchmaking service. We don't facilitate *meetings* between couples."

Trystan gritted his teeth. Had this guy always been such a smug, arrogant prick? Why was he only noticing it now? Not that Trystan generally minded people speaking their minds around him. He wasn't one of those assholes who needed to be surrounded by sycophants and yes-men, but he wasn't used to his bodyguards sounding off with such enthusiasm either.

They usually just stood silently in the background and looked menacing. He and Chance had been chatting more and had even bonded a bit during of their workouts and because of the fact that they were compatriots.

Part of Trystan wanted to put Chance in his place. Another—larger—part found that he didn't mind the honesty, even though it made him want to punch the guy in the nose. He briefly fantasized about what that would feel like, imagining using the man's own moves against him. Trystan sighed, as he acknowledged that Chance could likely paint the floor with his face if he chose to. Not that he would. Even more humiliating was the knowledge that Chance would probably simply side-step any attempt from him and watch him fall on his arse.

"It's clear that Iris and I aren't able to simply walk out of our homes to meet somewhere for coffee," Trystan explained with—what he felt was—the patience of a saint. "I need you or one of your colleagues to arrange a meeting with her in a neutral spot, free from prying eyes and ears."

"Again," Chance said, with equally exaggerated patience. "This is not something we would be able to do if Iris is not receptive to the idea. And she's not likely to be."

"How the hell would you know that until she's asked?" Trystan snapped out the question.

Chance took an infuriatingly slow sip from his coffee before replying, "She was just kicked out of her flat. I'm afraid, she's not going to be feeling particularly charitable toward you... sir."

Trystan's stomach dropped to the soles of his feet at the snippet of information. Oh God, this was going to be so much harder than he'd expected. He was desperate to have a conversation with Iris. He'd been calling her nonstop for days, and had been hitting a brick wall. His WhatsApp messages remained unseen and unread, a reliable indicator that she'd blocked his number. Her social media accounts had all been disabled.

The time for neutral meetings and rational discussions had passed. He'd allowed this to go on for longer than it should have. He should have reached out four days ago, after reading that article again. But he'd been a fucking coward. He'd wanted to have all his ducks in a row before he spoke to her. Now this news.

"Where is she staying?" Trystan asked, his voice shaky and

low. "Is she with her parents? I need you to take me there, right now."

"What?" For the first time Chance's slightly bored, smug demeanor slipped and he went from a relaxed slouch to upright in a second. "Take you where?"

"To Iris. At her parents' home."

"That's not a good idea, sir. We won't be able to control the environment, not at such short notice."

"It's better if I don't show up with a fucking entire army of bodyguards—"

"Close-protection officers," Chance corrected.

"Whatever the fuck! You know what I mean. We can call Quinny, take his car. It's a gray, ten-year-old Toyota. The most ordinary, nondescript car on the planet. It won't draw attention."

"But *you* will. You forget you're one of the most instantly recognizable people in the world."

"People see what they expect to see," Trystan said, warming to the mad idea. "And nobody expects me to show up to a house in Southfields at random-'o-clock on a Tuesday evening. I'll wear a hoodie, a baseball cap, something. I can pretend to be the pizza guy. Work with me here, Chance. I need to see her."

"No," Chance said, his voice adamant, his expression no-nonsense. "I can't let you do that."

"You forget that while I know that it's in my best interests to follow your instruction for my own safety, I don't actually *have* to do so. If I choose to walk out of here right now, you have no recourse but to follow me out that door."

Chance's lips tightened and he glared at Trystan.

"I expect this immature diva shit from the newly famous pop boys and girls, not from a seasoned professional who should know better."

"Sorry to disappoint you, Chance, but I'm out of options here. I have to speak with her. Before my interview on Thursday."

"Fine. I'll make a few calls and try to *facilitate* that meeting between you."

But that wasn't good enough for Trystan, not anymore. Not after what he'd learned about Iris being thrown out of her flat. He knew how much she'd enjoyed living there, how she'd prized the relationships with her flatmates. She must have been utterly devastated when they'd kicked her out.

"No. I'm going now. The longer I leave this, the worse it'll be."

"Can't really imagine how much worse it could get," Chance muttered, and Trystan tried to keep his panic at bay at the veracity in the man's words. It definitely couldn't get much worse. Iris wouldn't want to see him or have anything to do with him. But he had to try.

"I'll call Quinny for his car and get changed. Be ready to leave in fifteen minutes."

Chance heaved a long-suffering sigh and the sound gave Trystan pause. "That won't be necessary. She's not staying with her parents. I told you before, she didn't want to dump all of this shit right on their doorstep. She was desperate and felt like she had nowhere else to turn, so she took me up on the offer I made the day you kicked her out of your car. She moved into my spare room two days ago."

Chapter Twenty-One

"Iris is living with you?" Trystan asked, completely blindsided by Chance's statement.

"Yes. She had nowhere else to go."

"I didn't think you knew each other that well," Trystan said, not sure how to feel about this.

His sluggish brain was starting to finally put two and two together. No wonder Chance had been so uncharacteristically chatty and judgmental about Trystan's treatment of Iris. No wonder he knew so fucking *much* about what was going on in her life right now. Trystan should have questioned that knowledge long before now, but he'd had his head stuck so far up his own arse for too long. He'd been unable to see anything clearly since that fucking article was published.

"We don't," Chance said, in response to Trystan's absent-minded earlier comment. "But like I said, she was desperate."

"How is she?" Trystan asked, his voice a hoarse whisper, eyes intent.

"Sad, exhausted, defeated... angry."

"Angry with me?"

"What do you think?"

"I think..." Trystan paused and his brain stalled while his heart picked up the slack. "No. I *know* I hurt her. I know I broke her heart."

He'd known that since he'd reread that article and seen the inconsistencies in the writing styles between the journal and the rest of the article. He knew Iris's writing and that fucking article hadn't been written by her. Not one fucking part of it. The only words he'd known for certain were hers were the ones drawn directly from her journal.

Trystan had no reason to believe Iris *didn't* have a part in that story—she could have given that Evan bitch access to her journal—except for what his gut told him. And after recognizing how negatively this article had impacted her life, seeing how fiercely she'd clung to her privacy, her dignity and pride—Trystan had simply known that she was entirely innocent of any and all wrongdoing.

She was being so fucking brave in the face of overwhelming hatred and bullying. And Trystan, who had vowed never again to hurt her, to always give her the benefit of the doubt, had been the biggest fucking bully of them all.

He couldn't fix what they'd had before. He knew that. But he could make this better for Iris. That's what he was working on but he needed to speak to her first, to give her a heads up.

"Thank you." His voice was shaky as he said those words. "For doing that for her. For protecting her when I didn't."

"I didn't do it for you." Chance said, his voice frosty.

"I know that. But thank you nonetheless."

Chance didn't acknowledge his thanks with so much as a nod, and Trystan knew he deserved the man's contempt.

"Nobody knows she's at mine," Chance said. "So I guess it's the perfect neutral spot for that meeting you're so keen on. But we can't just show up. I have to clear it with her first. And if she says no, that's it. I won't bushwhack her."

"He wants to what?" Iris asked blankly.

"You heard me," Chance said.

"I did but I was sure I must've been mistaken. You *told* him I was here?"

Chance's sigh was a loud and noisy blast into the receiver. "I had no choice, Iris. He was dead set on going to your parents' house to see you."

"You should have let him," Iris retorted, her voice dripping with acid. "My dad would've kicked his arse."

The thought of her scrawny father kicking anyone's arse was incongruous, but the man was angry enough at Trystan to give it a good go.

"Uh... maybe," Chance said, the soul of tact and discretion. "Iris, you can say no."

"What does he want to talk about?"

"He didn't say."

"Why should I trust him not to hurl all kinds of unfounded, hurtful, and unfair accusations at me again?"

Chance remained silent, giving her the room she needed to rant and rave and work it out for herself.

"Put him on the line, Chance."

"Are you sure?"

"I'm sure," she said in her grimmest voice, happy that she sounded certain even though she was a mass of nerves and anxiety right now.

"Hold on." There were muffled voices and sounds as the phone was handed over.

"Iris."

Oh God, the sound of his voice damned near broke her barely healed heart all over again. And the pain of it merely confirmed that the decision she'd made was the right one.

"I don't want to see you."

There was a long silence at the other end before his voice taut and urgent replied,

"Please."

The word was a whisper. So faint she nearly didn't hear it, but it packed a punch. Because it was stripped raw of all Trystan's legendary confidence. It was denuded of his charisma and charm. It was the broken remnant of a word and yet, its impact was profound. Because—despite all that the broken single-syllable word lacked—it was steeped in despair, desolation and desperation.

But Iris hardened her heart against it. He couldn't do this to her. He couldn't ignore her for two weeks, while believing the absolute worst of her and abandoning her in the wreckage he'd made of her life and expect her to be swayed by just one word.

"No."

"Okay... you don't want to see me, yeah?" His accent was back and she knew it tended to appear only when he was at his most vulnerable. "What if we just talk? Like this?"

"I have nothing to say to you. And I can't imagine how anything *you* could say would interest me."

"I know you didn't write that article." There was an expectant pause after that statement and Iris sighed gustily, hoping the sound adequately relayed her feelings regarding *that* statement.

"You expecting applause?" she asked, breaking the—by now —awkward silence. "An award perhaps?"

"Iris, I fucked up."

She laughed at that, the sound harsh and bitter, but didn't acknowledge the admission in any way other than that abrasive, curt sound.

"Don't bother me again, Trystan. I'm trying to move on with my life. You can go back to being a remote, larger-than-life superstar and all of this can hopefully one day become a distant, unpleasant memory. I have nothing more to say to you."

"I promise I'll fix it."

"I don't care." Why was she still talking? Why didn't she just disconnect the call? Iris knew that was what she should do. And yet, she couldn't bring herself to sever what she knew would be the last contact with him.

"I'm sorry I hurt you, sorry I doubted you, sorry I was an arsehole. I'm so fucking sorry."

"You keep apologizing, Trystan," she said, a hot tide of bitter, acidic rage rising up inside her like a tsunami. And Iris discovered that she actually *had* a lot to say to him. And this was the last opportunity she'd ever have to get it off her chest. "That's all you've been doing since the day we met. It's a twisted, toxic cycle that pretty much defines our doomed non-relationship. You *fuck* up, you apologize, and I forgive you. But I'm breaking that pattern right now. I don't forgive you. I'll never forgive you. You *hurt* me, right after you promised never to hurt me again. Never to doubt me again.

"You gave me no opportunity to figure out what the hell had happened, no chance to defend myself. You literally kicked me to the curb, like I was a mangy dog you no longer wanted. No, you'd definitely treat a mangy dog better than you did me. I was expendable, easily disposed of, like so much garbage. You never trusted me, Trystan. You always believed I'd betray you somehow. You couldn't look past the fact that Stanford Carter was my biological father, and that I had the absolute nerve to show up at your den of solitude and manly sorrow, in search of—horror of horrors—an interview.

"And after all your pretty promises of sheltering me from the craziness of your life, you threw me in the deep end without so much as a life preserver. I was drowning, I was trapped, I felt like I was dying and you left me there to sink." The last six words emerged on a sob, as the angry tears she'd fought to keep at bay while she said her piece finally welled up and spilled over, adding a quavering thickness to her voice.

"God, Iris..." She heard the same thickness in his voice, but refused to acknowledge it. This was her moment and he didn't get to ruin it by making it about him. Her finger was poised on the red telephone icon, seconds away from finally ending the call. "You're right."

The two words made her hesitate.

"You're right. I let you down. I failed you and abandoned you. And it's something I'll regret to my dying day."

"Goodbye, Trystan."

This time she hung up without hesitation.

"ARE you sure they won't mind?" Iris asked for the umpteenth time as she smoothed her damp palms nervously over her '60s mod-style orange and yellow shift dress, with bright contrasting yellow and orange daisies printed all over the fabric.

The dress had a round neck, short sleeves, and a skirt that fell to mid-thigh., It was one of Iris's favorites and she paired it with white platform shoes. She knew it complemented her dusky skin and thick, curly brown shoulder-length hair—now styled in loose waves—perfectly, which made the friendly, brightly colored dress a much-needed confidence booster.

They were outside the door of a flat in a swanky, upmarket Victorian mansion block in Hammersmith. Iris had walked past this building often over the years but she'd never set foot inside of it before tonight.

Colby gave her a sweet, reassuring smile, before saying, "They won't mind at all. They're going to love you."

Iris wasn't so certain about that. This group of friends was so tight they apparently called their monthly get-togethers "family nights" and Iris—the perpetual socially awkward outsider who didn't make friends very easily—was extremely uncertain about gate-crashing, despite Colby's sincere assurances.

Still, Iris had literally been trapped in one way or the other for over a month—starting in South Africa—with limited social interactions. While, she'd never been particularly outgoing, she'd also never had her movements so forcibly restricted before. She was longing for the company of other people even though she feared that this outing was going to be a complete disaster. Especially since she was particularly wary of strangers right now.

Colby rang the doorbell and it was almost instantly opened by a slender, good-looking guy about Iris's age. He had wavy black hair, designer stubble, and his lovely dark brown eyes were outlined with black eyeliner.

"Thank *God* you're here," he whispered effusively when he saw Colby, enfolding both of her hands in his. "I swear to God I'm going to murder him tonight. You have to hold me back, Colbs! He's being insuffera... oh, *hello*."

This last as he finally caught sight of Iris hovering in the background.

"I know you," he said, staring at Iris like he couldn't quite place her. "Love your dress, by the way. *Groovy, baby*! But seriously, where the fuck do I know you from?"

Dismayed to already have been recognized and not at all sure how to respond, Iris stared back at him, her tongue tied in a knot.

"Oh, I've got it," he said, snapping his fingers. "You were a server at my brother's wedding last year."

Iris laughed, relief and incredulity making the sound a lot sharper than her usual easy-going chuckle. She had no clue what event he was referring to as she often helped her parents. But she was relieved the elephant in the room was in hiding for the moment.

"That's possible. My parents are caterers and I sometimes help out. I'm surprised you remember anybody on the waitstaff at such a significant family event."

He waved a hand dismissively. "I was bored out of my mind and you were noticeable. You kept swapping out Uncle Jos's vodka with water when he started getting loud and obnoxious. I was going to intervene before I realized you had the matter in hand."

"Oh my goodness," Iris laughed again. This time it sounded a lot closer to her regular laugh. "I think I remember that wedding. At some point he was grinding up against one of the bridesmaids."

"He's a gross old perve," the man said with a grimace.

"Jazz, how about you let them in, instead of blocking them at the door?" a woman's voice called from inside and the guy—Jazz?—made an *oops* face and waved them inside.

As Iris passed him, he draped a nonchalant arm around her shoulders, before confiding in a low voice, "I'm Jasper Cromwell, but everyone calls me Jazz. Well, everyone except that boring stick in the mud over there." He pointed his chin at an outrageously handsome man, dressed in a three-piece suit, who was trying to take a laden tray from the heavily pregnant woman in the kitchen.

"Nice to meet you, I'm Iris—"

"Iris Hughes, I know," he said

"But..."

"Well, I knew you were Iris Hughes the moment I saw you standing out there, but I didn't know where the hell I knew you from before all of this Trystan Abbott palaver. I always thought you looked familiar, but it didn't really click until I saw you in the flesh, so to speak. Come on, let's get you introduced."

He led her into the living room.

"Everybody, this is Iris. Iris, everybody."

There were five other people in the room excluding, Jazz, Colby, and Iris. They all looked mildly curious about her and they had warm enough expressions on their faces.

A chorus of greetings came her way before they went back to what they were doing before.

A massive guy was arguing with a lanky, slimmer one about whose playlist they should stream. The handsome man in the suit was still trying to persuade the short, curly haired pregnant woman to hand over the tray, and Colby joined them to add her protest to the man's.

Another woman, a leggy, beautiful blonde made her way over to Jazz and Iris.

"Hi Iris, I'm Bella Weaver... soon to be Bella Weaver-Sloane—"

"A ridiculous mouthful," Jazz said, rolling his eyes. "Just keep your own name, babe."

"*Soon* to be Bella Weaver-Sloane, when I marry that stud

over there," she said with a smug grin as she pointed toward the two men still arguing over the music.

Iris's eyes immediately went to the big, gorgeous man with the serious handsome features in appreciation.

"Ooh no, hun," Jazz muttered beneath his breath, when he saw the direction Iris's eyes had drifted. "Wrong stud. The big guy is married to the tiny pregnant dynamo over there."

Aah, okay. The couples seemed slightly mismatched, but a glance over at the gorgeous dreamy eyed blonde woman still staring at the two men confirmed that she'd locked eyes with the skinny, angular man in the ill-fitting suit and glasses. He was good-looking too, but in a less overt way than the other guys here.

"Excuse me," Bella said, not taking her eyes off her fiancé. "I think I'll add my voice to Pete's. Ty can be such a bossy arse sometimes." She drifted away, then paused to look over her shoulder with a smile. "It's really lovely to meet you, Iris. We'll chat more later."

Iris returned her smile and then focused her attention on Jazz. "So, who are you going to murder tonight and why?"

"Oh. Hugh, the uptight twat in the three-piece suit. Would it kill him to unbutton his collar? Maybe loosen his tie a bit?"

"You're pissed off because of the way he's dressed?"

"No, I'm pissed off because he thinks he's so much better than the rest of mankind. Mr. Perfect, never a hair out of place, lording it over the rest of us feeble-minded commoners."

It seemed like an irrational rant from someone so convivial. And she wondered what the underlying story there was. He soon abandoned the topic of Hugh and took her around the room to introduce her to Pete, Bella's fiancé, then the pregnant woman, Vicki, and her husband, Ty Chambers—their hosts this evening. Hugh, he ignored, and the man came over to introduce himself when Jazz left her chatting with Vicki and Ty to make a beeline for Colby who was pouring herself a glass of wine.

"Jazz and Colby are thick as thieves," Vicki confided in Iris after Hugh wandered off to get a drink as well. "They've bonded over the fact that they both have difficult relationships with a couple of members of the group. Specifically, Jazz with Hugh and Colby with Chance."

"Chance and Colby don't get along?" Iris asked in surprise.

She'd only been living in the house for four days, and she hadn't seen them together much in that time, but Chance struck her as the type of man who'd get along with everybody, and considering their unusual living arrangement, she'd assumed they at least liked each other. Surely you had to *like* the person you shared a house—and a bathroom! —with.

"Oh, I thought you'd have picked up on that since you're, uhm, staying with them..." Vicki's voice trailed off. She was clearly uncomfortable gossiping about her friends and Iris, people-pleaser that she was, immediately steered the conversation in a different direction.

"So, when's the baby due?" she asked.

The woman stared at her blankly.

"Baby? What baby? Oh my God, are you calling me *fat*?"

Iris's mouth dropped open in horror and she could feel her eyes bulging from her head in her desperation *not* to drop her gaze to the woman's protruding belly.

"Jesus, Vicki," Ty berated her, in his twangy American

accent. For such a big guy, he had a quiet voice, the timbre of it almost soothing. "Behave."

Vicki snorted and then guffawed, and before long she was howling. "I'm so sorry, Iris, I couldn't resist. The look on your face..."

Iris joined in the woman's infectious laughter after a few seconds.

"Fine, you got me," she said, after the laughter had died down. "For a second there I was convinced I'd committed the absolute worst social faux pas."

That set Vicki off again and when she finally stopped, she wiped tears from her eyes.

"In answer to your perfectly fine question, Iris," Ty said, giving his wife a pointed look. She rolled her eyes unrepentantly. Iris liked her a lot. "She's eight months along."

"And she *really* shouldn't be hosting tonight," Hugh—who'd rejoined them just as Ty replied—inserted, with a censorious glare at Ty.

"It's like you don't know your sister, Hugh," Ty scoffed.

"We entrusted her to *you*, Ty. This isn't what I call taking good care of her." Wow, Iris was starting to see why Jazz had said the man had a stick up his arse. Then again, he appeared legitimately concerned for Vicki, whom Iris hadn't realized was his sister until now.

"I don't need anyone to take care of me, Hughie," Vicki dismissed with a nonchalant wave, before refocusing her attention on Iris. "Do you have any over-protective big brothers, Iris?"

"A younger one, and he likes to act all tough and protective, but he's just a baby, really."

"I have two. In fact, you stayed in my older brother Miles's home last month with..." Her voice trailed off and her face paled.

And there it was...

That big old elephant came stomping right through the room to take a pachydermian-sized dump all over a perfectly good party.

Iris sighed. "So, I'm guessing everyone here knows about the Trystan thing?"

"Oh my God. I'm so sorry, Iris. You probably don't want to talk about it. You don't have to. I wasn't going to mention it, but my pregnancy brain is a foggy bitch lately." Ty palmed his distressed wife's nape and appeared to give it a gentle squeeze. Vicki leaned against him gratefully.

"It's fine, Vicki," Iris said, keeping her voice gentle. Because it really was fine. Nobody in this room had any malice in their hearts toward her. She'd sensed that almost immediately, and she was so grateful Colby had persuaded her to join them tonight. "It's impossible to avoid the subject and, really, this is the first time I've been out since... everything. And it's unrealistic to think people won't mention it, or be curious about it. I just hate that it's probably going to be the most interesting thing about me from now for eternity."

"Well, that's bollocks," Vicki said vehemently, and Bella and Colby—who had drifted over along with everyone else when the conversation had become awkward—made sounds of agreement. "You will *not* let what happened between you and that man define who and what you are, Iris. We refuse to allow that. You hear me?"

Iris's eyes misted as the unexpected kindness from these lovely people threatened to completely overwhelm her. She inhaled deeply and said, her voice a little shaky, "So, Miles Hollingsworth is your brother? Small world, isn't it?"

IRIS HAD A WONDERFUL EVENING. And when she and Colby finally left many hours later, everyone present had insisted she come to the next family night. Iris left feeling like she could become real friends with these people. It was an exciting, giddying prospect, and for the first time in weeks it felt like something in her life was going right.

Until it all came crashing down when—in the Uber on the way home—Iris's phone started dinging repeatedly. Dread immediately started eating away at her stomach lining again, recent experience having taught her that when her phone started blowing up, it almost always signaled some new catastrophe or the other.

"What's going on?" Colby asked and Iris shrugged.

"I'm not sure," she whispered, digging her phone out of her handbag. At least twenty messages from her parents, Robbie, her former flatmates, and a few of her clients. In addition to five missed calls from her mother, one from Robbie and several from Chance.

This couldn't be good.

MUM

Put on Mike Holmes. RHGT NPW!!

ROBBIE
ARE YOU WATCHING THIS?! 😳 👆
💪

NORA
OMG, Iris. Are you watching H@H?
Girl, this is epic.

The rest were of a similar vein. Not as awful as Iris had been anticipating but baffling nonetheless.

Colby's phone started buzzing and beeping and pinging as well, and when she checked, she grimaced.

"I'm getting similar messages from Jazz and Vicki and the rest, and one from Chance, who says... and I quote—*tell Iris to brace herself.*"

<hr>

"IRIS, maybe we should wait for Chance to come home to fill us in, before we..."

"No, we're watching it right now," Iris interrupted her friend a little rudely—resolve and determination adding steel to her voice. Colby sighed, and sat down next to Iris on the living room love seat. She reached for the remote.

"It's live, about half an hour into the show. Do you want to watch it from the beginning?" Iris hesitated and then nodded.

"Yes." Her voice had lost all its resolve and now emerged on a nervous whisper.

Colby tuned in to *Holmes@Home* and Iris tensed when the

cheerful theme music came on as she realized that Colby was right. They should have waited for Chance to come home and tell them exactly what went down. Or at the very least, Iris should've returned her mother's call before sitting down to watch.

That way she would at least be prepared for whatever she was about to witness. Instead, she was a nervous wreck, an emotional mess expecting the absolute worst.

She was so preoccupied and anxious that she missed Mike Holmes's usual hyper-enthusiastic opening chatter. She was staring down at the tightly clenched fists in her lap, barely recognizing them as her own, while she focused on her breathing in an attempt to remain calm.

"Iris?" Colby's concerned voice penetrated Iris's blooming haze of panic and jerked her back to the present.

"I'm fine," she said on a soft exhalation of breath. "Just needed a moment."

She shifted her focus to the large-screen TV.

The *Holmes@Home* set was meant to resemble a cozy sitting room. That iconic, three-meter-long, dark blue crushed-velvet Chesterfield sofa had seated uncountable toned A-lister bottoms in the two-and-a-half decades since the show had first aired.

Mike Homes, with his affable, startlingly white smile, perfectly styled light brown hair that never seemed to gray, and his trademark velvet smoking jackets—complete with a brown pipe tucked into the breast pocket—was a household name and one of the most instantly recognizable people in the country.

He was staring into the camera as he spoke—a move

designed to make viewers feel like he was speaking directly to them—his genial smile never fading.

"Tonight's first guest is an up-and-comer. Someone not used to the limelight, but partially responsible for one of the most shocking and impactful celebrity stories of the year. Please join me in welcoming the supremely talented Miss Evan Brooks to our sitting room!"

Chapter Twenty-Two

The air left Iris's lungs in a shocked gasp as she stared fixedly at the screen, dreading what was to come but unable to look away. Like a terrified doe watching a train hurtling down the tracks straight at her, but too stunned by the noise and light to move out of the way before it mowed her down.

Mike Holmes was standing, arm outstretched as Evan lithely skipped onto the stage, looking ethereally lovely under the lights. Her strawberry blonde hair was up in a top knot, emphasizing the elegant line of her neck and shoulders. She was wearing a form-fitting pastel blue dress with a knee-length skirt and a simple boat neck, giving her an understated, yet classy, appearance. The make-up artist had done a great job of making her too-pale complexion look dewy and fresh.

Holmes air kissed her cheeks, and she turned to wave at the

enthusiastically applauding studio audience, looking relaxed and confident. The man led her to the sofa and sat her down, before taking *his* seat—a massive winged armchair in the same color as the sofa.

"Oh my *God*," Evan squealed once the audience had settled down. She made a huge show of stroking the sofa and then resting her cheek on the arm. "It's just as comfy as it looks! I always wondered about that."

The audience laughed appreciatively, clearly warming to her.

"Well, we're happy you like it," Holmes said with a wink at the camera, as if inviting the viewers in on the joke.

Iris swallowed painfully. Evan was in her element here. She'd have the host, the audience, and the nation eating out of her hand by the end of this interview. It sickened Iris to see Evan reaping even more rewards from her and Trystan's misery.

"So, Evan, tell us a bit more about yourself. Where did you grow up?" Holmes invited, and Evan started talking about her family life, her adoring parents, her childhood cat—telling an amusing anecdote of the time Miss Pickles the cat had adopted a baby rat. It was all so frikking adorable.

Mike Holmes laughed on cue, listening raptly, prompting her with insightful questions, while expertly steering her toward the reason she was on the show.

"So where did you meet Iris Hughes?"

"At uni. She was always a bit of a misfit, you know? Not quite sure where and how she slotted in. She latched onto me almost from the first. But I didn't mind. She seemed like she needed a friend and she was nice enough, if a bit insecure. As I got to know her, I realized that she was absolutely *riddled* with anxiety."

"Oh, my God. That's not what happened," Iris muttered, feeling the need to defend herself, even if Colby was the only one there to hear her. "*She* approached *me*. She'd heard my father was Stanford Carter and she wanted to know everything about him. She asked if I had any of his notes. Yes, I don't make friends easily, and maybe I was too... *eager* to be liked by her. But she was so cool and confident. And—"

Colby reached over and squeezed Iris's knotted fists.

"You don't have to explain, Iris. She's not coming across as very convincing. Or sincere. Or likable."

"What?" Iris's head swung around to stare at Colby in disbelief. "She's got them hanging onto her every word. You're biased because you know me."

"I've got really good at reading people since working at Brand EPS. She's trying too hard to be coy and sweet. Instead, she strikes me as cloying and insincere."

"You're just one—albeit very astute—person. And, don't get me wrong, I'm really grateful that you see through her but everybody else seems to be buying her act.

"I'm not so sure." Colby shook her head, her expression thoughtful. "I've watched Mike Holmes's show a few times. I'm familiar with his interrogation techniques..."

"Interrogation?" Iris repeated with a startled laugh. "Interview, you mean?"

"I said what I said," Colby said with a slight grin and a lift of her chin. "Anyway, he's building up to something."

"And you and Miss Hughes—Iris—collaborated from the very beginning on this Trystan Abbott interview?" Holmes's question yanked Iris's attention back to the disaster unfolding on-screen. She recalled, with an unpleasant jolt, that this wasn't happening live. That everything she was watching right now, had already happened.

Evan had force-fed the world these lies already and Iris knew that any attempt she made now to fix it would be futile. She'd had so many opportunities to tell her own story, to possibly temper the catastrophic impact of this interview while mitigating the damage already done with the article and the leaked excerpts from her journal. But Iris had been too proud and too afraid to defend herself. Proud because she believed that those who loved her and knew her would surely not need to be spoon-fed the truth, while the rest did not matter. Meanwhile she'd really been terrified that nobody would believe her if she actually spoke up. Why would they? When Trystan hadn't.

While Iris had remained imprisoned at home, hiding from the world, the public had gone and made up their minds about the type of person they believed she was.

"Yes," Evan said in response to the man's question. "She approached Mr. Quinn, Trystan Abbott's manager. He agreed to the interview and we decided fairly early on that the article would be published by *Looker*."

"Because of your connections at the magazine, of course," Mike Holmes said with a sage nod and Evan smiled.

"Yes."

Holmes's eyes narrowed and he tilted his head, affecting a look of confusion.

"Now hold on. You make Iris sound like a bundle of neuroses and anxiety. Why entrust such an important interview to her? Especially since—as you said—she lacked experience. Why didn't *you* do it instead?"

"Uh..." Evan's relaxed smile slipped a notch, before she fixed it firmly in place. "Well, I would've loved to, of course. But I had commitments at work. I couldn't simply up and leave. Iris just does some freelance editing. It's easier for her to swan off to exotic destinations than it is for me."

"But surely your then-boss at *Looker* would have granted you some time off to pursue a story like this?"

"Iris and I decided that the fewer people who knew about this the better. I didn't trust my *then*-boss not to take the story from me."

"I understand your boss was fired and you have her job now?" Holmes inserted smoothly, with a warm little smile. Now Iris could see what Colby had meant. There was something watchful—almost predatory—in the host's dark gray eyes.

"I do. Yes."

"Congratulations," Holmes said and Evan smiled.

"Thank you."

"This story has been good to you. Recognition and respect at work, I assume a substantial pay rise, plus whatever you earned off the article—and you've become a recognized name in entertainment journalism. Not bad for one as young as you."

"I may be young, Mike, but I've worked my arse off for every opportunity."

"I'm sure," he said amenably. "And Iris? She's been cagey with the press. Not a single interview. Did *Looker* offer her a position? I'm sure you must be champing at the bit to have her working with you?"

"Iris isn't interested in working at *Looker*," Evan said, her voice as flat as the line of her mouth.

"Why not?"

"Who knows?" Evan's response was curt and dismissive. "She's a strange one."

"I agree. I do find it odd that someone would land the scoop of the decade, then not bask in the aftermath. She hasn't been seen in public much. Her family has closed ranks. It's like she fell off the face of the planet."

"Maybe she's embarrassed she slept her way into a story and that the entire world then got to read about it in her journal," Evan said snidely, then recognized that she'd miscalculated when a low rumble of mutters swept through the audience.

"Speaking of the journal... a lot of the information the excerpts revealed were deeply personal and not always flattering to Iris. I was baffled as to why anyone would want such intimate thoughts exposed to the public."

"You're going to have to ask Iris about that. I have no idea what motivates her sometimes." Evan tried for a wide, friendly smile, but she was starting to look a little frayed around the edges.

"I *would* ask her, only she's gone into hiding and, as her best friend, you're the only one who could possibly give us some insight into her thought process."

"I'd prefer not to discuss her, to be honest," Evan said. "I thought we would be chatting about *Looker*'s upcoming collaborative project with—"

"In a minute, but for now I'd like to remain focused on Iris, if you don't mind?" Mike Holmes's smile had become decidedly sharklike and Iris leaned forward on the sofa in anticipation. "How much of the article did she write?"

"Iris has never been a very good writer. I had to write most of it for her. It was a mess before I got hold of it."

"I see. Extremely generous of you to share the byline with her."

"Well, it *was* her story after all," Evan said with a modest smile.

"You merely wrote it for her," Holmes completed for her.

Evan laughed, looking flattered by the non-compliment, and made a zipping motion across her lips.

"It wouldn't be very *sporting* of me to say more than that, Mike."

Mike Holmes stared at her for a few beats, during which Evan actually squirmed a bit, before he dialed up his perfect smile again. "Well, Evan, as much as I've loved having you all to myself, the time has come to take a quick break and then welcome my next guest to the sitting room."

The screen went black for a few moments, which had obviously been a commercial break during the live show, and when the picture came back on Mike Holmes was staring directly into the camera.

"The team and I have been very sneaky about my next guest," he said, leaning forward in a confiding manner. "We've kept him off tonight's roster because we wanted to surprise you. After his last stormy visit, I must confess, I feared we'd never see him back on the couch. Which would have been a tragedy, since it's always *such* a pleasure having him here. But he very generously agreed to come back onto the show tonight. Ladies and gentleman, please welcome... The one! The only! The SUBLIMELY talented Mr. Trystan Abbott!"

The audience went wild as the live studio band struck up the show's theme once again, and Trystan strode confidently onto the set.

Iris's hands were up over her mouth as she gawked at the screen, not sure what to expect next. Trystan exchanged a warm handshake with the man he'd comprehensively shunned just ten days ago, and after a cool nod at a starstruck-looking Evan, who was now sitting on the other end of the couch, took his seat closest to Mike.

Trystan had lost weight since his previous interview and Iris wondered if he was preparing for a role or something. His cheeks had hollowed and the bones looked sharper beneath his taut skin. There were angles and shadows that had not been present the last time she'd run her fingers over his face. He was thinner, yes, but still devastatingly attractive. Iris sucked her quivering lower lip between her teeth to prevent the sob lurking in her throat from escaping.

"You okay?" Colby asked and Iris nodded, unable to speak. They heard the front door open and a few moments later Chance was in the living room, but Iris couldn't drag her attention away from the screen long enough to acknowledge him.

She heard him exchange a quiet greeting with Colby and

was peripherally aware of him sitting down in the easy chair on her left.

"Trystan," Mike Holmes gushed. "Welcome back."

"Happy to be back, Mike," Trystan said, clearly comfortable as he sat with his thighs spread and one arm draped over the back of the sofa. As always, he took up more than his fair share of space, but the couch was so large he didn't infringe on any part of Evan's space.

"Have you met Evan Brooks?" Holmes asked, gesturing toward Evan, whose eyes were sparkling with excitement. She had a winning smile on her face, and she'd angled her upper body toward his and was leaning toward him eagerly.

"I haven't yet had the pleasure," Trystan said with a cool smile that didn't quite reach his eyes. He turned that lukewarm smile on Evan. "Miss Brooks? Charmed, I'm sure."

"Oh, please call me Evan," the woman gushed and he nodded, but all that legendary charm was conspicuously absent.

Evan finally seemed to notice that he wasn't quite as receptive to her charms and she dialed down the enthusiasm a notch, before saying, face somber, voice throbbing with—what Iris knew had to be—feigned sincerity, "I've been meaning to reach out and apologize for any trouble my little article may have caused you."

"I doubt you would've managed to reach me. My team filters out all unsolicited attempts at contact." There was a smattering of laughter at the unequivocal put-down, but Trystan continued in that same devastating monotone. "But that's beside the point. You and I came out of this debacle none the worse for wear, didn't we? The public has been very supportive of me after the truth about Trish surfaced. Her family have suffered unnecessarily and I'd hoped to spare them that, so perhaps I'm not the one to whom you should be apologizing?"

"Of course," Evan backtracked hastily. "I did express similar doubts to Iris when I understood how troubled Trish Nesbitt had been, but she was adamant about leaving it in."

Iris made a choked sound of protest and Trystan's eyes narrowed as he stared at Evan in that assessing way of his. Evan visibly squirmed beneath that penetrative stare.

But Trystan merely said, "Was she?"

"It was quite impossible to dissuade her."

"The thing about Iris, Ms. Brooks—"

"*Evan*, please," she invited warmly.

"No." His icy, unequivocal response prompted nervous titters from the audience and Evan blinked in confusion.

"You were saying," Mike Holmes prompted. The focus had been on Evan and Trystan for so long that the host's interruption was almost jarring. Iris had nearly forgotten he was there. "About Iris? I know you were reluctant to discuss her last time, but I gather you're a little more open to speaking about her this evening?"

Trystan didn't reply, his focus still trained on Evan. Iris knew how it felt to be pinned beneath that relentless hawklike stare and she *almost* felt sorry for Evan.

"I was saying," Trystan continued. "The thing about Iris is that she never seemed particularly interested in journalism. The opportunity to interview me fell into her lap and she would have been foolish not to pursue it. She was filled with enthu- siasm and can-do-it-ness when she showed up on my doorstep, and everybody knows by now what followed. I treated her poorly and kept her locked in a room for days."

"She was intruding," Mike Holmes was quick to point out.

"No, she wasn't. My manager had okayed the interview and Iris had every right to be there. Funny how none of those *leaked* excerpts from her journal ever revealed the one snipped of information that would have entirely vindicated her from any whiff of wrong doing, isn't it? *I* was being the arsehole and people have been much too quick to dismiss my behavior, and divert blame onto her. She was properly terrified to be locked in that room and had I known—" He shook his head. "I would have behaved differently. I don't make a habit of terrorizing women and keeping them locked up in rooms. She caught me at a particularly vulnerable time, but that's still no excuse for my treatment of her."

"In the end you were correct to be wary of her though," Holmes said. "Considering everything that happened afterwards. She betrayed your trust."

"You have that backwards, Mike," Trystan said, his voice quiet, the studio audience—likely the entire nation, Iris included—so riveted by what he would say next you could hear a pin drop into the expectant silence. "*I* betrayed her trust."

"I'm not sure I follow," Holmes said and Trystan shifted his focus back to Evan who was staring at him with huge eyes.

"Thing is, Mike, I'm very familiar with Iris's writing. Familiar enough with her voice to know that there's no way in hell Iris wrote any part of that poorly constructed article."

The audience gasped, but Iris barely heard them over her own rough intake of breath. She hadn't been sure of his purpose in coming on the show this time, and certainly hadn't expected such a blunt denunciation of Evan's statements. It was unexpected but so welcome. Her sense of vindication and relief was overwhelming.

"I should have noticed it immediately," Trystan continued. "But I'll freely admit that I was too butt hurt at the notion that I'd been deceived and taken for a fool to think clearly. Too ready to accuse Iris and believe the worst of her when she'd never given me any reason to do so."

"Well, hold on a second now, Trystan. Evan did admit to writing a lot of the article, right Evan?"

"I did, because Iris..."

"I heard what you said earlier," Trystan interrupted. "About Iris not being a good writer. And I've never heard a bigger load of bollocks in my life. I've read her work and Iris is phenomenally talented. Decidedly more so than you are, Miss Brooks. And anybody who has read any part of those leaked excerpts from her journal could tell you that."

There was a quiet murmur of what sounded like assent from the audience.

"I wrote the article, I admit that, but everything from the journal came from her," Evan pointed out heatedly, her cheeks flushed an unbecoming shade of puce.

"Iris trusts the people she loves. Without doubt or hesitation. God, I wish she didn't, because it makes her completely vulnerable when some of those people turn on her. People like you. And me.

"When your story first broke, before she knew about it, I asked her for her laptop. It was password protected. When I pointed that out to her, instead of taking it from me and typing in the password herself, she told me what it was. Blind, unequivocal trust. And at some point, during your years-long friendship, she must have done the same with you, right? If not, you know her well enough to have gleaned her password. Easy enough to get into her cloud with that information."

Evan's jaw worked as she considered what to say next, but in the end she shrugged and sat back, folding her arms over her chest defiantly.

"Iris lacks ambition. She was sitting on a goldmine of information after the opportunity of a lifetime fell into her lap, and she refused to do anything with it."

Trystan's face contorted as her response confirmed what—up until that point—had been mere speculation on his part.

"You were jealous of her, weren't you?" Mike Holmes asked astutely, his voice low, non-threatening, as if he was afraid that any hint of condemnation would send her into retreat.

"Do you know who her father was?" Evan countered. "She owed it to him to do—*be*—better. But she looked down on his work, was ashamed of him. Thought she was so much better than him. And me. When *she's* the one who's an embarrassment—"

"The real embarrassment is the person who would publicize their friend's struggles with mental health and anxiety without their explicit consent," Trystan interrupted her on a low growl. "Iris has been persecuted, mocked, insulted, relentlessly attacked, and bullied online and in person. Her family has lost business and she has received dozens of death threats and has been kicked out of her home. Didn't you care how that would affect her emotional and mental health? She'd been trapped in her own home for weeks on end. She suffers from cleithrophobia." His voice broke on the word and he cleared his throat before continuing. "It must have been intolerable for her."

Iris was silently crying now, dimly aware of Colby's arm around her shoulder. Chance must have left the room at some point because he pressed a mug of hot tea into her cold hands.

"Iris is the real victim here. A victim of your ambition and greed," Trystan said. "And my weakness and distrust. And I wish with everything in me that I'd stood by her. That I'd believed in our love enough to overcome my doubt and fear."

"Look, it wasn't like that," Evan screeched in a panic, obviously only now understanding how badly this was going to rebound back on her. "I did it *for* Iris. That's why I added her name to..."

"Miss Brooks," Mike Holmes interrupted her firmly. "I thank you for joining us today, but I'm afraid that's the end of this segment."

"No, you *must* allow me to defend myself. This is slander. A vicious ambush. I demand—"

The screen went black and when the image reappeared a few seconds later, Evan was gone and only Trystan remained on the couch. Usually, Holmes hosted up to three guests and it was unusual to have only one person on the couch this far into the show.

"Trystan," Mike Holmes began, his voice almost tentative. "I understand that this is a difficult subject, but would you like to tell us more about your relationship with Iris Hughes?"

"Not particularly," Trystan said, his voice rough with

emotion. "It's—" He paused, then laughed, the sound devoid of humor. "I *was* going to say private but I realize how ridiculous that would sound in light of how much of it has already been revealed to the world.

"That horrible Brooks woman took something singular and beautiful and weaponized it. She then aimed that weapon at both Iris and me. I failed Iris. I can't forgive myself for that. She trusted me when I promised that I would protect her from the public eye and never hurt her." He stared down at the hands clasped between his spread knees and shook his head, the gesture slow and defeated. "The promise had barely left my mouth before I turned on her and left her vulnerable to the vultures. Who *does* that?"

"What would you say to her," Holmes said, his voice almost a whisper. "If she was watching right now?"

Trystan looked directly into the camera, his face so ravaged by grief and despair that the audience actually reacted in what sounded like a collective moan.

"Nothing I say can fix this, Mike. But if you *are* watching, Iris… I hope—I wish—" he shook his head, looking helpless and vulnerable. "I'm sorry. You deserved better. I know you can't forgive me. I don't blame you. I do—and *always* will—love you, Iris. So *so* much. And I hope in some way, this helps you claim back the life I stole from you."

"You want her back, don't you?" Mike Holmes murmured.

"It doesn't matter what I want, Mike," Trystan stated, his voice and face like granite. "What *I* want is unimportant. I fu—messed—up. I no longer have a say in what happens next. I hope Iris is able to forgive me someday, but if she doesn't… I'll understand. I don't deserve her. I never did. But—" He looked straight at the camera again, his heart in his eyes, his expression both vulnerable and hopeful. "Iris, if you *did* find it in your heart to give me another chance... I'd work my arse off every damned day of my life to deserve your love."

"Wow," Mike Holmes said, his voice shaky with restrained excitement and disbelief. "Thank you for returning to my sitting room this evening, Trystan, and laying your soul bare for the world to see. I do hope your Iris sees this and gives you another chance. That's all we have time for this evening, folks. I'm sure you'll agree with me that this has been one hell of a show. Thank you—"

Colby put the television on mute, while Iris continued to stare at the screen in disbelief, and no small amount of horror.

"How does he think this is going to make things better?" she asked, the question directed mostly at herself. "Now I'll be getting death threats if I *don't* take his sorry arse back."

Colby smothered what sounded like a laugh and rubbed Iris's back in comforting circles.

"Drink your tea before it gets cold," she instructed. "I agree that parting shot was a little ill advised, but the rest of it was pretty decent, right?"

"So... I'm supposed to just fall over myself and forgive him now?" Iris asked querulously, taking a sip of her lukewarm overly sweet tea. She wrinkled her nose and glared at Chance, out of sorts and irritable and willing to take out her frustration on anything male right now. "This tastes like syrup."

'Thought you'd need it sweet for the shock," he said with a nonchalant shrug.

"Did you know he was going to do this?" she asked him with a glare, pointing a shaky finger at the TV.

"I knew he had an interview, but I had no idea it was going to go down like that. I was backstage when they dragged Evan back there. She had a shell-shocked look, like she'd just been hit by a bus and didn't quite understand what had happened to her. Once the shock wore off, she started pacing, so furious you could practically see the steam coming off her. She was on her phone, sending frantic texts and making urgent, low-voiced phone calls. Got to admit, it was fun to watch her carefully constructed house of cards implode."

Iris was gnawing her cuticle again, and she hissed in pain when she hit a raw spot.

"Look, Iris, he asked me to give you this." Chance tugged a slim phone from his jacket's breast pocket. He didn't make any attempt to give it to her, merely held it in his hand. "I told him I'm not going to be his little errand boy, ferrying notes between you two like we're high school kids in the middle of some teenage drama. If you don't want this, I'll happily hand it back to him tomorrow and that'll be the end of it, okay? You don't owe him anything."

"Why does he want me to have that?" Iris asked, staring at the device like it was a venomous snake poised to strike.

Chance shrugged. "In case you want to talk, I reckon."

"I have a phone."

"Maybe he wanted to be certain you'd get his texts and phone calls. Since you've blocked and deleted him from your other phone."

"Not interested."

"Okay." Chance palmed the phone and moved it back to his pocket.

"Wait," Iris said, her eyes glued to the innocuous-looking device. She shook her head, furious with herself and held out her hand. "Give it to me."

Chance handed it over without comment.

"I don't want to talk to him," Iris maintained, sliding the phone between her thigh and the sofa cushion, and then tried her best to ignore the slight warmth emanating from the damned thing. "But I'll keep it in case I change my mind."

"You can smash it to pieces with a mallet if you want, Iris. It's your business."

"What's going to happen now?" Iris wondered.

"Hopefully this will all blow over soon," Colby said and then shook her head. "Frankly, after this interview, I don't see interest in you waning anytime soon, but it may be a lot less hostile and negative."

"I'm not sure how I feel about that."

"You'll have a security team, which means more freedom of movement," Chance said.

"A security team?"

"Trystan insisted."

Iris didn't like the thought of that at all. "I don't want to be beholden to him for anything."

"He got you into this shit. It's the least he can do," Chance said, his green eyes icing over. "It's not a permanent arrangement, Iris. But you'll be able to go for walks, go shopping, visit your parents, have some semblance of freedom again until things get a bit more normal."

"It's a good thing, Iris. Trust me," Colby said. "Our guys are so good you'll hardly even know they're there."

Iris gnawed uncertainly on her top lip before nodding.

"We'll see how it goes."

"You can go, Quinny." Trystan told his hovering friend, while he stared into the glass of cognac he'd been nursing for the past half hour. But Quinny continued to hover and fuss like an overanxious nursemaid. He sighed—the sound filled with impatience and irritation—and lifted his gaze to Quinny's concerned eyes. "I'm okay."

"You're not okay, mate," Quinny denied. "You're very fucking far from okay."

"I'm not going to run off into the WiFi-less wilds again, if that's your concern."

"My concern is that this is nothing at all like the Trish Nesbitt thing. Because, even though you felt guilty, you knew it wasn't your fault. You just needed time to figure that out."

"And this time, what?" Trystan sneered. "I'm guilty as fuck? You think I don't know that?"

"I think that despite what went down tonight, you still believe that you're the villain here."

"All that matters is what Iris thinks. And Iris hates me. So..." He pinched the bridge of his nose between his thumb and forefinger, trying to massage away the headache that was forming between his eyes. "Make of that what you will."

"You should fight for her." The words were an echo of the ones that had been rattling around in Trystan's skull for the better part of the week.

"Even if I did convince her to come back, what the hell do I have to offer her?"

"Seriously?" Quinny sounded incredulous and Trystan looked up in time to see his friend's eyes dart around the luxurious den they were in.

"Iris doesn't give a fuck about any of this crap." He waved a hand around wildly, and some of his cognac spilled onto his fingers. "I meant that she's already seen how bad it can get, what could ever induce her to willingly subject herself to such intrusive public scrutiny and criticism on a daily basis? The best thing I can do for her is to leave her alone. She's lost to me. And I have to figure out how to go on without her. Thing is, I don't know how to do that. I don't know if I *can* do that. I don't want to, Quinny. She's *everything*."

He directed his blurred gaze down into his glass, feeling defeated and so fucking sad. He thought about the phone he'd asked Chance to give to her, so hopeful even while knowing that it was a futile shot in the dark.

Defeat settled over him, weighing him down and smothering him like a sodden woolen blanket. He was barely able to breath. Suffocating beneath the staggering mass of his loss.

"Maybe after she sees the interview..." Quinny's voice trailed off when Trystan shook his head slowly.

"She deserves better, mate. Tonight wasn't about getting her back. It was about returning some semblance of peace and normalcy to her life. It was the least I could do."

Quinny poured himself a drink and sat down on the chair across from Trystan's.

"You don't have to stay. I'm fine."

"I'm not going anywhere," Trystan's friend said, resolve in his voice. Seeing the determination in Quinny's expression, Trystan nodded. And they sat like that for hours, drinking in stoic, companionable silence.

Chapter Twenty-Three

Iris didn't call.

Trystan—currently on his press tour for *Cryo Cop*—stared glumly at the phone in his hand. He'd tried his damnedest to leave her alone. Had succeeded for the most part, but he'd been unable to let her go completely.

He sent her texts. One or two a day. Usually pictures of Luna, who was part of his press tour entourage along with Chance, Quinny and Bee. Without them Trystan would likely have gone crazy by now.

His last text to Iris had been a picture of Luna sprawled on her back, legs akimbo, and tongue lolling out of her mouth as she slept. He'd added a message:

> I don't think she likes the Spanish heat 🥵👻

Like the two dozen or so messages that he'd sent previously, this one had been read but remained unanswered. It was driving him mad, those little blue *read* ticks. If nothing else, it strongly drove home the point that she wanted nothing to do with him. He understood that. He knew he should leave her alone, but perversely, while the blue ticks quite explicitly told him she wanted nothing to do with him, it also gave him hope. Because if she really wasn't interested, why did she keep the phone? And why was she still checking his messages?

He had yet another interview in half an hour and was exhausted just thinking about it. The tour had started a couple of days after his appearance on *Holmes@Home* nearly two weeks ago—and pretty much all anybody was interested in asking him about was Iris. And whether he'd reconciled with her yet. As if he ever would. As if she would have him back.

All he knew was that she was safe now, able to visit her family without fear of harassment, thanks to Brand's outstanding security team. Also, public sentiment had changed toward her after the interview. He saw a lot of positive posts about her. People lauded her for staying above the mud-slinging and for standing her ground and not running back to Trystan after his very public apology.

Looker magazine, fearing a lawsuit and the public condemnation that would likely result from keeping Evan Brooks in their employ, had printed an insincere apology to both Trystan and Iris for the breach of privacy and had fired Brooks without notice. Trystan didn't care enough to follow up on what she was doing now.

In fact, Trystan cared about very little these days. The only thing that remotely excited him lately were his chats with Bee and Quinny about restructuring his career. Both Quinny and Bee were as enthusiastic about the shift in gears as Trystan was and they were putting a solid plan of action in place as to how he should proceed when it came to choosing future projects.

It was the only positive thing in his life currently, and he had Iris to thank for it.

It was hard to believe that he'd now been apart from Iris for longer than they'd been together. He tried to tell himself it was ridiculous to be so crazy about a woman who clearly wanted nothing to do with him and whom—in all honesty—he'd barely known. Yet, he spent his days constantly thinking about her and his nights longing for her. He was lonely without her.

IT WAS after his press conference as he lay in his huge, empty hotel bed in Madrid, staring at a grainy candid image that a pap had shot of Iris just yesterday, that he finally caved.

She was laughing, out with her mum and a woman Chance didn't know. They were eating ice cream and she looked so fucking happy that his heart twisted in his chest. He loved that she was happy. He wanted that for her, but he could see that she'd lost weight, that there were dark circles under her eyes. So maybe she wasn't that happy. Maybe she missed him like he missed her.

And maybe Trystan was a fool who saw things that simply weren't there.

Icy Iris Ignores Idol! screeched the catchy headline.

He went back into his messenger app and stared at the

stream of one-sided messages from him to her. It was just after midnight, which meant it was after eleven in the UK.

> Please. Pick up.

He waited and within seconds... two blue ticks.

Trystan sucked in a huge breath, and shoving aside his doubt and better judgment, pressed call.

She answered on the second ring....

"Hello?"

...And all the breath left Trystan's body in a single harsh exhalation.

"You answered." He was unable to think of anything else to say in that moment because, honestly, he hadn't believed she would answer the call... and he was now unable to get his befuddled thoughts into any semblance of order.

"Well, you called," she pointed out.

"I did. I shouldn't have. I know that."

"So why did you?" She was giving him nothing, her voice neutral, unemotional.

"I'm lonely and I can't sleep. Why did you answer?"

A brief pause before, "I'm lonely and can't sleep."

"Iris..." His voice wobbled alarmingly and he sucked in a calming breath. "I miss you. Fuck, I miss you so damned much it actually physically hurts."

Silence.

"I know I shouldn't," he continued in a desperate bid to get it all out before she came to her senses and hung up on him. "I don't have that right. And by now you're probably wondering what the fuck you saw in me in the first place, right? And you've undoubtedly realized that what you felt for me in that house wasn't real. Just infatuation brought on by…"

"Proximity?" she finished for him and he frowned, a little disheartened by the fact that she hadn't denied any of what he'd said.

"Yeah."

"Are you wondering what you saw in me?" she asked.

"Not at all. In you, I saw forever. I saw us, old and gray, happy and fulfilled. And I loathe myself every day for throwing that away."

There was a long, lingering silence after his words and he heard her shuddering sigh, but she didn't respond.

"How have you been?" he asked, desperate to keep her on the line. He closed his eyes as he imagined her curled up on her side in bed, phone pressed to her ear. Hair messy, eyes droopy with exhaustion.

"Better. Thanks to that bonkers interview you did with Mike Holmes."

"You saw it. I wasn't sure you'd watch."

"I did. Thank you for doing that. It helped. Life is getting back to normal. I'm still staying with Chance and Colby at the moment, but I may be moving back into my old flat next month."

"That's fantastic news," he enthused, heartened to hear it.

Another pause, this one less awkward than the last.

"Why have you been sending me those texts?" she asked.

"Because I wanted to feel somehow connected to you still,

even though I know I don't deserve it. Why have you been reading them?"

"Curiosity. And also... I wanted to know how Luna was doing. Why didn't you stop when I didn't reply?"

"Because you kept reading them."

"Persistent, optimistic bugger, aren't you?" It was the first time since she'd answered that he'd heard a smidgeon of humor in her voice, and that lifted his mood.

"My one redeeming feature," he said injecting blatant false modesty into his voice. Her responding snort was as close to a laugh as he was going to get from her but he'd take it.

"It wasn't meant as a compliment," she clarified.

"No matter. I choose to see it as one." Another snort and he smiled into the darkness as he imagined her battling with herself in a valiant attempt to keep her humor at bay.

Iris had been staring into the night for what felt like hours, restless, with sleep an impossibility as always. Life wasn't the same. It would never be the same, but it was steadily returning to some semblance of normality.

Iris could still see the questions in people's eyes—from her family to her new group of friends to the grocer on the corner— questions Iris wasn't even sure *she* had the answers to.

Her family and friends didn't ask. They were waiting for her to break the silence, but the journalists who still dogged her steps—at a more respectful distance thanks to her security team —had no qualms about screaming them at her.

What did you think about Trystan Abbott's interview with

Mike Holmes? Would you ever take him back? How do you feel about him? Do you hate him? Do you love him? How much longer are you going to punish him?

Only Iris didn't consider it punishment. She was trying to piece her life back together. There was no room in that life for Trystan... or the insanity that surrounded him. She'd had a bitter taste of that life and it had nearly destroyed her. She'd be a fool to go running back to that.

Yet, when his text begging her to answer the phone had come through, the small, niggling part of her brain that kept revisiting his vulnerability in that interview and recalling the naked plea in his voice when he'd publicly begged for her forgiveness, had been unable to resist. Since that interview, Iris had lain awake every night, her restless mind always circling back to the fact that this awful, humiliating thing had happened to them *both*.

Yes, Trystan had promised to trust her and had broken that promise literal minutes after it had been made. He'd hurt her, humiliated her and abandoned her, but Evan's article had used *Iris's* words, thoughts, and even her emotions, to expose Trystan's deepest secrets. It had to have been hard for him to see past that and yet—even though it had taken him weeks to do so— Trystan *had* looked past all of that damning evidence to find the truth. Surely that deserved at least a conversation?

"How are your parents and Robbie?" Trystan asked, his deep voice wrapping around her like a warm, velvety comforter on a chilly night. She snuggled down in her bed—so damned happy she'd taken his call—and let it wash over her. She was disappointed when he didn't continue speaking after the question was asked, and then she rolled her eyes into the darkness as she realized she'd have to answer it if she wanted him to keep talking.

"They're fine. Business is picking up nicely again, and Robbie started dating that new girl my parents hired." She recognized how mundane her response was and wondered why on Earth Trystan, who was currently situated in—what was undoubtedly—a five-star hotel in Madrid, would possibly be interested in the boring details of her ordinary life.

"Yeah?" His voice raised a little, like his interest had been piqued. "I thought she wasn't that into him."

He remembered that?

"I'm not going to tell him, but I think she finds him a lot more interesting now because of his tenuous connection to you."

He snorted, the sound disdainful. "Then he's better off without her."

"I think so too. It'll run its course eventually and he'll move on, but he's like a lovesick puppy right now. It's kind of cute to see him like this, actually."

"Your parents? Did they get the third van?"

"Uh, yes. Last month."

"And you, Iris?" His voice deepened on her name. "Have you been writing?"

"I have."

"What have I missed? With Celestine?"

"I don't—" She began.

"Please, Iris," he interrupted. "Talk to me, just for a little while. Tell me what Celestine's been up to. Has she had the baby yet? Was it a wolf cub? Puppies?"

Iris stifled a laughed at the question and shook her head, unable to resist the plea.

"Where did you stop reading?"

He told her and—because she missed him as much as he claimed to miss her, because it was dark and she was lonely, and because this felt like a warm, safe cocoon made just for the two of them—Iris started talking.

TRYSTAN

Is it true you've been stepping out with Henry Cavill? 😬

IRIS

I should be so lucky 😍. Have you really been having secret coffee dates with Rihanna 🤭

TRYSTAN

She wouldn't be caught dead with my sorry arse 😩 😿 💔

IRIS

😹😹

IRIS

Moscow looks cold 😬

TRYSTAN

I'm fucking freezing my nuts off and
Quinny is driving me insane with this
ridiculous schedule 💀

IRIS:

I'm sorry 😔

TRYSTAN

No. I'M sorry. I sound like a whiny
bitch, I know. It's been a long month.
I'm exhausted.

IRIS

Still not sleeping well?

TRYSTAN

I only get a decent night's sleep after
talking to you. You?

IRIS

...

IRIS

...

IRIS

...

IRIS

Same.

TRYSTAN

What are you doing RIGHT now?

IRIS

Random. Lol. I'm in Gunnersbury Park
having a ham and cheese sandwich.
It's cold af. Winter is coming.

TRYSTAN

A GOT reference? Dated. And lame.

IRIS

Are you still salty because they didn't
cast you as Jon Snow?

TRYSTAN

Don't believe everything you read in
the tabloids, Iris!

IRIS

Oops, sorry. You'd think I'd know
better by now.

TRYSTAN

It was Robb Stark.

"MY MUM always makes the same meal my first night back," Trystan confided two weeks after that initial phone call to Iris from Madrid. "Sausages with onion gravy and mash. It was my favorite back when I was an ankle biter. Nobody makes it like Mum."

He always called Iris at the same time every night, even though *his* time zone kept changing with each subsequent stop on his tour. He'd been to ten countries throughout Europe and Asia in fourteen days. It exhausted Iris just thinking about it. He was currently in Cairns, his hometown. It would be a four-day stop, allowing him and his team time to rest and Trystan to spend time with his family.

Hunter Quinn had grabbed the opportunity to fly over to Christchurch to visit *his* parents and Chance had been temporarily relieved of duty as well, allowing him time to visit the few friends and acquaintances he had left in the Northern Territory.

"Do you have any special plans?"

"Nah, maybe have a barbie with some old schoolmates tomorrow. But nothing special."

"You must be happy to be home," she said with a smile.

"I'm not home." The sudden, overwhelming sadness in his voice made her heart stutter in her chest.

"Trys—"

"Iris... Home is where you are."

"You shouldn't say things like that. Why would you say that?" she asked in an appalled whisper, tears welling in her eyes. This was the first time, since they'd resumed communications, that he'd brought the conversation back to this place.

"Because it's true," he replied. "What do you think we're doing here? With the calls and the texts?"

"We're friends..."

"No," he said, his voice low, vehement. "*Fuck* that, Iris. We're not friends. If you think we're friends you're lying to yourself. I can't sleep unless I've heard your voice at night. And when we're not in the same time zone, I listen to your voice notes on repeat after I crawl into bed at night.

"*Tell* me that it's not the same for you. Every single one of your texts brightens my day... I dare you to say that you don't feel the same way about mine. This is not about friendship. I have enough friends. But I only have one *you*."

"You don't have me, Trystan."

"If that's true, then what are we doing here?"

"I don't know."

"I..." He stopped talking and they lapsed into silence. When he spoke again, she could hear the heaviness and despair in his voice. "I have to go."

"Trystan—"

"If you can't forgive me for my stupidity and weakness, Iris, tell me now. And I'll stop bothering you."

Iris hesitated and before she could speak, he sighed.

"I guess that's it then."

He hung up before she could reply.

THE MESSAGE REMAINED UNREAD.

"I'D LIKE TO STATE—FOR the record—that I think this is a terrible idea," Chance drawled, as he watched Trystan lift his hand to knock.

"Noted. I want you to talk to Brand about beefing up security in this building. It's disgraceful how that kid just let us in without even checking if we really belonged here."

"Worked in your favor though, didn't it?" Chance pointed out, and Trystan glared at him, recognizing the hypocrisy in pointing out a flaw that he'd just used to his own advantage.

"*I* don't mean any harm," he said.

"Iris might not agree."

"Shut up, Chance. I don't need you to tell me what I already know. Isn't your job to protect and *silently* observe?"

Chance merely lifted a brow at that slur but shifted his broad shoulders and sarcastically waved his hand at the door.

"Have at it, *sir*."

Trystan gritted his teeth at the sardonic emphasis on the honorific. Since Chance had taken to calling him Trystan or just *mate*, the deferential *sir* was not in the slightest bit respectful, and they both knew it.

Trystan would take exception to the man's familiarity if he didn't like him so much. He'd enjoyed Chance's company during the punishing press tour. Quinn was as exhausted as Trystan and their long-time friendship had taught them that when they were both tired, it was best to avoid each other to prevent petty arguments. And, while Trystan was fond of Bee, her esoteric tastes meant that they had little in common outside of work.

Chance, with his irreverent sense of humor and laid-back nature, was easy to be around. And since Trystan had to spend so much time in the man's company, it helped that they got along.

Trystan eyed the door again, before throwing back his shoulders and lifting his closed fist to knock.

Afterward he dropped his hand and tugged at his shirt self-consciously, straightening his cuffs, smoothing his palm over the cool fabric covering his chest. Seconds passed without any sound from inside. Trystan ran a nervous hand over his hair before trying again, knocking a little harder this time.

They heard the muffled grumbling of a woman approaching the door and Trystan's breathing stalled and his heart sped up when the key turned in the lock and the door swung inward.

The woman glowering up at them, wearing a robe, with a towel wrapped around her hair, was decidedly *not* Iris.

"What?" She snapped, before her eyes widened and her jaw dropped. "Oh. Wow. Hey... Trystan Abbott. This is—how's it hanging, man?"

She held up her fist and Trystan hesitated for a second before pounding it awkwardly.

"Is Iris home?" he asked, feeling like a child calling at his friend's house and asking if they could come out and play.

"Iris? No. She's not. She left early this morning. Said something about going to her parents' place. Why don't you try there? So this is it, huh? You're finally grand-gesturing?"

"What?" Trystan asked, wanting to get the hell out of here now that he knew Iris wasn't home, but not wanting to be rude to her flatmate. He was trying to mend fences here. Alienating her friends wouldn't be the way to do so.

"You know? Like at the end of every romcom when the guy —or girl—runs barefoot through the city, to the airport, bus station, train station, wherever... and proclaims his, or her, or their, love to the object of their affection? I must say as grand gestures go, merely knocking on her front door is a bit of a letdown."

"She's at her parents' place?"

"Yep. Nice to meet you, by the way, I'm Nora. I'm not into movies all that much, but yours aren't that bad. *Night of the Killer Wetās* was bitching. My mates and I have a viewing every Halloween. We're all allocated different roles and recite the lines while watching."

It sounded fucking horrendous.

"Yeah? Maybe I'll join in on the next one and read Adam's lines," he offered—Adam was his character in the movie—and cringed inwardly when her face lit up. Shit. Well, he might as well try and ingratiate himself to the people within Iris's most intimate circle. It could all form part of his not-at-all-thought-through Grand Gesture.

"That's cool, man. You're not too bad. I hope she takes you back. Although... I can't say I'm optimistic."

Neither was Trystan. But after her last message, which he'd seen two whole days after she'd posted it, he had to try.

"IRIS, we need refills on the *dolmades* and *spanakopita*. They're flying," Jason Hughes called across the bustling kitchen. It was organized chaos. Everybody knew their place and worked together like a well-oiled machine. Iris, who hadn't helped since before leaving for South Africa, had simply slotted back into the flow of things, familiar with the routine and the rest of the kitchen and waitstaff.

She was getting stares and a few rushed questions about *him* though, but for the most part she'd simply kept her head down and got the work done. There was some tension between Robbie and his girlfriend, Chloe, or Khlo—*with a K and a haich* —a seventeen-year-old with thick smudged black eyeliner around her vibrant blue eyes and badly dyed straight, limp black hair. She was constantly chewing gum and popping bubbles, which was both annoying and unhygienic. Iris's father had reprimanded the surly girl several times about the bubblegum, and each time she made a big, sulky show of spitting it out, but the discarded gum was always replaced with a fresh stick mere minutes later.

Robbie kept staring at her like a sad little whipped puppy. They'd clearly had an argument and Khlo was giving him the cold shoulder. It was pretty pathetic watching her lanky brother trail after the girl. He insisted on doing her work, and she wanted nothing to do with him, which meant that neither teen's work was being done and the rest of the team had to pick up the slack. Iris could tell that her father was getting annoyed by the way he constantly barked orders—uncharacteristic of him—at the pair of them.

Speaking of which... a kerfuffle broke out at the dessert workstation.

"Let me," Robbie pleaded, trying to grab a tray of *kataifi* from Khlo.

"No," the girl protested. "I can do it myself."

"Khlo... you..." She made a sharp movement away from him and the *kataifi* went flying off the tray in all directions.

Everybody froze for an instant and all eyes flew to Jason Hughes. Normally mild-mannered and an awesome boss, the man had zero tolerance when it came to incompetence in his kitchen.

Iris watched her father's jaw clench in that familiar way that said he was trying very, *very* hard to rein in his temper, and she winced.

"Robinson Burke Hughes," Uh oh, full name. Robbie was in deep shit now. "You and Chloe need to clean up that mess and then I want you out of this kitchen. You've both been useless today anyway!"

"But Dad," Robbie began, in his whiny I'm-so-misunderstood voice.

"No buts. We'll have to make do without you."

"Mum..." Robbie tried, swinging his gaze over to their mother who stood with her arms folded over her chest, her expression entirely unsympathetic.

"You heard your father. Clean this up and go home —*straight* home—right now."

Khlo glared at Robbie who gave her a surly look in return.

"You made the mess," she said stubbornly. "You clean it up!"

Oh *bravo*, Iris heartily agreed with that sentiment. Robbie was wholly responsible for the mess. He should have left Khlo alone when she gave him clear signals that she was angry with him. Iris would have a talk with her little brother later about respecting a woman's boundaries. If her parents didn't get to him first.

Khlo whipped off her white apron before flouncing out of the kitchen, nimbly sidestepping the sticky mounds of ruined *kataifi* scattered all over the floor. This was definitely not how Jason and Rosa Hughes ran their kitchen.

"F'fuck's sake," Robbie muttered beneath his breath and Iris grimaced. Their mother did *not* condone profanity. Even Robbie froze after saying it and slanted the woman a wary glance. Her expression had gone murderous. He uttered a hasty *sorry* and, showing more wisdom than Iris had ever given him credit for, meekly bent to clean up the sticky mess on the floor.

"Right, people, back to work!" their father commanded his troops with the confident authority of a seasoned general.

Everybody instantly obeyed and the small, efficient army of servers and kitchen staff began to ebb and flow around the surly Robbie, who was hunkered on the floor with a tray, gathering up broken bits of sticky dessert. Iris hopped to her previous assignment, loading up on the *dolmades* and *spanakopita* to refill the empty chafing dishes out in the grand ballroom where the buffet dinner service was in full swing.

Iris was happy this wasn't a sit-down meal service because she could flit in and out of the reception area with little chance of being noticed and recognized by the guests. Her thick hair was tightly gathered in a neat bun at the top of her head and she wore the company uniform of crisp long-sleeved white shirt, black waistcoat, black trousers, black bow tie, and polished black brogues on her feet.

After she deposited the food, she headed back to the kitchen, neatly dodging a pair of children playing tag on the dance floor, and careening straight into a solid male form in the process. His hands came up to steady her, loosely encircling her upper arms.

"*Oof,*" she gasped, rubbing her nose, which had hit the bony ridge of the man's clavicle. "So sorry, I wasn't loo—"

She looked up and the words died on her lips, as she registered exactly who it was she was staring at. But it was impossible. There was no way he could be here. *How* could he be here?

"Trystan?" she whispered as the world simply froze around her, ceasing to exist entirely while she tried to make sense of this impossibility.

Chapter Twenty-Four

"Why are you here? Do you know the Tavoularises?"

"What?" he asked, looking completely bemused as he stared at her as if he were seeing her for the very first time, and sounding perplexed by her question.

Well, as long as she wasn't the only bewildered party here.

His hands tightened briefly on her biceps, reminding her that he still held her in his grip and she wondered if she should protest that. She was so confused by his presence that she had no idea how to react to it.

"The—uh—bride and groom," she clarified, and his face cleared. He sent a preoccupied look around the room before shaking his head. He shifted slightly and angled his body so that his back was to the room, which meant—hopefully—that nobody would immediately recognize him. It was a miracle that his presence hadn't yet attracted any attention, but the guests were currently too engrossed in their food. Also, Trystan was wearing a white dress shirt and black jeans, and—despite his height—could have been mistaken for one of the staff. And, let's be real, a Greek wedding in Wandsworth was most assuredly the last place anybody would expect to find Trystan Abbott.

"I have no idea who they are."

"Then why are you here?" she asked again, irritation starting to outweigh the confusion and warring with the absolute joy she felt at seeing him again.

"To see you," he said, as if this was the most obvious fact, dropping his hands with seeming reluctance and Iris *hated* that she missed his touch as soon as it was gone.

"I'm working. You shouldn't have come here," she said in a low voice. "This is highly inappropriate. I won't have you hijacking this couple's day, and ruining my parents' professional reputation in the process,"

"I didn't know you'd be working," he said, casting his eyes around the room again. "Look, can we go somewhere and talk?"

"No. We're short-staffed. I can't simply up and leave because *you've* suddenly decided to do whatever this is."

"If you're short-staffed I could help," he suggested. "Then maybe we could talk afterward?"

She laughed incredulously at that suggestion.

"*Help?*" she repeated. "Do you even know who you are?"

"I have a disguise, and I can stay out of sight in the back if need be."

"A disguise?" she asked, but he was staring at her again, his eyes running over her face almost ravenously, then up to her hair, down over her body, his eyes flaring in appreciation at the sight of her figure-hugging uniform.

When he didn't reply, she prompted him, "Trystan? What disguise?"

"God, you're beautiful," he murmured, his eyes glinting with suspicious brightness beneath the lights. He lifted his hand to brush his knuckles down her cheek with a reverence that left her breathless. She leaned into the caress, before coming to her senses and jerking her head back.

"You want to help?" she asked, her voice curt as she tried to keep her emotions in check. He stared at her, eyes burning, face taut.

"Yes."

"Follow me," she said and turned to push through the swinging doors that led into the kitchen. He was so close to her she could feel the wash of heat from his body against her back.

"Surely you're not here alone," she said over her shoulder. "That would be irresponsible."

"Chance is with me. He hung back to give us some privacy." Even as he said the words, the doors swung inward again to reveal the big Aussie, who had a fierce glower on his face.

"Stay in sight, mate. That was the rule," Chance muttered beneath his breath, before levelling a warm grin at Iris. "Hello, Sunshine. I've missed you."

Iris returned his smile and stepped around Trystan to give Chance—whom she hadn't seen since he'd left to accompany Trystan on his press tour—a warm hug.

"Chance, it's so good to see you."

"Iris." Her father's voice snapped Iris back to the present

and her surroundings and she quickly became aware of the fact that all movement and chatter had stopped in the kitchen as everybody stared at the commotion that she and these two tall men were creating in the doorway.

She heard the collective gasp of recognition when Trystan turned to face the small crowd of people and sighed inwardly. Her parents were not going to be happy about yet another disruption to their service.

"Sorry, Dad, I'll get right back to work. But we have an extra pair of hands to help out," she said with forced good humor, determinedly ignoring the whispers and stares.

"*Two* extra pairs," Trystan volunteered.

"Nope," Chance disagreed cheerfully. "I'm already working right now. Need to keep my hands free. Besides, this is your penance tour, mate, not mine."

Trystan shot Chance a disgruntled look, but Chance ignored him to cast a professional eye around the kitchen, probably noting exits and potential weapons and threats.

"Just me then," Trystan said with awkward cheer.

Iris's father eyed him with blatant dislike on his face. "You're more likely to be a distraction and we're already running behind schedule today. I'm not sure what you're playing at, but I can't let you turn this wedding into a three-ring circus while we all pander to your ego."

Trystan's handsome features took on a determined cast as he met her father's eyes unflinchingly. "I understand why you would feel that way, sir. And I don't blame you. I promise you I didn't know that Iris would be working for you today, or I would have timed this better. But I'm here now, and I was a waiter at my uncle's Italian restaurant throughout high school and college. I know my way around a professional kitchen. I can help if you need it."

Iris's mum stepped forward, placing a hand on her husband's bony shoulder, to stop whatever he'd been about to say. She ran an assessing eye over Trystan's frame.

"Robbie, stop gawking and give Mr. Abbott—"

"Trystan, please."

"—Trystan, your waistcoat. And why are you still here? We told you to go home after cleaning up the *kataifi*."

"Mum," Robbie's voice was filled with hushed protest while his awed gaze remained glued to Trystan's face. "I can stay and help."

"No. Trystan will take your spot," she said implacably. Iris couldn't tell what the other woman was thinking or feeling right now. But part of her knew that her mum had to be relishing this opportunity to put Trystan in his place. She'd made her feelings on the subject of Trystan Abbott clear on very many occasions. Even after his public apology.

Robbie, his face contorted into a bad-tempered scowl, dragged off his waistcoat and handed it over to Trystan. The teen was tall and lanky, and Iris was pretty sure the waistcoat would be too tight for Trystan, but he took it without hesitation.

"Thanks, Robbie. Nice to meet you, by the way. I've heard a lot about you."

"Yeah?" For a second Robbie's face lit up like a little boy's— and he looked exactly like the adolescent he was, meeting one of his favorite movie stars—before it settled back into that familiar black scowl. "Well, you're a dick and my sister is better off without you."

Iris's heart melted at the grumbled words, and she watched with a fond smile as—after slanting a slightly self-conscious glance at her—Robbie skulked off muttering a few choice profanities that she hoped for his sake their mother didn't hear.

Trystan's smile faded and he nodded, taking Robbie's criticism on the chin, before shrugging into the waistcoat. As Iris had predicted, it was too tight, but he managed to get one straining button fastened.

"How many times am I going to have to tell you all to get back to work today?" Her father snapped at the staring, whispering staff. They all reluctantly returned to work.

"You," her mother pointed at Chance with an authoritative finger. "You can have a seat over there. It's out of the way but—since we can't let this one out of the kitchen for fear of him being recognized—you can still do your job from there. Help yourself to some food."

"Yes, ma'am," Chance said, in a twangy drawl that sounded remarkably like his best friend, Ty's. He ambled over to the corner her mother had indicated, picking up a plate and loading it with food on the way.

"Iris," her mother said, still in that no-nonsense voice. "Prep the champagne trays. The toasts will be starting after dessert. Trystan can help you."

Iris nodded and made her way to the relatively quiet corner where the empty champagne flutes were waiting. She knew her mother had assigned this task to her and Trystan because it would afford them some privacy to talk while they worked. But Iris wasn't sure she was ready to talk to Trystan. To say this day had taken an unexpected turn was understating it.

Her day had derailed and then tumbled off a cliff.

"So, how's Luna?" she asked, feeling a pang of loss as she thought of the sweet dog.

"She misses you. Almost as much as I do."

"Where is she now?" Iris asked, hoping to divert him.

"At home. She's tired and a little grumpy. We did a lot of flying over the last thirty-six hours."

A brief, uncomfortable silence settled between them.

"What did you mean when you said you have a disguise?" she asked, keen to keep things as impersonal as possible, even though she knew it couldn't possibly stay that way. She lined the glasses up in neat little rows in front of her. Trystan followed her lead and did the same.

"Oh," he said, his beautiful, big hands pausing in their movements while he reached into his chest pocket and produced—a pair of black-rimmed glasses. He propped them on his nose and gave her that famous, mischievous, heart-stopping grin of his.

"Clear glass, see? *Et voila!* Trystan Abbott is no more," he said, lowering his hands with a flourish.

Iris choked back a chuckle and shook her head with a roll of her eyes.

"I've got news for you there, Clark Kent. That disguise is not as effective as you may believe."

"You'd be surprised. Add a baseball cap to these and it's like I disappear."

"My father would kill you stone-dead if you wore a baseball cap at this event."

He held up his index finger, and then smoothed his short disheveled hair—which had grown out of the ruthless buzz cut—into the semblance of a conservative side-parted style.

"Luckily you won't be interacting with the guests," she said with another head shake.

"Pity, because you'd be amazed at how effective this can be." Another devastating smile that quite literally stole Iris's breath away. She didn't know how the silly man could think he could ever simply disappear thanks to a pair of fake glasses.

"Anyway, the timing needs to be perfect for this," she said, keen to change the subject. Her voice low, rushed, shaky and breathless. God, why'd she have to sound so damned breathless? "We need to have the champagne glasses filled, on trays and ready to be served in time for the toast."

Trystan eyed the sea of gleaming glasses—two-hundred-and-fifty of them to be precise—skeptically and asked, "How long do we have?"

Iris glanced at the clock.

"Fifteen minutes, according to the wedding planner's schedule, but these things rarely go according to plan. Still, we work according to the schedule. Everything else is out of our hands."

"I reckon we'd better get to pouring then," Trystan said, picking up a bottle of *Veuve Clicquot* and spinning it on his palm like a professional bartender.

"Don't show off," Iris warned. "My dad will lose his shit if you break a bottle. And he's on the verge of a meltdown already."

Trystan slanted a wary glance toward her father, who was reprimanding one of the younger waitstaff for not paying attention—Iris was very aware of the fact that many of the staff were still openly staring at her and Trystan—which was exactly the type of distraction she'd feared his presence here would create.

"He *is* a little terrifying," Trystan admitted beneath his breath and Iris's eyebrows rose to her hairline, shocked to hear him say that.

"My dad? The scrawny, balding guy over there?"

"He's your father, Iris. I'm trying to make a good impression."

Iris—who had been reaching for a bottle—froze at that admission and stared at him.

"Why are you here, Trystan? Aren't you supposed to be heading to New York today?"

"I cut the tour short." This bit of news stunned Iris and she wondered what Hunter Quinn's reaction to that had been. "And I think I made the why of this more than clear during our last phone call."

"But—"

"And on the Mike Holmes show." He poured while he spoke, keeping his gaze on the flute instead of her. Iris watched him while he did that, and the grave, studied concentration somehow gave him an irresistible, boyish appeal . He glanced up at her, a smoldering stare through his thick dark lashes. "I want you back, Iris."

"It's not that easy, Trystan," she said, her voice low and urgent. "Maybe in the beginning after our return from South Africa, if all of that awful shit with the article hadn't happened, we could have made a good go of it. But after everything—the humiliation, the pain, the fear, the harassment, your treatment of me—I can very definitively state that your life is not for me. I can't live like that."

She set to work pouring champagne, noting that Trystan—who obviously knew his stuff—was filling precisely two-thirds of each flute, and each glass was uniformly level. He held the bottle with practiced ease, thumb inside the punt to maintain a good grip.

He stopped pouring to meet her eyes and her breath caught at the naked vulnerability buried within the depths of his silver gaze.

"You said you forgave me." Which had to mean that he'd read her text... finally. Was that why he was here? When had he read it? After checking almost every hour on the hour for a day and a half, Iris had given up on him ever seeing it, thinking he'd finally moved on. It had left her feeling hollow and devastated and heartbroken all over again, but ultimately, she'd decided that it was best for *both* of them to move on with their lives. She'd very determinedly muted and archived the conversation, and had resisted the impulse to check it again.

"I *have*, Trystan. I didn't want to walk around with resentment, bitterness and anger in my heart toward you. I wanted to move on with my life and remember our time together with warmth and affection."

"Warmth and affection?" he repeated, his voice acidic and scathing. "Like a comfy blanket. All *nice* and *pleasant*. What about the passion, Iris? The soul-deep connection? The off-the-charts chemistry? What about the fucking *love*? Is *that* what you'll be remembering with this warmth and affection?" The volume in his voice had increased, drawing attention, but this time Iris didn't even care that they were creating a scene, or that it was interfering with their work. How could she care about that when confronted by this much outraged, affronted, clearly wounded male?

"What do you want me to say, Trystan?" she snapped back, furious now. Angry that he was pushing this, that he wouldn't just let it—the notion of *them*—die a dignified, silent death. "Do want to hear how truly fucking pissed off I am with you for *ruining* what we had? Do you want to hear every detail of how much you hurt me? Of how I couldn't eat, couldn't sleep, couldn't function because of how much I missed you? How I held out hope for the longest time—while I was trapped in my room too terrified to leave home for fear of being harassed and accosted—that you would realize your mistake and come and save me from the madness? But you never came. And when you finally *did* come to your senses the damage had been done. I can't live like that again. I can't. I refuse to. I forgive you Trystan, but I can't be in your life."

"I wish I'd been the man you needed me to be," he said, his voice dropping to a low growl. "I wish I'd been stronger, more confident of what we had. I wish I hadn't allowed external forces to tear us apart. But I'm just a man. A weak, dumb, often foolish, human male. I'm smaller than my fame, more ordinary than my legend, and I'm fucking *nothing* without you, Iris."

Iris's trembling hand lifted to her cover her mouth, hoping to force back the sobs that threatened to tumble into the void between them.

He put the bottle down, gently palmed her cheeks, and bent his head until his forehead came to rest on hers.

"I'm so sorry, baby," he whispered, his warm breath washing against the back of her hand. "I didn't treat you well. I know that. I should have cherished you, and I didn't. But I love you so much, Iris. I always will. I know my timing is shit, I know this puts you on the spot and I'm sorry about that too. You don't have to say anything right now. Or ever. We'll go back to pouring this champagne before your dad kills us but I couldn't let another second go by without telling you that I love you. If you tell me today that you don't love me, it'll break my heart but I'll leave you alone. But if, by some miracle, your love survived the apocalypse of my doubt, then I'll announce my retirement and we'll figure out the rest together, okay?"

"You know I don't want you to do that, Trystan. I never wanted that. That's not how it should be. Like I told you in my text I don't know how *we* could possibly work... but I'm fairly certain that you starting with a sacrifice of such magnitude is not the key to a successful relationship. One person shouldn't have to give up *everything* to be with the other."

"You're still not getting it, Iris. Losing *you* would mean losing everything. All the rest? It's just noise."

He let her go and stepped away from her.

"So this is what a penance tour looks like, huh?" she murmured, remembering Chance's words and Trystan managed a wry smile, despite the somber fear in his eyes.

"Go big, or go home, right?" he said, picking up the bottle again. He peered at the clock. "We have ten minutes to finish this."

Iris glanced around the room, and heads and eyes suddenly averted, while the silence was filled with sudden inane chatter. For once, her father wasn't yelling at everyone to get back to work. Instead, he was watching Iris and Trystan with a speculative frown on his face. He met her eyes and nodded cryptically, before going back to organizing the kitchen clean-up crew.

Iris managed to get her quota of glasses filled on time, despite her shaky hands and poor concentration. Her glasses were much less uniform than Trystan's and to her chagrin, he topped up the too-low ones without saying a word.

Once they'd completed their assignment, with three minutes to spare, she excused herself and rushed to the staff bathroom, needing a moment to compose herself. Once there, she stared at her reflection in the mirror, trying to make sense of Trystan's words in her confused brain. He loved her. She'd known that already. She'd known it all along, but somewhere along the line, probably right around the time he'd dumped her at the side of the road, she'd convinced herself that their love wasn't enough to overcome all these obstacles.

It had been easy to believe that while they'd been apart and even easier to persuade herself that the gaping holes in her heart and her soul were wounds she would get used to eventually. Like a bum knee, or chronic back pain, it would always be there, but she'd have to simply... live with it.

Now here he was telling her that it didn't *have* to be that way. That they could both walk out of this healed, renewed, pain free. All she had to do was believe in him and trust that *this* time his love was strong enough to overcome any obstacle.

And that's where she hit a wall because how was this

different to last time? How were these promises and confessions of love more sincere than the last? Because she'd believed and trusted him then. She'd had faith in the power and strength of their love and look where that had got her.

She rinsed her face, needing the shock of cold water to heighten her senses.

She so desperately wanted to believe in his promises but how could she? How could she ever trust him again?

TRYSTAN WAS ACUTELY aware of the scrutiny of every pair of eyes in the kitchen, but kept his head down and his hands busy. He made sure each round silver tray was loaded with exactly ten evenly spaced, full champagne flutes, and when that was done he tidied up their workstation, wiping surfaces with a damp cloth, then rinsing and discarding the empty bottles.

He should have known after his bread-crumb trail search for Iris this morning—going from her flat, to her parents' house where a nosy neighbor had informed Chance that the family was at this address in Wandsworth—that she'd probably be helping out her parents today. But in his eagerness to see her, he'd totally ignored Chance's warnings when they'd pulled up to this restored manor with the dozens of cars parked outside, and had unknowingly gate-crashed a wedding.

There'd been no security to speak of and he'd simply walked in, expecting to see Iris having lunch or something with her family. He'd had a moment of disorienting confusion when he'd walked into a massive hall full of milling, jovial people, all so focused on their food that they hadn't even realized that he didn't belong there.

And then he'd spotted her—in that sexy form-fitting tuxedo-like uniform— across the room, hands laden with platters of food. By the time he'd reached her, she was turning away toward the doors at the back of the room, and he'd hurried to get ahead of her, only to have her walk right into him. He'd known immediately that confronting her while she was working was wrong, but seeing and *touching* her after all this time had renewed his sense of urgency. Now it felt like he'd—once again —fucked everything up. Approached her in the wrong setting, pleaded his case at the worst time. He'd had one shot and he'd blown it. He knew it. And when she'd hastened away from him after they'd finished with the champagne, it had confirmed his worst fears.

She'd been gone for nearly five minutes and—not sure what to do about the filled glasses—Trystan wiped his hands, straightened his cuffs, and tugged at the hem of the snug waistcoat, before throwing back his shoulders and making his way to Jason Hughes.

"The champagne is ready for service, sir," he informed the man quietly. "What else do you need me to do?"

The man, who'd been inspecting the clipboard in his hand, met Trystan's eyes in a long, uncomfortable stare.

"Why did you come here?" Blunt. Trystan liked that.

"To beg Iris to take me back." The older man's eyes narrowed on his face. It was evident that he wasn't remotely impressed by Trystan's words.

"And why should she do that? After what happened the last time?"

"She probably shouldn't," Trystan admitted. Jason Hughes's gray eyes flared in surprise at Trystan's words. "She deserves better than a foolish arsehole like me. But I believe that she loves me... and if she's been even half as miserable as I have without her these last few weeks, then she's in a lot of pain. We're stronger together and happier together, but we didn't get a fair shot at making a success of our relationship. I just wanted —*hoped for*—another chance."

"From what I gather it won't be the first time you've needed *another chance*. What makes this time different?"

"What I had with Iris always seemed too good to be true... and I reckon I—subconsciously—was always waiting for the other shoe to drop. I *should* have known better., I should've trusted her, but after everything I'd just been through with the press after Trish's death—" He scrubbed a hand over his face and shook his head. "It felt inevitable. Like I'd been waiting for the betrayal since day one. I have the same fears and doubts and insecurities as every other man, and I succumbed to my fear in that moment. My fear of being hurt and betrayed. I went on the defensive and I said and did the most unforgivable things."

"And yet you expect to be forgiven?" the man said, his face unreadable.

"It's not expectation. It's hope."

Jason Hughes's eyes drifted away from Trystan's face and a gentle smile tilted the corners of his lips as he nodded at whomever was behind Trystan.

"Iris, why don't you and Trystan go someplace private to talk? We can manage here. There's not much more left to do."

Trystan spun around and found Iris standing a few feet behind him, her eyes bright with unshed tears. The sight of those tears tore at his heart and he stumbled toward her, hand outstretched—his instinct to comfort her—before he came to an uncertain halt. Knowing that he didn't have that right.

Instead, he stood before her, shoulders hunched, hands hanging limply by his sides, as he waited.

"Are you sure?" For a second Trystan was almost certain her question was for him, until she averted her gaze to her father's face.

"I'm sure. Between the gawking and the eavesdropping, this lot isn't going to be much use to me unless you and Trystan get out of sight while you talk."

Iris nodded and turned those beautiful, bright eyes back to Trystan. It was like being brushed by the sun, and he could bask in her gaze all day long.

"Follow me," she said, and turned away from him, her movements tight, the line of her narrow shoulders taut and tense. He meekly followed her slender body as she weaved through the silently staring crowd. Chance, who'd been watching while wolfing down some pretty tasty-looking Greek food, sat upright as they passed him.

"Relax, Chance," Trystan heard Iris murmur. "We're just going to the pantry."

Great, his entire future was about to be decided in a banquet hall pantry of all places.

Well, at least it was private, he noted as he stepped into the quiet, gloomy interior of a mid-sized pantry. It was empty save for a few crates of alcohol and several discarded cardboard boxes that still retained the aroma of the fresh fruits and vegetables they had transported.

Iris shut the door behind them, and switched on the overhead light. The fluorescent tube buzzed and flared to life, producing a stuttering flicker that surged and waned without any kind of predictability. Iris turned toward him and Trystan took a step back, to give her some room, and waited for her to speak.

"I heard what you said," she began, after a few moments of pensive silence. "To my dad."

Chapter Twenty-Five

Trystan nodded gravely, shoving his hands into his pockets to prevent himself from reaching for her.

"You were afraid of being hurt?" The lilting intonation in Iris's voice made the statement a question.

"Of course I was, Iris," he admitted, his hands bunching into fists in his pockets. "I'd just served my heart up to you on a silver platter. I'd never been more vulnerable in my life. I was terrified."

"So when the article came out—"

"All my deepest, darkest fears came to life in that one moment. I was so fucking blindsided by the sweeping pain, the panic and the fear of even more hurt to follow that I lost all ability to think rationally. I lashed out at you—the one I mistakenly believed was the source of all that pain—it was a nuclear response based wholly on emotion. I wanted to punish you. I wanted you to feel what I'd felt... and after that I retreated into myself. I functioned on autopilot. I refused to think about you, refused to consider how you must have felt, what you were going through. It was only at the first interview with Mike Holmes—when he dared ask me about you—that I finally started to come out of that daze and began to think clearly again. Before that, I'd managed to sanitize my surroundings, my interviews, of your presence—having him ask about you was like having a bucket of ice water tossed directly into my face.

"It was brutal and my reaction was visceral, instinctive. I walked out because I was physically unable to talk about you. It hurt too much. But after that, you were all I could think about... More and more I had the uneasy feeling that I had things completely wrong. That feeling grew and grew until it consumed me and I was asphyxiated by my own stupidity. I started hearing about what you were going through. And that's when the repercussions of my scorched-earth reaction in the car that day truly hit me." He choked up and bowed his head to stare at the polished floor between his feet, fighting for control. "I'd abandoned you. I promised you I'd be there for you and then I wasn't. Iris, I can't..."

He lost his battle with the sob that forced its way up past the blockage in his throat and out on a guttural moan.

"I'm sorry," he whispered, daring a glance upward, not sure what he'd find, not sure he wanted her to see the despair on his face, but unable to help himself. Her eyes were gleaming with unshed tears, her expressive face nakedly vulnerable. "I'm so fucking sorry. I wish there were bigger words than *sorry*. I wish there were massive, mountain-sized epic fucking words to describe my regret and despair. But I'm stuck with *I'm sorry*. I can promise you the world, only I know you don't want it... I don't know what you want. But I kind of hoped you would be okay with just me. Trystan Abbott. I know I'm weak and flawed, and kind of an arsehole. I make mistakes, I say and do dumb shit, but my one true redeeming feature was being loved by you once. And the only thing I'm capable of doing truly right in this world is loving you back."

"Trystan," Iris murmured, her voice throbbing with emotion and regret, and Trystan shook his head in a panic, certain she was about to reject him, absolutely sure he was seconds away from losing her. He took a step toward her, his hands coming out of his pockets and reaching toward her, wanting to stop her, to somehow physically prevent her from sending him away for good. But in the end, he knew he couldn't stop her. He needed to let her speak and then he had to let her go and allow her to move on with her life.

Iris watched the frustrated aborted movement of his hands as they strained toward her for a second and then fell limply to his sides.

His words, spoken in that harsh, broken voice, still echoed through her mind, and gave her a clarity she'd been missing for weeks.

"I once told you that if you wanted a life with me you have to be prepared to live it with me, remember? Out in the real world, where everybody thinks they own a piece of you."

He nodded warily.

"Well, I got a taste of that now and I can't say I like it

much… that ownership people seem to think they have over you, that possessiveness where I'm seen as competition or a threat, as an easy target to take potshots at."

"Iris, I'm so—"

"Ssh," she interrupted gently, stepping toward him and placing her fingers over his lips. "The time for apologies has passed now. Let me speak, okay?"

He swallowed, and his lips moved against her fingers, but he said nothing, just nodded.

She dropped her hand and folded it into a fist, trying to alleviate the tingle caused by that brief brush of his mouth against her skin.

"I also told you that I don't want you to give up your career and live a life of obscurity because of me, that I refused to let you use me as an excuse to hide from your demons. Well, *I'd* be the hypocrite I once accused you of being if I turned you away and gave up our shot at happiness because I allowed my fear of the public and press to dictate my decisions. The decision I have to make right now is twofold: do I love you enough to trust you with my heart again? And do I love you enough to live in the public eye, possibly under constant scrutiny, having everything from the way I dress, to my mental and emotional health discussed and criticized and mocked."

"Iris, I told you, I'll resign…"

This again, she sighed impatiently and held up her forefinger, effectively shutting him up.

"Trystan, do you love what you do?"

He was saved from replying by the perfunctory knock at the door.

"Christ," Trystan barked beneath his breath, running an unsteady hand over his short, spiky hair. "Yes?"

The door opened and Chance's head popped around it.

"Sorry to disturb, but word's gotten out that you're here."

"What the fuck?" Trystan blurted. "*How?*"

"Sorry, Iris, seems you have a mole in your operation," Chance said somberly, then ruined the effect by grinning like a dopey kid. "I've always wanted to say that. Anyway, seems like someone called the press on the sly. Brand EPS's pap insider alerted head office and the word's filtered down that the vultures are headed this way. So, you're going to have to continue this discussion someplace more secure."

Trystan sent Iris a tortured look, and she knew it was because he believed this confirmed everything she'd just said about his life.

She offered him a small, reassuring smile.

"Should we continue our discussion at your place?" she asked, and his face just about melted with relief. "I'd love to see Luna again."

"Are you sure?"

"Yes, I've missed her."

"About continuing, I mean. Because... Iris, I need you to be sure."

She cupped his jaw, her thumb finding the familiar ridge of the completely healed cicatrix slicing through his stubble.

"I'm sure."

His Adam's apple bobbed as he swallowed heavily and he covered her hand with his own, pressing it against his skin for a second, before nodding.

"Let's get out of here," he murmured, bringing their joined hands down between their bodies and interlinking their fingers.

IT WAS RELATIVELY easy to slip away from the wedding. Chance brought the car round the back entrance and Iris's parents both hugged her before slanting equally menacing warning looks at Trystan, and ushering them out.

By mutual, unspoken agreement, Iris and Trystan didn't talk much in the car. Saving the weighty conversation they needed to have for when they had more time. Instead, Trystan told her about his visit home, about his family and friends, while Iris talked about her new group of friends, her writing, and her brief stay at Chance and Colby's.

While they gently and tentatively filled in the blanks of their time apart for each other, they couldn't seem to stop touching and staring as if they were unable to believe that they were actually here, together, close enough to touch, breathe, feel and caress each other.

It wasn't at all how Iris had planned this discussion to go. She'd hoped to remain emotionally distant until they figured out what the future held for them, but to be here with him like this with no words, no conflict or confusion, or chaos to muddy the waters between them...

It was sublime.

They were each so entranced by the other's mere presence

that the privacy glass unceremoniously sliding down between them and Chance was jarring and intrusive.

"Sorry, guys, but we're going to have to battle our way through this tide of shit," Chance announced cheerfully and they both looked away from each other long enough to understand that there was a veritable *sea* of people outside the car.

"Fuck, what about the underground parking?" Trystan asked, his voice terse, while his white-knuckled hold on Iris's hand threatened to bruise her skin.

"Can't get the car through them. They got here much faster than we'd anticipated and backup's not here yet, so we either sit here and wait—although it might take a while for them to get here through this throng. The police might get here first—*or* we strong-arm our way through them."

He gave them an unholy, slightly unhinged grin, and cracked his knuckles.

Trystan's gaze dropped to Iris's face, his eyes dull with fear and concern.

"No. I won't risk Iris getting hurt in the mayhem. We'll wait."

Just then some *wanker* thumped on the Maybach's bonnet and yelled: "Are Trystan and Iris in there? Are they getting back together? Is—hey, fuck you, man!" the last when Chance restarted the car and released the clutch enough for the vehicle to lurch, causing the reporter to leap back.

"I don't want to wait," Iris decided, tilting her chin up and meeting Trystan's gaze resolutely. "I refuse to let these bastards dictate a single moment more of my life."

"Iris..."

"Trystan you once promised me a safe space within your life, remember?" she reminded. His face contorted and he swallowed thickly.

"I remember."

"That offer still stand?"

He exhaled, a soul-deep shuddering exhalation of pure relief.

"Always, baby. Fucking always and forever."

"Well, that starts right now," she warned, and his eyes widened when she nodded at Chance. "Let's go, Chance."

"Wait a second—" Trystan protested, but it was too late. Chance was out of the car, literally shoving people out of the way as he headed toward the curbside of the car. Once there, he used one long, muscular arm to sweep away two invading paps, dragged the door open, and then positioned his massive body so that he was between Iris and the crowd. Trystan hastily followed, ensuring she was protected on the other side as well.

The reporters went rabid at the sight of Iris, then frothed at the mouth when Trystan joined her seconds later and wrapped a protective arm around her slender shoulders.

A lot of jostling and shoving—at least one punch from Trystan, and a well-aimed kick to a crotch from Iris—later they were in the peaceful foyer of the apartment block.

Chance was still grinning maniacally as he ushered them toward the elevator.

"Saw that palm heel strike, mate," Chance told Trystan as they all stepped into the blissfully empty and quiet lift. "Sloppy technique, but that weedy little fucker is going to feel it for days."

Trystan ignored Chance and turned Iris to face him. He ran his hands over her body, smoothing down her hair, straightening her waistcoat, his eyes grave with concern.

"You okay? Did they hurt you? I'm so sorry, baby. That shouldn't have happened. We should have stayed in the—"

"Did you see me kick that gropey bastard right in the testicles?" she asked, brushing aside his hands. "Can you believe that arsehole used to be a friend of my dad's? I met him when I was a child and actually called him *uncle* at one stage, for God's sake. He was going straight for a boob brush, the dick."

Trystan's face went frigid.

"*Who?* I'll fuck him up."

The elevator dinged to a stop and Iris cupped his jaw and went onto her toes to kiss his scar.

"Don't worry about him. He's not worth a second more of our time, not when we have more important things to think about and discuss."

Chance silently led them toward the front door of Trystan's apartment but remained outside.

Iris stopped in confusion and stared at him.

"Chance? Aren't you coming in?"

"The penthouse is secure. I can stand guard out here. Just don't try to kill my principal, Iris, or I'll have to intervene."

Trystan impatiently took hold of her hand again to tug her inside before shutting the door with a definitive thud.

"Iris, we—"

"Oh my *God,* Luna-puppy. I've missed you so much," Iris's squeal interrupted him as the big dog came lumbering over with more pep in her step than Iris had ever seen from her before, the entirety of her hindquarters vibrating with the force of her tail wagging. She rubbed her big head against Iris's body, clearly demanding scratches and pets, and Iris was only too happy to comply.

She bent slightly and wrapped her arms around the dog's neck, giving her a hug.

"I'm so happy to see you," she said into the dog's bristly fur and Luna snorted into her ear, presumably returning the sentiment. When she surfaced from the hug, it was to find Trystan leaning against the marble countertop of a huge open-plan kitchen, watching them with a soft, almost adoring, smile on his face. Luna shook herself and ambled back to her basket, clearly content now that her people were in the same room again.

"Sorry," Iris muttered, wiping at her damp eyes self-consciously. "I just—" her voice hitched unexpectedly and she shook her head, fighting for control before speaking again. "I never expected to see her again."

"Oh, baby," he whispered, his voice fraught with regret and sorrow. She offered him a wobbly smile of reassurance, but— when he opened his arms to her—she stepped into them gratefully and accepted his hug.

After a long moment, he dropped his arms, and stepped back toward the marble- topped island, allowing her some breathing room. She appreciated the space, giving herself a moment to get her emotions under control by casting her eyes around the luxurious penthouse apartment curiously. She tucked a strand of hair behind her ear, feeling self-conscious beneath his scorching perusal.

"How do you feel?" he asked. Iris—who hadn't really been

taking in anything of what she was looking at—latched onto the abrupt question gratefully.

"About?"

"What just happened."

"That hug?" she asked, genuinely confused.

"With the paparazzi," he clarified. "Downstairs."

"Oh. *That.*" She considered the question, examining it and her reaction to the situation in the moment from all angles. "It was better with you and Chance there. I didn't feel threatened, or afraid, or alone. I felt... protected. Safe. Like you promised I'd be."

She moved closer to him, trailing her finger over the expanse of the cool granite countertop as she walked toward him. She traced that same finger over the back of the hand he had resting on the counter, up over his shirt sleeve, then over one twitching pec, before flattening her palm in the center of his chest, where she could feel his heart pounding too hard and too fast against his ribcage.

"It felt like—together—we can overcome anything. If we just *trust* each other."

His jaw twitched and his lower lip quivered before he brought himself under stern control.

"Quinny and I... we've been talking a lot. About my career, about the future projects I want to take on. I was reading scripts, comedies—not straight-up slapstick stuff—that's not for me. But dramadies, y'know? There are a few I'm really excited about. I can't remember the last time I felt eager and enthusiastic about my work. There are other quirkier dark comedies that I love. There's also this science-fiction script that landed on my desk. It has a small role in it that I'm dying to play but I'm mostly keen on producing and directing it. Quinny and Bee—my PR manager—have been supportive of the direction I want to take with my career, and are moving mountains to facilitate the shift."

"You don't want to give it up?" Iris asked quietly, and his brow furrowed above those tormented eyes. As if he wasn't sure what the right answer was.

"I would, Iris, in a heartbeat, if it meant being with you."

"I would absolutely *love* to see what you could do in those roles, Trystan. I'm excited to see how far you can stretch your-self and how high you can fly. I don't want you to give that up for me. I would hate it."

He pressed his hand over hers where it still rested on his chest.

"I've had a taste of life without you, Iris... and I hated every goddamned second of it. I felt empty, lost. I could barely func-tion. And I despised myself for driving you away. If my career is what keeps us apart, I would despise that too."

She sighed. The sound was soft and resigned.

"I love you, Trystan. More than enough to risk my heart again. But I warn you, it's fragile and I'm trusting you not to break it again... because I don't think I'd recover from a next time."

He lifted her hand to his face, nuzzling his stubbled cheek into her palm, before turning his head to press a worshipful kiss on her soft skin. His eyes were screwed shut, but that did not prevent a silvery bead of moisture from escaping and streaking down his lean cheek to catch in the dark stubble on his jaw.

His chest was shuddering and it took Iris a moment to comprehend that what she was hearing were sobs, and what she was seeing were tears.

Her throat closed up and she tugged her hand from beneath his to wrap her arms around his waist and hold him close.

He collapsed against her, weak and helpless in her arms as he buried his head on her shoulder and shook in her arms. The storm of emotion passed after a few endless moments and when his lips sought hers, Iris welcomed them with heartfelt enthusiasm.

His big hands came up to cradle her face, while his thumbs tilted her jaw upwards to better accommodate his demanding, scorching kiss.

By the time their tongues got involved, he'd somehow marched her backward toward a bedroom. Iris only realized where they were when the backs of her knees hit the edge of a mattress.

She jerked her head up and cast him a narrow-eyed glower.

"Mr. Abbott, have you lured me into your bedroom?" she teased and he looked uncertain for a second before his kiss-swollen lips spread into a wide, happy smile.

"Why, yes, I have, Miss Hughes..."

"And do you have *seduction* in mind, sir?" she asked in a scandalized whisper.

"I'm gonna seduct you so hard you won't be able to walk straight for a week, ma'am," he affirmed lazily.

"*Seduct* isn't a word, sir."

"It should be," he said. "It rhymes so very nicely with fucked."

She laughed, the sound giddy and lighthearted. After the intensity of the past hour, as well as the days, weeks they'd been apart, the humor was a welcome relief.

"Well, then," she said, running her fingers through his short, silky hair. "Seduct me long and hard, babe. I'm ready."

He growled, the sound was low and feral and sent a thrill of anticipation up Iris's spine. It reminded her of that wounded beast she'd first met all those weeks ago and her pussy throbbed in reaction to the sound, already wet and swollen, while her nipples tightened to the point of pain.

He nudged her onto the bed and kneed his way between her thighs, taking her mouth in another deep, suctioning kiss that turned her bones to jelly.

"Don't think I told you how sexy I find this uniform," his said, voice guttural, while he clumsily pawed at the buttons of her waistcoat. "You have an outstanding arse but in this getup, it's positively sinful." He dropped a hand to her butt and squeezed, almost roughly. Iris whimpered, loving his dominant possessiveness. Something told her she was in for a wild ride. He seemed unable to get himself under control, and she *loved* it.

He unsnapped the button on her trousers, and slid the flat of his hand down the front, inside her panties until he'd palmed her crudely. His long fingers skirted over her throbbing clit and headed straight for her entrance, where he found her soaking wet and scalding hot. He sank two fingers into her without any warning and Iris keened and arched into his touch, her clit pressed into his palm while her swollen flesh clenched around his invading fingers and she orgasmed without any warning whatsoever.

She muffled her scream against his bicep and then bit down on the taut flesh when her brain shut down and white-hot light blinded her to anything but the intense pleasure of her climax.

By the time she drifted down from that amazing peak, he had her waistcoat and shirt unbuttoned and spread open, and was busy peeling her trousers off. She could do nothing but watch him, as she lay limp and sated on the bed, feeling a little like an unwrapped present waiting to be thoroughly enjoyed by its recipient.

When he finally managed to tug the black pants free, Iris lay there waiting, legs splayed, arms outstretched, nipples big and hard, a smug, contented grin on her face. She felt decadent, lazy, pampered and spoiled... while the sexiest man in the world stared at her like she was the most beautiful woman he'd ever seen. And then he started to strip and she moaned as she watched more and more of that perfect body come into view.

All hers, always, and forever.

By the time he was completely naked, gorgeous cock hard and throbbing for *her*, she was panting, and hungry for him, aching for what she knew he would give her.

He fumbled with a condom, not as suave as he liked to think he was, and she loved that too... loved that he was clumsy in his eagerness to be with her. Loved that her perfect man was not so perfect after all, but flawed and human.

When he pushed into her, she cried out, helpless to stop the sound from spilling out into the reverent silence that had fallen between them, and when she tightened around him, a similar sound tore itself from his chest.

Their union felt familiar, yet new, the craving and urgency

after so long apart lending a frenetic pace to their coupling that had been absent in their previous lovemaking. But that didn't matter. Nothing mattered except that Iris loved Trystan. And Trystan loved Iris. Together they could and would conquer mountains.

Trystan swore softly, a low, urgent *fuck* as he lost control, and seemed barely able to restrain himself as he pounded into her harder and faster. Iris loved it. She raked her nails down the length of his back, then dug her fingers into his rapidly thrusting tight arse as she brought her knees up and pushed her feet down on the backs of his thighs.

"Harder, Trystan," she urged and he groaned, burying his face into the cove of her neck as he complied.

She wailed, the sound high, wild, as her orgasm crashed into her like a freight train and derailed her. Trystan, one hand braced on the mattress beside her head for balance, and the fingers of the other digging—tightly enough to bruise—into one of her butt cheeks, groaned. It was a quiet, helpless sound and it was followed by a shudder, then her name.

Every muscle in his body tightened as he froze and then came, in a series of hard, violent jolts.

IN THE SILENCE that fell after their fierce bout of lovemaking, Trystan held Iris close, terrified that if he let her go he'd wake up and find himself alone to discover that this had been yet another one of his tormented dreams.

She'd drifted off after her orgasm, body limp, limbs spread with the abandon of a carefree kid. He loved the unguardedness of her sprawl. It meant that she felt safe with him and that made him proud as fuck. He wanted her to feel protected around him. Wanted her to know that he could take care of her and always would.

This moment felt a little too good to be true. That he could have Iris *and* his career. It was more than he'd hoped for. That was why he was afraid to sleep. Because if this was a dream, he wasn't sure he'd survive the devastation when he woke up from it. So he lay there, staring at the ceiling, holding her close, stroking her hair, fighting the somnolence with everything in him.

Until his eyes drifted shut.

And he slept.

WHEN TRYSTAN next opened his eyes, the room was gloomier, telling him it was close to sunset, probably just gone six pm. As his eyes adjusted, he searched for Iris, pushing himself up frantically when he didn't see her anywhere in the immediate vicinity.

He got up, dragging on his boxer briefs and nothing else as he hastily made his way to the kitchen.

He froze when he spotted her, curled up on the sofa, Luna stretched out next to her, with her massive head resting in Iris's lap.

Iris looked up with a smile when she saw him.

"Hey, you were out like a light, and I figured the jet lag was probably hitting you hard."

She looked adorable, wearing his shirt and nothing else. Her hair was a mess and she was sipping something from a mug, while leafing through a magazine.

"Trystan?" she prompted, concern laced through her voice. And Trystan knew he was behaving strangely, just staring at her like she was some kind of apparition.

"I thought it was a dream," he confessed, his voice gruff with sleep and embarrassment but she didn't look confused. Instead her smile widened in understanding.

"I was scared it wasn't real too," she said, then patted the empty space beside her. "Pour yourself a cup of cocoa from the saucepan on the stove and join us."

He complied with almost indecent haste, getting a mug full of the chocolatey drink before sliding into place beside her. He tucked his arm around her shoulders and she dropped her head into the dip between his chest and his armpit.

"You staying the night?" he asked into the fragrant cloud of her hair.

"Since the reporters seem to have camped out downstairs that would probably be best. They'll have a field day speculating about what we're doing up here."

Trystan took a sip of his chocolate.

"Does that bother you?" he asked cautiously and she laughed, turning her head to press a kiss against his chest, just above his nipple.

"Nope, they can't even begin to imagine what we're like together. Anything they come up with would pale in comparison to reality."

"Yeah?" He couldn't help feeling a little smug about her comment.

"Yep."

After a companionable silence, broken only by Luna's snores, Iris tilted her head to look up at him.

"I'm happy."

His heart clenched at those two small words and then brimmed to overflowing with joy and love for this woman.

"I am too, Iris."

So fucking happy.

"You said something a while back that I didn't quite get. But I know what you mean now because I feel the same way."

"Hmm?"

"Being with you feels like home."

Epilogue

NEWS

)L.XI - NO.4350   NEW ISSUE   SINCE 1865

Trystan Pops the Question

After nearly two years of living with popular author Iris Hughes, Trystan Abbott has finally popped the question. Interest levels in the couple's relationship have been off the charts ever since Abbott's now-legendary pair of interviews with Mike Holmes a couple of years ago, shortly after which a video clip of Abbott begging Hughes to take him back surfaced on several social media platforms simultaneously. The clip, shot anonymously while Hughes was working at her parents' catering company, went viral, amassing millions of views in just a day. The fiercely private couple was spotted dining at a well-known Soho eatery last Friday night, with Iris sporting a massive emerald and diamond engagement ring. Sources close to the pair confirm that Trystan proposed on—

NEWS

OL.XI - NO.4350   NEW ISSUE   SINCE 1865

Trystan and Iris Tie The Knot

Academy Award winner Trystan Abbott and bestselling author Iris Hughes have married in a small, private ceremony in South Africa. The wedding is rumored to have taken place at billionaire entrepreneur Miles Hollingsworth's home in the Western Cape. Adorably, the couple's dog, Luna, is said to have been the ringbearer. Guests included—

NEWS

OL.XI - NO.4350   NEW ISSUE   SINCE 1865

Trystan and Iris Welcome Twin Tots

Acclaimed actor and director Trystan Abbott and his wife, award-winning playwright and bestselling author Iris Hughes-Abbott, have recently become the proud parents of twin girls. Mother and babies are said to be perfectly healthy and doing well. The notoriously media-shy couple have not yet released images of the infants to the public, but Abbott made the announcement via his Instagram account, with a picture of the family dog, Luna, snuggled between two small plush bears, captioned: Welcome to the world, baby sisters Fern and Willow. I can't wait to meet you. included—

Welcome to the world, baby sisters Fern and Willow. I can't wait to meet you.

With nearly a million books sold, Natasha Anders has been drawing praise and attention as a unique voice in romance since 2012. Her first novel, The Unwanted Wife, was a bestselling sensation and remains a consistent favorite among readers. Her 2017 novel, The Wingman, the first in her new Alpha Men trilogy, was a finalist for a 2018 Romance Writers of America RITA Award.

Born in Cape Town, South Africa, Anders spent nine years as an associate English teacher in Niigata, Japan, where she became a legendary karaoke diva. Anders currently lives in Cape Town with her temperamental chihuahua, Maia; her moody budgie, Baxter; sweet little chihuahua Hana; and her little wingman, adorable parrotlet, Mason.

Readers can connect with her through her Facebook page, on Twitter at @satyne1, or at www.natashaanders.com

Natasha Anders

* 9 7 8 0 7 9 6 1 8 2 8 0 7 *